TRUTH
OR
DARE

Also by M.J. Arlidge

M.J. Arlidge has worked in television for the last twenty years, specialising in high-end drama production, including prime-time crime serials *Silent Witness*, *Torn*, *The Little House* and, most recently, the hit ITV show *Innocent*. In 2015 his audiobook exclusive *Six Degrees of Assassination* was a number-one bestseller. His debut thriller, *Eeny Meeny*, was the UK's bestselling crime debut of 2014 and has been followed by nine more DI Helen Grace thrillers – all Sunday Times bestsellers. *Truth or Dare* is the tenth novel featuring his much-loved lead detective, Helen Grace.

🐦 @mjarlidge
❘ /MJArlidge
📷 @m_j_arlidge

TRUTH
OR
DARE

M.J. Arlidge

ORION

First published in Great Britain in 2021 by Orion Fiction,
an imprint of The Orion Publishing Group Ltd.,
Carmelite House, 50 Victoria Embankment
London EC4Y 0DZ

An Hachette UK Company

1 3 5 7 9 10 8 6 4 2

A CIP catalogue record for this book is
available from the British Library.

ISBN (Hardback) 978 1 4091 8845 2
ISBN (Trade Paperback) 978 1 4091 8846 9
ISBN (eBook) 978 1 4091 8848 3

Typeset at The Spartan Press Ltd,
Lymington, Hants

Printed and bound in Great Britain by Clays Ltd,
Elcograf S.p.A.

www.orionbooks.co.uk

For Jennie, Chloe and Alex,
who shared this lockdown novel with me.

Day One

Chapter 1

He didn't want to move, but he knew he had to. He had come too far, risked too much, to back out now. Steeling himself, he crept forward, his eyes scanning the gloomy yard. If there was any movement, any possibility of being detected, then he would turn and run without a second thought. But there was nothing, no sign of life at all, so he pressed on.

The Portakabin lay directly in front of him, lonely and isolated in the darkness. A dull glow crept from beneath the blinds, the sole indication that it was inhabited. Anyone stumbling upon this yard might easily have missed the anomaly – this was a place where things came to rot and die; a dumping ground for abandoned cars and household junk. Curiosity was not encouraged, the entrance gates were chained and, though he had snapped the padlock easily, he was sure no one else had been tempted to try. You wouldn't set foot in this place unless you had to, nor would you assume that a treasure trove of secrets lay just beyond the stained door of the Portakabin.

The ground was littered with rusting exhaust pipes, empty packing cases and abandoned white goods. It would be easy to kick something in the darkness, alerting his victim, so he moved forward carefully, teasing his way through the detritus. In the distance, a siren wailed, startling a bird which took flight, squawking loudly, but he ignored it, grimly focused on the task in hand.

Reaching the Portakabin, he paused, pressing himself up against its filthy carapace, craning around to peer through the window. The glass was grimy, coated in bird mess and dirt, so his view was blurred, yet he could still make out the figure inside. Overweight, sprawling, a bottle of Jack Daniel's clamped in his hand, Declan McManus slumbered on a tired sofa. McManus looked totally out of it, utterly at peace with the world, which seemed profoundly odd given the grave danger he was in. Surely he wouldn't have been so relaxed had he known that his hiding place had been discovered, that someone *else* knew his secret?

He counted silently to ten, wanting to be *sure* that McManus was asleep, then quietly stepped up to the door. Still there was no sound within, so reaching out a gloved hand, he turned the handle. His heart was thumping, his hand shaking, as he teased it downwards. This was the point of maximum risk, when his approach was most likely to be detected, but the handle slid down easily. Cautiously, he eased the door open, preparing to cross the threshold. As he did so, however, the aged hinge started to protest, screaming out in alarm. Horrified, the intruder froze, uncertain what to do, then acting on instinct, he yanked the door fully open. The hinge squeaked briefly, then was silent once more. Stepping inside, he cast an anxious eye towards the sleeping man, but McManus hadn't stirred, the near-empty bottle of bourbon having done its work.

He closed the door, the sounds of the night suddenly dying away. Now it was just the two of them, cocooned inside this sad space. It was even more unpleasant and odorous than he'd anticipated, a fitting backdrop for the grubby individual in front of him. This was where McManus hid his spoils, conducted his business, brought young girls. He shuddered to think what had occurred within these four walls, but he was not here to dwell on past crimes, he was here to do a job. To do what was *necessary*. Many lives had been blighted by this man, but perhaps after tonight he would do no more harm.

Stepping forward, he looked down at the comatose figure. Part of him still expected McManus to rear up, wrapping his sweaty palms around his neck... but he lay still, undisturbed and unsuspecting. There was nothing stopping him, no imminent danger, no chance of detection. This was it.

It was time to kill.

Chapter 2

The pale face stared up at her, tranquil but lifeless. Detective Inspector Helen Grace had encountered many bodies in Jim Grieves's mortuary, but this one brought a lump to her throat. They always did when they were young.

The girl lying half hidden beneath the crisp white sheet was only sixteen years old. Eve Sutcliffe, a gifted student at the prestigious Milton Downs Ladies' Academy, still awaiting the results of her GCSEs. Long auburn hair framed a pretty face still touched by teenage hormones, a cluster of spots decorating her left cheek. The beauty in her features, the serenity of her expression, however, hid the brutality of her murder.

'Blunt force trauma,' Jim Grieves growled. 'From the shape and size of the impact wound, I'd say we're talking about a hammer. Was anything recovered from the scene?'

Shaking her head, Helen leaned forward as Jim Grieves turned the deceased to reveal a bloody mess at the back of her skull. The young girl's half-naked body had been found in bushes in Lakeside Country Park five days ago. No weapon had been discovered, no witnesses unearthed, nor did they have any offenders under consideration. Helen had been hoping Jim Grieves would give her something to work with, but he quickly put paid to that notion.

'Not much more to tell you, I'm afraid. She was struck eight, possibly nine times, with considerable force, fracturing her skull and leading to massive internal bleeding. She probably wouldn't have been conscious after the second blow, but even so…'

'Any hairs? Sweat? Blood?'

Grieves shook his head.

'Nothing under her fingernails, no sign of a struggle. I imagine that she was approached from behind and subdued before she had a chance to fight back.'

'What about semen? On the body, on the clothes?'

'You'll have to ask Meredith about her clothes, but there's nothing on or in the body; in fact, there's no sign of sexual assault per se, no scratching or bruising around the genitals. She *was* sexually active, but not in the days, possibly weeks, leading up to her death.'

Already Helen's mind was turning. Was there a boyfriend on the scene? Someone she'd recently broken up with? Someone who felt angry and spurned? Or was this a random act of violence, a young girl falling victim to a vicious, sexually motivated stranger?

'So, her attacker was intent on assaulting her, but lost his nerve? Got frightened off?'

'You tell me, you're the detective,' Grieves fired back, with grim relish.

Helen took the hit, privately acknowledging that the title had never felt more like a millstone. So much bloodshed, so much heartache of late, yet so little to go on. Recently, Helen had felt like she was swimming with one hand tied behind her back, drowning in a rising tide of violence and brutality.

'I've got a couple more bits and pieces to do,' Grieves continued, in conciliatory mode, 'and if I find anything significant, I'll let you know. I just wanted to give you my initial findings.'

7

'Thanks, Jim. I appreciate it.'

And she did. But it didn't help her. The memories of Eve's devastated parents – their desolation, their agony – were still fresh in Helen's mind. It was a case that *demanded* to be solved, not just for Eve's sake, but for others who might yet be in danger from this violent offender, but so far they had nothing. Staring down at the girl's innocent face, Helen was filled with guilt and sadness – for the loss of all that Eve might have been, all she might have become.

For a young life brutally snuffed out.

Chapter 3

The lighter sparked in his hand, then died. He wanted to scream, to spew out his rage and anxiety, but there was no question of that – his victim lay only a few yards from him, docile but dangerous. If McManus awoke now, if he took the fight to his assailant, there would only be one winner.

He tried again, the lighter clicking out its quiet, hopeless rhythm. Still it didn't catch, remaining lifeless in his hand. It made no sense, he'd only bought it yesterday – it was *full* of fuel. He'd used it on the way here, one last cigarette, and it had worked perfectly. So what was the problem now? Yes, his hand was shaking, but surely not enough to disable the device?

He tried again, aggressively, persistently. It sparked, more encouragingly this time, but the flame burnt only briefly before going out. And now McManus stirred, snorting and rubbing his nose, disturbed by the click, click, click of the lighter. He was moving, shifting his substantial weight on the tired faux-leather sofa, which squeaked loudly in response, disturbing him still further. A frown, a cough and then he dropped the bottle of bourbon, which landed on the floor with a heavy thunk. Now his body shivered, as if juddering back into consciousness. There was no doubt about it – he was about to wake up.

Trying to calm himself, the intruder stared at the lighter,

willing it to work. He pressed the small metal wheel and pushed down hard. Once, twice, three times and now – miraculously – a flame sprang up. A strong, steady flame. His breath hissed from him, tension flooding from his body, and he didn't hesitate, raising the flame to the milk bottle he was clutching in his left hand. The dirty rag hung, moist and heavy, in the bottle's mouth, asking to be ignited. Carefully holding it to the flame, he watched with excitement as the homemade fuse took. Now the fire was working its way up the primed rag towards the petrol inside.

Taking a step back, he looked down at the man in front of him. His eyelids were flickering, he was only moments from consciousness, so, raising his arm, he hurled the bottle down. Smashing on the hard floor, it exploded into flame, greedily latching on to the spilt whisky, the aged sofa, the man's clothes. The ferocity, the heat, was far greater than his attacker had expected and he stumbled backwards, away from the conflagration, suddenly fearful for his *own* safety.

Retreating, he grasped the door handle gratefully, yanking it open. He was about to run through the open doorway – run away as *fast* he could – but now something, some semblance of calm, some fragment of his planning – made him pause. Refusing to look backwards at the scene of horror, he gathered himself, reaching down to pull the key from the lock. Then, moving swiftly and silently, he stepped out of the Portakabin, shutting the door behind him and turning the key in the lock.

Stepping out into the cool night air, he hurried down the stairs, desperate to be away from this awful place. But even as he did so, a sound from within the burning cabin stopped him dead in his tracks.

A single, agonized scream.

Chapter 4

He hurried down the alleyway, eagerly searching for his prize. A sharp-eyed constable had spotted it half an hour earlier and Detective Sergeant Joseph Hudson had wasted no time in responding. Running to the bike park, he'd raced across town, determined to have something to show for the day.

The officer now came into view, standing guard over the abandoned BMW. Hudson was convinced the stolen car would've been stripped, then dumped, and his instinct had been proved right. Here was the prestige vehicle he'd been seeking, the proud status symbol that someone had been prepared to kill for.

'I haven't touched it,' the constable ventured quickly, as Hudson approached. 'I just clocked the number plate and called it in.'

'Thank you, Constable...?'

'Atkins, sir.'

'Well done, Atkins,' Hudson responded, giving him a hearty slap on the shoulder. 'Good work, but I can take it from here...'

The constable nodded, pleased with the compliment, then headed off. Hudson watched him go, gratified to have cultivated another foot soldier, then turned his attention to the abandoned vehicle.

Unsurprisingly, it wasn't locked. In fact, it wasn't even secured, the driver's door hanging ajar. Donning a pair of gloves, Hudson teased it open, crouching down to peer inside. It was a BMW 5 Series, four years old, but top of the range and, before it had been stolen, it would've had a state-of-the-art entertainment and navigation system to compliment the hand-stitched leather interior. Now, however, it was a mess. From the outside, with its striking, metallic paint and tinted windows, it still looked impressive, but the view from the inside was very different. It had been cannibalized – the screen ripped out to leave hanging wires, the main armrest removed, even the chrome handles had been lifted. He was surprised to see the leather seats still in place, but perhaps the thief was an amateur, keen to make a quick buck. If so, he hoped he'd got a good price. The cost had been high and the reckoning would be severe.

Hudson's eyes were now drawn to the dark stains in the driver's footwell, then to the rust-coloured smears on the window next to it. Up until ten days ago, this prestige vehicle had belonged to Alison Burris, an administrative manager at Southampton's Children's Hospital. It had been an extravagant anniversary present from her besotted husband and it was her pride and joy. She always parked it in a discreet car park, a couple of blocks from the hospital, and it was there that she was targeted one Wednesday night, shortly after midnight.

It was perhaps foolish of her to be alone in the car park so late, but still she should have had every reason to feel safe. As it was, she was set upon by a car jacker as she attempted to drive home. A struggle ensued – her clothing was torn, a clump of hair ripped out – as Burris battled to fight off the thief. It had proved a bad call, the young professional stabbed twice in the heart, before her attacker made off with her vehicle.

Alison Burris was found by a businessman just after midnight, but by then she was long dead. Hudson was the SIO on the scene and was quick to put the pieces together. There had been a spate of luxury car thefts in Southampton of late, another front in their battle against rising crime in the city, though few of them had been as violent as this one. As Hudson had crouched down over the poor woman's body, his eyes had been drawn to the narrow, cylindrical wounds in her flesh. He was still waiting on the post-mortem – Jim Grieves had a backlog of bodies – but Hudson had a pretty good idea of what killed Burris. She had been felled by a sharpened screwdriver, rammed into her heart at close quarters. It was a sickening way to die and for what? There was a thriving market for black-market car parts in Southampton, had been ever since the post-Covid downturn, but even so, what would the thief have got for the parts he lifted? Five thousand pounds? Six? It seemed a paltry payback, but in these troubled times perhaps it was about right. Looking down at the brutalized interior of the car, the blood smears on the window, Hudson reflected that of late one thing had become abundantly clear.

Life was cheap.

Chapter 5

His eyes were glued to the Portakabin, transfixed by the sight in front of him. Through the thin blinds, he could make out the flames reaching for the ceiling, desperate to satiate their appetite for destruction. And even above the crackling of timber, chipboard and plastic, he could hear the screaming.

He had never heard a man shriek before. In his line of work, it was not something you came across. And he'd certainly never heard a man shriek like *that*. It didn't sound human – it was so shrill, so insistent, dragged from the pit of his stomach. It was at once terrible and wonderful.

He would be the sole witness to McManus's last moments, the extinguishing of a life. Yes, he should have left immediately, sneaking through the gates and disappearing into the night – that would have been the *sensible* thing to do. But he had to stay, to see that the job was done. There was too much riding on this to leave anything to chance. So he stood his ground, positioned at the far corner of the yard, watching and waiting for the screams to cease, for the Portakabin to collapse in on itself, for the flames to leap up into the night sky.

As soon as they did so, he'd be off. As soon as he could be *sure*, he would put as much distance between himself and this awful place as possible. And then he would celebrate, happy that his nerve had held, that he'd been capable of doing what was necessary. He might regret it at some point in the future, but not yet. For now he would simply reflect on a job well done.

Dragging his eyes away from the scene, he glanced at his watch. The pristine Omega showed him it was just before eleven – there was plenty of time to get where he needed to be without arousing suspicion. Such was the virtue of having a plan, of taking suitable precautions, of doing something right—

A loud noise made him look up. There it was again – a heavy, repetitive banging. And now he became aware of something else – the Portakabin seemed to be shaking. What the hell was going on? Was the fabric of the tired office finally cracking, splintering under the vicious assault of the flames? Then, suddenly and unexpectedly, he had his answer, the locked door bursting open, the unmistakable form of Declan McManus crashing out onto the scrubby ground below.

For a moment, he couldn't believe what he was seeing. He'd never expected his victim to *survive* the initial assault of the flames, let alone have strength enough to break out of the Portakabin. But there he lay on the ground, his clothes still burning, large as life. Immediately, the attacker's eyes fell on a discarded tool, a rusting wrench that lay next to the shell of a Ford Mondeo. Should he pick it up? Rush over and cave the injured man's head in? He reached towards it, but his attention was now drawn back to his victim. And what he saw chilled his blood.

McManus had risen to his feet. He was stumbling, raging, screaming, but he was upright. Even now he was blundering forward, bumping into old chassis, clinging on to packing cases. As he did so, zigzagging from obstacle to obstacle, he left a flaming trail in his wake, the discarded boxes and packing paper catching light as he passed. It was a bewildering, horrifying procession, but surely it would be short-lived? The man was on fire, for God's sake, surely he would succumb to his injuries soon ... but on he went, staggering away from the Portakabin, searching for salvation.

He watched on, horrified, transfixed, but worse was to follow. McManus had been stumbling towards the main gates, but now suddenly changed direction. Even in his agony, the flaming man had been casting around for help, any means of saving his skin and now he'd spotted *him*, standing across the yard in the shadows, passively watching his torment. Now McManus was making directly for him, speeding up as he did so, lurching towards his potential rescuer.

The man's eyes widened, even as vomit crept up his throat. Never in his worst nightmares had he imagined something like *this*. McManus continued to gain momentum, barrelling towards him, his flaming arms reaching out, even as the fire continued to consume his hair, his limbs, his skin. He knew he should turn and run, flee a man whom he had badly underestimated, yet for some reason his feet remained rooted to the spot. McManus was only twenty feet from him, now fifteen, now ten. Any minute now, he would throw himself upon his attacker, locking him in an agonizing embrace. So why wouldn't his feet obey him? Why did he continue to stand there, waiting patiently for oblivion?

He felt tears prick his eyes and he clamped them shut, bracing himself for the impact. Then he felt a rush of air, followed by a hefty thud and, opening his eyes a fraction, he saw that the portly aggressor had suddenly collapsed, falling in a crumpled heap by his feet. Relief now flooded through him, a high-pitched laugh exploding from his lungs, as he stared down at the twitching man. He couldn't believe it – McManus had made it all the way across the yard, only to fall just short of him.

It scarcely seemed believable, but the burning trail of

destruction in the yard was testament to his amazing progress. And even now as he looked at his wake, drinking in the blazing boxes and packing cases, he saw the Portakabin roof collapse, sending a great shower of sparks up into the air.

The alarm would soon be raised. The whole yard was catching alight, thin trails of smoke climbing up into the sky. It was no time to linger, so turning on his heel, he made for a sizeable tear in the chain-link fence, squeezing through it and hurrying away.

Chapter 6

She wrenched open the door and pushed inside. The incident room was deserted, which was how Helen wanted it. She needed time to gather her thoughts, following her trip to the mortuary.

Crossing the room, she headed not for her office, but to the murder board. Here, pictures of victims and suspects were displayed for analysis, surrounded by a spaghetti of supposition – marker pen lines linking individuals, leads and theories. Usually the sight excited her – as the board filled up, the different jigsaw pieces of the truth inexorably came together – but tonight it left her feeling like she'd been slapped.

Southampton was a vibrant city, with its fair share of crime, so it was customary to have two or three serious investigations on the go. Currently they had four – four murders that they had made no tangible progress on. A fatal mugging in Ocean Village three weeks back, an aggravated burglary in Upper Shirley shortly after that, a carjacking in the city centre and, of course, the recent murder of Eve Sutcliffe. All these cases had made headlines in different ways – the mugging victim was a mother of two, the middle-aged man who'd tackled an intruder was a self-made millionaire, the carjack victim was a young NHS manager and as for Eve … well, she was a 'gift' for tabloid hacks and vampires like Emilia Garanita, the local journalist who used her newspaper columns to dwell on Eve's beauty, her talent, her tender age. With each new case, with each new banner headline, the pressure ratcheted up a notch, placing Helen and the team under severe scrutiny.

The unit's murder board had never been so full, yet so empty – a point Chief Superintendent Alan Peters had made forcibly on his recent visit to the incident room. Helen couldn't remember a time when the city had felt so febrile, so dangerous, and it wasn't hard to figure out why – numerous local businesses having gone to the wall since Covid. Unemployment had spiked, as had divorce, domestic violence, child abuse and countless other serious offences. There was a general sense of fear, anger, even desperation in the city, but it was the recent spate of murders that brought the situation home most starkly.

The mugging, the burglary, the carjacking – these were economic crimes, laced with violence, perpetrated by those who thought there was more money to be made in the shadows, on the black market, than in the regular working world. Even the attack on Eve Sutcliffe was a testament to the profound legacy of the downturn, sexual crimes and crimes against women having also sky rocketed – powerless, desperate individuals taking out their fury, resentment and despair on the vulnerable.

'Not a pretty sight, is it?'

Helen turned, her body tensing. Joseph Hudson had slipped into the room without her noticing and was standing close by.

'I'm sorry?' Helen queried, annoyed.

Hudson held Helen's gaze for a moment, enjoying her discomfort, then shifted his attention to the varied photos on the murder board.

'All that pain, all that suffering. And for what? A few pounds in the pocket, a fleeting moment of pleasure ...' He shook his head ruefully, but there was a ghost of a smile on his lips. 'It's like the old rules don't apply any more,' he continued. 'Decency, respect, humanity. It's a dog-eat-dog world out there now. Every man – or woman – for themselves.'

Hudson wasn't looking at her, but Helen could hardly miss his point. Several months ago, Helen had called time on their relationship, intimating that it might be a good idea if Hudson moved on from Southampton Central. Her former lover had taken this suggestion very badly, making it clear on a number of occasions since that he had no intention of going anywhere.

'Did you have anything to report, DS Hudson?' Helen countered. 'Or have you just come here—'

'We found Alison Burris's BMW,' Hudson interrupted, crossing to the murder board. 'In an alleyway just off St Mary's. Stolen, stripped and dumped, just as I said it would be. I've asked forensics to take a look at it for us.'

Picking up the marker pen, Hudson wrote the details on the board, linking this development via a crisp line to the photo of the unfortunate Burris.

'Least one of us is making progress, eh?'

Replacing the pen, he smiled broadly at Helen, then headed for the door.

'Don't stay too late, Helen. All work and no play…'

Helen watched Hudson go, desperately fighting the urge to tear a strip off him. In normal circumstances, she would have reprimanded him there and then, but these *weren't* normal circumstances. DS Charlie Brooks was still on maternity leave, meaning that Joseph Hudson was her only remaining senior officer. Given the situation, given the crime wave that was now engulfing the city, Helen *had* to rely on him, even though she was becoming increasingly troubled by his 'contribution'. He was frequently insubordinate, even hostile – something she feared the rest of the team had picked up on – and, worse, seemed to be actively enjoying her predicament.

Of late she'd even begun to wonder if Hudson was actively working *against* her, enjoying the empty murder boards, the nasty headlines, the growing pressure. It seemed a crazy idea, her own DS torpedoing their investigations out of spite, but it was a notion she couldn't shake. In her darker moments, she even began to wonder whether Hudson might be conspiring with Emilia Garanita – the thorny reporter appearing extremely well informed of late.

The truth was that Helen had never felt so isolated and exposed. Each new day seemed to bring fresh problems rather than answers. The team were looking to her for inspiration, for leadership, but for the first time she felt uncertain as to what to do. Nothing seemed to be working, the tried and tested tenets of modern policing coming up short, as her overstretched team battled a growing lawlessness in the city.

As ever, when Helen stood in front of the murder boards, she yearned to see patterns, clues, lines of enquiry, to divine a clear route to justice. But tonight, as she gazed at the empty space in front of her, she saw only the faces of the dead staring back.

Chapter 7

She pulled the scarf over her mouth and nose, then tugged hard on the drawstring of her hoodie. Carefully, she ran her fingers around the edge of the fabric, checking that her disguise was securely in place, then, satisfied that even her own mother wouldn't recognize her, she emerged from the shadows.

She had been skulking in the basement stairwell for nearly two hours, waiting for the right moment to break cover. Several times she'd ventured up to the street level, but each time something had given her pause – the bark of a dog, a door slamming, and, most alarmingly of all, a couple wandering by. They had been happy – drunk, laughing, amorous – but their sudden appearance had set her heart racing.

Fortunately, the danger had passed, the couple walking on, oblivious, but she didn't want to push her luck by outstaying her welcome. Nervously checking that the coast was clear, she stepped out onto the pavement and, keeping low, scurried across the road, concealing herself between parked cars on the other side. Here again she hesitated, convinced something was about to go wrong – a nosey neighbour spotting her, a beat copper passing by – but Ashley Road was as quiet as the grave.

She looked at her watch – half midnight – then fixed her gaze on the house in front of her. Her attention had been glued to

Number 21 since she'd arrived, watching the comings and goings inside – figures flitting behind the drawn curtains, lights turning on and off, before, finally, the house settled into contented darkness. There had been no movement, no signs of life, for over three quarters of an hour now. With luck, the inhabitants were slumbering peacefully, unaware of the vitriol and hatred that lurked outside.

Another quick check, scanning the upper windows of the neighbouring houses, then the figure emerged from behind the parked car, cresting the pavement and hurrying up the steps to the front door. Lilah and Martin Hill didn't have a dog, an alarm, or any security cameras, but even so, this was still a very dangerous moment. Given everything that had happened recently, who was to say that they *wouldn't* be on their guard? That the door wouldn't suddenly spring open? That she wouldn't be caught *red-handed*?

But there was no movement inside, no sound anywhere, so reaching into her pocket, she pulled out the aerosol can. Shaking it, she held it up to the door and pressed down hard. Immediately, a jet of black paint spewed forth, spoiling the fashionably grey door. The eruption made her start, but gathering herself, she pressed on, sketching out the first line. It was hardly a polished effort, looking uneven and irregular, but it was at least clear, so she continued, carving out the second line with one vicious sweep of her arm.

Now she was getting the hang of it, gaining confidence with each passing second, moving swiftly and smoothly. She was reaching the end of the door, so aimed the paint onto the white wall, then onto the living-room window, sketching out the vile symbol deftly. The design was nearly complete now, so doubling back once more, she concluded her handiwork with a grim flourish.

The whole operation had taken no more than a minute, but still she stood breathless in front of her handiwork, the adrenaline coursing through her. She'd achieved what she came to do, defacing the pretty terraced house, but could she get away without being spotted, or worse, challenged? Replacing the aerosol in her pocket, she scuttled back down the steps and away down the street.

She didn't dare look back, couldn't bear to see if Lilah or Martin were even now throwing open the front door and setting off in pursuit. She'd never done this kind of thing before, felt certain she would mess it up ... yet each step took her closer to safety. She had put fifty yards between herself and the house already, maybe more. Even if someone *did* challenge her now, could they be sure that she was the culprit? Only a body search would reveal that – another good reason to dump the tell-tale aerosol as soon as possible.

She was nearing the end of the street. Once she was back on the main street, blending in with the human traffic, she would feel better. Covering the last few feet in a matter of seconds, she swept around the corner, making one final burst for freedom. But even as she did so, an ear-splitting wail arrested her progress.

Sirens. She could hear sirens, close by and insistent. It didn't seem possible – how had they got here so quickly? *Had* someone been watching her? Hidden away behind the curtains, surreptitiously dialling the police as they took in her wanton act of vandalism? She thought she had been so careful, so cautious. Was it all going to unravel before it had even begun?

The sirens were getting louder, but still she remained frozen on the spot. She was paralyzed by uncertainty, not knowing what to do for the best. The approaching vehicles were nearly upon her, their remorseless wail growing louder with each second.

Now instinct took over and she hurled herself backwards into the shadows, shielding her face with her arm, even as a pair of fire engines raced past.

She could have laughed out loud, if she wasn't so scared. Panting heavily, she watched the speeding fire engines slowly grow smaller, before eventually disappearing from view altogether. Only then did she emerge from the shadows, turning on her heel and sprinting away down the street as if her life depended upon it.

Chapter 8

She padded across the smooth, wooden floor, enjoying the deathly calm of this silent space. Helen hadn't lingered in the office following her encounter with Joseph Hudson, too aggravated and unnerved to achieve anything there. Instead, she'd hurried back to her flat.

Joseph Hudson had spent much time here during their brief romance – in her kitchen, her living room, her bed. Relationships between police colleagues were seriously frowned upon, so they had conducted their liaison in secret, mostly within these four walls. Hudson's imprint on her flat, and, in truth, her heart, had been minimal, however, and she'd successfully expunged any lingering trace of him, meaning her flat was still the one place where she could relax, where she could truly find some peace.

Tonight, however, her phone started ringing almost as soon as she'd sat down on the sofa. The TV remote was still in her hand, pointing forlornly at the blank screen, but she tossed it aside, scooping up her mobile instead. To her relief, it was just her immediate boss, DCI Grace Simmons, on the other end.

'You're up late, ma'am.'

'Can't sleep. And you can drop the "ma'am". It makes me feel like I'm eighty.'

'Sorry.'

'Though on present form that might be about right...' Simmons joked breathlessly, before changing tack. 'Anyway, how are you? I'm sorry I couldn't make it in today, just wanted to see how you got on.'

'Slow but steady...'

Helen would've loved to be able to give her friend and mentor better news, but there was no point offering false hope. In truth, they were no further on than they'd been this morning, but even so, Helen was glad of the call. Grace Simmons was a fitful presence at Southampton Central these days, but she remained a firm friend and ally.

'We've got so many lines running that, honestly, we're a bit thin on the ground at the moment. I keep hoping Charlie will get bored of changing nappies and return to the fray...'

'I'm working on getting you some reinforcements. But you know what Peters is like, always keeping a close eye on the pennies.'

'We'll be fine,' Helen reassured her. 'We just need to get a break, something to give us some forward momentum.'

This was only partially true. There was much more Helen *could* have shared with her boss – her problems with Hudson, a growing sense of discontent within the team – but she wasn't ready to confess these just yet.

'Well, you have my full confidence,' Simmons replied warmly. 'If anyone can do it, you can.'

DCI Simmons rang off shortly afterwards, leaving Helen alone with her thoughts. Their brief conversation had cheered her, but she knew she wouldn't be able to relax just yet, nagging fears and anxieties continuing to circle. Abandoning the TV, she marched into the kitchen to grab a drink of water, before heading out onto her small terrace.

Her flat was on the top floor, commanding fine views of the

city. Helen often ended her evenings here, letting the warm breeze comfort her, as she listened to the muffled sound of the shipping in the Solent. Southampton was a boisterous city, but nights like this could be very still, soothing even, a necessary tonic after a tough day's work.

Gripping the rail, Helen looked out over the city, eerily beautiful tonight in the glow of the full moon. The wind was strong, the hot air smothering her, and normally she would have found its warmth comforting. But tonight the breeze carried a disturbing note in her direction, the sound of sirens. Listening intently, Helen oriented herself, turning slowly in the direction of the sound. And now she saw it. Not as she'd expected, a collection of flashing lights speeding through the streets, but something much more alarming. For even at this late hour, in the silvery half-light, Helen could make it out – a huge plume of smoke rising up into the night sky.

Day Two

Chapter 9

The morning sunlight streamed through the windows, illuminating the kitchen. The Miele appliances glistened, the quartz worktop sparkled, even the Quooker was getting in on the act, winking sunbeams around the spacious room. It was an impressive sight – a bright, welcoming modernization of an attractive period kitchen – but generally this vista depressed Robert Downing, especially when it was so devoid of life.

Previously, it had been the heart of the family, Alexia, he and the boys spending many happy hours together, making pancakes, throwing soap bubbles, tucking into a Sunday roast. Then the marriage had foundered, with the result that it was usually just him and the boys, and occasionally, as today, just him, the twins having spent last night with their mother. Usually this isolation put Robert in a funk, gripped by a low-level feeling of anger and dissatisfaction, which often lasted the whole day. Today it seemed worse still, as if the opulent, echoing room was a vision of the future, a snapshot of what his life *might* be like if he came off second best in their forthcoming custody hearing. It didn't bear thinking about – the serenity, the silence in the large room, was crushing.

Plonking the coffee pot on the hob, Robert fired up the burner, then angled a look at his watch before flicking on the radio, keen to distract himself from these negative thoughts. It still seemed impossible that his life had unravelled so quickly, so completely. Often, he couldn't help himself, poring over the details, the cracks he should have seen, the things that had gone unsaid. Yes, he'd had his suspicions that Alexia wasn't happy, but he'd never have guessed that she would seek affection elsewhere and that before long that bastard Graham would be playing daddy to *his* boys. Even now the thought made him seethe...

In a flash, Robert had gone from being the thrusting, success-ful barrister with the glamorous wife, lovely boys and desirable home to being the lonely bachelor carving up ownership of the house and custody of the twins, even as he tried to be a good dad to two very confused boys. He was now the kind of man women took pity on, bringing food, comfort and *plenty* of advice on how to cope. It all seemed so wrong, yet somehow this was the bitter reality – a man alone with his thoughts, staring down the barrel.

The coffee pot was starting to bubble, even as the local weathercaster droned on, confirming that it would be another sweltering day in the city. That was all he needed, another stultifying session in an airless court, but at least there was one small crumb of comfort today. He was picking up the boys later and bringing them home. How long he would continue to do so was in question, but he would make sure they had a great time tonight. Once they had done their homework, he would spoil them rotten – cookie dough ice cream, a family-size pack of Sours and whatever they wanted on Netflix. The thought made his heavy heart sing.

The weather report had finished, replaced by the sombre tones of the newsreader, reminding Robert that he had to get a move on – he was due in court at ten. Scooping up his brief, he slid it into his case. Then he moved over to the worktop to grab his phone from the charger, but even as he did so, something grabbed his attention, the newscaster's words cutting through his self-absorption.

'...attended a major fire in the Locks Heath area of the city.'

He paused in his preparations.

'The blaze, which took hold in a scrapyard, burned for several hours, driving local residents from their homes, but is now under control. Hampshire Police have confirmed that there was one casualty, forty-two-year-old Declan McManus...'

Robert hurried over to the radio to turn it up.

'He is currently being treated in the burns unit of Southampton University Hospital and though there has so far been no update on his progress, hospital staff have confirmed that his condition is critical...'

He stood stock still, uncertain whether to be worried or pleased. He had never wished harm on anyone, but he made an exception for McManus, who was a blood-sucking parasite. And now he was on the verge of death, crippled by life-changing injuries. The reporter continued, outlining the police response and the possible theories concerning the provenance of the blaze, most of which seemed to centre on foul play. Robert remained where he was, drinking in the detail, even as the coffee pot clanked and bubbled noisily in the background, spilling its sticky, boiling contents all over the immaculate surface. He had no interest any more in this kitchen, his breakfast, or indeed the court hearing that he was due to attend. Now he had only one question on his mind.

Would Declan McManus live or die?

Chapter 10

She took in the scene in front of her, scarcely believing what she was seeing. It was a picture of utter desolation.

Helen had called Southampton Central as soon as she spotted the conflagration last night – the hassled desk sergeant confirming that a major fire was raging in Locks Heath. Helen's initial hope was that the incident would be of interest purely to Hampshire Fire Service, but once the identity of the victim had been established, it immediately became clear that her team would need to investigate. Declan McManus was an ex-Met copper, drummed out of the Force following a lengthy corruption investigation, who'd now taken up residence in Southampton, working as a private detective. Helen had run into him on a couple of occasions over the past few years, but had never been sure where he operated from. Until now.

Dispatching DS Hudson to interview McManus's shocked girlfriend, Helen had headed to the site. The yard, which up until two years ago had been owned by a scrap-metal merchant, was littered with the wreckage of a major blaze. Picking her way through the charred detritus, her scarf over her face to shield her lungs from the acrid aroma, Helen moved cautiously towards the Portakabin, keen to see if anything had survived of what she now assumed was McManus's nerve centre. Hovering in the doorway, however, taking in the smouldering ashes, Helen knew she was destined to be disappointed.

'Well, it's not to everyone's taste, but it's cheap and with careful renovation...'

Helen looked up to see their chief forensics officer, Meredith Walker, approaching. As ever, she was clad in a sterile suit, latex gloves and mask.

'Think we'll be able to salvage anything?' Helen responded, smiling.

'Not sure. We haven't had a chance to conduct a fingertip search yet. But by the looks of things, nothing in this place was fire retardant...'

Helen surveyed the burnt desk, the ravaged sofa.

'Any sign of any files? Computers? Hard drives?'

'I can't see any evidence of a filing cabinet. Be just our bad luck if he kept his files in cardboard boxes. Computers and hard drives wouldn't have survived a blaze of this magnitude... We can only hope that somewhere underneath all this mess there's a safe that he kept his paperwork in...'

Helen nodded, but knew Meredith was scrabbling to find something upbeat to offer.

'And are we saying the Portakabin was the seat of the fire?' Helen replied, sniffing the air.

'Yes. There's fragments of glass and a strong residual odour of petrol. I'm guessing it was arson, though I'll have to do some more digging to be sure.'

'If it was,' Helen said, taking in the blackened interior, 'the place would have gone up like a tinderbox.'

'Taking Mr McManus with it.'

Helen nodded, but said nothing. She had encountered arson attacks before and they always left her unnerved. It was such a callous, cowardly crime.

'What about the rest of the yard? Was that torched as the attacker left?'

'I don't think so,' Meredith replied, gesturing to Helen to follow her away from the Portakabin.

The pair descended back to ground level, picking their way through the burnt carcasses around them.

'The team haven't found any traces of petrol outside the cabin, but there are fragments of burnt clothing – burnt denim, to be precise – at several spots where the cardboard boxes and packing cases went up, sparking secondary fires.'

'So, presuming the arsonist wasn't incredibly clumsy during his retreat,' Helen added, 'we can assume the clothing belonged to McManus.'

'Looks that way. The guy's on fire, in agony, desperate. In his attempt to escape the blaze, he cannons into several obstacles ...'

'... setting the rest of the yard on fire.'

'That's more or less the face of it,' Meredith confirmed. 'In fact, you can get a pretty good picture of his progress by looking at the course of the fire, not to mention the scattered fragments of clothing.'

Helen followed Meredith's gaze, picking up the evidence markers that *did* seem to illuminate the injured man's erratic progress away from the Portakabin. And even as she did so, something struck her.

'The main gates were open when uniform arrived, right?' she asked, turning to Meredith once more.

'Yup. The padlock had been broken.'

'So why didn't McManus head directly for them? That would have been his quickest route to safety, to the street ...'

Meredith followed Helen's gaze, noting how McManus had started out towards the gate, then veered abruptly left, towards the far corner of the yard.

'Perhaps he lost momentum, lost focus? His injuries were pretty severe by all accounts...'

'Or perhaps he saw something more interesting over there...'

Helen was already moving in the direction of the perimeter fence on the eastern edge of the yard, following McManus's crazy dance. Soon she had reached the spot where McManus had face-planted, his clothes still alight, his life hanging by a thread. The paramedics had reported finding him face down in the dirt, unconscious, his skin blistered and raw. Given that, it seemed incredible, impossible almost, that McManus was still alive, battling for his life at Southampton University Hospital. The ex-copper was clearly a fighter, though there was no question that the outlook was uncertain for him, even if by some miracle he *did* manage to survive.

Crouching down in the dirt, Helen examined the earth, mentally outlining the shape of McManus's prostrate body.

'What were you after, Declan...?'

Helen was aware that Meredith was watching her; moving forward, she examined the ground just beyond the fall site. And now she spotted something. The weather had been punishingly hot of late – a proper summer heatwave – but two nights ago there had been a vicious storm, the like of which you seldom see in the UK. Rain had lashed the city, leaving it dirty and besmirched and here in the cracked, dusty yard, residual traces of the storm remained. Just in front of McManus's resting place, just out of reach, was a small muddy puddle, on the fringe of which was what looked like a partial footwear mark.

'Look here.'

Meredith did as she was bid, crouching down to investigate.

'It's a trainer of some kind, I'd guess. Size eight, size nine?'

Already she was gesturing to a photographer to join them.

'You're thinking it's our arsonist?'

'Makes sense. He does the deed, retires to a safe distance to watch the blaze, then, against the odds, McManus escapes. Perhaps he makes for the gates, then changes course when he spots someone standing here. Perhaps he thinks this person's going to help him. Or perhaps he knows that this person wants him dead and means to confront him...'

'He would have been quite a sight, heading towards you, his clothes on fire, his hair ablaze.'

'Exactly,' Helen murmured, even now looking for signs of retreat.

Stepping away from the puddle, Helen scanned the ground. It was harder here, the slope rising towards the perimeter fence, but even so the progress of the fleeing arsonist was obvious, the disturbed dust patterns and partial prints of that familiar trainer illuminating his escape route.

'Now we just need to discover how he got out...'

Helen petered out, having already answered her own question. The footwear marks led straight to the boundary, where she spotted a tear in the chain-link fence. Soon they were both crouched down by it, scanning the torn wire, the ground beyond it, hoping for some further evidence of the arsonist's retreat. In the event, it was Meredith who spotted it first.

'There.'

Helen followed the line of her outstretched finger. At first, she couldn't see what Meredith was trying to indicate, then, suddenly, she spotted it. Caught on the ragged edge of one of the torn wires was a single, navy-blue thread.

Chapter 11

Sandra Keaton was teetering on the edge, liable to break at any moment.

Sucking hard on a king-size cigarette, McManus's youthful girlfriend stared at DS Joseph Hudson, her red-rimmed eyes threatening more tears. As far as Hudson had been able to make out, her relationship with McManus had been on and off at best, but she'd nevertheless taken news of the attack on him hard, unable to rid herself of the image of her lover lighting up the night sky, his skin and hair crackling in the intense heat.

'So, when were you last with Declan?' Hudson continued gently, trying to refocus the conversation.

The young woman sniffed, wiping her nose aggressively, as she considered her answer.

'Couple of days ago, but he didn't stay or nothing. He was in a right strop—'

'Because?'

'Nothing to do with me,' she countered defensively. 'He'd been having a few problems at work, that's all. Comes with the territory, I guess...'

'What kind of problems?'

'Someone had been trying to get at him.'

'Who?' Hudson replied, leaning forward.

'That was just it, he didn't know...'

She took another drag on her cigarette, running a hand through long, lank hair. They were an odd couple, no question; she was a good twenty years younger and considerably more attractive than McManus. She was, however, criminally lacking in confidence and might have been impressed by Declan's past career as a police officer and the mysterious 'glamour' of his current incarnation as a private detective.

'What exactly had happened?'

'Nothing major. About a week ago someone tried to break into his house. He's got a flat he rents over in Thornhill—'

'We know.'

'Well, someone tried to force the window when he was out. Made a pretty shit job of it, by all accounts – still needs replacing though...'

She lingered on the thought, perhaps wondering if Declan would ever again be fit to supervise the repair, whether she should perhaps do something about it.

'What were they after?'

'His laptop. Keeps all his files on there.'

'Why are you so certain that's what they were after?'

'Cos they got it two days ago.'

'They?'

'Him, She, It, whatever...'

'How?'

'Forced the boot of his car. He'd left it in there, when he came in to visit me.'

Clearly McManus didn't stay long with Sandra, making Hudson wonder what the exact nature of their relationship was, but he knew he couldn't afford to get distracted.

'Someone stole his laptop?'

'All of his work, his records, gone, just like that...' she said knowingly, as if she was contributing a major piece of the jigsaw to the case. 'He had some paper files elsewhere, but they were mostly of old investigations.'

'You seem to know a lot about it.'

'He told me bits and bobs.'

'Details of his investigations?'

'Not names or nothing, he said that wouldn't be "professional".'

She wrapped her mouth around the word, as if it was something exotic.

'So you had no idea who he was working for then – recently, I mean?'

'He took on loads of stuff, whatever paid, really. Private companies, insurance firms, individual clients, women who thought their husbands were playing away, employers who were being ripped off by their staff. He wasn't fussy.'

Hudson could well believe it.

'And Declan had no idea who might have taken the laptop?'

'That was just it, that's what made him so mad. He's made a lot of enemies over the last couple of years. People he'd showed up, whose businesses he'd threatened, who he'd got arrested, even. Truth is, there's a dozen or more people who would willingly have attacked him . . .'

Now she petered out, the image of her martyred lover fracturing her composure once more. A single tear ran down her cheek, even as she dragged the nicotine into her lungs, trying to master herself. Hudson maintained a cheery, professional expression, but inside he knew exactly how she felt. Sandra clearly thought the case was hopeless, that it would be nigh on impossible to whittle down the number of possible suspects and Hudson couldn't disagree with that assessment. Declan McManus was a grubby chancer, with few morals or scruples, willing to expose anyone in order to make some easy cash. He had been sticking his nose in where it wasn't wanted for too long and perhaps it was no surprise that someone had tried to silence him for good. Whether this was to stymie an ongoing investigation or to settle an old score was unclear, but as Hudson wrapped up the interview, he was left in no doubt that, unless McManus made a miraculous recovery, finding his attacker would be like looking for a needle in a haystack.

Chapter 12

Squeezing through the gap between the gates, Helen walked away from the yard, deep in thought. Her time with Meredith had been fruitful – she felt they had a pretty clear idea of what had happened and might even have garnered some valuable forensic evidence – but the motive for this crime was shrouded in mystery and likely to remain so, unless they could unearth some credible intel on McManus's recent goings on. The intent had been to kill, that was clear, and the fact that McManus was still clinging to life might yet prove useful. It was unlikely he'd be fit to be interviewed for days, possibly weeks, but his continuing survival might prompt his attacker to do something rash. Would they be tempted to contact the hospital? Perhaps even pay a visit there to check up on the ailing detective's condition?

Even as she thought it, Helen knew it was a long shot. DC McAndrew was currently at McManus's flat in Thornhill, whilst Hudson was talking to his girlfriend – perhaps they would turn up something, but the idea of chancing on a single, stand-out suspect seemed a fond hope, given McManus's chaotic lifestyle and multifarious investigations. The thought depressed Helen – how they could do with an easy case, an open-and-shut investigation, to bolster morale and remind the powers that be that they *were* good at their job. Lucky breaks, however, seemed thin on the ground of late.

Helen trudged towards her bike and as she neared it, her mood plummeted still further. Ranged in front of her, lounging provocatively on *her* Kawasaki, was Emilia Garanita.

'Off!' Helen barked, enraged that the journalist should even think of touching her ride.

'And a good morning to you, Helen,' Emilia chirped back, running her hand over the leather saddle, before reluctantly straightening up. 'What's cooking?'

Even as she said it, an impish smile tugged at her lips, her gaze drifting towards the smouldering wreckage beyond.

'Any *hot* leads?'

'You're hilarious,' Helen muttered, pushing past her towards her bike.

'So I'm told. But this isn't a laughing matter, is it?' Emilia gestured towards the crime scene. 'Arson, attempted murder, destruction of property,' the journalist continued. 'Any idea who had it in for McManus?'

As ever, she was irritatingly up to speed.

'We'll be holding a press conference later today, Emilia. If you're interested—'

'Oh, I know that,' the journalist returned dismissively. 'I was just wondering if *you* had a particular suspect in mind. Was it someone who was targeting him specifically? Or was it a random attack? Should the public be worried?'

'No, the public are perfectly safe.'

Climbing onto her bike, Helen turned the ignition, signalling the end of the conversation. But Garanita wasn't finished.

'Really? That's not the vibe I'm getting, not *at all*. Muggings, burglaries, carjackings, fires, you name it. And what's your clear-up rate? Zero. From what I can see, it looks very much like the city is out of control, that we're losing the battle in the midst of an unprecedented crime wave ...'

For once, Helen was inclined to agree with her. Things *did* feel out of control at the moment. But there was no way she was going to admit it.

'Been nice talking to you, Emilia. Now I really do hav—'

'Ever feel that you've been in the job too long? That perhaps you've got nothing left to give?'

The directness of the question brought Helen up short. She had been wondering the exact same thing earlier in the week, until DCI Grace Simmons had put a stop to her crisis of confidence, reminding her of her *many* past successes. Yet the questions, the doubts, remained. Emilia Garanita seemed to sense this, smiling broadly as she awaited Helen's response. But Helen was not going to play ball – not today, not ever – instead sliding down her visor and roaring away, spraying Garanita with a cloud of dust as she went.

Helen moved away at speed, but as she did so, her eye crept to her side mirror. And there was the journalist, looking utterly unperturbed by her sudden, aggressive departure. In fact, Garanita seemed to be enjoying herself, a broad grin gracing her face. It was an image that made Helen feel nauseous – not just Emilia's knowingness, her confidence, her enjoyment of their current predicament, but also her very presence. Garanita had always been a thorn in her side, but now more than ever she seemed to be an agent of persecution. She was always ahead of the pack, always hot on the scent – in fact, whenever Helen was under the cosh, reeling from yet more bloodshed and tragedy, she could be sure that when she looked up, Emilia Garanita would be standing there, a smile plastered across her face, ready to stick the knife in.

Chapter 13

She stared up at the graffiti, sickened and scared.

Lilah Hill had risen late, bolting down her breakfast, before grabbing her cycle helmet and racing down the hall, desperate not to be late for work. But as she'd approached the front door, she'd seen through the glazing that something was wrong, that someone had defaced their little home. Angry, unnerved, she'd yanked the door open, wanting to see the damage, wanting to confirm to herself that it was just some kids messing about. In her heart, however, Lilah suspected this desecration had a more sinister root and the sight that met her had confirmed that, dashing her fond hopes. Daubed across the front door and adjacent window was a large, black swastika.

It took her breath away. A symbol that contained so much hatred, bigotry and contempt. As a young black couple, she and Martin had experienced abuse and prejudice before, but never anything so pointed or personal, never at *their home*, and it left her feeling shaken and fearful.

She'd remained there for a minute, maybe two, her arms wrapped around herself, before she became aware that others had noted the attack on their house. A clutch of neighbours had gathered in the street, watching and talking whilst local schoolkids walked by, pausing en route to take in the awful image. Oddly, ridiculously, Lilah felt embarrassed, ashamed even, as if somehow this wanton act of vandalism was *her* fault. They were the only black couple living in the street, a fact that had always made her uncomfortable, and this attack increased her unease tenfold.

'Martin!'

Her voice sounded weak and fractured, but it must have conveyed her shock and distress, for moments later her husband appeared. Stepping outside, he turned to take in the damage.

'Look what they've done,' Lilah whispered, her voice shaking.

Martin scrutinized the swastika, his expression unreadable.

'They must have done it whilst we were sleeping...' Lilah continued, tears pricking her eyes.

It was a terrible thought, the idea of someone creeping up to their front door whilst they were slumbering, and she was expecting Martin to react with anger, expletives, outrage. But to her surprise, he simply shook his head and walked back inside.

'Martin? Where are you going?'

She sounded pathetic, desperate, which was more or less how she felt. Realizing what a spectacle she was now making of herself, Lilah tried to master her emotions, to regain her composure. Taking a few steps away from the house, she raised her mobile phone, snapping photos of the defaced exterior. But as she did so, Martin returned, ruining her shot. To her great surprise, he was carrying a bucket of soapy water and a sponge.

'What are you doing? We can't wipe it off!' she exclaimed, hurrying towards him.

'You want to leave it like this?'

'No, of course not. But I need to take some pictures. Plus, the police will need to see it.'

'You're calling the police?'

47

It was hard to tell if he was being sarcastic or was simply surprised.

'Of course I am. We *have* to report this.'

'For all the good it'll do.'

'We can't just let this go.'

'Well, call them if you want, but *you'll* have to clean it up, then.'

He plonked down the bucket, making to leave. And now Lilah clocked the crisp white shirt, the smart navy trousers.

'You've got a job interview...' she said, kicking herself for forgetting.

'And you wouldn't want me to miss it, would you? *You've* been the one who's been on at me to get a job.'

'Of course not.'

'Good, because I'm not going to let anyone stop me.' He looked up at the graffiti, as he spoke. 'Especially these brainless idiots. Wish me luck?'

She did as she was asked, kissing him warmly on the cheek, but her heart wasn't in it. Of course Martin had to go, he couldn't let himself be intimidated, but was he really going to leave her here alone?

'What if they come back?'

'They won't, they're cowards,' he reassured her.

'They could have done anything last night. Poured petrol through the letterbox or—'

'They wouldn't have the balls. We won't be seeing them again, trust me.'

Turning, Martin carried on down the road, checking his phone as if nothing had happened. Upset, Lilah turned away, once more taking in the front of the house. The sight punched her in the guts and this time a tear slid down her cheek. Suddenly, she felt out of control, as if she didn't know what was going on or who, if anyone, she could trust.

'Jesus, look at that…'

The schoolboy's muttered exclamation snapped her from her introspection. Gathering herself, wiping away her tears, Lilah dialled 999. In spite of Martin's disapproval, she would do the right thing. But as she waited for the operator to answer, as her eye alighted once more on the bucket and sponge in front of her, she realized that she wanted *none* of this – the attention, the hassle, the silent judgement. No, in truth, she just wanted it all to go away.

Chapter 14

Lee Moffat threw back his head and laughed, a deep, wicked roar that filled the room. This was far better than he could possibly have hoped for.

'What's it say?' he said, finally mastering himself, turning to face his companion.

'That McManus is in intensive care, that his injuries are possibly life-threatening, that he's burnt to a fucking crisp, basically,' Darren replied, his thick Scottish accent coating the words. 'It's all over local radio, the internet, everything.'

'And they've named him?'

'Aye. "Declan McManus, a local private detective, formerly of the Met Police…"'

'Show me.'

Lee gestured at him to hand over his phone, which his companion did, albeit somewhat reluctantly. Darren's new iPhone, borrowed from a Porsche they'd lifted three days ago, was his pride and joy.

Swiftly, Lee scrolled through the news feeds, drinking in the pictures of the blaze, chuckling at the photo of McManus, whose plump, scowling face stared back at him.

'I wonder what odds you'll get on him pulling through,' he muttered.

'Best call Ladbrokes, eh?' Darren joked confidently, even as his feeble words died in the air.

Lee ignored him, lost in his own thoughts. Maybe McManus *would* die of his injuries, silencing him for good. Else he'd survive, ruined, cowed, far too concerned for his own hide to poke his nose in where it wasn't wanted. Honestly, happily, Lee didn't care which.

Either way, his life had just become *a lot* easier.

Chapter 15

'I know we need another case like a hole in the head, but these are the facts we have so far.'

The team had gathered in the incident room at Southampton Central and watched as Helen pinned a photo of Declan McManus to the murder board.

'Declan McManus, aged forty-two. Born in Belfast, but spent most of his working life in London, first as a detective sergeant in the Met's financial crimes division, then as a *disgraced* detective sergeant, dismissed from the Force for fraud, false accounting, accepting bribes and perverting the course of justice.'

There was an ironic clap from the rear of the group, one of the junior members trying to lighten the atmosphere.

Smiling briefly, Helen continued: 'He's been resident in Southampton for two years now, working as a private detective. Last night, he was the victim of an arson attack at his Portakabin office in Locks Heath. He's currently in an induced coma at Southampton University Hospital – they're saying he's critical, but stable – so for now we're treating this as attempted murder.'

'Who knew he worked there?' DC Malik asked, on the front foot as always.

'Very few people, according to his girlfriend,' Joseph Hudson spoke up. 'Sandra Keaton, a couple of people that he used as scouts on more complicated cases, but other than that—'

'What do we know about these "scouts?"' Helen queried.

Hudson didn't look up, instead scrolling through the notes on his iPhone.

'Lauren Jackson and Samuel Taylor. We've got addresses and are chasing them down now.'

Nodding briefly, Helen carried on: 'The fire was intense, as you'll have seen from the extensive coverage in the press. These are *our* photos of the scene...'

She pinned up a series of carefully framed shots, which outlined the devastation.

'Almost nothing was spared. There may be fragments of files we can muster, but I wouldn't count on it. Did we find anything at his flat in Thornhill?'

DC McAndrew shook her head. 'Dirty clothes, empty take-away boxes and a bundle of newspapers. This guy travelled light...'

'Go through all the newspapers. See if there was a particular case, person, incident that he was interested in. Anything he might have circled, articles he's torn out. Did the girlfriend have anything interesting to say?'

This time, Helen turned to face Hudson. Any residual sense of antagonism, of triumph, after their encounter last night remained well masked as he raised his eyes to meet hers, responding in a professional, considered manner.

'She was in bits and, to be honest, she didn't know much. It was very much an on-and-off thing, a relationship of convenience, nothing more.'

His gaze didn't waver for a second, a knowingness creeping back into his expression. Breaking eye contact quickly, Helen turned back to the group.

'OK, so in the absence of any obvious leads, we're going to have to go back to basics. Who was McManus seeing? Who was he talking to? Where was he going? We've already pulled his call history from the phone company.'

Helen held up a sheaf of papers, all of which were studded with telephone numbers and call durations.

'This gives us an idea of who McManus had contacted recently, though obviously not the content of those conversations. We'll need to talk to everyone on this list, but we should also canvas neighbours and local residents near the yard. Did they see anyone loitering, near his flat, his car, the Portakabin? Was he arguing with anyone in the days leading up to the arson attack? Let's also go through the obvious CCTV pinch points – the train station, the Westquay shopping centre, the hospitals. Was he tailing anyone? He has no immediate family locally – his ex-wives live in Belfast and Durham respectively and have no contact with him – so let's really dig down into his professional life. We know that someone tried to access his flat a week ago, that his laptop was stolen from his car the day before yesterday, and that pretty much all of his casework files went up in the blaze. The manner of the attack suggests that his attempted murder was not impulsive, but instead a carefully planned attempt on his life, so, for the moment, I'm assuming that it was linked to his job. What was he doing that people didn't like? What did they want to *stop*?'

'What sort of thing was he known for?' DC Osbourne asked.

'Anything and everything. Financial crime, corporate fraud, insurance scams, infidelities, bigamy, will disputes. He did some work for lawyers' firms too—'

'It's got to be financial,' Hudson interrupted abruptly. 'Something active, something ongoing that threatened some lowlife's scam or enterprise.'

'Not necessarily,' Helen retorted. 'He could have been silenced to protect someone's marriage, their family, their livelihood—'

'Or it could be revenge for something he'd done on a previous assignment,' DC Bentham offered. 'The settling of an old score, by someone whose life had *already* been ruined by McManu—'

'I don't buy it,' Hudson interjected once more, cutting him off. 'You'd have to be pretty pissed off to go to such lengths over an old score. I think whoever did this was desperate, up against the wall, a person or organization who wanted to send out a message that this is what you get if you meddle in their business.'

'You think it was a gang, then? Organized crime?' Helen responded calmly, determined not to be riled by Hudson's aggressive manner.

'I think it's to do with *money*,' Hudson replied firmly. 'Look at the board. Pretty much every major investigation we've got on has a financial motive at its core. Whether it's iPhones or laptops or luxury vehicles that people are after, they're just look-ing to make some easy cash. The job market is screwed, people's savings are gone, the insurance companies aren't paying out, so people are going to the black market. The only people making money currently are those who can supply that market with stolen goods, car parts, whatever. Now we know McManus had a number of retainers with major insurance companies, that's where most of his work came from. All I'm saying is, that if someone had a good racket going, and McManus threatened to expose them, then the obvious step would be to shut him down, close down his operation *for good.*'

'And that may well be what happened. But I want us to keep our options open at this early stage of the investigation.' As she spoke, Helen turned away from Hudson to face the group once more. 'So we do the boring things, the obvious things. A crime of this brutality doesn't come from nowhere. Something's happened – a threat made, a word spoken out of turn, the fracturing of a relationship – and last night Declan McManus paid the price. Maybe we'll get lucky with CCTV or a witness, but my guess is that the culprit is someone who was connected to McManus, who *knew* him.' As she concluded, Helen held up the victim's call log once more. 'So, let's chase down everyone he was talking to and find out what they wanted, because, odds on, one of them had a motive to kill.'

Chapter 16

She felt as if the eyes of the world were upon her, but, turning, she saw that no one present had paid her so much as a second glance. She was utterly anonymous in the home depot store, which is how she wanted it.

Pulling her baseball cap down, she carried on. Picking up the pace, she strode past wallpaper, past lighting, past the stacked pyramids of paint tins, until eventually she came to kitchenware. This was not a store she was familiar with; she found the layout frustrating and confusing, and it took her a few minutes to orient herself. There were great piles of frying pans and blenders for sale, flanked by cheap cutlery and colourful colanders. Wandering through them, as if browsing for bargains, she slowly zeroed in on the kitchen utensils. Spatulas, whisks, tongs, fish slices and, finally, knives.

For a moment, she let her eyes skim over the familiar names – Sabatier at the top end, the store's own brand at the bottom. Many of the more expensive items had security tags on them, so she breezed past these to the bargain buys. Now she paused, assessing the options, before finally settling on an eight-inch kitchen knife that fitted the bill.

She was tempted to reach out and grab it, but she held back, taking a moment to calm herself. Remembering the drill she'd rehearsed, she looked at her watch, then down the aisle, as if searching for a tardy partner. There was no one to her right, so she turned to her left, hoping for the same empty vista. But to her horror, a security guard now stood at the end of the aisle, looking directly at her.

Had he spotted something unusual in her behaviour? Did he *know* she was up to no good? She smiled at him, despite the fact that she was quaking inside, and to her immense relief, he smiled back, before heading on his way. Again she ached to snatch up the knife and run, but she stopped herself, angling a glance up at the ceiling, searching for cameras. There were no specific cameras in the vicinity, just a general surveillance unit, housed in a clear plastic dome, some thirty feet away from her. Satisfied, she examined a spatula on a higher shelf, in the process angling her body towards the camera, so that the cheaper kitchen knives were hidden from view. Replacing the spatula with her right hand, she now gathered up the kitchen knife with her left, slipping it smoothly into her handbag. With a theatrical little shake of the head, she left the spatula where it was and walked away, zipping up her bag.

To all and intents and purposes she was just another shopper going about her business. In reality, of course, she was anything but. She'd been terrified on arrival, convinced she would bungle this petty act of criminality, but now felt giddy and excited, bestowing a smile on the checkout girl, before striding off with her bottle of white spirit, past the security barriers and through the exit, convinced that no one was any the wiser.

As the warm air hit her, she felt her spirits soar. The adrenaline, the relief, coursed through her as she marched across the car park. Again, she was tempted to cut loose, to sprint across the tarmac, putting as much distance between herself and the home store as possible. But again, caution and calculation won out, so she walked on with a measured step, suppressing a smile and trying her very best not to look suspicious.

Chapter 17

They strode along the pavement, their feet perfectly in time with one another.

'To what do I owe this unexpected pleasure?'

Helen was parallel to the speaker, so could not tell whether Robert Downing's cheerful greeting extended as far as his eyes. His gaze was fixed straight ahead, walking fast away from Southampton Crown Court, his brief, gown and wig clutched tightly under his arm.

'I'm assuming you heard about the fire over in Locks Heath last night?'

'Sure, it was on the radio. Some kind of scrapyard, wasn't it?'

'Used to be. More recently it was the hideout-cum-office of Declan McManus, a local private detective.'

'I see.' His tone was studiedly neutral.

'Anyway,' Helen continued, 'we're just running a rule over his movements, his contacts, during the last few weeks. And your number came up.'

She was looking for a reaction, a flicker of recognition, guilt, alarm perhaps, but there was nothing. Downing's face remained a mask of professional disinterest. Helen wasn't surprised – she knew the barrister well from the Southampton circuit – and knew that he was always friendly, polite and unruffled. Privately, she wondered if he ever let his guard down.

'The name doesn't ring a bell,' he answered eventually. 'Can you describe him to me?'

'Short, wide, thinning red hair, Belfast accent. Used to be a Met copper—'

'OK, yes … I think I know who you mean,' Downing cut in. 'He had a very strong accent, as I recall. Was quite hard to make out what he was saying…'

'What was the nature of his contact with you?'

'Well, he rang me on my mobile,' Downing continued. 'No idea how he got the number.'

'And?'

'Well, it was about ten days or so ago now. I was at home with the boys, so I was tempted not to answer, but you never know who it might be, so I took the call.'

'What was he after?' Helen pressed him, beginning to feel that Downing was deliberately wasting time, his parked car just a hundred feet away now.

Clocking her urgency, Downing turned to face her for the first time. 'He was looking for work.'

'What sort of work?'

'Well, he gave me a brief résumé of his clients. I'm sure you know all this already, but on top of the work he does for insurance companies, he occasionally works for local law firms. Surveillance, background checks, door-stepping, that sort of thing – ascertaining whether people suing big organizations really *are* as injured, depressed, aggrieved as they claim to be, whether the children they're claiming benefits for really exist. Basically, if you can't get out of something via standard legal methods, you employ someone like McManus to see if there's *another* way around it…'

'And this was the first time he'd contacted you?'

'The only time,' Downing clarified.

'And what did you say to him?'

'Not a lot. After his initial pitch, I thanked him and hung up. I wasn't going to waste my Saturday talking to a cold caller.'

'And that was it? There were no follow-up calls? On your landline, to your office?'

'No, nothing,' Downing confirmed. 'I wasn't exactly encouraging, so I think he got the message.'

They had reached his car, Downing slowing as he turned to Helen once more.

'Now was that everything, or...?'

'For now.'

She could have pressed him further, but his story seemed to stack up. McManus's call log showed only one call to Downing's number, the whole exchange lasting less than a minute.

'Well, then, I must run,' Downing concluded. 'But it really has been a pleasure, Helen. You take care of yourself now.'

Nodding warmly at her, Downing turned and flung open the car door. Stepping back, Helen watched him drive away, impressed in spite of herself. Others might have been flustered by her unexpected appearance, but Downing had never broken stride, remaining cordial, helpful and efficient throughout. He'd appeared eager to help, answering her questions smoothly and fluently, keen to clear up any misunderstanding about the nature of his 'relationship' with McManus. Whether Helen would have been able to tell if he was deliberately misleading her, however, was debatable. This was a man who lied for a living.

She was still mulling over their exchange when her mobile buzzed. She was intrigued to see that it was Meredith Walker calling.

'Morning, Meredith. What can I do for you?'

'It's more what I can do for *you*,' she replied cheerily. 'Any chance you could pop over to the lab?'

Helen was already hurrying to her bike. Experience had taught her that when Meredith called, you came running.

Chapter 18

She forced a smile, but couldn't hide her irritation, as DS Joseph Hudson made his way across the café towards her. Emilia Garanita had finished her lunch over half an hour ago and was keen to be away from the busy builders' pit stop – the smell of brown sauce and bacon was beginning to affect her.

'You're late,' she chided him, as he took a seat opposite her, darting a quick look around to check they weren't being watched.

'Nice to see you too, Emilia,' he replied, turning to face her. 'And sorry for keeping you, but we do have rather a lot on at the moment.'

'You working on the McManus case?'

He nodded. 'Helen's had the whole team checking out McManus's contacts. Pretty pointless, really, he seems to have spent most of his time chasing teenage girls who wouldn't give him the time of day.'

'It's that bad, is it?' Emilia replied, surprised. 'I thought with someone like McManus there'd be an obvious suspect, an investigation he was about to break, someone he was going to expose…'

'Nothing obvious about it. All his files were destroyed, his computer nicked. We've got some info from his phone, but he changed SIM card and devices regularly in case he was hacked, so it's not given us much…'

'What about CCTV? Witnesses?'

'There's very little coverage in that part of town and you don't wander around there late at night, so—'

'So unless he wakes up and points the finger, you're clutching at straws.'

'Something like that,' Hudson replied dryly. 'Jesus, what do you need to do to get served in here?'

He craned his neck round, searching for a waitress, but Emilia didn't have time to be diverted.

'So if I highlight the lack of leads, the vast array of possible suspects, the huge stretch on resources, and the general lack of direction, that would be about right?'

'That's the size of it,' Hudson answered, returning his attention to her.

'Because I don't want to be surprised by a sudden rabbit out of the hat,' Emilia continued.

'You won't be.'

'Good,' she said, rising. 'Call me if there are any developments.'

Nodding, Hudson resumed his hunt for a cup of tea, but Emilia didn't linger, striding through the café and out the door. She was glad to be away – the sun was strong already, making the greasy spoon uncomfortably stuffy – and, besides, she had work to do. She had seldom felt more excited, more energized. Since the downturn, the only growth business in Southampton had been crime – for perpetrators and reporters alike. She had never been so busy – the murders, rapes, muggings piling up, providing a never-ending carousel of misery and fear for their readers. Her output was up, circulation was up, and the *Southampton Evening News* was turning a nice profit, increasing its space for adverts peddling home-security equipment, rape alarms and pepper spray, not to mention divorce lawyers, employment experts and pay-day lenders.

For every cloud there was a silver lining, but that wasn't even the best bit. The really delicious part was still to come. This was not something she could brag about, it would have to remain a close secret for years, but in some ways that added to the enjoyment. Since the Justin Lanning investigation six months ago, Emilia had had DS Joseph Hudson in her pocket. He had leaked information to her regularly in the intervening period and she even had a recording of him promising to do so, during a snatched conversation from the earlier investigation. She had him in her thrall, but ambitious man that he was, he'd decided to turn this to his advantage, making an ally of his captor.

Hudson was intent on bringing Helen Grace down, willing to provide Emilia with all manner of damaging material on his boss, as well as regular, detailed updates on the investigations. Not only was Emilia ahead of the pack when bringing news of the latest murder or rape to the *Evening News*'s loyal readers, but she also now had DI Helen Grace well within her sights.

Ever since the recent spike in crime, Emilia had been on hand to lambast Helen Grace. Everyone likes to have someone to blame and in the beleaguered detective inspector, Emilia had found the perfect fall guy. Grace had been in place at Southampton Central for years, during which time she'd enjoyed many spectacular successes, but now easy victories seemed elusive. For the first time ever, Grace seemed to have lost her grip on the city, struggling to marshal the forces ranged against her, including Joseph Hudson. Did she know he was after her job? That he was intent on damaging her reputation irreparably, before going in for the kill? Either way, it made no difference. Helen Grace was on the back foot. Joseph Hudson had made it his life's work to take her chair, to cast the wounded beast into the wilderness and supplant her as the new head of Southampton Central's Major Incident Team.

And Emilia was going to help him do it.

Chapter 19

'So what have we got?' Helen enquired, still a little breathless from her sprint up the stairs.

'We've got something rather unexpected,' Meredith replied, smiling at Helen's obvious excitement.

Directing Helen's attention to the blue thread that lay on the microscope slide in front of her, the forensic scientist continued, 'I was assuming it would be a strand of fabric from a coat or a hoodie, a bit of cotton that snagged on the wire fence as our arsonist fled the scene.'

'Right...'

'And that is basically what we're looking at, except that it's not cotton. It's cashmere.'

Helen nodded, but couldn't conceal her surprise. Cashmere was the preserve of the wealthy, not the garb of a shadowy arsonist in a rough part of town.

'It appears to be new. We've had a good look at it, and it's not been washed yet. Nor does it have any ingrained dirt or dust.'

'So it's fresh off the peg?'

'Looks that way, but that's not the interesting part. What intrigued me was the colour.'

'Go on,' Helen replied, ever more curious.

'Well, at first glance it appears to be a navy-blue thread.'

'Sure.'

'But we've taken a look at the dye and it's a very unusual mix. It's basically a kind of midnight-blue, but with traces of jade and silver, to give it a richness, a sheen. It's fairly sophisticated and I would guess expensive, so I'd say you're really looking at the upper end of designer on this one. Prada, Gucci, Stella McCartney, Fendi, or perhaps something even more bespoke, something you can't buy on the high street. Whoever this belongs to, he or she was a snappy dresser. I'd love to be able to give you chapter and verse on where they got it, but, as you know, I'm more of an H&M girl.'

'You'd never guess,' Helen said laughing, taking the printed breakdown Meredith offered her.

'We've also had a bit of joy on the footprint; details are outlined here,' Meredith continued, indicating another entry on the piece of paper, 'but that's all we've got for now. Obviously, I'll buzz you if we turn up anything else.'

Thanking her, Helen was soon on her way, speed-dialling the incident room. Now that they had something to go on, she wanted the whole team on the case. The sooner they could get a lead on last night's arsonist, the greater the chance of apprehending them and bringing them to justice.

As she relayed the details to DC Malik, Helen's mind continued to turn on this surprising development. She had expected the thread to be a lead of sorts – especially if they could find CCTV footage of someone fleeing the scene in a dark-blue coat or hoodie – but the information Meredith had provided was surprising and detailed. In her head, she'd imagined McManus's attacker as a low life in tatty clothes and scruffy trainers, someone hired perhaps to do this nasty, cowardly job. But the evidence they'd gathered pointed the other way – the partial footwear mark appeared to have been made by a Philipp Plein trainer, which Helen knew cost north of £400, whilst the jacket or top probably cost several times that.

It didn't make sense, but the evidence was undeniable. The perpetrator of this brutal and cowardly attack on McManus was not a scruffy assassin or desperate hired hand. No, they were someone who took pride in their appearance, in how they presented themselves to the world.

Someone who dressed to kill.

Chapter 20

'So we think the fibre comes from a Rick Owens hoodie.'

DC Malik presented her findings without fanfare, in her customary matter-of-fact tone. It was one of the reasons Helen liked her – for Malik, it was the end result that was important, not personal glory. After a day spent chasing down McManus's contacts, the team had regrouped for a final debrief. Prompted by Helen, Malik had been focusing primarily on Meredith's lead, digging that had now born fruit.

'We're waiting for a call back from the firm themselves to confirm it, but we're pretty confident we're right. Their hoodies are one hundred per cent cashmere and the colour dye is *exclusive* to them. They call it Midnight Silk because the dark blue is offset by hints of green and "argent", which is a posh way of saying silver.'

'And where can you buy these hoodies?' Helen queried.

'Mail order only, retailing at roughly one thousand pounds.'

There was a low whistle from the back room, this sort of garment way beyond a DC's paygrade.

Unabashed, Malik continued, 'We've managed to get a print-out from the company of all the Southampton residents who've purchased one in the last two years.'

Helen looked at the handout. There were only fifteen names

and she scanned them quickly. Downing's name was not on it, but fifteen other individuals were, men who might hold the key to unravelling this baffling crime.

'Lee Moffat.'

Helen looked up to see that Joseph Hudson had spoken.

'We should look at him.' He suddenly seemed excited, as if he was onto something.

'Because?'

'Because he's a violent, immoral thug, who'd think nothing of torching McManus if he interfered with his business. Moffat and his crew have a nice line going, lifting and stripping prestige vehicles, before selling the parts to body shops, garages or private individuals. It may be that McManus was investigating them, had something on them, *plus* it might link back to the Alison Burris murder. Her BMW was taken off her by someone who didn't give a damn about human life or decency, who was happy to kill to make a quick buck. Which pretty much sums up Lee Moffat.'

Helen couldn't deny that it sounded intriguing, so, much as she hated to let Hudson take the lead on anything these days, she replied, 'OK, run with it. See if you can smoke him out.'

'I'd like to suggest that DCs McAndrew, Edwards and Reid assist,' Hudson responded. 'Moffat's got several known addresses, several aliases—'

'You can have one additional officer,' Helen replied. 'We have a lot of different names to chase down and I want them all contacted *today*.'

'But this guy has form,' Hudson insisted angrily. 'And if we can link him to two outstanding investigations—'

'Then that would be great, but that's *pure speculation* at this point. The neatest solution is not always the right one, so we check out every one of these names, see if any of them has a motive, a weak alibi, a link to McManus, *anything* that might put them in the frame. OK?'

Hudson stared at her, saying nothing, clearly displeased. Sensing the antagonism between DI and DS, the other team members lingered, seemingly uncertain whose lead to follow.

'Well, what are you waiting for? Let's get to it,' Helen continued sharply, determined to remind them of the chain of command.

Now the officers reacted, hurrying away to their work stations. Helen, too, was on the move, determined to avoid a showdown with Hudson and keen to make the most of their new lead. She was impatient to start interrogating the handful of names that DC Malik had unearthed, but even as she turned to head into her office, DC Osbourne hurried up to her.

'Sorry to interrupt, guv, but Chief Superintendent Peters' office is on the phone. He'd like to see you as soon as is convenient.'

'In other words, straightaway,' Helen grimaced.

Osbourne shrugged in rueful agreement. Being summoned to the headmaster's study was never good news. In fact, it meant only one thing.

Trouble.

Chapter 21

'Could you explain to me what the *bloody hell* is going on?' Chief Superintendent Alan Peters' blood was up and he wasted no time in getting straight to the point. 'If an alien landed in Southampton today and took a look at the newspapers, he'd think he'd touched down in Gotham City.' He gestured to the latest issue of the *Southampton Evening News*, which lay open on his desk. 'Last night's arson attack is covered in great detail on pages one to three. Eve Sutcliffe's murder is rehashed on page five, Alison Burris's fatal stabbing is on page six. Shall I go on?'

He looked up now, his frustration and anger clear. Helen remained standing, flanked by her immediate boss, DCI Grace Simmons, and their new media liaison officer, Abigail Miller, who'd both been given the courtesy of a chair. Helen had not and stood between them, looking every inch the errant child.

'I know the coverage in the papers has been extensive, sir—'

'Extensive? It's bloody *exhaustive*. There's nothing else in the paper. Even the editorial is aimed at us, a rather pointed attack on our methods, motivation and clean-up rate. The prose is terrible, but you can't deny the thrust of the argument. Things *do* appear to be getting worse, rather than better. Which may help to sell newspapers, but doesn't do much for public confidence in

73

this force. I had the police commissioner on the phone earlier, making that very point.'

Helen stared at Peters, surprised and concerned. She had seldom seen the station boss look so rattled.

'We need some progress, DI Grace. Some *results*. Where are we at with the arson attack?'

'Early stages, sir. We have some tentative leads which we're chasing down—'

'Any specific names?'

He was staring at her, challenging Helen to disappoint him. It was very tempting to give him what he wanted – to offer up Lee Moffat's name – but Helen refused to do that, not when they were still trying to establish if the young thug had any involvement in the crime.

'Not yet, but we're moving very fast—'

'And what about the victim? Any chance that he might recover consciousness? Identify his attacker, perhaps?'

'That's certainly a possibility,' Helen replied cautiously. 'I took a call from the hospital earlier. They're saying that he's responded well to treatment, that the antibiotics appear to be having an effect… but obviously they have to take things very slowly, given the severity of his injuries, hence why he's in an induced coma—'

'So, Emilia Garanita is right, is she? We've got *nothing…*'

'I don't follow, sir…'

'Garanita rang me this morning,' Abigail Miller answered, taking up the cudgels on the chief superintendent's behalf, 'asking if I would confirm that Hampshire Police were "baffled" by McManus's attempted murder and "had no tangible leads". She seemed to know the identity of the victim *and* had good detail about the incident itself, which made me wonder if she's simply chancing her arm—'

'Or whether she has a direct source of information,' Peters added.

'Meaning?'

'Don't be obtuse, DI Grace. Do we have a leak?'

'I think it's highly unlikely that anyone in the Major Incident Team would throw in their lot with Garanita,' DCI Simmons interjected. 'DI Grace and I have discussed this before and—'

'Then perhaps she'd be good enough to share her thoughts with *me*,' Peters snapped. 'Garanita does seem to be *spectacularly* well informed about our current investigations.'

Helen hesitated before replying, a dozen conflicting thoughts colliding. She *had* had the same thought herself, wondering whether Joseph Hudson might have been tempted to leak material to Garanita. Or whether one of the younger, greener DCs had been bribed or pressured into giving out privileged information. Previously, Helen had dismissed the idea – it would be career suicide – but now, for the first time, she began to have her doubts.

'Well?' Peters barked.

'I appreciate it might appear that way, but I think it's highly unlikely,' Helen replied, sounding much more confident than she felt.

'Then how do you explain it?' Miller countered, on the attack once more.

'Garanita is a very experienced, very manipulative journalist,' Simmons responded, but again was cut short.

'My question was directed to DI Grace,' Miller cut in.

Helen marvelled at Miller's front, batting DCI Simmons down like that. She would only be doing so if she'd been given authority to do so by Peters, a dangerous precedent.

'DCI Simmons is right,' Helen responded. 'Garanita has had years of experience shaping stories to make Hampshire Police look bad. She's also adept at exploiting any and every avenue of information. In the past she's targeted police constables, data analysts, even members of the media liaison team—' she shot a gimlet eye at Miller – 'and there's nothing to suggest a member of *my* team is helping her, nor that there's a leak. So instead of focusing on Garanita, can I suggest we redouble our efforts to deal with the investigations in front of us?'

'You can give us your personal guarantee, then, that the team is functioning as it should? That everyone's pulling in the same direction?'

There was something in Peters' tone which suggested he was setting her up for a fall, preparing to hang her out to dry, should that become necessary.

'Absolutely,' Helen replied firmly.

'Then we won't detain you any longer.'

Peters rose, gesturing Helen and Simmons towards the door. It had been as bad as Helen had expected, but thankfully their punishment was at an end.

'Thank you, sir.'

She nodded at the station chief, then pivoted on her heel. Abigail Miller was looking at her expectantly, hoping for some form of farewell, some acknowledgment of her importance and stature, but Helen was damned if she was going to afford her that. So, instead, she marched across the room and out the door, without once looking in her direction.

Chapter 22

'I'm sorry, that was childish of me. I should know better really...'

Helen made her apology to Grace Simmons when they were comfortably out of earshot, marching away down the deserted corridor.

'Don't sweat it,' Simmons replied, shaking her head furiously. 'I was tempted to swing for her myself.'

Helen laughed, in spite of herself. Somehow her old mentor always knew how to cheer her up.

'I mean, *really*...' Simmons continued, 'where does she get the nerve to talk down to you like that? Not to mention talking *over* me...' She gave another curt shake of the head, though this time accompanied by a wicked smile. 'Just because she's had a couple of prestigious jobs previously, a couple of safe, *corporate* gigs, suddenly she's an expert on policing? It makes my blood boil. And why Peters lets her get away with it, heaven only knows...'

She raised an eyebrow suggestively, but Helen ducked the inference, didn't want to go *there*.

'I totally agree,' Helen responded, 'but be that as it may, I will *attempt* to play nice in the future. I don't need to open up another front, trust me...'

The smile faded somewhat on Simmons's face now. For a moment, Helen thought her boss was going to pick her up on this, asking her uncomfortable questions about the state of the investigation, the mood of the team, but, instead, she slowed to a halt, laying a comforting hand on Helen's arm.

'You'll do what you think best. But know this. I've got your back. And if a jumped-up "Media Relations" graduate wants to pick a fight with you, then she'll have to go through *me*.'

Smiling once more, Simmons departed, walking briskly back to her office. Helen watched her go, comforted by her support, but nevertheless unsettled by the afternoon's developments. Helen had the distinct impression that Miller was intent on furthering the chief superintendent's hostile agenda, with no care for the cost – either in terms of her team's morale or their ability to bring the current crime wave to an end. Helen hoped that her obvious anger at Miller's line of thinking, plus her insistence that the media chief's fears were baseless, would give Miller pause. But walking back to the incident room, Helen wondered how effective her denials had been. It's hard to sound convincing when you're far from convinced yourself – and Helen could sense the suspicion and unease she'd left behind. She had fought her corner, with Simmons backing her up, but she had a nasty feeling that this was just the first battle in a long war, that the vultures would continue to circle.

Watching and waiting for their moment to strike.

Chapter 23

Her hands were shaking as she clipped the padlock shut, chaining her bike to the railings. Several hours had passed since Lilah had reported the desecration of their house to a sympathetic WPC, during which time she'd been to work, participating in two major pitches, yet the intervening period had done little to quell her anxiety, paranoia or fear. Indeed, if anything, it had got *worse*, Lilah constantly shooting anxious looks over her shoulder as she cycled home, fearful that someone might be following her.

Abandoning her bike, she walked quickly up the stairs to the front door, keeping her eyes glued to the floor, desperate to avoid the sight of the tarnished brickwork, the stained door. She had laboured hard to remove the graffiti this morning, working her fingers to the bone with sponge and soap, but the grim outline of the swastika remained visible. They were still marked by someone else's hatred.

Sliding her key into the lock, she hurried inside. She'd received many WhatsApp messages during the day, from neighbours and friends, asking if she and Martin were OK. First, she'd felt embarrassed, then angry for feeling awkward about something that was not her fault, then just anxious and depressed. She was able to let them know how she felt, was happy to do so, in fact, but she couldn't answer for Martin, who hadn't been in contact with her since he'd left for his interview at the start of the day.

'Hello?'

Lilah hurried down the hallway as she spoke. She was about to dart into the kitchen, when, suddenly, she checked herself, spotting Martin's familiar form in the living room.

'There you are,' she said, diverting into the cosy room. 'I've been messaging you all afternoon. How did the interview go?'

Martin Hill lay on the sofa in joggers, staring at the TV, but as Lilah entered he turned to face her.

'As well as could be expected.'

His resigned tone sent Lilah's heart tumbling into her boots, but she continued in bright tones.

'That's good. When will you hear?'

'End of the week.'

'Great. Well, I'm sure you've got as good a shot as anyone. Someone's got to get it, right?'

She manoeuvred his legs off the sofa, seating herself next to him, as she placed her handbag on the floor.

'And how was *your* day?'

Martin's tone had a mocking edge, as if they were merely playing at being a happy suburban couple, as if this was some kind of game.

'OK, I guess,' she lied. 'I was diabolically late for work, but they were all right about it when I explained what had happened.'

'And how were the police?'

She was hoping he wouldn't bring it up, but there was no avoiding it now.

'They were fine – good, actually. Came quickly, seemed very concerned...'

'And?'

'Well, they took a statement, some more photos. They're going to talk to the neighbours, check local CCTV—'

'We'll be the talk of the town.'

'It's not like that...'

'Anything else? Any other leads?'

Lilah retained her cheerful expression, but felt her body suddenly tense.

'Well, they... they did ask about the fight.'

Martin nodded, but said nothing.

'Obviously, they've got a record of it on their files, so they're wondering if there's a connection.'

She said it cautiously, but in Lilah's mind there was no doubt that the two events *were* linked. A month ago, she'd been racially abused by a bunch of neo-Nazi youths outside a bar in the town centre. Martin had intervened and a fight had ensued, all those involved, barring Lilah, ending up at the local police station. The teenagers had been cautioned and released, as had Martin, but his treatment at the hands of the police still rankled.

'So they think this—' he replied, gesturing to the front of the house – 'is *my* fault.'

'No, of course not.'

'Because *I* stepped in to protect you, to protect my girlfriend from being attacked, somehow *I'm* responsible?'

'You're twisting my words. All I'm saying – all the police are saying – is that it's a possibility that they're linked, that those guys have found out where we live and are now targeting us.'

'Targeting me, you mean.'

'No, targeting *us*. We're in this together, you know we are.'

'Are we?'

'Yes, of course.'

'That's funny, because lately I've been picking up a very different vibe from you. You've been avoiding me, working late, going to bed early, doing whatever you can to escape spending time with me...'

His words were measured and calm, but they still felt like a slap in the face.

'Come on, Marty. You know that's not true.'

'Really?'

'*Really*. I love spending time with you.'

'And I with you.' As he spoke, he slid his hand into hers, stroking her fingers. 'But you've got to admit you've been distant.'

'Just preoccupied with work, that's all.'

'It's more than that. In fact, ever since that fight in town, it's like you don't want to be seen with me. We never go out, you never hold my hand in public...'

'You're overthinking this—'

'Are you scared? Is that what it is?'

She stared at him, wrong-footed.

'Does *this* scare you?' he continued urgently, gesturing towards the window.

'Of course it does. Someone is targeting us.'

'Because of my actions, because I stuck up for you.'

'No.'

'Perhaps you think you'd be better off without me?'

'Of course not...'

'Maybe you think that if you put some distance between us, you'd feel happier, safer...'

As he said it, he extricated his fingers from hers, wrapping them around her wrist instead, as if binding her to him.

'Have I ever said anything to make you think that?' she protested.

'No, but you've thought it, I know you have...'

The pressure of his grip was increasing, his fingers pinching her skin.

'That's not true. I love you, I love this place, it's our home...'

'Admit it, you want *out*. You want to leave me behind, cut your losses—'

'No, no. Please, Martin you're hurting me...'

The pain was getting worse, his nails digging into her flesh.

'Then admit it.'

'No, no I won't. Because it's *not* true.'

She was determined not to crumble, not to play his game.

'I love you. I'll never leave.'

Without warning, the pressure dissipated, Martin releasing her wrist and breaking into a relieved smile.

'And I love you too. Always will.' Leaning forward, he kissed her gently on the forehead. 'And ignore me. Guess I'm more wound up by this stuff than I thought...'

Lilah nodded, but said nothing, cradling her throbbing wrist.

'Now how about we order a pizza? I could eat a horse...'

Without waiting for an answer, he headed into the hallway. A moment later, he called through, asking what she wanted. Lilah answered mechanically, but in truth she didn't care what he ordered. Her nerves were shot and her spirits at rock bottom – food had no appeal.

'Yes, can I place an order please?'

Martin was in the hall, safely out of view, in conversation with Domino's. Lilah paused for a moment, wrestling with herself, then she leaned down to clip open her handbag. Delving deep into the interior, she retrieved a half-bottle of vodka, cracking open the lid in one, practised movement. She knew it was the wrong thing to do – reckless, stupid, weak – but it was what she needed right now. So, swallowing down her distress, she pressed the bottle to her lips and began to drink.

Chapter 24

His eyes remained glued to the road as he jabbed the accelerator repeatedly, bullying the cars out of the way. It was late, but there were still a few stragglers on the streets, commuters wending their way home. Joseph Hudson ached to put the siren on, to scatter them, but he dared not announce their presence, not when success was so close at hand. Instead he had to rely on the blue light and some audacious overtaking manoeuvres to keep them on track.

'What's our ETA?' he demanded, without turning to his companion.

'Two minutes,' DC Reid replied, his eyes fixed on Googlemaps. 'The traffic thins out after this.'

'Where are the others?'

'McAndrew and Edwards are just behind us. A minute or so max...'

Angling a look in the rear-view mirror, Hudson spotted a small blue light in the distance.

'Good. Any word from base?'

'Nothing yet. Do you want me—?'

'No, we can handle this.'

'Course.'

Hudson stole a look at his companion, seeking signs of

disaffection. But, unlike that perennial pain in the arse Malik, DC Reid appeared unconcerned – in fact, he seemed excited. Hudson was pleased he'd spent so much time cultivating him. Reid was a talented and ambitious officer, with one eye to the future, who might in time prove a valuable ally.

Returning his eyes to the road, Hudson raised his speed. The traffic had cleared now and he was determined to take full advantage. Like Reid, Hudson's blood was up. Ever since they'd got a possible address for Lee Moffat, he had been energized and focused, mentally spooling forward to the young thug's apprehension and arrest. With any luck, he'd be picked up, processed and safely in the interview suite before Helen Grace was any the wiser. The less she had to do with this successful result, the better.

They were approaching the junction and, signalling left, he swung around the corner, diverting off the main road. Not all such operations were enjoyable – he'd had a high-speed car chase six months ago that had gone disastrously wrong – but when the wind was at your back, few things could compare. Tonight he felt in control, in command, as if he could bend the world to his will.

'It's this next street on the right. You might want to—'

Hudson was one step ahead of him, killing the strobing light. A gap now opened up in the adjacent lane and Hudson didn't delay, executing a long, slow lazy turn across the road and into the narrow street.

They were deep in Woolston now, never a particularly attract-ive part of town and even less so after dark. Ocean View was visible across the water, but the affluent harbour apartments and eateries seemed a world away from the decaying houses and warehouses on this side of the Solent. This was not an area of town where you came to be seen. It was a place where you came to hide.

'Which one is it?'

'Hold on...'

Reid was scanning the darkened doorways, trying to make out numbers.

'Bit further, keep going. There, that's the one...'

Dropping his speed, Hudson brought the car to a halt, killing the engine. Looking out of the window, he took in the sad building opposite him. Perhaps it had once been full of life, a happy, noisy dwelling for dock workers, but now it seemed lonely and forgotten. The windows were boarded up, the door secured with a steel shutter. It appeared to all intents and purposes to have been abandoned, but their intelligence was specific and clear – Lee Moffat had met several body-shop owners here recently to make deals, one of whom had, under duress, revealed that Moffat actually resided here. This latter witness had clocked him here not two days ago, claiming he could usually be found here early evening, getting high. Which suited Joseph Hudson perfectly.

A sound made him look up and he spotted McAndrew and Edwards pulling up. He nodded at Reid and they both climbed out, hurrying towards their colleagues.

'Phones to silent.'

Reid responded, fiddling with his phone settings. As he did so, Hudson took advantage of his distraction to send a swift message, before silencing his phone too. Content, he turned to the reinforcements, who approached, looking tense but focused.

Without further conversation, Hudson led the way to the front door. He was not surprised to see that the padlock had been severed. Gently wrapping his fingers around the metal handle, he teased it open, making sure not to drag the door's heavy frame over the hard floor. And now the interior opened up before them, pitch-black and unwelcoming.

Turning to his colleagues, a smile spread across his face, Hudson whispered: 'Ready?'

Three nodding heads, so, turning, Hudson pulled his baton from his belt and stepped into the darkness.

Chapter 25

Helen pushed into the room, then ground to a halt. The incident room, which should have been pulsing with activity, was virtually deserted. Three lonely faces, isolated and intent at their terminals, were the only officers present.

'Where is everyone?' Helen demanded, marching up to DC Malik.

'Boss?'

'The rest of the team. Where are they? I don't remember telling anyone they could clock off.'

'Oh, they haven't gone home,' Malik countered, springing to her colleagues' defence.

'So where *are* they?'

'Following up a lead, guv.'

'What lead?'

Now Malik hesitated, apparently uncertain how to proceed.

'Well... DS Hudson, he – he and DC Reid got a possible last-known address for Lee Moffat, so they've headed there to pick him up.'

'That doesn't account for everyone else.'

'DC Edwards and DC McAndrew have gone to assist...'

'And the others?'

'They're investigating two other possible addresses for Moffat, in Portswood and Fremantle...'

Helen didn't know how to respond, couldn't quite believe what she was hearing. DS Hudson, her deputy, had scrambled pretty much the whole team to chase up *his* lead, without bothering to consult her. She suspected he'd have taken the entire team if he could have, but he knew not to push it with DC Malik, who was *not* a fan. This was perhaps not surprising, given that he'd nearly killed her in a high-speed car chase not six months ago. Spinning on her heel, Helen retrieved her phone, but even as she punched in Joseph Hudson's number, she heard Malik clearing her throat.

'Yes?' Helen asked, her finger hovering over the call button.

'There *was* something else, something I wanted to show you...'

Her manner was tentative but insistent and Helen knew to take this intervention seriously. Tucking her phone away, Helen returned to her desk.

'What have you got?'

'Well, so far, we've managed to chase down seven of the fifteen local people who bought the Rick Owens hoodie. Five of them check out, they've got strong alibis, but there are a couple more I think we should look into. There's a Sam Becker, who appears to be declining our calls, and this guy...'

She handed Helen a printout, which was dominated by a glossy profile picture of a handsome middle-aged man, with a neatly trimmed beard and a bright orange turban.

'Amar Goj,' Helen intoned, scanning his particulars.

'He's Southampton born and bred, well known in the Sikh community. Very involved at the main temple and with local charities, features a lot in good news stories in the *Evening News*...'

'Seems an unlikely arsonist...'

'Sure, but he *did* buy one of these hoodies, about three months back, and here's the curious bit. He works at Southampton Children's Hospital, as a manager in procurement...'

'Isn't that where our stabbing victim worked?' Helen asked, her eyes darting to the murder board. 'Alison Burris was in the same department, I think.'

'Better than that,' Malik replied. 'Amar Goj was *her boss*. She worked under him for the past year or so.'

And now Helen looked down at Goj's smiling, confident face again. It was certainly true that the handsome professional didn't look like a midnight assassin, but the link between him and the recent murder victim was too intriguing to ignore.

'Well done, DC Malik. You can get off now.'

Turning away, Helen walked swiftly to the door, grabbing her helmet and keys en route. Hudson could chase his lead, she would chase down *hers*.

It was time to meet Amar Goj.

Chapter 26

He was in here somewhere. The question was where.

Padding across the uneven floor, Hudson kept his torch steady, slowly arcing it left to right. The beam was strong, throwing up huge, sinister shadows, the outlines of numerous engines, car seats, even whole chassis projected onto the walls. At first it looked like a wrecking yard, but on closer inspection turned it out to be a kind of showroom, Hudson's torch picking out the insignias of BMW, Mercedes, Audi, even Porsche. It was like an Aladdin's cave of cannibalized car parts and accessories. No wonder black-market dealers and mechanics beat a path to Moffat's door.

The four police officers spread out, keeping pace with each other, never letting their guard drop. Moffat and his crew had no fear of the police – they'd been in and out of prison since they could crawl – and as recent events had shown, were happy to mete out extreme violence. Their only real anxiety was getting caught – their liberty to enjoy their ill-gotten gains paramount in their minds – and they would fight tooth and nail to avoid this fate. Hence the need for extra caution.

Hudson scanned the vast room in front of them. It was an old dockside warehouse, littered with car parts and chassis, all of which might provide cover for anyone wishing to remain hidden. Was Moffat in the room even now, concealed, waiting to run, waiting to *pounce*? Hudson's heart was thumping, he sensed victory, but it wouldn't do to get a screwdriver in the guts, so he approached each obstacle cautiously, ensuring the coast was clear, before moving on. Any slip now could cost him or his colleagues dear.

On he went, past the chassis of a BMW saloon, stripped clean like a carcass in the desert. It seemed wrong, sinister even, the luxury vehicle now just a skeleton, and it made Hudson shiver. Somehow, illuminated by his piercing torch beam, it seemed to presage decay, even death. Faster now his eyes scanned the path ahead, fearful of ambush.

They were nearing the far end of the room now. If Moffat had scurried away as they'd entered, then it would be here that he would make his final stand. Again, Hudson wondered if he should have called for armed backup, but he pushed the thought away. There was no way of doing so without alerting Helen Grace, so they'd have to handle the situation alone. Still, he felt exposed with just a police baton to protect him, as he crept towards the shadowy corner of the room.

At the very rear of the room, by some barred double doors, was a new vehicle. A black Lexus, seemingly intact. Unable to see through it, Hudson paused, wondering if Moffat had hunkered down behind the boot, weapon in hand. Gesturing towards McAndrew, Reid and Edwards, he watched as they spread out, approaching the vehicle in a wide, trident formation. If their quarry was here, this was the moment he would bolt – but still he made no move.

Nodding to the others, Hudson held up three fingers, silently counting down. Three, two – Reid pre-empted him, suddenly moving forward, nerves overcoming him. Now Hudson moved too, Edwards and McAndrew just behind, racing around to the back of the vehicle. The adrenaline was coursing through Hudson, his baton raised and ready, even as a loud noise to his right made him spin round – but it was just a false alarm, an apologetic-looking McAndrew having just crushed an empty Coke can.

Angry, distracted, Hudson turned his attention back to the gloomy space behind the vehicle ... but there was no one there. Just the four of them standing breathless and frustrated, the echo of the crushed can hanging in the cavernous space, insistent and sinister.

Hudson cursed silently. Any element of surprise was gone, now it was all about speed. The building was on several levels, with any number of potential exit points and, picking out a pair of rickety stairs leading up, Hudson hurried over to them. He took them nimbly, two at a time, ascending to another vast storage area. This too was littered with car parts – just how big was Moffat's operation? – and in the corner another staircase led up to a further floor.

Hudson's heart sank. Maybe Moffat was on this level, maybe the one above, or even the one above that. Or maybe he'd already slipped out of one of the old loading bays, making good his escape. It didn't bear thinking about – having to return to base empty-handed to explain himself to Helen. He stared out into the inky darkness, his spirits plummeting, but even as he began to accept the possibility of defeat, an idea struck him. Something simple, but effective, something he should have thought of at the very start.

Retrieving his phone from his pocket, Hudson scrolled quickly through his emails, until he alighted on Lee Moffat's most recent mobile number. He clicked on it, pressing 'call'. Now it connected, but no sound was heard in the building – in fact, nothing at all disturbed the sepulchral quiet of the warehouse. But over in the far corner, in a pool of deep shadow, a bright yellow light suddenly glowed, illuminating a tall, skinny figure.

'Hello, Lee.'

Chapter 27

It was as if she'd stepped into another world, a world where only love, happiness and laughter were allowed.

Helen Grace paused on the threshold, marvelling at the sight in front of her. Having failed to raise Amar Goj at home, Helen had resorted to seeking out his neighbours, in the process discovering that Amar, and pretty much the entire local Sikh community, had decamped to an events suite at St Mary's Stadium, home to the much-loved Saints. Hastening there, Helen was surprised to find that not only was Amar Goj present, he was also *hosting* the affair – a lavish party to celebrate the engagement of his eldest daughter Kaya to local businessman Chirjot Bajwa.

Parties at St Mary's were often sober, corporate affairs, but not this one. The whole room was a riot of colour, scores of bright red and orange turbans perfectly complimented by the ladies' elegant salwars. Everyone was resplendent, decked out in their finery, yet even so it wasn't hard to divine which of the attendees was the object of Helen's interest. Amar Goj, slightly more portly in real life than in his profile picture, stood in the centre of the room, surrounded by well-wishers. His daughter and her fiancé were nominally the stars of the show, but you wouldn't know it, with Goj holding court at the heart of the proceedings, receiving congratulations from one and all. He looked every inch the happy paterfamilias and local dignitary, confident, respected, beloved.

A young couple walked past Helen, shooting her a curious look, giving her pause for thought. She had at least taken off her biking leathers, but even so, she looked curiously out of place in her navy work suit. This space, full of music, jollity and chatter, was a happy place, a sanctuary from the world's ills and she knew no one would thank her for intruding. But then she remembered the hideously injured Declan McManus, and Alison Burris's lifeless corpse, reminding herself that she had not joined the police force to make friends.

Crossing the floor, she skirted a waitress offering her a fantail prawn, before diving into the crowd. It seemed to shift and weave in front of her, a rainbow of vivid colours forming a protective sea around the party's host. Eventually, however, Helen glimpsed Goj, deep in conversation, a phalanx of patient well-wishers surrounding him.

'Excuse me.'

The music was so loud, nobody even reacted.

'EXCUSE ME.'

A couple of heads turned, displaying first confusion, then a dawning apprehension that her business here was official, not social. Helen took full advantage, manoeuvring her way to the front. Even as she did so, Amar Goj turned towards her. He was no doubt expecting more praise, more back-slapping, more *love*, and his face was a picture as it turned from benign condescension to consternation. He had no idea who this woman was or what she was doing here – she certainly *wasn't* on the guest list.

'DI Grace from Southampton Central. Might I have a quick word?'

'I'm sorry?'

'DI Grace,' she repeated, discreetly offering him her warrant card. 'I was wondering if I might have five minutes of your time.'

'Now?' He couldn't conceal his incredulity.

'It won't take long, I can assure you.'

'DI Grade—'

'Grace.'

'I'd obviously be happy to help you at a later date, but as you can see—'

'I'm afraid it can't wait.'

Now Goj faltered, aware that the hum of conversation had died away, the crowd of well-wishers watching their exchange.

'Very well, then. Can I suggest we talk at 9 a.m. tomorrow morning? I'm sure I'll be able to help you then, with whatever minor police matter this is concern—'

But Helen hadn't come all this way to be bullshitted.

'I'm conducting a murder investigation, Mr Goj,' she interrupted. 'And actually I need to talk to you *now*.'

Chapter 28

They stared at each other, a gulf of darkness between them. Hudson fixed his torch on Lee Moffat, picking out his thin, weasel features. His target was squinting, offended by the penetrating beam, looking like a cornered animal.

'Nice to see you, Lee.'

'Likewise,' was the grunted response.

'I'm DS Hudson, by the way. I've tried calling you, several times, but perhaps you've been busy ...'

'You know how it is ...' His reply was half-hearted and distracted.

Even at this distance, Hudson could make out Lee's small, dark eyes, darting hither and thither, seeking an escape route. Behind him, Hudson heard McAndrew, Reid and Edwards cresting the staircase and he waved them forward.

'Got a couple of questions for you, Lee.'

'What about?'

'About a woman called Alison Burris. She owned a BMW until fairly recently.'

'Don't know her.'

'And Declan McManus. You might have heard he had a nasty accident, a fire—'

'Means nothing to me.'

'Then perhaps you'd care to accompany us to Southampton Central, so we can straighten it all out. If you've got nothing to hide, then I'm sure we won't detain you...'

The word 'detain' seemed to give Moffat pause for thought, the young man taking a step backwards, as if scared by the very word. Hudson, by contrast, took a step forward, keen to conclude this dance. Even so, he went carefully, his eyes glued to Moffat, alive to the danger of a concealed weapon or sudden burst of activity. But Moffat was retreating now. Hudson couldn't understand it, the boy was backing himself into a corner, seemingly conceding defeat... then suddenly he got it. Their suspect was simply giving himself options, backing away past a pile of car seats that currently blocked his path. And now Moffat made his move, darting sideways and scurrying across the room.

It happened in a flash, catching Hudson and his colleagues off guard. Moffat was halfway across the room and moving fast, eating up the ground towards the far wall. Startled, Hudson broke into a sprint, pursuing the fugitive, but he was too slow to stop Moffat reaching the staircase in the far-right-hand corner of the room. Already Moffat was ascending it, driving higher and higher, away from capture, away from *them*.

Raising his speed, Hudson skidded to a halt at the bottom of the stairs, scrambling up them in pursuit. He was making good progress, warming to his task, but even as he began to gain on Moffat, his foot crashed through one of the steps, the rotten wooden board snapping clean in two. Hudson's knee dashed into the step above, even as his other leg hung helplessly in the air. Grabbing the bannister, grimacing in pain, he hauled himself upright and carried on, treading lightly on each step as he climbed higher and higher.

Stumbling onto the second floor of the building, he saw Moffat in the far corner, desperately trying to lever open a shuttered window. He was wrenching at the board with all his might and now Hudson spotted his chance. Cantering towards him, he braced himself for the impact, determined to bring the fugitive down. But Moffat was a street rat, with well-honed survival instincts and, realizing that his task was hopeless, he waited until Hudson was almost on him before bolting once more. Unable to arrest his momentum, Hudson sailed past him, crashing into the boarded window. Cannoning off it, Hudson turned, winded and embarrassed, to see Moffat sprinting away.

Was there another escape route? Somewhere on the roof, perhaps? Hudson levered himself off the wall and gave chase, falteringly now as his lungs burned and his chest heaved. Moffat was putting considerable ground between them, confident of escape... but then suddenly and unexpectedly he hit the deck hard, DC McAndrew emerging from the shadows and executing a perfectly timed rugby tackle, bringing the fleeing suspect crashing to the ground.

Surprised, elated, Hudson struggled over to them, to find Moffat squirming on the dirty floor, even as McAndrew applied the cuffs. Now she hauled him upright, reading him his rights, swiftly and professionally. Moffat appeared unable to take it in, stunned by what had just hit him.

'Right, boss,' McAndrew said, her face streaked with dirt. 'Shall we get him back to base?'

'Absolutely, but allow me...' Hudson responded, moving to take possession of the prisoner.

'It's OK, I've got him, boss.'

'No, no, I insist. You've done enough.'

McAndrew looked reluctant to relinquish her hard-earned prize, but Hudson's tone brooked no argument.

'And well done, I'll make sure you get mentioned in dispatches,' Hudson continued warmly, wrapping his hand round the man's cuffed wrists and marching him away towards the stairs.

The operation had had its tricky moments, but had ended in triumph. Barring a jarred knee, Hudson had got exactly what he wanted. A suspect in custody, his name on the arrest sheet and, assuming Emilia Garanita was in position as arranged, *his* photo in tomorrow's newspapers.

Chapter 29

'I just don't see what this has to do with *me*. I've never heard of the guy...'

Amar Goj's discomfort was genuine, but was his outrage? He was certainly putting on a good show – the aggrieved host dragged from his daughter's engagement party – but Helen wasn't sure she was buying it. In similar circumstances, when innocent parties had been questioned at inconvenient moments, there had been real anger on display. Taking in her companion now, Helen felt that this was the vibe Goj was *trying* to give off, yet somehow he only managed to come across as defensive and flustered.

'What did you say his name was? McKenzie?'

'McManus, Declan McManus. He's a private investigator.'

'Well, I don't know him. What need would I have for a private eye? I'm the Chief Operating Officer at Southampton Children's Hospital...'

'Yes, so you said.'

'My interest is in saving lives, in helping people. Not spying on them.'

'So you can account for your whereabouts last night? Between 10 p.m. and midnight?'

'Of course,' Goj said firmly, without any intention of elaborating.

'So ... you were at home? At work?'

'Neither,' was the crisp reply. 'I was sourcing some last-minute items for the party.'

'Right ...'

'Kaya decided she wanted some keepsakes for people to take away, sweetmeats and the like. It was very last minute, but I knew a shop over in Hedge End that stays open late, so I went there.'

Helen scribbled this down, without taking her eyes off him.

'And they'll confirm that, will they?'

'You'd have to ask them. But they are always very busy. It's popular with cab drivers and the late-night crowd, so picking out one middle-aged man in a turban from the rest might be tricky ...'

Helen nodded, curious as to why he'd already given his alibi an 'out', but she didn't push it. There was no point pinning him to the wall until she had cause to do so.

'Did you drive?'

'Yes, I took the Jaguar. Check the cameras on the road, you should be able to see where I went.'

He was smiling at her, trying to look relaxed and confident, but his eyes betrayed his disquiet.

'Now unless there's anything else, I really should be getting back to my guests.'

'Of course,' Helen ceded, stepping back to let him pass. She allowed him to take a few steps towards the door, then spoke up once more, 'There is one last thing ...'

Goj paused, pivoting slowly towards her once more. Helen was intrigued to see that he was perspiring heavily, sweat clinging to his craggy forehead.

'Do you own a Rick Owens cashmere hoodie?'

There was a long pause as he stared at her. He seemed utterly poleaxed by the question.

'Do I look like the kind of guy who wears hoodies?' he finally joked.

'It's just that their records show you purchased one three months back. You used a Visa credit card to purchase it; I have the number here somewhere ...'

'It's perfectly possible,' he conceded. 'I have many items of clothing; fashion is something of a hobby of mine.'

'And what about a pair of Philipp Plein trainers?'

'Again, it's possible. I do generally wear trainers, designer ones—'

'And you'd be what ...?' Helen continued, dropping her eyes to his patent-leather shoes. 'Size nine? Size ten?'

'A size nine,' Amar replied quietly, looking more confused and unnerved than ever.

'Great, thank you. That's very helpful. Enjoy tonight, but maybe stick around town for a few days; we might need to talk to you again.'

Goj nodded awkwardly at her, then turned, hurrying away. Helen watched him go, amused to see that with each step he appeared to gain speed, as if desperate to be out of her sight. This wasn't uncommon, she often had that effect on people, but somehow the NHS manager's desire to flee struck her as significant. His whole performance had been just that – an artificial display of confidence, ebullience and innocence, designed to throw her off track. But it seemed contrived and unconvincing, Goj giving the lie to his protestations by the urgency of his retreat. He was clearly rattled, unnerved by Helen's unexpected intervention – even now the NHS manager couldn't resist a brief, nervous look back over his shoulder, before finally making his escape, plunging back into the noise and colour of the function room, pulling the door firmly shut behind him.

Chapter 30

'You're early.'

Alexia stood in the doorway, arms folded, barring him entry.

'We said *8 p.m.*, the boys are still eating. Graham's only just got home...'

'Hey, boys, Daddy's here!' Robert shouted over her shoulder, ignoring her.

In the middle distance, Alexia heard chairs scraping as the twins left the dinner table. Seconds later, they were haring down the hall towards them. Alexia was raging inside, certain that Robert had deliberately messed up the timing to make trouble, but she swallowed her fury down, determined not to argue in front of the boys.

'Daddy!'

They threw themselves at him, falling into his outstretched arms. Despite herself, Alexia felt a pang of sadness. She didn't want to step back in time, she was done with being Mrs Downing, but privately she yearned for the days when life was simpler, more straightforward.

'It's *so* good to see you. Have you missed me?'

Robert was laying it on thick, ruffling their hair and kissing them repeatedly, but Alexia kept her counsel. He might have been putting it on for her benefit, but there *was* real love there, so she would let it go. Besides, if it was designed to rile her, or even soften her, he was wasting his time. *She* knew what was best for the kids and she wouldn't countenance backing down now.

'Why don't you grab your things, so we can scoot off?'

Freddie and Joshua turned to her, appealing.

'You haven't had your pudding yet, boys...'

'I'm happy to feed them at mine,' Robert cut in. 'I've got cookie dough *and* phish food...'

The words hung in the air, delighting the hungry boys.

'Please, Mum, can we?'

She knew she should say no, that Graham would be pissed off, but over time she had learned which battles to fight.

'Go on, then.'

They scampered away, barging each other aside to be first up the stairs.

'Your bags are packed, just grab your toothbrushes,' she called after them, before turning to face her husband. 'You know, for a mature, intelligent man, this is just a tiny bit juvenile...'

'Wanting to see my sons?'

'Point scoring, buying people's affection, reneging on our agreements—'

'Oh, you're the expert in that department, my love. You see when *I* married, I married for life...'

He held up his left hand, his wedding band still in place.

'*Really?* You want to have that conversation again?'

'Why not? I find slut-shaming so entertaining.'

Before she knew what she was doing, she'd taken a step towards him. Shock and anger pulsed through her. He had never spoken to her like that before, nor could she allow him to get away with it now. Raising her hand, she made to slap him hard across the face, but even as she did so, she heard the boys charging across the landing to the top of the stairs.

Dropping her hand, she took a step back, hissing out her anger.

'Say what you like, Robert. Do what you like. But it won't make one iota of difference.'

'We'll see.'

'This is one fight you *won't* win.'

'Keep telling yourself that, Alexia...'

'I mean it, Robert, don't push me.'

Her ex didn't bat an eyelid, seeming oddly calm, even triumphant. And now the boys hurried down to join him, kissing their mum distractedly, before racing out to the Mercedes. Alexia eyed Robert shrewdly, suddenly alarmed. Something was different tonight, something had *changed*. She'd always had the upper hand in their arguments, always been able to force him onto the back foot, but now he seemed willing and able to go on the offensive, to take the fight to *her*. And as if to underline this fact, he leaned in close now, his lips almost brushing her ear, as he whispered:

'See you in court, Alexia.'

Chapter 31

'When was he brought in?'

Helen wouldn't usually have been so abrupt with a custody officer and immediately regretted her sharp tone. Anthony Parks was a genial presence at Southampton Central, a friendly bloke with whom she'd often shared a joke, but Helen's sense of humour seemed to have deserted her tonight. On the way back to the station, she'd got word that DS Hudson had arrested Lee Moffat, relentlessly pushing ahead with *his* agenda, ignoring her explicit instructions.

'About half an hour ago,' Parks responded carefully. 'I took him down myself. DS Hudson was going to let him stew for the night, question him in the morning, but I'll happily bring him up, if you want?'

Helen took a moment to consider. Moffat *was* a person of interest and there was perhaps a point to be made by taking control of his questioning. But to do so would be to hijack another officer's line of enquiry *and* distract her from pursuing other important leads. So, reminding herself not to let station politics cloud her vision, Helen replied, 'You're all right, let him sweat for the night. Thanks, Anthony.'

'Always a pleasure, DI Grace…'

Normally Parks's parting shot would have raised a smile

– he had a fine line in clumsy flirting – but Helen's mind was turning on other things. Pushing into the stairwell, she was already processing the night's developments, thoughts of Goj, Moffat and Hudson tumbling over one another. There was much to digest and a strategy to consider – how to push forward numerous different lines of enquiry whilst dealing with Hudson's insubordination. It was not an easy circle to square, especially as her former lover seemed to have friends, allies even, in the team. No, this battle would require carefu—

Her phone rang, making her jump. Helen realized she had been so lost in her own thoughts that she'd tuned out the wider world, walking well past the seventh floor up to the very top of the building. Cursing her stupidity, Helen looked down at the caller ID, expecting some problem, some new setback, but suddenly her face broke out into a smile, as she realized who was calling.

'Charlie, how are you?'

'I'm the walking dead, of course. How are you?'

It was so good to hear Charlie's voice, the warmth in her tone, her gentle, self-deprecating humour – the perfect tonic after a trying day. Leaning back against the cold wall of the stairwell, Helen continued eagerly, 'Fine, fine. And what about those lovely girls?'

'Oh, they're horrible, hideous, and totally lovely. Honestly, I've never worked so hard in my life, or looked so awful. From now on, it's strictly phone calls only, no Zoom, no Facetime...'

'I know the feeling.'

'Don't be silly, you never look anything less than amazing...'

It wasn't true, of course, but it was nice to hear. Since DS Charlene Brooks – Charlie to her friends – had been on maternity leave, juggling Jessie and newborn Orla, she and Helen had spoken only intermittently, but whenever they had, there was a warmth, generosity and informality that wouldn't have been possible were they working a case together. Helen had come to cherish these conversations; they were the perfect antidote to everything that was going on at Southampton Central.

'So what's the gossip? What am I missing out on?'

'Oh, just a general breakdown in law and order, trust in the police, team morale. Believe me, Charlie, you're better off out of it...'

'I know and, of course, there's no way I could be doing what you're doing *and* bring up these two critters... but there's a part of me that *would* like to be there. Helping the team, helping *you*...'

It was said tentatively, even a little awkwardly. And now Helen realized why Charlie had rung. She was worried – worried about *her*. Had she picked up on the numerous crime reports in the local paper of late? Talked to DC Bentham or another long-serving member of the team? Whatever had prompted the call, she'd felt compelled to reach out to Helen, which cheered and moved her more than she could say. Charlie's concern for her was simple, heartfelt and honest and suddenly Helen yearned to have her back at Southampton Central.

'Well, nothing would please me more,' Helen said, her voice sounding oddly thick, as emotion ambushed her. 'But you've got a more important job to do, bringing up my god-daughters to be law-abiding, constructive members of society. God knows there are precious few of those around these days...'

'Well, I'll do my best,' Charlie laughed, 'but I'm not sure what three hours of Peppa Pig a day is doing to their brains. Given their parentage, they didn't have much in that department to start with.'

They continued to chat, relaxed and happy, for over half an hour. It was the perfect way to unwind, but when eventually she rang off, Helen felt mixed emotions. Relieved that Charlie, Steve and the girls were OK, happy to have heard from her old friend, but aware of just how isolated she'd become at Southampton Central. Helen felt as if the sands were shifting beneath her feet, old loyalties being tested, new challenges rising up to face her and, without Charlie, her rock, she suddenly felt exposed, even vulnerable, counting only Grace Simmons as a firm, trustworthy ally.

Helen would front up to these challenges – what else could she do? – but she would have been happier, far happier, if Charlie had been by her side. There was no question of that happening, however, so for the time being, Helen would have to soldier on as best she could.

This was a contest, a battle, that she would have to fight alone.

Day Three

Chapter 32

She awoke with a start, suddenly aware that someone was in the room. Disoriented, uncertain in the dull gloom whether it was morning or the middle of the night, Lilah sat bolt upright, pulling the duvet around her. But to her surprise it was only Martin, holding a heavily laden tray.

'What's all this?' she enquired, pushing the stray hairs from her face.

'What does it look like?' he returned, happily. 'Coffee, croissant and freshly squeezed orange juice. A breakfast fit for a queen...'

He slid the tray in front of her.

'Yesterday was pretty rough. Thought you deserved a treat.'

'Well, that's very nice of you...'

Lilah picked up the orange juice, draining it in one go. She knew Martin was expecting her to be grateful and gushing, but she wasn't sure she could summon the energy. It had been a disturbed night, Lilah tossing and turning as Martin slumbered, hearing all sorts of noises, imagining all kinds of unpleasant scenarios. She'd had at least two nightmares in which shadowy figures invaded their home, nightmares that seemed terrifyingly real. Even when fatigue finally overtook her, her body begging for sleep, the vodka hangover started to kick in, her brain pulsing with low-level pain. How she regretted her weakness now.

'This is delicious,' she said, mustering what enthusiasm she could. 'But you didn't need to go to so much trouble.'

'It's no trouble. You know I want things to be good between us, for us to be happy. So what's a little effort, a little consideration?'

It was as close to an apology as Lilah was going to get, so, nodding gratefully, she took a bite of the croissant. It was crisp and sweet and the feeling of the rich dough hitting her empty stomach immediately made her feel better. So she took another bite, then another, devouring the whole pastry in less than a minute.

'You *were* hungry...' Martin laughed, climbing on the bed next to her.

Lilah raised the coffee to her lips, but as she did so, Martin stopped her.

'And so am I.'

Taking the cup from her, he placed it on the bedside table, then turned back to her, sliding the strap of her vest top from her shoulder, kissing her skin gently.

'Martin, I've got to go to work...'

'It's only seven o'clock, we've got plenty of time.'

He kissed the top of her chest, gently sliding the strap down to reveal more skin.

'But I was so late yesterday, I wanted to get in early...'

'Forget about them. They've had more than their pound of flesh from you over the years.'

He caressed the edge of her breast. In spite of herself, Lilah felt a shiver of desire.

'And besides,' Martin continued, 'what's a reconciliation without a bit of making up?'

Hauling his powerful frame upwards, Martin straddled her, pushing her back gently down onto the bed and kissing her urgently. Lilah submitted, part of her wanting it, part of her not, yet knowing there was no point fighting his desire. In days gone by, she had held the upper hand in their relationship, but no longer, and today, as so often recently, she was powerless to resist.

Chapter 33

He looked small, vulnerable even, hunched on a broken chair, framed by the expansive backdrop of the interview suite. But the expression on Lee Moffat's face gave the lie to that notion. A night in the cells had not softened him – he stared unflinchingly across the table at Joseph Hudson, defiant and scornful.

'I'll ask you again. Where were you on the night of the twelfth of August? Between the hours of 10 p.m. and midnight?'

There were three of them in the room, DS Hudson and DC Reid playing bad cop, bad cop with their truculent suspect. Moffat had declined a lawyer, declined refreshments and, so far, had declined to comment. In response to Joseph Hudson's question, he simply chewed his gum, loudly, aggressively, the white, rubbery substance snapping and crackling in his mouth.

'Were you in the Locks Heath area between those hours?'

Moffat shrugged, but said nothing.

'OK, how about the small hours of the second of August? Between midnight and 2 a.m.?'

Lee Moffat narrowed his eyes, as if thinking hard, then leaned back in his chair, running a hand through his long, lank hair, in the process revealing a vivid snake tattoo on his forearm.

'That *is* when you're generally out and about, right?' Reid spoke up.

'From what we hear, you've been very busy,' Hudson added. 'But nicking other people's cars comes with certain risks, doesn't it?'

Click, click, click, the chewing gum going round and round.

'Especially if your victims don't want to give up their vehicles. Does the name Alison Burris mean anything to you?'

Now there was a reaction, the chewing ceasing briefly, before resuming, more aggressively this time.

'She was murdered in the Carlton Road car park in the early hours of the second of August. Can you explain to me why you had two screwdrivers on you when we picked you up last night?'

Moffat stared at him, looking slightly less amused now. 'Tools of the trade. I'm a handyman ...'

The scorn was back and Hudson was quick to slap it down.

'The screwdriver heads were sharpened, Lee. They weren't tools, they were weapons.'

'Nah ...'

'What's more, they're being examined right now in the lab. If we can link them to the attack on Alison Burris—'

'Knock yourself out.'

It was said decisively, as if ending the conversation. Hudson stared at Moffat for a moment, saying nothing in response. Was Moffat dismissive of the accusation because he was innocent? Or because he was confident no trace of his crime remained?

'I will, Lee, don't worry. Because I intend to prove that you killed Alison Burris *and* Declan McManus.'

'Fuck off. I never touched them ...'

'Makes no difference if it was you, or one of your guys. That doesn't matter in the eyes of the law. You're the ringmaster, the instigator ...'

'You don't know what you're on about—'

'Your warehouse has got parts from thirty, forty luxury vehicles, maybe more. You must be turning a tidy profit...'

Click, click, click. The gum was back, Moffat retreating from the fray.

'Was that why you targeted McManus?' Reid asked, picking up the baton.

'You've lost me...'

'Declan McManus was working for ARG Insurance. They'd hired him to look into car thefts in Southampton, Portsmouth, Bournemouth. They're having to make a lot of payouts and, trust me, they're not happy about it. McManus had been working for them for *over three weeks*, visiting the mechanics, body shops, black-market dealers, trying to figure out who was the source of all this unpleasantness. The head of the snake...' Reid said.

'Which threatened your interests, didn't it?' Hudson added. 'Is that why you chose to do it with petrol?'

Moffat stared at him, determined not to break eye contact.

'Lighter fluid, or meths, would have been easier, certainly less dangerous. But using petrol – well, that sent out a clear message, didn't it?'

Moffat shook his head slowly, but said nothing.

'Is that why you killed McManus? To stop his investigation? To deter others from poking their noses into your business?'

'You've got the wrong man,' Moffat replied, turning his palms upwards in a show of innocence. 'I don't know the guy.'

'OK, Lee, have it your way,' Hudson said. 'Do you own one of these?'

He slid a photo of the Rick Owens hoodie across the table. Moffat paused, then looked down at it. As he did so, first a frown of confusion, then consternation, passed across his face.

'It's designer wear, something you're very keen on. Got to do something with all those ill-gotten gains, right?'

Moffat's eyes were glued to the picture.

'Well, guess what? Fibres from a hoodie like that were found at the crime scene in Locks Heath, snagged on a fence as the perpetrator fled. You got one like that?'

'No.'

'Yes, you do. I've got a copy of the order form. Paid for by a debit card registered to a "Lee Moffat" and delivered to your mother's address six weeks ago.'

Moffat kept his counsel, the chewing stilled for now.

'Other than that, it was a very professional job, I must say…'

'Wasn't me.'

'So where's the hoodie?'

Silence.

'I'd love to take a look at it, see if it's got a tear in it, traces of petrol…'

'Haven't got it.'

'You only bought it *six weeks ago*.'

'Must have lost it or given it away or something…'

'It cost a thousand pounds.'

'So?'

'Well, I know you're loaded, Lee, but surely that kind of money means *something* to you. People have been killed for less.'

Moffat said nothing, eyeballing Hudson venomously. All traces of amusement, of cocksureness, were now gone.

'Look, Lee. I know you did it. And I know why. So let's cut to the chase, shall we? I want you to take me through your movements on the second and the twelfth, minute by minute. Where you were, what you were doing, who you were with. We've got your phone now, we can track your movements, so don't even *think* about lying to me. This is it, mate, the end of the road…' He stared at Moffat, smiling as he concluded: 'It's time for you to tell me the truth.'

Chapter 34

Helen had the distinct impression he was stalling, attempting to deflect her questions by asking some of his own.

'Can I ask the nature of your interest in Mr Goj?'

Helen took him in, amused by the polished slickness of Jeremy Blake. CEOs of hospital trusts tended to look more like Forbes 500 execs than healthcare providers and Blake was no exception. Southampton Children's Hospital was one of the biggest in the country, providing outstanding care, support and hope to young people all over the South Coast, but the meeting room they were ensconced in would not have been out of place in Silicon Valley. It was modern, expensive, impressive, much like the CEO who sat opposite her.

'It's an incident involving threat to life,' Helen replied crisply. 'You don't come to the attention of the Major Incident Team unless it's something serious.'

Blake was taken aback, clearly he had not been expecting this.

Helen let her words linger for a moment, before continuing. 'Before we get into that, however, I'd just like to double-check a few of the basics. So, Mr Goj started work here in 1992, as a trainee manager in procurement.'

'That's right,' Blake replied cautiously. 'Procurement is a huge operation for a hospital of this size, so we're always taking on new staff.'

'So his job was to source surgical gowns, nurses' uniforms, computers—'

'Cleaning equipment, lanyards, blankets and sheets, pens, paper clips, printer paper, whatever we need to run the hospital safely and efficiently.'

'I see. And over time, he rose up the ranks, eventually becoming Chief Operating Officer, right?'

A marked reaction from Blake – confusion and concern.

'Or perhaps I've got that wrong,' Helen added, looking at her notes.

'Well...' Blake replied tentatively. 'Amar is a long-standing, loyal member of hospital staff, been here nearly twenty years... but he's not exactly scaled the heights. He's a good worker, but he was promoted to the position of departmental manager in procurement in 2006 and he's been doing that ever since.'

Helen stared at Blake, taken aback.

'I can run off his service record and pay slips. I'll get HR to do it now, if you like...'

Helen nodded absently, her thoughts turning to the larger-than-life figure she had met last night. He certainly presented himself as a man of importance, of means, but appearances could be deceiving. Gathering herself, she slid the printout of Goj's Facebook page across the desk towards him.

'You can see why we were confused...'

Blake took in the page, his face ashen. 'Jesus Christ, I had no idea...' He handed it back to her. 'The current COO's going to be none too pleased, I can tell you.' It was an attempt at humour, but felt forced.

'And is Mr Goj a good employee?'

'Yes. By and large.'

'Meaning?'

'Meaning nothing. He is what he is. A middle manager in procurement.'

'And have you had any problems in that department? Recently, I mean.'

'Well, you'll know that we suffered a tragic bereavement recently. One of our deputy managers—'

'Alison Burris.'

'That's right. Such a sad loss, she was a very able administrator and a popular, valued colleague. Have you made progress with your investigation? We were supposed to get an update from someone in your team but—'

'Presumably that means extra work for Mr Goj now,' Helen interrupted, cutting off Blake's attempt at diversion. 'As her direct superior, he'll have to do two jobs basically, until such time as you can find a replacement?'

'That's about the size of it. It'll be tough for him, but I'm sure he'll cope.'

'That's funny, because I checked with reception when I arrived. Mr Goj is not expected in today,' Helen fired back. 'In fact, his security clearance has been revoked.'

Blake stared at her, caught out.

'Would you care to explain why that is, Mr Blake?'

There was a long, heavy silence.

'Inspector, can I suggest that we reconvene with lawyers present. I want to provide what assistance I can, but it must be done in the right way. I could meet you tomorrow or the day after at their offices—'

'No.'

'I'm sorry?'

'I'm sure you'd love to delay this conversation, but I have two serious crimes to investigate – the murder of one of *your* employees and the attempted murder of another man. If Amar Goj is in any way connected to these crimes, if you even *suspect* he had any involvement, I need to know. And I need to know now.'

She glared at him, challenging him to push back. She half expected him to do just that, but now she saw his body sag. The smart suit and power glasses were just for show – Blake was weak and scared.

'Look, I can't say... I don't *know*... if Amar has any involvement in these matters, what he may or may not have been up to—'

'But—' Helen interrupted, impatiently.

'But, we had to suspend him following allegations of financial impropriety.'

'When?'

'Yesterday.'

Now it was Helen's turn to be surprised. The man she'd met last night, who'd appeared so ebullient, so popular, so successful, had only hours earlier been suspended from the job he'd held for nearly twenty years.

'Why? What had he done?'

'Well, we don't know the ins and outs of it. A full internal enquiry is just getting under way.'

Helen noted the way he stressed the word 'internal' as if privacy and discretion were paramount.

'But it appears he may have been defrauding the Trust.'

'How?'

'Well...' Blake replied, giving every impression of not wanting to elaborate, 'procurement is a very complicated business. There are thousands, tens of thousands of transactions every month. We can't double-check every single one, there has to be a certain amount of trust extended towards the managers, and their staff—'

'And?'

'And we think that trust might have been betrayed. We believe that Amar might have set up a shell company – a fictitious supplier – then started procuring items from them, at significantly inflated prices.'

'A company that he in fact owned.'

He nodded.

'How long has this been going on?'

Blake looked sick now.

'We've no idea, but it could be five years, ten, maybe more.'

'And what sort of sums are involved?'

'Well, it was a few hundred here, a few hundred there, but – if it's as bad as we fear – then it might be upwards of a million pounds.'

Helen sat back in her chair. She'd thought that Goj's lavish display last night was a one-off to celebrate his daughter's wedding, but perhaps his largesse, his wealth, ran far deeper than that. Blake didn't meet her eye and she could well understand why. Such a massive fraud would be a huge blot on the hospital's reputation, not to mention his own. But she wasn't finished yet.

'And how did you come to learn of this fraud?'

'It came to light following an internal audit. After the PPE fiasco during Covid, we did a route-and-branch investigation into our procurement systems – which is when some anomalies were spotted.'

'Who by?'

There was another long pause, then: 'Alison Burris.'

Helen lean forward, her mind suddenly whirring. 'When she spotted these "anomalies", the seemingly fake supplier, whom would she have taken her concerns to?'

'To her boss, to Amar Goj, of course.'

'And what happened?'

'Nothing, that was the problem. She raised the issue a few weeks ago and tried to follow it up with him several times thereafter. Amar said he was dealing with it, would raise it with the Board, but ... he did nothing. In the end, I'm afraid Alison came to the conclusion that he was stalling, deliberately soft-pedalling the enquiry.'

'And did she say anything to you? Or any other member of senior management?'

'No – well, not to my face at least.'

'So how do you know about this?'

'She sent me an email, outlining her concerns.'

'And what did you do?'

'Well, I didn't do anything,' he replied, before quickly clarifying. 'I didn't have time to. She was killed only a couple of hours after she sent it.'

Blake stared at his feet, looking exhausted, as if he had nothing more to give. But in truth, this was just the beginning for both of them. Blake was facing a protracted, damaging, public examination of his leadership – a long, dark road. For Helen, by contrast, things were looking up.

Finally, she had a possible motive for Alison Burris's murder.

Chapter 35

'Look at the photos.'

Hudson drummed his fingers on the stills that lay on the table between them.

'This is what you did to that poor woman.'

Reluctantly, Lee Moffat stole a look. There were five photos in total, three wide shots of Alison Burris lying crumpled on the ground, the others close-ups of the stab wounds. Two angry, pink, puckered holes, staring up at him.

'It *wasn't* me.'

'Lee, we're going around in circles here. Burris was killed because someone wanted her BMW, right?'

'If you say so.'

'Do you know of any other operations in Southampton that are lifting cars to order?'

'No, but—'

'That would be *so* brazen, dragging a woman from her car—'

'I've never done that shit.'

'That would have no qualms about stabbing someone in order to take what was wanted. There is no one else, Lee. You have the motive, you have the weapons and now we can link you to the McManus crime scene—'

'No way.'

'So where were you? You keep protesting your innocence but you won't tell me your whereabouts on the night of the twelfth…'

'I was out, all right?'

'Where?'

'Just *out*.'

'Doing what?'

'This and that.'

'Not good enough. What about the second?'

'The same. I'm always out nights…'

'Well, that's convenient. And you've no memory of where you were?'

Moffat shook his head, but couldn't meet his eye.

'This was *two nights ago*. Is your memory really that bad…?'

'Must be the drugs. What can I say?'

'You expect me to believe that?'

'Believe what you want. I ain't bothered…'

It was said defiantly, dismissively, in the hope that it would take the wind from Hudson's sails. But Joseph Hudson regarded Moffat for a second, then leaned back in his chair, clasping his hands behind his head.

'Would you like to know a little secret, Lee? Something the wider world doesn't know?'

Moffat shrugged, feigning disinterest.

'Declan McManus's condition is *improving*.'

A small, but marked reaction from the suspect.

'I spoke to the hospital first thing this morning. He's been in an induced coma since the attack, but later today they are going to attempt to bring him out of it. He'll be weak, of course, and in pain, but the doctors have assured me that he should be able to *talk*. And I'm sure he'll have plenty to say…' He fixed Moffat with a stare. 'He'll know who wanted him out of the way. Who doused him in petrol. Who set him alight. And I'm betting he's going to point the finger directly at *you*.'

Moffat stared back at Hudson, his anger clear.

'You may think you can dodge this one, Lee, but you can't. Make no mistake, we *will* place you at the yard, we *will* prove that you were responsible for killing Alison Burris and for the attempted murder of Declan McManus—'

'So charge me.'

The words shot out from the suspect, angry, defiant. 'Go ahead. If you're so sure you can pin this on me, then do it now. I'm ready for you.'

Hudson hesitated, surprised by this aggressive counter-attack, and Moffat was quick to take advantage.

'But if you can't, if you haven't got the *balls*, then you'd best get my coat . . .'

His eyes locked onto Hudson's, challenging, triumphant, as he leaned back in his chair.

'Because we're done here.'

Chapter 36

'I'm afraid I can't let you in. You'll have to come back later...'

Arsha Goj stood in the doorway, blocking Helen's entry. The proud matriarch was determined to protect her husband, her family, to keep bad news from hearth and home. But Helen wasn't going to be denied, not today.

'As I said, this is a serious police matter,' Helen responded, sliding her warrant card back into her pocket.

'So serious that you interrupt our daughter's engagement party, that you come to our home again this morning, waking up half the street with your banging...'

Helen didn't know whether to be angered or amused by Arsha's inference that she was simply a nuisance, an inconvenient intrusion to be shooed away, rather than a police officer executing her duties.

'We have relatives staying with us—'

'And once again, I'm sorry to disturb you, but I do need to talk to your husband.'

'What about?'

'I'm happy to come back later today with a warrant,' Helen continued, ignoring the question. 'But then I'll have to bring the whole team with me, which will create a lot more disruption, be much more *visible*...'

Helen was pleased to see a crease of concern cloud Arsha's expression.

'So why don't we just do this now? Half an hour tops, then I'll be on my way.'

This was a lie – Helen had no idea how long she'd need to question Goj – but it seemed to cut some ice with his wife. She was clearly worried about Helen's presence and the thought that this might all be done and dusted before the rest of the street took note was clearly appealing.

'Thirty minutes and no more,' she said sternly, as if she was the one in charge.

Smiling politely, Helen wiped her feet and stepped inside.

A minute later, Helen was striding down the garden path. She had been intrigued by the interior of the elegant five-bedroom house, one of the largest she'd seen in Bevois Mount, noting that it had been completely redecorated recently, perhaps in anticipation of visitors during the wedding celebrations, but a proper interrogation of Goj's lifestyle and spending would have to wait. Now she had more pressing concerns.

Goj's theft, his long-term defrauding of the children's hospital, seemed nailed on, Helen realizing now why he had had to pass himself off as a COO to justify his impressive income. What was less clear was his role in the attack on Declan McManus and his potential involvement in the murder of Alison Burris. For the first crime he appeared to have no motive, and the second seemed wildly out of character, Goj appearing to be a thief, rather than a killer. He certainly had no criminal record, no past offences to speak of and Helen was keen to confront him with these anomalies. You could tell a lot about someone's innocence or guilt by the way they reacted to a direct accusation.

Helen had expected to find Amar sitting at the breakfast

table holding court, sucking up the approbation from last night's lavish party, but perhaps she shouldn't have been surprised when Arsha told her that actually her husband was closeted away in his garden office. This was presumably where he lived out his double life, where he plotted, covered and concealed, keeping the money flowing in with an ever-growing number of fake invoices. If, as seemed likely, his back really was up against the wall, if he was staring down the barrel of an internal enquiry and possible criminal proceedings, then he would presumably have retreated here to try and plot his next move.

Rapping on the shed door, Helen took a deep breath. She was excited but also tense – this could go easily, with a swift collapse or confession, or could be long and hard, lies and obfuscations frustrating their investigation. The next few minutes would decide which.

There was no movement inside – Helen could picture Amar cowering, alarmed by the aggressive knocking – so Helen tried again. Still there was no response, so now she tried the handle. It turned easily, the door was not locked, and as she pushed forward, she announced:

'Mr Goj? It's DI Helen Grace, I'm coming in ...'

Except she wasn't. She was pushing against the door, but it wasn't moving. This made no sense, the catch was up now, meaning that there must be some kind of obstacle inside. Had Amar barricaded himself in? Had he spotted her coming and made defensive preparations? It seemed absurd, ridiculous, but still ...

'Amar, this isn't helping. Obstructing a police officer in the execution of her duties is a criminal offence ...'

She put her shoulder to the door, but still it didn't yield, so stepping back, she took a short run at it, cannoning into the warm wood. Now the door did shift slightly and, carefully, Helen poked her head into the gap. She had expected to see a startled Amar backed into the corner, but instead she saw that it was Amar himself who was blocking the entrance, lying prone on the floor just inside the door.

Redoubling her efforts, Helen eased the door open a fraction more, then slid inside the shed. Quickly, she crouched down by the prostrate figure.

'Amar? Amar, it's DI Grace. Can you hear me?'

No response. Craning over him, Helen took in his blank expression, his glazed eyes.

'Amar, please...'

Her heart was beating sixteen to the dozen, but her training now kicked in, Helen placing two fingers on Amar's carotid artery in search of a pulse. But there was nothing, no vital signs at all.

Amar Goj was dead.

Chapter 37

She watched the dumb show, with a sinking heart. From her office on the tenth floor, DCI Grace Simmons had a perfect view of the main entrance at Southampton Central. All human life came in and out of those doors – police officers, victims of crime, offenders, social workers, press – and many a drama had played out below, in full view of the building's occupants.

Today's performance was muted, but still provoked a reaction. Lee Moffat, the suspect DS Hudson had pulled in last night, had just been released without charge. Hudson was convinced there was more to learn about Moffat's involvement in a couple of recent murders, but they didn't have enough to hold him, let alone charge him, so they'd had to let him go. Moffat was making the most of this, dawdling on the main steps, enjoying a smoke whilst taking phone calls, no doubt crowing to his mates. It made Simmons's blood boil – the casual, innate confidence of seasoned criminals always did.

Breaking away, Simmons returned to her desk, but there was little solace to be found here. Every day she got the local and national newspapers delivered to her office, determined to keep abreast of the press's latest preoccupations and machinations. The headlines seldom offered cause for optimism and so it proved yet again today. The front page of the early edition of the

Southampton Evening News was particularly loaded and personal, the banner headline asking: *Has DI Grace lost the plot?*

Flicking it open, Simmons scanned the accompanying articles, but she could have guessed the contents. The local rag, which was trusted by its readers, had of late been conducting a sustained campaign against Helen, and Hampshire Police in general, questioning their competence in the face of a marked rise in crime. And whilst the accusations they made didn't worry Simmons unduly – she was sure Helen would make progress in time – she was concerned about the effect on public morale, on their willingness to engage with the police. Without the eyes and ears of the local population, their ability to fight crime and keep the public safe would be severely compromised, something they could ill afford at the moment.

Slumping down in her seat, Simmons shoved the papers away, determined to get stuck into her groaning in-tray, but in truth she had no energy, no drive this morning. She had felt increasingly like that, general fatigue exacerbated by a growing feeling of disquiet. Until recently, she had never once doubted her methods, her instincts, but now she was plagued by doubts. The public were worried, the press troublesome and Chief Superintendent Peters openly concerned. Worse still, there *did* seem to be problems at Southampton Central, within Helen's Major Incident Team specifically, problems which, for now, Helen seemed determined to keep to herself. She would never have admitted this to anyone else, but to Simmons it seemed for the first time as if perhaps they were being overwhelmed, as if they *had* lost their grip on the city.

If this *was* the case, then it was not Helen's fault, but *hers*. Ultimately, she was in charge of operations and, had she been ten years younger, would've worked night and day to turn the ship around. That was still her instinct, but reality was biting. She was well into her sixties and able to provide only fitful leadership, given her health problems and general sense of exhaustion. She now regretted being coaxed into taking the job at Southampton Central – she should have stuck to her original plan to retire. She regretted not having been more honest with her superiors, and indeed with Helen, when offered the post. She had lied about her health, shielding them from her personal problems, in order to help them. Or so she'd thought. Now it appeared a selfish, cowardly act which only served to hinder Helen's efforts, leaving her old friend to do Simmons's job as well as her own.

The sensible thing to do would be to step aside, to make way for a younger, more vital presence. But to do so now, amidst the storm of criticism and scrutiny, would look like an admission that the ship was sinking, inadvertently making a bad situation much worse. The alternative then was to stay, to dig in and try to make a difference, but did she have the energy, the life force to do that? Some days it was hard enough just to get out of bed.

How she missed her late husband then, cheerily chiding her for her lethargy, forcing her to face the new day. Now she was alone, exhausted and dispirited, torn as to what to do for the best. She used to pride herself on her resolve, her clarity of thought, her ability to predict the future and bend it to her will. Now she had none of that foresight, none of that vision.

Now all she could see was a situation that was rapidly spiralling out of control.

Chapter 38

So much poverty, so many desperate people. Looking at the long list of names on his spreadsheet, it did genuinely seem as if the world was going to hell in a handcart. Well, if it was, so be it. So much the better for him.

Running a grubby finger down the columns of figures, Gary Bleecher did a quick mental calculation. Some of his clients would default on their repayments, no question, but if even 70 per cent of them paid what they owed him, then he would still turn a very tidy profit. That was the way of things – when times were tough, it was the man with cash who was king. He was no Rockefeller, but he had means and, what's more, a reputation for accepting *any* new client, regardless of their circumstances. This meant he had a constant line of customers, a dozen enquiries every day. Some tried to put on a proud front, confident that new funds, fresh employment, were just around the corner. Others begged or even cried, but it made no difference. You could tell straight away that they were all desperate, hence why they were willing to accept a scandalous rate of interest on their loan.

The newspapers moaned about the downturn, the politicians vowed to turn it around, but Gary hoped this wouldn't happen any time soon. There were only two thriving industries these days – debt and crime. He was in the vanguard of the first and on the fringes of the second, occasionally having to use force to remind people of their financial responsibilities. Yes, people looked down at him, calling him a parasite, a lowlife, scum, but they could go hang. He was the one lining his pockets, the guy who would come out on top in the end.

Staring at his computer screen, Gary was startled from his thoughts by the noise of the letterbox snapping shut. Curious, he angled a glance towards the front door. The postmen around here were so lazy, they never made it to his house until early afternoon, meaning that this was something special, hand-delivered to his home. Unusual for someone to drop and run, usually they wanted a face-to-face meet, either to beg for more time or to ensure the money found its way into the right hands.

Confused, he rose, making his way cautiously to the window. Teasing the curtain gently to one side, he peered out – but whoever had deposited the letter had already gone. There was no one in the immediate vicinity, nor any car that they might be concealed behind. Confident there was no immediate cause for alarm, he hurried into the hallway, where an envelope lay on the mat. Greedily, he scooped it up. Odds on there would be cash inside.

He was disappointed, however, to find that it was exceptionally thin and light. In fact, there barely seemed to be anything in it all. Irritated, he ripped open the seal and ferreted inside. At first, he found nothing, but then, right in the corner, his fingers alighted on something. Something hard and metallic. Once more his spirits rose – perhaps it was a gold ring, or a valuable keepsake, some heirloom being donated to pay off debt. Turning the envelope upside down, he tipped it into his hand, fixing his expectant eyes upon it.

And now excitement turned to confusion. Because nestled in his sweaty palm was not a valuable trinket, or a nugget of gold, but a single, shiny bullet.

Chapter 39

'What is all this stuff?'

DC Malik was standing in front of the spacious wardrobe, Helen hovering just behind her. The forensics and pathology teams were busy in Amar Goj's office, so Helen and her officers had retreated to the main house. Goj's shell-shocked wife and relatives were currently closeted away with a Family Liaison Officer in the living room, leaving Helen's team free to roam the house. They had investigated the main bedroom and were now standing in the guest room, which appeared to be little more than a collection of wardrobes stuffed full of clothes.

'The spoils of fraud,' Helen murmured, taking in the rows of jackets, knitwear, trousers and shirts, beneath which nestled countless shoe boxes.

Kneeling down, Malik's gloved hand teased open one of the boxes, to be confronted with a box-fresh pair of Gucci trainers.

'What size are they?'

Malik plucked one out and looked inside.

'Nine.'

'OK,' Helen responded, pleased. 'It's unlikely that Goj kept the trainers or the hoodie he was wearing on the night of the arson attack, but have a thorough look anyway. Failing that, any receipts, any proof of purchase for those items, would be extremely useful. Obviously, those items are our top priority, but I would also like a full inventory of everything that's here.'

Already Malik was pulling a face, looking pained.

'I know, I know,' Helen responded. 'It'll take you all morning, but I'd like to get a sense of what he's got, how much he must have spent to accumulate all this...'

'Unusual for a bloke to be such a clothes horse,' Malik said, blowing out her cheeks. 'He must have been seriously into his fashion.'

'Except most of the clothes haven't even been *touched*. Look, the majority of them still have the tags on and some of the shoes boxes haven't been opened...'

'Money to burn...'

'But to what end?'

They stood in silence. There was something sobering, tragic, even, at the sight of Goj's pristine clothes, prizes that he had apparently ruined his life to amass.

'Anyway, if you're OK, I'm going to leave you in charge and head off.'

Malik turned to Helen, surprised, though pleased by the vote of confidence.

'Call me if you turn up anything interesting,' Helen continued, 'otherwise, I'll see you back at base.'

'Sure thing. See you later...'

Malik was clearly curious as to where Helen was going, but didn't want to ask. Helen was glad of her discretion; she didn't intend to advertise her destination and wouldn't do so unless it turned up anything useful. There was no point distressing his grieving relatives further.

Descending the stairs, Helen heard hushed, faltering voices in the living room. The grief, the anguish of the family was plain, even through the walls, and Helen didn't linger, hurrying down the stairs towards the front door. It had been a terrible scene – the irascible, protective Arsha suddenly reduced to a tear-stricken wreck. She had begged Helen to be allowed to see inside the shed, to learn what had happened to her husband, but there was no way Helen could allow her to see him like that, rigid and cold, an empty pill bottle clutched in his hand. Nor could she allow Arsha to disturb the scene. It was *possible* that Amar had been murdered – though on the face of it, everything pointed to suicide. This was a man who had worked hard to create an image of himself as a successful, respectable member of society, who in the space of twenty-four hours had found himself suspended from work, pending slow, excruciating exposure, *and* a key suspect in an ongoing police investigation, the subject of close interest from the Major Incident Team. If he was guilty of both offences, as Helen heavily suspected he was, then surely this double whammy, this pincer movement of catastrophe, was more than enough to push him over the edge. That he had done so alone, without anyone close to him having the slightest inkling of what he was contemplating, was evidenced by the shocked, hysterical reaction to his death.

Closing the front door gently behind her, Helen hurried down the path and out onto the street. The family would no doubt provide some useful background information, but Helen strongly suspected that Amar Goj was a man who liked to keep his secrets close, hence her urgent departure now. Climbing onto her Kawasaki, Helen fired up the ignition, but even as she did so, she couldn't resist one last look back at the house.

On arrival, it had appeared to be the opulent status symbol of a popular, well-heeled family. Now it felt very different, now it was a house of grief, pain and death. In the last couple of days events had spiralled out of control, leaving this once happy family unit shattered, unable to understand the calamity that had befallen them. Helen feared there was worse to come, that there would be more slingshots to absorb and, now, right on cue, Arsha Goj appeared in the living-room window, her eyes locking onto Helen's. When they had first met, there had been hostility, resistance, even pride there. Now this spirited matriarch, this freshly minted widow, stood staring out at the world hollow and empty, her face a picture of perfect desolation.

Chapter 40

He sprinted down the street, his feet pounding the pavement. It felt good to be away from the house, away from those complex, troubling emotions, working his body hard on his daily lunch-time run. Martin Hill had always been a keen jogger, it had been his survival mechanism in the past when he needed some time to himself, and even now that his life was more settled, he still craved the hit of endorphins and the adrenaline.

He always pushed himself hard, constantly trying to better his time. He'd had a set route of late, a punishing circuit of the city, but on each outing he managed to shave a few seconds off his personal best. Today, however, he was off the pace. He was working hard, his Nike Airs hammering the concrete, but he was distracted, out of sorts, his mind not on the task. Morning sex, followed by a long run, would pretty much be his perfect day usually, but his coupling with Lilah had been dissatisfactory and frustrating, despite his inevitable climax.

Lilah had said all the right things, done all the right things, but through it all he'd sensed that she wasn't really present. It was as if she was imagining herself elsewhere, thinking of something else, *someone* else. Was it possible that, despite everything, she was considering leaving him? It would be a bold move, hardly seemed creditable really, given how tentative and cautious Lilah normally was. But it was a feeling Martin couldn't shake.

He knew it was possible that he was overreacting, that he was being paranoid. Being robbed of your parents at a young age, being brought up by an aunt who didn't want you, was liable to make you suspicious, even paranoid. But that didn't mean he was wrong, that he was imagining things. He had trusted his instincts before and had been proven right. Once more his gut was telling him that trouble lay ahead and he knew from experience that forewarned was forearmed.

Darting off the main street, he hurried down Butler's Passage, a small cut-through in the heart of Portswood. The alleyway wasn't well known – he always had it to himself – so he powered down it now, trying to claw back some of the lost seconds. Even being close to his personal best would be an achievement today. He ached to cut loose, to hit top speed, to drive the demons away ... but even here, he was destined to be disappointed, suddenly grinding to a halt, swallowing a silent curse as he did so.

Someone was blocking his way. His first reaction was territorial, this alley had always been *his* little secret, his private thoroughfare, but this was swiftly followed by a wave of annoyance and impatience. The woman in front of him had clearly been struggling up the alleyway with shopping, overloaded, one of the Sainsbury's bags having split, spilling tins of soup and canned fish onto the ground. Even now she was cursing, bending down to scoop them up. Martin's overriding instinct was to try to step around her and be on his way, but it would be virtually impossible to do so without knocking her over, so instead he slowed. And as he did so, he noticed something else – this unfortunate woman was incredibly pretty. Blonde hair cut in a neat bob, sharp cheekbones and full pink lips. She was looking at him, offering an embarrassed smile that had the least noble part of his brain firing.

'I don't suppose you could give me a hand, could you? I'm such a klutz…'

Even before spoke, he found himself bending down to retrieve an errant tin of tomato soup.

'No problem at all, I'm not in a rush.'

Smiling, he set about scooping up the rest of the tins, keen to make a good impression. Then, having completed his task, he straightened up to hand her back her groceries. As he did so, he was surprised to find that she had moved close to him, much closer than he was expecting. For a wild moment, he thought that intimacy was in the offing, that this was one of his fantasies come true, but then something strange happened. With a look of intense concentration on her face, the woman stepped forward and punched him in the stomach.

Stunned, Martin stared at her, the cans tumbling from his grasp. Now she withdrew her hand and suddenly, with piercing clarity, Martin noticed three things. First, an intense pain in his belly. Second, that the woman was wearing gloves, despite the cloying heat of the day. And third, that she appeared to have a knife in her hand, a knife that was covered in blood.

Now she lunged again, her blade sliding into his chest. Martin was rocked back, the air punched from his lungs, but there was no respite. The knife slid out, then arrowed towards him again. Desperately, hopeless, he flung out an arm, but the knife sped past, plunging into his heart.

Now everything seemed to stop. The knife was raised, ready to land again, but before it could do so, Martin Hill crumpled to the ground, suddenly consumed by darkness.

Chapter 41

'Dead?'

The word hung in the air, dull, disbelieving.

'I'm afraid so. His body was found at his home earlier this morning. We believe Mr Goj took his own life.'

Dr Alex Blythe's face was a curious mixture of shock and anger, as if he somehow blamed Helen for his patient's death.

'That's partly why I'm here,' Helen continued quickly. 'It appears he took an overdose of antidepressants, perhaps as much as a whole bottle, medication that was prescribed by you...'

Another body blow, the psychiatrist's face was a shade paler now. He was, Helen guessed, around thirty-five years old, but he looked much younger today. She wondered privately whether this was the first time one of his clients had taken his own life.

'Can I ask how long he'd been seeing you?'

'Around six months or so. That's when I prescribed the Naltrexone. I would have assumed they'd be long gone by now...'

'You hadn't given him a repeat prescription?'

'No, he said he didn't need them anymore. We were making progress. Slowly, but progress nevertheless.'

'And what *was* his condition?'

Helen knew she was on shaky ground here. Immediately, she noticed the psychiatrist stiffen.

'Look, inspector, doctor–patient confidentiality pertains even after death...'

'And I respect that, Dr Blythe, but Mr Goj is a key suspect in an ongoing police investigation, so it's important we get a clear picture of what kind of man he was, what might have driven him to take his own life.'

'Can I ask what crime you suspect him of?'

'Attempted murder.'

This time, Blythe looked like he'd been slapped.

'No, no, that's not possible... Amar had his issues, but he was a kind, gentle man. He wouldn't hurt a fly.'

'Stranger things have happened, which is why I'm asking the question.'

The psychiatrist looked at her, saying nothing. It was obvious that he wasn't convinced, not yet willing to remove the veil that separated their professions.

'I'm guessing it was financial,' Helen added. 'His house is stuffed full of luxury goods, designer clothes and his outgoings far exceeded what he could have earned from his job at the children's hospital. I should add that he was recently suspended from his post there, following the discovery of a major fraud, so clearly *something* was pushing him to accumulate, to spend, to project a certain image of himself. Whatever *was* driving him had clearly got out of control, as he was prepared to break the law, perhaps even commit murder, to keep the ship afloat. All I need from you is a little background – about his health, his state of mind, whether you noticed anything odd about his behaviour in recent weeks.'

Helen came to a halt, breathless after her quick-fire burst. Thankfully, her words seemed to have landed, Blythe's demeanour noticeably less hostile than a few moments before. Rounding the desk, he sat down heavily in his chair, shooting a glance at a framed picture of a pretty young woman, who beamed back at him. But it was not she who came to his aid now, but a cute springer spaniel who hopped up onto his lap. He petted her for a moment, grateful for the distraction, before replying.

'To be honest, I'm not sure there's much more to add; you've hit the nail on the head. Obviously, I can't go into detail about our sessions together, but what I can tell you is that Amar contacted me six months ago and that we met weekly, usually on Thursday evenings. As you've worked out, Amar had issues with his spending. He was heavily in debt, he told me, felt out of control, unable to stop, even though the things he acquired often went unused and certainly didn't give him the satisfaction he hoped they would.'

'Did he ever mention how he was getting the money?'

'No, he was the Chief Operating Officer at the children's hospital, so I assumed—'

'Actually, he was just a middle manager.'

'Right... I didn't know that,' the psychiatrist replied, flustered. 'Well, anyway, I knew he was spending more than he was earning, but he certainly didn't infer that he was resorting to – to criminal means to finance his lifestyle. If he had, I would have contacted the police immediately. The rules are very clear on that.'

'And do you have any sense of *why* he felt compelled to spend in this way, to have the very best of everything, the most fashionable clothes, the most up-to-date phones?'

Once more Blythe hesitated. He was an attractive, articulate young man, whom Helen imagined would have been a very reassuring presence in his smartly designed, pet-friendly office, but today he looked uncertain and ill at ease, uncomfortable sharing the inner workings of his client's troubled mind, offering up Amar Goj's soul for inspection.

'It's hard to pin it down *exactly*, but I think, I think that Amar had always used money to earn – no, to *buy* – respect. It started at school, I believe. He'd steal from his mum's purse in order to flash the cash with his mates and, later, when he was dating, he'd give his girlfriends lavish gifts, take them to expensive restaurants, drive them around in a hired Mercedes... and it kind of worked. People *did* seem to like him. He got married, bought a nice house, an expensive car... though I suspect in his heart he always wondered whether they really liked him.'

'Or whether they were just in his pay.'

'Exactly.'

'What drives something like that?'

'Chronic lack of self-esteem, basically. Though what the basis of that anxiety was, I'm afraid I never got close to working out. We just didn't have enough time together.'

'But you said you were making progress?'

'Yes. When Amar came to me, he was very depressed, could only dispel his anxiety by spending more, getting deeper and deeper into trouble. We managed to get a grip on that, stabilize the situation.'

'But he was still in a bad way?'

'Of course. This was learned behaviour, something he'd been practising since childhood. You must understand that when people make the decision to consult a psychiatrist, they're often seeking a quick fix. They want you to wave a magic wand and make it all go away. But it doesn't work like that. Conquering problems of this magnitude takes months, even years of counselling and CBT, supported by medication, help groups, pledge schemes and so on. It's not an easy ride, it *really* isn't, especially if you're hiding your issues from your family and friends and I'm afraid that – that I barely got past first base with Amar.'

Blythe petered out, the reality of his patient's death finally sinking in. Helen could see that the psychiatrist was receding into himself now, as the full weight of his responsibility, his failure, made itself felt, so she asked a couple more probing questions, then took her leave. She had what she wanted, a clear picture of the net that had slowly tightened around the unfortunate Amar. She was particularly intrigued by the fact that the NHS manager had sought professional help at around the same time as the hospital announced its internal review of procurement post-Covid. Did the fraudster see the catastrophe that lay down the line? Was he hoping that he could somehow cover his tracks, get a grip on his spending and perhaps start again? It seemed highly likely, but of course they would never know for sure now.

Trotting down the stairs, Helen hit the door release, pushing out into the quiet mews street. As she did so, a wall of heat hit her, the temperature outside a marked contrast to the air-conditioned interior. Hauling off her jacket, Helen walked quickly to her bike, flicking open the saddle to toss the leather garment inside, but even as she did so, her phone started to buzz. Retrieving it, she saw it was DC McAndrew calling.

'Hi, Ellie. What's up?'

There was a long pause. Immediately, Helen knew it was bad news but even so, she was still rocked back on her heels, as McAndrew replied: 'There's been a fatal stabbing in Portswood.'

Chapter 42

She was close now. If she could just hold her nerve for a couple more minutes, she would be free and clear.

So far everything had gone according to plan. She had stationed herself in the alleyway, carefully laying out the tins on the ground, before sliding her hand inside the torn plastic bag, her gloved fingers fumbling for the reassuring bulk of the knife's handle. No sooner had she got a grip on it, however, than she'd heard footsteps approaching.

Martin Hill was a man of habit, running down the lonely alleyway at pretty much the same time every day, enjoying the privacy, isolation and free passage it afforded him. This lunchtime, these qualities had served *her* well, rendering the cut-through the perfect spot for an ambush. Her victim had suspected nothing, nor was there anyone to witness the attack, as she slid the knife into his stomach, catching him off guard.

This was the point where it could all have gone wrong, had he fought back. But such was his shock, that not only did he *not* tackle her, he also failed to make even the slightest noise as he slid to the floor. It was all over in less than a minute. It had been easy – terribly, sickeningly, easy.

For a brief moment, she'd stood and stared, awed by what she'd just done, then her survival instinct kicked in. Dropping the bloody knife into the torn bag, she wrapped it up tightly, depositing the package in the other shopping bag. Then, reaching down, she'd scooped up the tins and flung them in too, before hurrying away. She made swift progress to the northern end of the alleyway, where she was sure there were no tell-tale CCTV cameras. She kept her gaze fixed ahead, driving onward with zealous enthusiasm and it was only right at the last, as she reached the mouth of the alleyway, that she felt compelled to steal a look back.

Nothing had changed; Martin Hill lay lifeless on the floor, a fallen giant. It was a pitiful sight and, stung by a sudden sense of regret, she turned, needing to be away from the scene of her crime. Now she was back on the main drag, alarmed to see people, cars, *life*. She realized that she was sweating heavily – she could feel the clamminess under her armpits, beads of perspiration gripping her forehead. She was convinced that her guilt was self-evident, that everyone would stare at her, calling her out for her callous crime. But in fact everyone was going about their business as usual, as if nothing of consequence had happened.

Lowering her head, she pressed on. Her car was parked several streets away, a five-minute march at the most. If she could get there, if she could drive to her chosen disposal site without arousing suspicion, then it would be done.

The traffic was busy this morning, and she was held up at one pedestrian crossing after another, muttering impatiently under her breath each time for the cars to pass by. Each wasted second felt like an eternity, her right arm, her conscience, weighed down by the knife that nestled in her shopping bag.

'Come on, come on...'

Now a gap opened up and she was on her way again, but even as she broke cover, she realized that she'd badly misjudged the situation, that a car in the far lane was speeding towards her, would *hit* her if she carried on. Grinding to a halt, she just had time to step back, as the car roared past, horn blaring. Rattled, she shot another look to her left, but the road was now clear. Moments later, she was back on the pavement and away, hoping nobody had clocked this near miss.

On she marched, half walking, half running in an ungainly lope. To sprint would be too attention-grabbing, too suspicious, but somehow she couldn't just walk. So, she hurried along as she best she could, hoping she looked like a regular professional running late for a meeting.

With each passing minute, she was putting more distance between herself and the crime scene. With each road crossed, she was a little safer. The sweat still clung to her, but her breathing had stabilized now and it was with a sense of profound relief that she reached Lena Gardens. Her car was parked at the far end and soon she would be away, safe and sound.

But even as she turned into the street, she ground to a juddering halt. Someone was standing by her car, someone in uniform. Suddenly her heart was in her mouth. Was it possible that she had been discovered *already*? That she would be caught, arrested, charged? Terrified, she tried to get a grip on her panic, to find some semblance of calm and now, even in her fevered state, she realized that the tall figure by her vehicle was not a police officer. He was a traffic warden.

'What the hell ...?'

The man was bending down to examine her front tyre, taking great interest in its positioning. And now she understood. There had been fewer spaces than usual in the street this morning, so she'd had to park up close to a double yellow line. It wasn't ideal, but she was sure her wheels were merely kissing the yellow paint, hardly a ticket offence.

The traffic warden clearly disagreed. Even now he was

getting out his camera, taking pictures of the car registration, the offending tyre, the position of the car. Worse still, he was consulting his watch, starting the ten-minute grace period which had to elapse before he could issue his ticket. Dear God, he was even whistling now, looking around happily, evidently in good humour.

She turned away, stepping behind a tree, desperate not to be seen. What should she do now? Stand and wait here until he was finished? No, there was no way she could do that, anyone might see her loitering in the busy residential street, might even approach her, asking her what she was up to. Suddenly she felt sure that if someone *were* to stop her she wouldn't pass the test, wouldn't be able to lie her way out of the situation, with the bloody kitchen knife swinging by her side. No, she needed to get out of here, returning for the car when the coast was clear. Relieved, she hurried off, back towards the main street, but she had barely walked a few paces, before she stopped once more. She almost couldn't believe it, but she wasn't seeing things – two police officers were now standing at the top of the road, at the junction with the main street.

Where had *they* come from? And what were they up to? She felt caught between the devil and deep blue sea, danger behind her, danger in front. One of the officers now cast a glance up the road towards her and instinctively she turned away, busying herself with her phone, desperately trying to buy herself some time. There was no way she could stand here in full view; she needed to move, to get away. The simple thing to do would be to cross to the other side of the street and move off, using the phone to shield her face from view. Yes, that was it. She would take it at a steady pace, composed and purposeful, like any other morning commuter. All she needed was a little nerve, a little composure.

Taking a deep breath, she took one step off the pavement into the road, but even as she did so, she paused. Something had hit her foot. Looking down, she was horrified to see that it was a drop of blood. A single drop of blood.

The bag was leaking. Somehow the blood had escaped its plastic wrapping, pooling in the corner of her shopping bag. Even now it was seeping from a tiny hole in the plastic, leaving a trail of guilt. Panicking, desperate, she looked up to see the police officers walking towards her. They had been chatting to a local resident, but now had broken off to continue their rounds. Any minute now they would be upon her, their curious gaze drawn to the shaking, terrified woman, with her blood-stained shopping bag...

Casting around for some means of salvation, her eye now fell on a rainwater drain next to the curb, hidden between two parked cars. Moving forward, she deliberately dropped her phone, swore loudly, then crouching down, retrieved the bloody Sainsbury's bag and shoved it through the wide metal grate. With an enormous sense of relief, she felt it fall from her grasp. She was hoping to hear a reassuring splash, but was not altogether surprised when she heard a dull thud instead, the weather having been so dry recently. Relieved nevertheless, she pulled off her gloves, grabbed her shopping bag and scooped up her phone, clamping it to her face, before hurrying over to the other side of the road. From there it was just a minute's walk to the main street and safety, but she made it there in barely thirty seconds, never once looking back. This was not how she'd planned it and it might yet come back to haunt her, but right now that didn't matter. Her heart was pounding fit to burst, her forehead was dripping with sweat, but she had done it. She was free and clear – for now at least.

Chapter 43

'This is a massive account, so every agency worth its salt is going to be after it. We're going to need to be at our very best, our most innovative, if we're going to land it...'

Joel Jenkins was in full flow, challenging the team to respond to his directive, to seize the prize that lay before them. In the past, his directive would have fired Lilah up, would have inspired her to work harder, longer, better, to ensure that they won the contract, but she had heard too many such speeches and knew instinctively that their efforts were most likely doomed, given the odds. It didn't help that she'd heard a rumour that the hotel chain in question had already made up their mind to go with another agency, thanks to a cosy relationship between the respective CEOs.

Even if she *had* felt there was a chance of victory, it's unlikely she would have been able to rise to the challenge. She was in a bad way today, no question, and besides, everyone in the room was so much younger, sharper, hungrier than her, so keen to clamber over each other's corpses to get to the top. She had been like that once, but not anymore, life having intervened forcefully in the interim. Now she felt spent, lifeless, barely able to put one foot in front of the other, let alone compete with the agency's young guns.

Looking around the well-appointed meeting room, she felt completely out of place, wondering if she'd ever really fitted in here. Although the company was split evenly along gender lines, the atmosphere was overwhelmingly masculine – aggressive, assertive, Darwinian. The look on the faces of her colleagues, so eager and acquisitive, used to make her feel intimidated. Now it just made her feel ill.

Perhaps that was the answer. She had been trying to soldier on, concealing her problems from her colleagues, but perhaps it was time to admit that she needed a break. She had used up her paltry holiday allowance, so perhaps the thing to do was to take sick leave, a proper chunk of time off. It would damage her reputation for sure, perhaps even her career, whatever HR might say, but suddenly she didn't care. The illusory goals she'd been chasing for so long appeared to be just that. What she craved now was space – space to think, heal, perhaps even start over. How would the request go down? she wondered. Would there be endless discussions and meetings, or could it all be done over email, formally, clinically? If so, she would write the email today, as soon as the meeting was—

'Lilah?'

She looked up to find Joel looking at her intently.

'Yes, sorry, I was just letting an idea turn over in my head. But basically I agree with what Sam was just saying—'

'I wasn't asking for your input.'

'Right, sorry...'

'I was just alerting you to the fact that Louise has been knocking on the window for the last minute, trying to get your attention...'

Embarrassed, Lilah turned to see their departmental PA tapping on the glass wall.

'Sorry, sorry, I was just—' she mumbled, rising.

She was aware that all eyes were on her, that she appeared foolish and distracted, so moved quickly, sliding across the hard, wooden floor and out into the corridor. Keen to maintain some semblance of professional dignity, she fixed a smile on her face as she turned to their long-serving PA.

'Thank God for you, Louise. Joel is in full flow in there, so you've saved me from a fate worse than—' She petered out as she saw that Louise seemed tearful, even nervous.

'I've just had the police on the phone for you,' she said tentatively.

Immediately, Lilah felt her insides constrict. Had something happened to her mum and dad? To Eric?

'It's about Martin…'

Even as she said it, Lilah knew it was over. That her husband was dead. And that her life would never be the same again.

Chapter 44

She stared down at his face, her gaze drawn to his lifeless, bloodshot eyes.

Helen had wasted no time in racing over to the crime scene in Portswood, determined to get on top of the situation immediately. It didn't seem possible that yet another violent crime had been committed, so hot on the heels of the attack on Declan McManus, and only a matter of hours after Amar Goj's suicide, but the reports had proven accurate, a horrified schoolboy stumbling upon a dead body whilst sneaking into an alleyway for a crafty smoke.

The teenage boy was being looked after by DC Reid, and Helen hadn't broken stride to talk to him; there would be time for that later. She'd been impatient to see what they were dealing with, ducking under the police tape and picking her way carefully towards the corpse. Meredith Walker and David Spivack were not yet on the scene, meaning that, for now, Helen had the victim to herself.

The uniformed officers who'd secured the scene had spotted a wallet in the victim's tracksuit pocket, using this to identify him as Martin Hill. Crouching down, Helen took in his lifeless body. Hill was tall, muscular, and would have been an attractive, arresting presence in normal circumstances. But now he seemed disquieting, repellent even, his features locked into an expression of agony and horror, as if shocked, sickened, that his life should have ended this way. Moving in closer, Helen saw that his face was otherwise untouched, so too his large, open hands, which appeared smooth and without signs of abrasions. The same could not be said for his torso, however, and Helen's gaze drifted there now.

The victim was wearing a white T-shirt, crisp and brilliant on the arms and collar, but sodden and crimson around the stomach and chest. Tracing a gloved finger just above the fabric, Helen discovered three significant tears, one around the stomach, two further up, near the heart. Death would have been swift but savage, three sickening blows robbing the victim of breath, consciousness and ultimately life itself. Helen shuddered, it was an awful way to die.

Stepping away, she straightened up, scanning the alleyway. The heat was stifling this morning and she angrily clawed the hairs away from her face, which even now clung to her cheeks. Surveying the length of the alleyway, Helen saw immediately that Hill's attacker had chosen the site well – no CCTV, no over-looking windows and very little chance of being disturbed. Had they lain in wait, then, biding their time until their unfortunate victim approached? And if so, to what end? The man's wallet was still on him and his iPhone 12 remained strapped to his left bicep, a pair of AirPods still nestling incongruously in his ears. Given this, robbery didn't appear to be the motive, so why had Hill been so viciously dispatched? What did his attacker stand to *gain*?

Standing alone by the body, Helen felt unsteady on her feet. The temperature was rising steadily, the sun forcing itself into the alleyway, but it wasn't that which made Helen's head swim. It was fear, a rising sense of panic, which she'd felt often recently.

The innocent faces of Eve Sutcliffe, Alison Burris and Declan McManus seemed to dance in front of her, reminding her of the relentless tide of bloodshed. Had the city lost its mind? If so, what chance did Helen have of wresting back control of the situation?

Turning away from the body, Helen hurried back down the alleyway, hoping against hope that the team might have turned up something. A sighting, a witness, a motive, anything – but in truth they looked as shocked and forlorn as she did. They were already working flat out on other investigations, running on fumes, and now they had to deal with this – another high-profile murder case.

Lifting the police tape, Helen ducked underneath, pivoting towards the team, but even as she did so, she was confronted by a familiar figure.

Snap, snap, snap.

It took Helen a moment to process what was happening, a moment more for the anger to surge within her. Emilia Garanita was standing there, bold as brass, intent on capturing an image of Helen – sweaty, anxious, worried – her camera lens trained upon her.

'What the hell is *she* doing here?' Helen barked in the direction of DC Bentham, who looked flustered and embarrassed.

Snap, snap, snap.

Helen was tempted to bat the camera from Garanita's grasp, to smash it on the ground, but she knew this would only add fuel to the fire, so instead she pushed angrily past.

'Any comment to make, DI Grace? Anything to say about this latest outrage?'

Helen spun round, unable to contain her anger.

'I'll remind you that this is a crime scene. If you're not out of here in thirty seconds...'

'Just doing my job,' Emilia said, smiling broadly, as she backed away. 'At least one of us is, right?'

Now Helen really was tempted to go for her, but Emilia was wise to the danger, dropping her camera to her side and casually walking back towards her car. Even as she did so, Helen turned on DC Bentham.

'Would someone *please* explain to me what the bloody hell's going on here? Do we have no site management anymore? No protocols? She shouldn't have got past uniform, let alone you lot...'

'She just appeared from nowhere,' Bentham protested. 'I – I didn't see her.'

'Well, it's not good enough. And if it happens again, I'll be holding you responsible, *all* of you.' She gestured at the assembled team, who seemed to shrink back as she spoke, looking aggrieved, even a little scared. 'This is *totally* unacceptable. A young man is dead in that alleyway and somehow Emilia Garanita has the run of the scene, before forensics, before pathology – I mean, what part of you thinks that's OK? Have you forgotten *everything* you were taught at police college?'

Her accusation, angry and aggressive, hung in the air. No one spoke, no one moved, though whether this was out of embarrassment or fear was unclear. Helen was torn, wanting to lambast the team, to vent all her anger and anxiety on them – yet also painfully aware of the strain they were *all* under.

'Look, just – just secure the site,' she continued, moderating her tone. 'And get to work. Let's find out what happened here.'

She marched off towards her bike, intent on getting to Martin Hill's next of kin as quickly as possible. Helen was trying to look purposeful, in control, but knew she looked anything but. Every day of her working life, she tried hard to be a good leader, to be decisive, inspiring, calm. But recently she'd forgotten how, misplacing the strength and resolve she used to be famous for, in the process losing the battle for hearts and minds. Now, when the stakes couldn't be any higher, when the eyes of her team, her superiors and the wider world were fixed upon her, she looked anxious, desperate and scared.

Chapter 45

He kept a beady eye on them, even as he punched in the numbers.

The boys were in high spirits today, animated and boisterous, cavorting around in the garden, laughing and whooping. The sight pleased him – pleased him more than he could say – but he was still scared that they might suddenly burst into the house, which of course he could ill afford. This was a phone call he needed to make alone.

Moving away from the window, Robert Downing returned his attention to the handset. He had entered the phone number, now all he needed do was hit 'call'. Such a simple action, but still he hesitated. Was he really ready to do this? It would change his life, the boys' life forever. Yet what choice did he have? To do anything else would be madness. He *had* to make the call.

He stabbed the button and waited. He half hoped that it would go straight to voicemail, but now the call connected, a dull ringing filling his ear. Even now, he was tempted to stab 'end', to cut his losses and run, but courage prevailed and he hung on. One ring, two, three... would she never answer?

And now her voicemail *did* click in, her strong, authoritative voice reaching out to him.

'Hi, this is Helen Grace, please leave a message...'

A moment's silence, then a strong, decisive bleep. This was it, then, the last chance to back out, but instead he spoke swiftly, decisively: 'Helen, hi, it's Robert Downing. We need to talk.'

Chapter 46

'It started a week ago ...'

Lilah Hill was speaking slowly, as if it was an effort to join one word to the next. She was in shock, her body shaking, her voice quivering, desperately trying to make sense of the terrible tragedy that had suddenly befallen her.

'Can you talk me through it? I need to know *exactly* what happened.'

Helen sat opposite her, in the house she had shared with Martin Hill. Lilah had retreated there, having received the awful news at work, and Helen was keen to see if *she* could cast any light on this morning's brutal murder. And no sooner had she pulled up outside the attractive terraced house, than she got the first inkling of what lay in store – the imprint of a recently painted swastika still just about visible on the exterior.

'Well, about a week ago, we had a couple of odd calls. Silent calls, someone hanging up as soon as we answered the phone. We didn't think much of it – maybe a wrong number or kids mucking about. Then three or four days ago – it was the tenth, I think – things got much worse. Martin picked up the phone and this woman just went for him, calling him every racist name under the sun, before hanging up.'

Helen made a note of the date and replied: 'Do you think

those earlier calls were her too, plucking up the "courage" to abuse your husband, perhaps?'

'Maybe.' Lilah shrugged dully, still trying to process the events of the last few days.

'How long did the call last?'

'Thirty seconds, no more.'

'And were there any more calls?'

'No, for the next couple of days there was nothing. We thought maybe it was a one-off, just a nasty, stupid incident. But then we woke up two days ago to find ... well, you saw what they did to the front of the house.'

'They?'

'They, he, whoever. We didn't see them doing it.'

'And none of the neighbours saw anything?'

'I asked a few people but nobody had anything to say, so I gave up, didn't want to keep going on about it.'

Helen thought for a moment, then asked: 'Just doubling back to the phone calls, can I ask whether the woman mentioned Martin by name? Did she know the identity of the person she was abusing?'

Lilah nodded. 'Yes, totally. She used his name, knew where he lived. Said someone like him shouldn't be living on a nice, "white" street ...'

Helen's heart sunk. Every murder was a tragedy, but some had more impact than others. A racially motivated murder was the last thing Southampton needed right now.

'Did Martin recognize the voice?'

'I don't think so.'

'Could it have been someone from the bar, someone involved in that altercation?'

'Well, there *were* girls in the group, so it's possible, I suppose ...' Lilah Hill petered out, as Helen's suggestion landed.

'Is that what you think this is?' she continued nervously. 'That whoever made the calls, graffitied the house, also ... also did this to Martin?' Lilah was staring straight at Helen, her anger fuelling some kind of composure now, even though tears still filled her eyes.

'Honestly? I've no idea,' Helen replied. 'But it's obviously a strong possibility. And it might explain why they seemed to target him specifically, rather than the pair of you. I take it Martin hasn't had any other problems recently? Any other altercations or racially motivated incidents? On public transport? When he was out and about?'

'No.'

'He wasn't conscious of any hostility towards him?'

'No.'

'Or anyone following him home?'

'No, nothing like that.'

'And as regards the youths whom Martin confronted at the bar, had there been any *other* contact with them since that initial incident? Any threats made in weeks gone by? Any further confrontations?'

'Not that he told me about. Honestly, we thought it was over, finished. Which is what we wanted. We didn't ask to be abused, to be assaulted. We never asked for *any* of it. I spent three hours scrubbing that shit off the front of the house, for all the good it did me. And now *this* ...'

She opened up her hands as she spoke, as if indicating the breadth of her tragedy, but it seemed woefully inadequate, given how hollow, how shell-shocked she obviously felt.

'And can I ask how things were between the pair of you?'

Lilah looked up sharply, suspicion writ large on her face.

'Were you happy? Was it a loving relationship?'

'Of course, we've been together nearly ten years now. We were happy, are happy...'

'It's just that I can't help noticing that you have a nasty bruise on your wrist.'

Immediately, Lilah pulled her arms in, perhaps regretting exposing herself to view.

'That's nothing.'

'It doesn't look like nothing.'

'It was just a domestic accident, that's all. I got my arm caught in the door...' It sounded weak and unconvincing. 'Martin and I, we had our ups and downs, like any couple,' Lilah continued quickly. 'But we were solid, happy...'

She looked entreatingly at Helen, as if asking her, nicely, to shut down this topic of conversation.

'Look, Lilah, I know this kind of thing is hard to talk about, especially now Martin's gone. But if I'm going to work out why this happened, I need *all* the facts. Chapter and verse on you, Martin, your time together, what you did, where you went, how you were together...'

'The state of our relationship has nothing to do with what happened this morning, I swear. We were *fine*. Martin was attacked by mindless, racist thugs—'

'Lilah, I've been doing this for over twenty years now. I've been in dozens of homes where there has been tension, even violence, between couples. It's absolutely nothing to be ashamed of and I can tell you from experience that *not* talking about it is the very worst thing you can do. So please, if there were any issues, any conflict within your relationship, tell me now.'

The bereaved woman stared at her, as if appalled by the request. 'There is *nothing to tell*, because we were happy.' She glared at Helen, challenging her to come back at her, before reiterating: 'We were *happy*.'

Chapter 47

'You might want to take a look at this...'

DC Edwards kept his voice low, which pleased Joseph Hudson. DCI Simmons had paid an unexpected visit to the incident room – to rally the troops and raise morale – and, clearly, Edwards knew where Simmons's loyalties lay. The ambitious DC had summoned Hudson discreetly and appeared keen to keep his discovery between the pair of them. Encouraged by this display of loyalty and discretion, Hudson leaned in, carefully examining the photo on his terminal.

'What am I looking at?'

'Well, following this morning's incident, DI Grace asked me to do some background research on recent incidences of hate crime, activities of local far-right groups, online trolling and so on...' Edwards was speaking fast, as if keen to get through this preamble. 'And as you can imagine, there's a lot to take in.' Edwards maximized a couple of tabs. 'There're reams of xenophobic and racist abuse on line, most of it pedalling a line about the rights of white Anglo-Saxons. The Chinese come in for a lot of abuse, but so does anyone else who's not deemed to be properly "British".'

As Edwards spoke, Hudson's eyes darted to the head shot of Martin Hill on the murder board.

'There's also a lot of activity amongst the neo-Nazi and far-right groups. Much of it driven by unemployment, anger, desperation, but also by a fear of crime. Groups of disaffected young men are mobilizing, promising to weed out "disruptive elements" in their communities.'

He gestured to the screen, pulling Hudson's attention back to the terminal. On it was a web page belonging to a group called Albion, whose credo was clear. The Union Jack provided the backdrop to the screeds of racially charged text and dire predictions of a future apocalypse, the red in the flag slowly running down the page like dripping blood.

'If you can imagine a neo-Nazi version of Reclaim the Streets, this is it. They are actively recruiting, taking on anyone they deem racially "pure" to help them make Southampton "White again". It's completely confused and contradictory – the guys who run it seem to admire Churchill *and* Hitler – but their message has proved popular. They've got over four hundred followers, many of whom are happy to take up arms.'

Once again, Edwards clicked, minimizing this screen and pulling up the photo again. Hudson drank in the detail – twenty or so young white males, most with shaven heads and animal-istic expressions, berating Asian store owners and shoppers in Thornhill. Their victims looked scared and it wasn't hard to see why – the young men were carrying baseball bats and looked ready to use them. Due to the hot weather, most of the aggres-sors were stripped to the waist, their Iron Eagle and Swastika tattoos clearly visible.

'The prime mover in Albion is a man who calls himself Panzer, from the German word—'

'Meaning armour,' Hudson interrupted. 'I know my history, DC Edwards.'

'Sure, sorry. Anyway, he's been very active of late. Organizing marches through deprived areas, making a number of inflammatory speeches and posting endless web messages urging his followers to fight back, to rid the streets of the "coloured vermin".

'Nice…'

'We think his real name is Michael Sergeant. He's been booked a number of times for hate crimes, though never charged. He's currently under investigation for a hammer attack on a group of black teenagers on the Common three months ago—'

'I remember it.'

'—but that hasn't stopped him urging his followers on to bigger and better things. In his last post, written three days ago, he actively calls for mob violence, telling people to fight back, to spill blood in the streets, to defend the British way of life, blah blah blah.'

'And this is relevant *how?*'

Hudson was intrigued by Edwards's discoveries, but keen to get to the point.

'Sorry. So, yeah, in this photo, we've got a clutch of his followers, smashing up local shops, scaring women and children. Some of them are known to us, some of them are new, but at the back I spotted this guy—'

Hudson leaned in closer, scrutinizing a young man at the rear group. Stripped to the waist, his tattooed torso proudly displayed, the man had his fist clenched in some sort of salute, even as he screamed at an elderly Asian man. His face was turned away from the camera, but even at an angle, his features were distinct and familiar.

'It's Lee Moffat…'

'Exactly. Turns out he's got history in this area. His older brother, Jason, was a member of a group called Final Solution and Lee himself posts fairly regularly on Albion and its sister sites. He's flirted with the English Defence League, the BNP in the past, but is now a full-time advocator for a race war.'

Hudson stared at the young man's features, which were contorted with hate.

'Strange how his name keeps popping up, right?' Edwards's question was leading, seeking affirmation and approbation. Hudson was happy to oblige – this discovery another small but important part of the jigsaw.

'Spot on. You've done well. Can you prioritize this line of enquiry, please, reporting back *directly* to me?'

'Of course.'

'Any links to Martin Hill, to planned hate crime in Portswood, anything that might link Lee Moffat to this morning's murder, I want to know about it. And I want to know about it *first*.'

'Course, boss. I'll get right on it.'

'Good man. You're too experienced for grunt work, but sometimes the devil's in the detail, right? You never know where it might take you.'

Patting him on the back, Hudson walked back to his desk, passing DCI Simmons, who remained locked in conversation with DC Bentham. Having started the day angry and frustrated, Hudson now had a spring in his step. He had information that Helen Grace didn't possess, evidence potentially linking Lee Moffat to *three* current investigations, plus a new ally in DC Edwards. The experienced officer's career had plateaued under Grace's leadership and if Hudson could encourage disloyalty, by seeming to offer better things ahead, then he wouldn't hesitate to do so.

Every ally was vital. And when the moment came to take Helen down, he would need *all* of them by his side.

Chapter 48

'You have one new voicemail message.'

Helen could barely hear the words over the roar of her bike. Her Bluetooth-enabled helmet was top quality, but she was riding fast and loud, having been urgently summoned by Meredith Walker to a cul-de-sac not half a mile from this morning's crime scene.

'Helen, hi, it's Robert Downing. We need to talk.'

Surprised, Helen strained to hear, but the message now ended, as the caller hung up. Tapping her headset, Helen listened again, doubting she'd heard the message correctly, but there was no question that it *was* Downing. He sounded tense, agitated even, which intrigued her. Downing had seemed so cool, so collected when they'd last met. Had something happened in the interim?

Helen's first instinct was to call him back, in order to satisfy her curiosity. But even as she reached out towards her phone, she clocked activity ahead. A dozen uniformed officers, fluttering yellow crime tape and a handful of search officers in their distinctive sterile suits. She had reached Lena Gardens.

Ditching her plans to call Downing back, Helen parked quickly, slipping on shoe coverings and eating up the yards to where Meredith Walker now stood, mopping her brow. Working in high temperatures was not pleasant for any forensics officer, but for once Meredith had a smile on her face. Lena Gardens was a quiet residential street, unused to fevered police activity, but today it had heralded an important discovery.

'Where'd you find it?'

'Down the drain,' Meredith replied with a rueful smile. 'Not very imaginative, perhaps, but needs must…'

Helen kneeled down, taking in the murky hole in front of her. The grate had been lifted off, revealing a deep cavity of dried earth and rubbish, at the centre of which lay a stained Sainsbury's bag.

'What made you look here?'

'Well, I pulled most of the team down to help with the fingertip search. Knives are usually dumped close to the scene, people don't like to carry them once they've been used. They're often disposed of in out-of-the-way places – parks, alleyways, cul de sacs, that sort of thing – so we ignored the main thorough-fares to look at the quieter, residential streets. One of our guys spotted blood on the pavement, then a short trail of deposits leading to the drain. To be honest, it wasn't very well hidden, just stuffed down there without much thought…'

Helen nodded, intrigued. The actual murder had been very well planned and executed, leaving no obvious traces of the perpetrator behind. This was different, careless, even amateurish, which set her mind wondering. Was this a mistake, an oversight? Or were they *meant* to find it?

'You're convinced it *is* our weapon?'

'We won't know for sure till we get it back to the lab, but odds on. The blade is the right width, the handle shape looks right, given the bruising on the body and, as you can see, the blood is fresh.'

Helen peered into the bag, the knife visible at its heart. The blood on the long blade had dried now, but its rich crimson hue and sticky sheen strongly suggested that Meredith was right.

'OK, let's fast-track it, please,' Helen suggested, straightening up.

'Of course.'

'And let's scour every inch of this road.'

'Already on it.'

'Anything, however small, I want to know about it *straight-away*.'

Taking her leave, Helen paced back to her bike. It was an intriguing development, which might yet lead to a breakthrough, and it was with something approaching optimism that Helen climbed onto her Kawasaki. But as she did so, her phone rang. For a moment, she thought it might be Robert Downing trying her again, but the caller ID indicated otherwise.

'DC Malik?'

'Boss.'

'I'm at Lena Gardens, but on my way back now.'

'That's great, but I thought you'd want to know – we've just taken a call from the hospital...'

Helen tensed, sensing that a day that had already delivered several surprises was not done yet.

'Apparently, there were complications with McManus when they tried to bring him out of the induced coma. He suffered multiple organ failure, which resulted in cardiac arrest. He died just after two o'clock this afternoon.'

Chapter 49

'What's got into you?'

Carol looked pleased, but surprised, as Belinda descended upon her, kissing her neck, her nose, her forehead.

'Do I need a reason to seduce my girlfriend?' Belinda countered, kissing her on the lips, even as she undid a button on her shirt.

'No ... but it's the middle of the afternoon. I've got to teach soon, so have you ...'

'It won't matter if we're a little bit late ...'

Even as she spoke, Belinda slid her hand inside Carol's shirt, her deft fingers running over the soft fabric of her bra, seeking out her nipple. Carol reacted, aroused now, but even so she took hold of Belinda's hand, stopping her.

'I'm not saying it wouldn't be nice, I just want to know what's going on ...'

'I would have thought that was obvious,' Belinda teased, struggling in her grip.

'Seriously, Belinda. What's this about?'

Reluctantly, Belinda relented, removing her hand.

Carol continued, 'You've been weird and distant all week. You refuse to spend the day with me, won't tell me why, then suddenly you burst in, out of the blue, wanting to shag my brains out. You'll forgive me for being a little confused.'

'You're right and I'm sorry,' Belinda replied, running a hand through Carol's hair. 'I have been a bitch. Honestly, I don't know what's been wrong with me.'

She was trying hard, but felt self-conscious under Carol's shrewd gaze. Her lover had been hurt by her before, the wounds still sore, and was clearly not going to give her an easy ride.

'I don't know if it was pupil exam stress,' Belinda explained, 'or my hormones, or just my bloody mother bugging me out – probably all three. But I had no right to take it out on you, to be so distant and cold. This is just my way of saying sorry…' Running her hand across Carol's cheek, she chanced another gentle kiss. 'You know I'm not very good with words, I find it hard to say the right thing.'

'But you know how to fuck, right?' Carol shot back. There was an edge to her voice, hurt and suspicion undercutting her desire.

'No, I know how to love.' Belinda let the word hang in the air, enjoying the look of surprise on Carol's face. 'Because I do love you, I really do. And I never want you to feel worried or anxious. I want to make your life better, happier, every single day…' She kissed her again and this time Carol allowed it. 'I really mean it, I want us to work – and if, you know, if you want to talk again about family, about kids…' Belinda didn't know where the words were coming from, hadn't planned any of this, wasn't sure she even meant it, but it felt right in the moment – 'then we should do it. I want what you want, end of story.'

Now Carol kissed her back, fierce and passionate. Belinda was surprised to see tears in her partner's eyes, but something else too. Love, burning, aching love. Responding to her touches, she tugged off her own shirt, then Carol's. Now they were tumbling onto the bed, pulling at each other's trousers, happily giving in to sensual abandon. Carol was biting her earlobes, kissing her nipples, caressing her tummy, now going lower still. Belinda lay back, surrendering to her lover's desire, nestling on the soft, plump duvet – happy, elated, alive.

Perhaps everything *was* going to be all right, after all.

Chapter 50

The atmosphere in the room was tense. Helen had pulled the whole team back to base to bring them up to speed on the latest developments. These end-of-the day catch-ups were often incredibly productive, the various threads of the investigation weaving seamlessly together to reveal important clues or vital breakthroughs. They could be charged, adrenalized, exciting, but today the team looked like Helen felt – hot, irritable and dog-tired.

'So Declan McManus died earlier this afternoon. Given the extent of his injuries, it was touch and go whether he was going to survive, but even so I can't pretend that it's not a bitter blow…'

No one present disagreed.

'Obviously, this means it's now a murder enquiry, with all the attendant publicity that that's going to generate. So I want us to move fast on this one.'

A couple of team members nodded, putting their last vestiges of energy into mustering a modicum of enthusiasm, which Helen was grateful for. The team had not been pulling as one, hadn't covered itself in glory of late, but there were still some committed, determined officers around her.

'I'm particularly interested in Amar Goj, who until recently was a procurement manager at Southampton Children's Hospital.'

She pinned his photo just beneath McManus's leering face.

'We're now sure that he bought a Rick Owens hoodie recently – we found the receipt in a shoebox at his house. Also, Meredith's team have confirmed that the partial footwear marks found at the crime scene match a brand that Amar Goj favoured – he had two box-fresh pairs of Philipp Plein shoes in his wardrobe at home. The search team haven't recovered the actual shoes used during the attack, but I'm assuming he dumped those along with the hoodie.'

A couple of the team nodded, but Helen's eye was now drawn to Joseph Hudson. He stood at the back of the group, saying nothing, his face betraying little emotion. His still, heavy presence unnerved her, but she pressed on.

'DC Malik also uncovered something interesting during her questioning of the Goj family...'

'Maybe something, maybe nothing, but his wife confirmed that he had refilled the petrol canister they use to supply their lawn mower three days ago. Goj has only mown the lawn once since then, but when we checked, the canister was almost empty...'

'There could be a dozen different explanations for that,' DC Reid responded, unimpressed.

'True, but it's interesting circumstantial,' Helen countered, trying to hide her irritation at Reid's casual dismissal of Malik's findings. 'And, if you'll pardon the pun, adds further fuel to the fire.'

'But what's the motive?' Hudson spoke up, finally breaking cover. 'What's the link between Goj and McManus?'

'Well, that's what we need to work out,' Helen replied firmly. 'I'm going to go back to Jeremy Blake, the CEO of the children's hospital, first thing tomorrow. He seemed reluctant to co-operate with us, more interested in shielding his Hospital Trust from negative publicity. He claims he only found out about the fraud recently following an email from Alison Burris. But he's not yet provided the email, or any other corroborative evidence to back up his account, and I'm wondering if there might be some connection between the hospital and McManus. Had they set McManus on Goj's trail, wanting to conduct their own private investigation rather than involving the police? Perhaps they wanted to deal with this entirely "in house" so that no one would be any the wiser?'

'I don't see it,' Hudson said dismissively. 'Why would they go to someone like him? A low-rent gumshoe? They'd have brought in a professional audit team, someone to do a forensic financial analysis of Goj's work transactions, his personal spending and so on—'

'Maybe, but we know McManus was the discreet arm of corporations and companies wishing to look into potentially criminal behaviour without getting their own hands dirty—'

'But that was mainly insurance firms and banks, companies who regularly had to pay out because of fraudsters,' DC Reid protested. 'There's no evidence that McManus worked in the healthcare sector.'

'There's a first time for everything, DC Reid,' Helen shot back, just about keeping her temper in check. 'And if McManus *was* keeping tabs on Goj, and he somehow got wind of that, then he'd have every motive to—'

'I'm sorry, I just don't buy it.'

Joseph Hudson's tone was measured, but firm, as if he was determined to shut down Helen's line of enquiry. And he wasn't alone, DCs Edwards and Reid acting as loyal wingmen, helping to shoot holes in her argument. Looking at them, Helen had the distinct feeling that they had already decided on their line of attack, knew *their* version of events which they were intent on prosecuting. And now, right on cue, Joseph Hudson changed tack.

'I think we should prioritize Lee Moffat.'

'Surely we've been down that road,' DC Malik responded tersely.

'We've questioned him once,' Hudson fired back. 'And he was hostile and evasive, failing to account for his movements or the missing hoodie.'

'That's not enough...'

'And we now have concrete evidence that McManus was investigating him *specifically*. The insurance company that was employing him sent over the reports submitted by McManus to them, reports in which he singles out Lee Moffat as the prime mover in a luxury-car-theft gang.'

Malik was silenced by this bit of news, which appeared to please Hudson.

'Moreover,' he continued confidently, 'DC Edwards has turned up some interesting links to far-right organizations, who are actively targeting ethnic minorities in Southampton.'

DC Edwards distributed a printout of his earlier discoveries, the dissemination of this new lead carefully choreographed for maximum impact.

'We're digging down on his online activity as we speak,' Hudson continued. 'I've got the data analysts on it and if we can find a link between Moffat and Martin Hill, then we can potentially link him to *three* current investigations.'

'But what's the motive?' DC Malik challenged, her antipathy to Hudson clear, perhaps *too* clear. 'I thought he was just interested in making money.'

'A man can be a thief *and* a racist, DC Malik,' Hudson

responded coolly, his eyes lingering on the young Asian officer. 'We know he has a penchant for violence, so it's perfectly possible that he murdered Alison Burris whilst "at work", that he killed McManus to protect his interests *and* heeded Albion's call to arms by murdering Martin Hill...'

'It's too much of a stretch; Moffat doesn't have it in him,' Helen intervened.

'I don't agree,' Hudson countered quickly. 'He's cocky, aggressive and growing in confidence every day. I think he's thriving off this atmosphere of lawlessness. I think he believes he can get away with anything, that he's untouchable.'

'He really has got under your nose, hasn't he?'

'He's a vicious, amoral thug with strong motives for all three murders.'

'With *possible* motives,' Helen countered. 'Moffat is a chancer, a thief. He hasn't transformed into a serial killer overnight. No, something, or someone else, is responsible for these murders.'

'Goj?' Hudson shot back, his tone withering.

'Goj and A.N. Other. Perhaps even someone we haven't alighted on yet. Which is why I want us to prioritize three areas of enquiry. First, McManus's movements. We've only a patchy tapestry of his activities during the last days of his life. I want more detail on these, to see if there was a specific trigger for his murder. Second, his connection to the children's hospital – is there any evidence McManus had worked for them, previously or currently—'

Hudson shook his head slowly, theatrically, but Helen pressed on, ignoring him.

'And finally, Lilah Hill. We know she and Martin were racially abused outside the Marquee Bar in Queen's Street a month ago. The identities of the perpetrators are on file and obviously our first priority is to talk to them about today's attack, to interrogate their movements, their recent call history... *but* I think there were also problems in Lilah's relationship with Martin and I want to know more. Did *she* have a motive? Was she seeing someone else? Had Martin threatened *her* in the past? Let's focus on these three areas and see what we can turn up. Everyone clear?'

Helen was keen to conclude the meeting, but Joseph Hudson had other ideas.

'Crystal clear, but I want to put on record my strong objection to the direction of this investigation. I think we are dismissing a very credible suspect, in order to follow up fanciful notions of Goj as an arsonist and a killer.'

Helen tried to interrupt, but Joseph talked over her.

'And I should say that several other members of the team feel exactly the same way as me.'

No one moved, no one spoke up in support, but they didn't have to. DC Edwards, DC Reid, even DC McAndrew were grouped around Hudson, silently providing support and affirmation.

'Be that as it may, I am the SIO in this room,' Helen hit back. 'And these are the lines of investigation we *will* be following. I expect every officer to do so willingly, vigorously and to the best of their abilities, or they'll have me to answer to. There have been too many breakdowns in protocol recently, too many lines of investigation pursued without my knowledge or authorization and it stops *today*.'

She ran an eye over Hudson, then Edwards, Reid and McAndrew in turn. The last of these at least had the wit to lower her head in embarrassment.

'Anyhow, it's late now and it's been a long day. Go home, get some sleep and be back here, bright-eyed and bushy-tailed, first thing in the morning. Meeting adjourned.'

Turning, Helen strode back to her office, determined not to get drawn into further arguments. She could hear the buzz of reaction, whispered exchanges, even the odd expletive, but she had no desire to get sucked into the fallout. The meeting had not gone well and it was better to draw it to a close than risk a full-on confrontation with Hudson, not least because she had no idea who would win such an encounter. Yes, she had carried the day, but she'd had to pull rank in order to do so, which left her feeling profoundly uncomfortable. She had never had to do so before, reliant on the loyalty and good sense of her team, but now, with rival power blocks forming, and Hudson determinedly recruiting fresh allies, she'd been left with little choice. She knew, though, that this displayed her vulnerability, weakness even, rather than her strength. She was still in charge of the team, still determined to drive the investigation forward, but there was no doubt now that her position was under threat.

Mutiny was in the air.

Chapter 51

'If you don't go to bed right now, there will be serious trouble...'

Robert's grim warning seemed to cut no ice, Freddie and Joshua continuing to bounce on their beds, their bare feet dirtying the pristine sheets.

'Come on, guys, please. You're making an awful mess here...'

His voice was weary, laced with irritation, but still the bouncing continued.

'Look at the clock, it's way past your bedtime. Clothes off, teeth, then bed, please...'

Now they swapped beds, leaping across the divide to continue bouncing.

'I'm warning you...'

They cocked their heads, as if mocking his ability to discipline them. He was seriously tempted to shout at them, but wisdom prevailed and he changed tack.

'I'll smack your bottoms...'

Much giggling at the mention of *that* word.

'I'll hang you out the window by your ankles...'

Now they paused, seemingly *excited* by this idea.

'OK, forget that, I want you in to bed in two minutes – or there'll be no Xbox tomorrow.'

And now his words seem to cut through.

'Really?'

'Not a single minute.'

That decided matters, the two six-year-old boys jumping off their beds and racing to the bathroom. Miraculously, one minute and fifty-five seconds later, they were back in bed, pyjamas on and teeth brushed. Their feet were still dirty, but that was one of the few benefits of being a single parent – you could set your own standards of hygiene.

Switching off the main light, Robert knelt down between their beds. Kissing one, then the other, he said: 'Straight to sleep now. And if you're lucky, I might let you play Fortnite whilst eating your Cheerios in the morning...'

Tucking them in, he kissed them again, then retreated to the doorway. Pulling it gently closed, he stole a look back. To his immense surprise, they already seemed to be asleep. Bathed in the soft glow of their night lights, they seemed relaxed, calm, totally at peace. When do we lose that, he wondered, that ability to sleep easily at night, without a care in the world? It's a precious gift, lost before it's fully appreciated, then gone forever.

Resting his cheek on the door, he stared at his boys, enraptured by the sight of them. It had been a deeply troubling day, fraught with anxiety, confusion and fear, but as he stared at Freddie and Joshua slumbering in their beds, he felt none of these things. He felt only love: deep, all-consuming love.

One last look, then he turned away, padding across the landing and down the stairs. As he did so, he retrieved his phone from his pocket. Staring at it a minute, he hesitated briefly, then made his decision, holding the power button down firmly until the screen went blank.

Chapter 52

'Nothing? Nothing at all?'

Helen couldn't hide her dismay.

'Nothing apart from the obvious,' Meredith responded, her voice tinny on the other end of the phone line. 'Martin Hill's blood was all over the blade, but there are no traces of anything else. No sweat, no prints, no other blood traces, the blade *and* handle are clean as a whistle.'

'It's not been used before, then? In a domestic setting, say, for chopping food or—'

'There's no bacteria on it and, in fact, the protective coating that the knife has to prevent it from rusting in store is still intact.'

'So the knife was acquired recently, perhaps specifically for this crime…'

'Makes sense to me. Anyway, that's all I've got for now, and the new series of *Succession* is calling, so…'

'Of course, you go. We'll speak in the morning.'

'I've no doubt,' the forensics officer replied ruefully.

Ringing off, Helen leaned against the corridor wall, digesting Meredith's news. The disposal of the knife had been crude and ineffective, but otherwise Martin Hill's murder had been carefully conceived and perfectly executed. No witnesses, no forensic evidence, no CCTV – the ideal way to dispatch the unfortunate Hill. To Helen, this argued strongly against his attacker being a neo-Nazi aggressor, as Hudson believed, or a half-witted youth intent on revenge, as Lilah Hill suggested. No, there was something sophisticated, pre-meditated and neat about Hill's death that suggested the culprit wanted to remain hidden. A racist thug would seek the acclaim of the kill, might even claim responsibility for his murder via some online forum, rather than remaining in the shadows. Ditto an old adversary, who might brag to mates, parading his bravery and strength for all to admire. Who was responsible, then? Lilah Hill might yet prove to possess a strong motive, but she had a rock-solid alibi, thanks to her colleagues. Was it possible, then, that she had hired someone to kill her husband? The thought seemed fanciful, but what other possibilities were there?

Exhaling heavily, Helen pocketed her mobile and resumed her march to the incident room. The rest of the team had gone now, but she wanted to remain a while longer, to sift the day's developments, to see if she could chance upon any leads, any avenues for investigation that they'd overlooked. As she stalked along the corridor, however, her eye was drawn to the window, to some activity in the courtyard below. Slowing, she realized that the tiny figure at street level was Joseph Hudson, walking across the tarmac to his bike.

He was alone, having presumably stayed after everyone else had departed, though to what end Helen wasn't sure. Watching him stride confidently across the bike park, Helen was filled with a riot of emotions. Sadness, suspicion, disappointment, but, above all, anger. Anger that this reckless, lying narcissist should challenge her so openly in *her* incident room. She had been at Southampton Central for years, driving this team, *her* team, to become one of the best in the country. What had he done except spread division, lies and disquiet? What right did he have to take a wrecking ball to her unit, her reputation, when he was just a faithless try-hard, with no inkling of the importance of teamwork, loyalty and respect? What right did he have to take her on, when it was *he* who was in the wrong?

And now, without intending to do so, Helen found herself moving. Along the corridor, through the fire exit and down the stairs towards the bike park.

Chapter 53

Hudson looked up as Helen approached, her urgent footsteps alerting him to her arrival. She saw surprise there, then something that looked very much like self-satisfaction, even conceit.

'So what was *that* all about?' Helen demanded, dispensing with any pretence of formalities, as she slipped her phone back into her pocket.

'What was what …?'

'You know perfectly well what. That little performance in there, that gross insubordination.'

'Steady now, Helen.'

'Challenging my authority, in front of the rest of the team. I mean, that's page-one stuff, Joseph. You just don't do it.'

'Except when it's necessary—'

'Oh, come off it …'

'To get an investigation, a team, back on track.'

'And you're best placed to make that judgement, are you? Having been here for, what, two years?'

'Sometimes a fresh pair of eyes is what's needed.'

Now Helen couldn't conceal her scorn, openly laughing at him. 'So this has nothing to do with us? The fact that our brief fling came to a rather sorry end?'

'It's to do with leadership, Helen. A quality you used to know something about.'

'You really are unbelievable.'

'For caring about the cases we're running, for caring about the team's reputation?'

'No, for caring about yourself and your own bruised ego so much that you're prepared to destroy the team.'

'It's not about that.'

'That's exactly what it's about. At least do me the courtesy of being honest about it.'

The words flew from her, sharp and angry. Hudson looked momentarily taken aback by her aggression. Softening a little, Helen continued, 'Look, Joseph, we're all in a tough place at the moment. You don't want to be working for me, I don't particularly want you in my team, but for the time being we're going to have to make the best of it. We're under intense pressure, intense scrutiny, and it's taking a toll on *all* of us. We're all exhausted, all frustrated, all feeling the heat. God knows, I had a drink the other day, for the first time in twenty-odd years ... so I get it, I *really* do. This is tough for everyone.'

He was regarding her curiously, uncertain where this was going. But he didn't interrupt, so Helen continued: 'So this is me making a peace offering. Can we put our differences aside until the current investigations are concluded? Then, we can sit down and sort this out properly, sensibly, so that everyone's happy. Can you live with that? Can you do that for me?'

'No.' A single word, but loaded with defiance.

'I'm sorry?'

'You'd love me to come running back to Mummy, wouldn't you? To be a good little boy because you're feeling the pressure. Well, you can forget it, Helen. I wouldn't piss on you if you were on fire.'

'What the hell?' Helen exploded.

'I mean it. We had something, could have been great together, but you dismantled all that with your clumsy accusations, your paranoia, your lies. Which is why I'm going to bring you down.'

'Nothing I said was untrue,' Helen shot back. 'You *did* abandon your wife and child.'

'Oh, change the record, Helen. I've heard it all before. And I didn't like it then. So no, I won't be your patsy, I won't play ball. I will do my job.'

'Well, just make sure you have one to keep hold of.'

'Are you threatening me, Helen?'

'No, I'm simply letting you know that if you deliberately sabotage these investigations, if you openly flout my authority or undermine the chain of command again, then I will have no alternative but to instigate disciplinary procedures.'

She had been hoping this would shut him up, for if there was one thing that was important to Joseph it was his professional standing, his rank, his status. But to her immense surprise, he broke into a broad, mocking smile.

'Go on, Helen, I *dare* you. I dare you to report me. Because if you do, the truth will come tumbling out.'

'What do you mean by that?'

'Simmons, Peters, the team, the whole world will find out what you're up to.'

'You've lost me.'

'I'll tell them how you slept with me, then discarded me when you lost interest.'

'It wasn't like that and you know it.'

'How I wasn't happy, how I felt used, how I complained to you. How you then decided to drive me out of Southampton Central.'

'My God, Joseph, are you delusional?'

'How you tried to suffocate my career, undermining me at every turn, giving me grunt work—'

'Stop right there, Joseph, before you say something you'll regret.'

'It's constructive dismissal, pure and simple. The union will be all over it and do you know why? Because I'm the victim here, Helen.'

Helen stared at him, speechless. His gall was staggering, as was his determination to twist the truth to suit his own ends.

'So go ahead, report me if you dare. But if you *do*, then the powers that be will learn all about your tawdry liaison with a junior officer, your misuse of office to try to suffocate my career and force me out. How you've broken every rule in the book to satisfy your own desires.'

He fixed Helen with a glare as he concluded: 'They'll know *everything*.'

Day Four

Chapter 54

She wandered through the living room, her bare feet slapping the polished wooden floor. Save for the customary morning sounds of the refuse trucks and car horns outside, her progress was the only noise breaching the sepulchral quiet of the house, her footfall echoing gently off the walls.

Coming to a halt, Lilah took in her surroundings, achingly familiar yet somehow deeply strange. She had bought this place with Martin, decorated it with him, marked and scuffed it during their rows, their love-making, the business of everyday life. It was their place, their home, and now it seemed profoundly empty without him.

He was generally first up, rising at 7 a.m., regular as clockwork, whether he'd gone to bed early or been out partying till late. Often, he'd mock Lilah for her inability to rise, her deep, enduring love of her bed. Come what may he'd be at the breakfast bar when she stumbled in, bleary-eyed and gasping for coffee. Sometimes he'd provide it for her, sometimes he wouldn't.

But there was no one to fire up the coffee machine this morning, no one with whom to pick the bones out of last night's events. So how was she supposed to make sense of it all? Martin was gone and she was alone, struggling to understand what had befallen him. Or what lay in store.

Her firm had signed her off sick – they had no choice in the circumstances, even though it was exceptionally ill-timed – and the police had told her to stay local, in case they needed to talk to her again. Meaning she was stuck here, in this oppressively quiet house, with only her thoughts for company.

The police officer   DI Grace – had been sparing with the detail at first, but Lilah had persisted, finally learning that Martin had been stabbed three times, once in the stomach and twice in the chest. The thought of it, the image of a long blade puncturing his heart, had made her feel physically sick. Their relationship had been complicated, fractured – on occasion she'd even thought she hated him – but still, the idea of him being attacked like that, of his body enduring such a brutal assault, was beyond awful. What must he have felt like when he knew he was in mortal danger, how terrified and shocked must he have been? Was death instantaneous or was he conscious throughout, aware of his life force ebbing away? The thought of his suffering brought tears to her eyes, which surprised her. She'd thought she was all cried out.

Crossing to the sofa, Lilah tucked her legs beneath her, even as she wrapped her fluffy dressing gown around her. The curtains were drawn, the reporters who'd hassled her last night having departed, so for now this place was safe enough, her cocoon and sanctuary. It was just her and the odd, empty atmosphere. Had it not been for DI Grace's instructions, she'd have been tempted to flee, to head to Durham to be with her parents. She'd spoken to them briefly last night and they'd urged her to do just that. How nice it would have been to be in their uncomplicated embrace, bathing in their love, support and affection.

But there was no hope of that. She had to stay put to deal with the grim practicalities of death – telling colleagues and friends, organizing the funeral, dealing with the legal stuff and, worst of all, talking to Martin's aunt.

This was the bit she was dreading, but it couldn't be avoided. Having had a brief, fraught conversation with her last night, she was due to call her again this morning. Now she would have to give her the full story, the brutal, unvarnished truth about her nephew's murder. It would be hideous, heart-rending and all the worse because the whole charade was sickeningly pointless. His aunt had never shown Martin any love, reminding him every day that he was a burden and an inconvenience, forever prioritizing the needs of her own children at his expense. She would play the grieving relative now, any chance to enjoy the anguish and attention, but it would all be fake. Nevertheless, Nessa would seize the opportunity to fight Martin's corner, to protect his interests, his legacy. She would no doubt question Lilah's role in proceedings – what she knew, why she hadn't protected Martin, why she hadn't gone to the police after the abusive phone call – but, worse, she would question Lilah's feelings for him, casting aspersions on the depth of attachment to Martin, her loyalty, the level of her distress. This, without question, would be the hardest part. Not just because it would be hurtful, aggressive and relentless, but because amidst all the barbs and insults, there would be a kernel of truth.

This was why she was dreading the call, why she wished with all her heart that she could avoid it. Because deep down she knew that Nessa was right – that despite all the misery and heartache, there was a part of her that felt liberated and relieved.

A part of her that was glad Martin Hill was dead.

Chapter 55

'Did you have feelings for Joseph?'

DCI Grace Simmons scrutinized Helen shrewdly, looking for any hint of evasion or duplicity.

'I'm not really sure,' Helen replied honestly. 'I think I was developing some kind of affection for him, I enjoyed his company, but obviously his secrecy about his former life, his lies about his wife and child, put paid to that.'

Simmons nodded thoughtfully, but said nothing. She looked pale and anxious, clearly shocked by what Helen had told her. Helen hadn't wanted to burden her with this – hadn't wanted to drag her old friend into her mess – but after last night she'd had no choice. Joseph had gone way beyond insubordination, he was trying to leverage her, no, he was trying to *blackmail* her into keeping quiet about his rebellion whilst he slowly set about destroying her unit, a team she'd spent years constructing.

There was no question of taking him on at his own game, of resorting to underhand tactics. If need be, that would come later. Her first step was to come clean, to confess to their clandestine relationship, hence why she'd requested a private interview with DCI Simmons first thing this morning. She was an ally, a mentor, but she was also her boss, and it was vital that this situation was handled properly, by the book. Which was why they were now closeted away together in her office.

'So what happened then?' Simmons queried.

'Well, I confronted him with my discoveries and he basically went nuts. He blew his top, accused me of conspiring with his ex-wife, bitching about him, denigrating him.'

'And do you think he was in any way justified in his reaction?'

'In what way?'

'Well, you'd contacted his ex-wife without his knowledge or permission, asked her deeply personal questions about their relationship, about DS Hudson himself. Do you not think he was justified in being angered by this invasion of his privacy?'

'Well, possibly, yes—'

'Dangerous too for you professionally. What would have happened if his ex-wife had become upset, reported you to the Force?'

'Look, it was a stupid thing to do, I admit that. And I regretted it afterwards, but it revealed something which I had suspected all along – that Joseph Hudson couldn't be trusted, was interested only in himself, which was important for me to know both personally and professionally. He's not a team player.'

'Which you might have discovered in time through more legitimate means.'

'Yes, for sure. Look, I know I shouldn't even have been in a relationship with him in the first place and, yes, I could have handled it better—'

'And after that?'

'Well, we rowed and he left,' Helen said, her mind arrowing back to that bitter confrontation. 'Then the Justin Lanning investigation took over and I didn't speak to him again until after it had concluded, when I was recovering in hospital.'

'And what was that conversation like?'

'Deeply unpleasant. I suggested that perhaps our continuing to work together was not a good idea—'

'Did you threaten him?'

'No, *absolutely* not. I just pointed out that our relationship – the trust between us – had completely broken down and that would not be good for the team, especially as he would effectively be my deputy whilst DS Brooks was on maternity leave. I suggested he might look elsewhere for a suitable position, one befitting his talents, and that I would do whatever I could to facilitate that move.'

'And what was his response?'

'He told me in no uncertain terms that he was going nowhere. That I could leave if I wanted to, but that he was staying put.'

'And that was the last conversation you had on this matter? Before last night, I mean?'

'Yes. Since then he's been doing his job – on the face of it, at least – taking orders, running down leads, but actually he's been cultivating allies, attempting to turn officers against me, prioritizing his own investigations over mine and generally trying to undermine me at every turn.'

'And do you think he would go to Peters, take this all the way to the top, if you *did* call his bluff? Does he have the stomach for a full disciplinary enquiry?'

Helen thought for a moment. 'Yes, I think he would. It would damage him, of course, professionally. But – but I think he feels we're at war now. I think he'll take it all the way.'

It seemed profoundly odd to be saying these words, but it was true. Joseph Hudson did seem intent on bringing her down, whatever the cost to himself. Looking up, she saw Simmons appraising her, weighing up the situation, clearly deeply troubled by what she was hearing.

'Look, ma'am, I'm really sorry for my actions. The relationship was entirely inappropriate and the fallout has been deeply damaging. Worse, I've now dragged you into this, when I know you've got enough on your plate—'

'No, it was the right thing to do,' Simmons responded.

'Anyway, I felt it was important that I apologized to you personally, whilst making it clear what's happened.'

'I think I understand the situation and I'm fairly sure we can handle it.'

'I don't expect you to fight my battles.'

But her superior held up her hand to silence her. 'It's not a question of that, Helen. It's about doing what's right, but being smart about it. You need to concentrate on your investigative work, on the things that really matter—' she paused briefly, before adding – '*I'll* deal with Joseph Hudson.'

Chapter 56

'Are you absolutely certain?'

DC Reid squirmed in his seat, uncomfortable under DS Hudson's unforgiving glare.

'Yes. I've checked and double-checked, but it seems clear that Moffat was in a pub when Martin Hill was attacked.'

'Which one?'

'The Horse and Groom, on George Street, by the docks.'

'How many witnesses?' Hudson demanded, frowning.

'Two.'

'Who?'

'Mates of his.'

'*Criminal* mates?'

'Yes, but—'

'Which means we should hardly take their word as gospel.'

'Of course not, but the CCTV grab kind of proves it.' DC Reid offered Hudson a grainy printout. 'The clothes are right, the cap too, and look, there on his arm, the snake tattoo...'

Hudson stared at the image angrily, prompting DC Reid to continue quickly: 'It's not all bad news, though.'

Hudson turned to him once more. 'Go on.'

'So, the racist attack on Lilah Hill at the Marquee bar a month back. The thugs who abused her were all cautioned and released, then a few weeks later, Martin Hill was a victim of racially motivated abuse – the phone calls, the graffiti—'

'What's this got to do with Moffat?' Hudson interrupted, impatiently.

'Well, the instigator of the fight at the bar was Darren Moorfield, Moffat's best mate from school. He still runs with Moffat, is part of his crew.'

'So even if Moffat didn't physically attack Hill himself,' Hudson added, picking up the thread, 'that doesn't mean he wasn't the instigator of the attack.'

'Moorfield is small fry,' Reid agreed. 'He wouldn't have the balls or imagination to commit a serious crime. But what if he was put up to it? Challenged to prove himself? Moorfield must have told Moffat about the incident in the bar, how Hill got him and his pals arrested. Lee wouldn't have liked that, for a number of reasons, so—'

'This is good, DC Reid,' Hudson purred. 'And where's Moorfield now?'

'No idea, though we think he's living in Freemantle.'

'Find him. Make that your top priority.'

Reid nodded obediently.

'And as soon as you've got eyes on him, let me know.' He looked directly at Reid, as he concluded, 'Because if we can get him to cough for the Hill murder, then we'll have Moffat *exactly* where we want him.'

Chapter 57

Helen strode past, barely acknowledging Hudson's presence. As soon as she'd re-entered the incident room, she'd spotted Hudson in a huddle with DC Reid, but she was determined not to react. She had no interest in what they were cooking up and certainly didn't want to create a scene. No, as far as the rest of the team were concerned, it had to be business as usual. Helen could betray no agitation, no weakness, no uncertainty. She had to project confidence, leadership and, crucially, industry, so she continued to march towards her office, even as she punched redial on her phone. As before, however, her call went straight to voicemail.

'Hi, this is Robert Downing, leave a message.'

Helen waited patiently for the beep, then responded to the prompt. 'Robert, it's Helen Grace again. Call me back.'

Ending the call, she slid the phone into her pocket, thoughts of Downing preoccupying her. He'd seemed determined to get hold of her yesterday, but now wasn't taking any calls. It was an intriguing development, but one that would have to wait, for as Helen reached her office, she spotted DC McAndrew gesturing to her. If the long-serving officer felt any awkwardness at being lumped in with Hudson's rebels yesterday, she didn't show it, seeming focused, even a little excited.

'What have you got for me?' Helen asked, crossing to her work station.

'I think we might have a lead on the knife.'

DC McAndrew said this firmly, but quietly, as if not quite believing that she'd stumbled on a possible breakthrough.

'Go on.'

'Well, you know you asked us to look at eight-inch own-brand B&Q kitchen knives, bought or stolen in the last seven days...'

Helen nodded.

'Well, we've been calling all the stores this morning. And one in Hedge End turned up this...'

Helen squinted at the fuzzy grey image. It was a CCTV shot of an aisle in B&Q, taken from on high, showing a tiny figure, in baseball cap and jacket, loitering in the kitchenware section.

'They realized that an eight-inch knife had been lifted whilst they were doing their stock check last night. They looked back through their security footage and...'

She hit play and the quiet drama played out, the capped figure approaching the knife section and checking the coast was clear, before slipping something into her bag whilst pretending to be examining a spatula.

'Can we go in any closer?'

'Not without losing all resolution. She's concealed her identity pretty well, but we can say that it's a woman, probably thirties, forties, with shoulder-length blonde hair. And, of course, we've got a good look at the clothes...'

'Did anyone in the store get a look at her?'

'Well, after this, she heads to the cashier, purchases some white spirit, but as you can see, the girl on the till barely looks at her, more interested in her phone.'

'You've spoken to the cashier?'

'Briefly. "Blonde, middle-aged, posh," was the best she could do.'

Helen considered this, intrigued, then replied: 'Anything in the store car park?'

'No, she leaves on foot, which is interesting because she had her car with her.'

McAndrew hit some more keys, bringing up a different image.

'This is in Beaumont Road, about a five-minute walk from B&Q.'

'It's definitely her, isn't it?' Helen said, excited.

'No question. Same trainers, jacket, cap. Same-length hair . . .'

'Where's this feed from?'

'Traffic camera, they've had accidents on this road before, as it's a bit of a cut-through. Anyway, we see her get into the parked car and drive off and as she does so—'

'We see the car registration,' Helen interrupted, leaning over to freeze the image.

'Exactly.'

'So who is she?'

'Well, the car belongs to a Belinda Raeburn.'

As she spoke, McAndrew maximized another tab. A glossy head shot of an attractive, forty-something blonde with shoulder-length hair filled the screen. Helen scrutinized the image carefully – this glamorous, self-possessed woman didn't seem the dictionary definition of a racist thug.

'And where can we find this Belinda Raeburn?'

'Well, that's the fun bit,' McAndrew replied, clearly having saved the best until last. 'She's the principal music teacher at Milton Downs Ladies' Academy.'

Chapter 58

Helen swept through the open gateway, gliding up the wide tarmac drive. The speed limit was twenty miles per hour, affording Helen a chance to take in her surroundings. What she saw beggared belief; the school campus was more like a luxury hotel than a place of education. It was certainly unlike anything she'd experienced during her early years in South London and even in Southampton it stood out as a beacon of excellence, affluence and inspiration. From the moment you entered the gates, it was as if you'd entered another world.

Established over three hundred years ago for the sons of the Admiralty and rich merchant seamen, it was now a prestigious co-educational secondary school, where places were in high demand – if you could afford the fees. In addition to a first-class academic education, pupils enjoyed top-notch sporting, media and art facilities and pinpoint career advice and assistance – the school's contacts in London, Paris, Washington and beyond second to none. If you lived in Hampshire and had money and ambition, this was where you sent your children.

Helen rode past the open-air swimming pool, the lacrosse and hockey pitches, then, lowering her speed still further, slid past the croquet lawn that stood just in front of the main entrance. Parking beside the magnificent Palladian portico, Helen slipped inside, entering a world that was as intriguing to her as it was alien.

'May I ask what it's regarding?'

The school secretary was polite but cautious, her nose wrinkling slightly as she looked Helen up and down.

'It's a police matter.'

Helen's reply was firm and, before long, they were on the move, the secretary hurrying her along the perfectly polished corridors, as if keen to keep her out of sight.

'She's very busy running our music summer school,' the secretary protested, as if expecting Helen to back down. 'In fact, right now she's in the middle of a solo tutorial.'

'I'll be as quick as I can,' Helen lied, as they reached the door to the well-resourced music department.

They pushed inside, the heavy doors closing gently behind them. It was as if they had stepped into a cocoon, perfectly shut off from the outside world. How cossetted, how protected the pupils were, Helen thought, and what a strange world to inhabit – the practice rooms were so well insulated that the occupants seemed to be playing instruments that made no sound.

'She's just along here, room fourteen...'

Helen said nothing, her mind now focused on the task in hand. Grasping the handle, the school secretary knocked on the door and stepped inside, forcing Helen to follow.

'So sorry to interrupt, Ms Raeburn. But I have a – visitor for you.'

Helen rounded her chaperone to find a pretty, blonde woman of forty-plus years, locked in conference with a student, who cradled a clarinet in his hands.

Surprised, Belinda Raeburn turned to face them, a smile lighting up her attractive features. She seemed surprised, but not unhappy about the intrusion, taking in Helen with unbridled curiosity. Tall, striking and clad in biking leathers, Helen often had this effect on people, yet, as she held up her warrant card for inspection, the teacher's smile faded.

'DI Helen Grace. Could I have a word?'

Chapter 59

'This isn't me.' Raeburn tapped aggressively at the CCTV image, looking perplexed and angry.

'It certainly *looks* like you,' Helen countered gently. 'Right height, right build and from this angle the shape of the face is spot on ...'

'Yes, well, "like" isn't the same as "is",' Raeburn fired back, taking refuge in semantics.

'So you're saying you didn't visit B&Q in Hedge End two days ago?'

'Do I look like a DIY nut? I never visit those kinds of stores—'

'This isn't you stealing a kitchen knife?'

'Categorically *no*. Why would I do such a thing? If I needed a new kitchen knife, I'd buy one.'

Her gaze locked onto Helen's, defiant, challenging.

'Anyway, I hope that's cleared things up. Now if you'll excuse me—'

'I should add,' Helen countered, 'that the woman who stole that knife was seen driving off in a car registered in your name. Has your vehicle been stolen?'

'Of course not. I drove to school in it this morning. There must be some kind of mistake.'

'There's no mistake.'

'And I must say,' Raeburn continued, her tone sharpening, 'I'm surprised that such a trivial crime warrants this kind of intrusion. I'm supposed to be teaching now. I've got back-to-back tutorials...'

Raeburn's sunny disposition was long gone. She obviously wanted to be out of Helen's presence, the latter intrigued by how keen Raeburn was to shut their conversation down.

'We believe the knife in question was subsequently used in a serious crime.'

'Right...' Raeburn responded reluctantly, clearly disappointed the conversation wasn't over.

'A man called Martin Hill was murdered, around lunchtime yesterday.'

Raeburn didn't react.

'He was stabbed to death in an alleyway in Portswood.'

'I heard about that on the radio, but I don't see what it's got to do with me.'

'Did you know Mr Hill?'

'No, not at all. Besides, according to the radio, it was a racially motivated attack, some mindless thug preying on an innocent guy.'

Helen maintained eye contact, but said nothing, letting the silence do the work for her.

'You can't seriously think *I* had anything to do with this,' Raeburn protested. 'I don't have a racist bone in my body. Talk to my friends, my family, if you need to, look at my posts online. I'm a card-carrying Labour Party member, who's actively campaigned against anti-Semitism, racism – in fact, bigotry of any kind.'

Helen didn't doubt that this was true, but noted how the words poured from her, a torrent of self-justification and denial.

'We're still investigating possible motives for the attack,'

Helen responded. 'But you're saying you had no animus against him, no reason to wish him harm?'

'I didn't even know him, for God's sake. Why would I attack him?'

Nodding, Helen pulled her notepad from her jacket. 'Can you tell me where you were, then, between the hours of noon and 2 p.m. yesterday?'

'Well, I... I popped into town during at lunch time. I had some things to pick up.'

'Precisely, please.'

'OK, so I dropped a violin into a repair shop in St Denys around 12.30 p.m., then I dropped into the university on the way back to pick up some sheet music – some arrangements a friend had done for me. I can give you their details...'

'Were you in Portswood at all during those hours?'

'No. I mean, I drove through it on my way out of town...'

'But you didn't stop?'

'No, I had lessons to get back for.'

'It's just that your car was ticketed in Lena Gardens at 1.14 p.m. yesterday.'

Now there was a slight reaction from Raeburn. Had she been hoping the police wouldn't make the connection? That the link between the various agencies was *that* fragmented?

'A traffic warden spotted a minor infringement and issued a Penalty Charge Notice to a car registered in your name. I'm assuming it can't have been your partner Carol Shepherd driving because she was in Portsmouth at that time, at a seminar.'

Raeburn looked stunned, shocked that the police had obviously checked out her partner's movements.

'And besides, you've just said you drove into town, so...'

'Actually, you're right, I did stop briefly in Portswood on my way back.'

'I see.'

'Totally slipped my mind. Yes, I needed to pick up some yoghurt, so I parked and went to the supermarket.'

'Obviously the parking ticket didn't register...'

'I get them all the time, I'm afraid.'

'And which supermarket did you visit?'

'I didn't really look, to be honest. Tesco Metro, I think.'

'Did you use a card to make your purchase?'

'No, cash.'

'And would anyone have seen you there?'

'I don't know. I used the automated check-out, but maybe the security guard will remember me, though it was pretty busy...'

'Well, we can check out the CCTV from Tesco Metros in that area. That should help us clear this up.'

'Of course. Great.'

Raeburn was smiling fiercely, trying to appear confident, relaxed. Helen wondered how she'd react when she discovered there were no Tesco Metros in Portswood.

'And did you go anywhere after that? Stop off anywhere else?'

'No, that was it, sorry. I came straight back here. I'm sure the school can confirm what time I returned.'

Helen nodded and made a note, confident that this part of Raeburn's alleged alibi would stack up at least. Looking up, she saw that the teacher was tense, alert, as if expecting more questions. Her urgency, her desire to bring proceedings to a close, seemed to have evaporated now, sensing perhaps that she was in a serious fight, one she needed to see out, so as not to provoke further suspicion. Deciding to spare her any more discomfort, Helen snapped her notepad shut and rose once more.

'Well, that's plenty for me to be getting on with. Thanks very much for your time.'

'No problem at all,' the teacher gushed. 'Happy to help.'

The relief in her voice was clear, the sense that perhaps she had seen off Helen, unscathed. Smiling her thanks, Helen headed to the door, but as she opened it, she paused.

'Actually, there was one other thing...' she said, turning to face the teacher once more.

The smile was still fixed on Raeburn's face.

'Am I right in thinking you knew Eve Sutcliffe?'

Raeburn looked utterly stupefied, as if Helen had just punched her, then she recovered herself.

'Yes, of course. Such a terrible loss...'

'And you knew her because...?'

'Because I taught her. She was the finest musician in her year. In fact...' Raeburn's voice seemed to tremble now, as she raised her gaze to Helen's one final time. 'She was the best musician in the school, full stop.'

Chapter 60

Helen hurried to her Kawasaki, sliding onto the saddle and firing up the ignition. Flicking off the brake, she eased away down the drive, watched carefully by the school secretary. The old woman scented trouble and, following her interview with Belinda Raeburn, so did Helen.

Two murders had been committed in Southampton in the last four days, deaths which seemed to defy logic. Both were very well planned, but amateurish in execution, Amar Goj and Belinda Raeburn bungling their escapes, drawing attention to themselves in the process. These mistakes highlighted their lack of experience – neither Goj nor Raeburn had any previous record of violence. So what had suddenly possessed them to commit murder?

This was the other peculiarity. Neither seemed to have any *motive* for the attack. Goj had no historical connection to McManus and, as far as they could ascertain, wasn't currently being investigated by the private detective. So what did he stand to gain by killing him? Likewise, Belinda Raeburn, whose communications history showed no contact with Martin Hill, who didn't overlap professionally or personally with the victim and who, on the face of it, had no truck with racism of any kind. Yet Helen was convinced she'd stabbed Hill to death – her feeble alibi and defensive body language adding fuel to Helen's suspicions. Was she then also responsible for the abusive phone calls, the foul graffiti? It seemed unlikely, improbable, perhaps, but what other explanation could there be?

Tapping her Bluetooth, Helen dialled the incident room as she sped away down the drive.

'McAndrew, incident room.'

'Ellie, it's me. I need you to do something.'

'Sure thing.'

'I want us to go back over everything we have on Eve Sutcliffe...'

'OK...' McAndrew said, surprised by Helen's desire to return to a case that had hit the buffers.

'Specifically, I want us to look for any connections between Eve Sutcliffe and Belinda Raeburn. Raeburn taught her, had prepped her for her GCSE exam, but I want to scratch beneath the surface, see what we turn up.'

'I'll get onto it right away.'

'Thank you. Quick as you can, please.'

Clicking off, Helen continued her progress towards the school gates, lost in thought. On the face of it, the two murders appeared random, inexplicable even, but Helen was intrigued and alarmed by a possible link which now presented itself. Amar Goj gained nothing from McManus's murder, but could have stood to gain from the death of Alison Burris, who'd been stabbed to death in a city centre car park ten days earlier. Likewise, Raeburn's attack on Hill seemed utterly out of character and without purpose, *yet* she knew Eve Sutcliffe, the victim of a brutal, apparently sexually motivated attack in Lakeside Country Park eight days ago. Was it possible that Raeburn was somehow involved, perhaps had even *ordered* the young girl's murder?

It seemed a crazy notion, yet the coincidence was curious, to say the least. Of course, this potential line of investigation threw up as many problems as possibilities. There were so many moving parts, so many missing pieces of the jigsaw, that at present it was impossible to say how – *if* – the whole thing knitted together. Yet it was clear to Helen that something *was* badly wrong, that there were forces at work in Southampton compelling ordinary citizens to commit murder. As she roared down the gravel drive, Helen knew for certain that the stakes had risen still further and that unless she could work out who was behind this orgy of violence, more blood would be spilled.

Chapter 61

'I'm telling you the truth.'

Darren Moorfield spat the words out, angry and aggrieved. But Hudson wasn't fooled for a second, tightening his grip still further. Having traced Lee Moffat's best friend to a squalid dwelling in Freemantle, he was determined to get what he wanted.

'You don't know the meaning of the word. I *know* you were involved, I *know* you did it, so start talking...'

'Get off me, man. I've got nothing to say to *you*...'

Moorfield tried to wrench himself free, but Hudson was expecting this move. Using the young man's own momentum against him, he swung him around, disorienting him still further, before marching him backwards across the room. Moorfield's crummy attic flat was littered with discarded pizza boxes and empty beer cans and he cursed viciously as he stumbled backwards, out of control and off balance.

'You can't do this, you stupid fuck...'

'I don't see anyone who's going to stop me,' Hudson replied coolly.

It was true, they were quite alone in the dilapidated flat, perhaps even the building. Whatever money Moffat made from his rackets clearly didn't go to his foot soldiers. Despite being

Lee's best mate, Moorfield lived alone in a crumbling block of flats in a scruffy part of town. There would be few witnesses to stop Hudson, certainly none who would want to engage with the police.

'This is harassment, assault...'

'By the time I'm finished, you'll wish that's *all* it was...'

They were moving fast. Directly in front of them was a dirty window that looked down onto the cobbles three floors below. Darren Moorfield was protesting, cursing, but Joseph didn't stop, ramming the skinny young man against the glass. It cracked instantly, but even so Hudson *increased* the pressure, the glass threatening to break.

'Jesus Christ, are you mad?' Moorfield shrieked.

'No, mate. I've never been able to see things more clearly. Which is why you're not going to wriggle off the hook...'

'But I've told you I never touched Martin Hill. I was at the bookies that day.'

'I don't believe you.'

'Honest to God—'

'I think you embarrassed yourself, embarrassed Lee, that night at the Marquee. Trying to play the tough guy, picking on Lilah Hill. And what did you get for your pains? A night in the cells. Did Lee have to bail you out?'

Moorfield shrugged, avoiding eye contact, confirming Hudson's suspicion.

'I bet he *loved* that,' Hudson laughed. 'Having to rescue your sorry arse from jail.'

'So what?'

'You must have been humiliated, Darren, embarrassed, ashamed. I bet you were *desperate* to prove yourself to Lee after that, prove that you could be more than just a foot soldier, that you could be his main man.'

'Sure, but—'

'I also know that you wouldn't do anything without his say so. You don't have the imagination. Were the phone calls and the graffiti his idea?'

'What are you talking about?'

'Did he give you the knife? Challenge you to put things right?'

'Please, I don't know anything…' Moorfield moaned, struggling to wriggle from Hudson's grip.

'Don't lie to me, Darren.'

'I'm not, I swear—'

'I know what you are. You're a liar, a thief and a killer. And I intend to prove it.'

'Please, no, I—'

Moorfield was lost for words, fear strangling his senses, the glass continuing to creak behind him.

'Look, I'll… I'll cough to nicking the cars—'

'Not good enough. I want a full confession. I want you to give me Lee.'

'But I didn't do it. He never asked me to.'

To his surprise, Hudson now saw tears in Moorfield's eyes.

'On my life, I never did it. I haven't killed anyone – I couldn't. I'm a thief, that's all.'

Moorfield was crying properly now, tears sliding down his cheeks. He seemed resigned, defeated, as if he knew Hudson would eventually push him through the glass down onto the cobbles below. Hudson was seriously tempted to oblige, wanted to see the look of horror and fear on his face as he fell, but against all his better instincts, he now hauled the young man away from the window, throwing him down roughly on the floor.

'This isn't over.'

Hudson arrowed the words at him, angry, determined, but in truth he knew it was. If Moffat *had* ordered Hill's death, then the pathetic Moorfield clearly knew nothing about it. He was a worm, nothing more, nothing less. Even now he was staring up at him, rubbing his neck, looking aggrieved and scared. But Hudson didn't linger, he'd wasted enough time here already.

Marching out of the flat into the dingy stairwell beyond, Hudson considered his next move. He could pull Moffat in again, but it might make better sense to seek out his other lieutenants, see if *they* were willing to sacrifice their leader to avoid a prison sentence. It would be time-consuming and potentially fruitless, as there was always the possibility he and Reid *were* barking up the wrong tree with this line of enquiry, but they had to try. Retrieving his phone, Hudson was about to call Edwards when suddenly the device came alive in his hands. Taking in the caller ID, Hudson took a moment to compose himself before answering Grace Simmons's call.

'Morning, ma'am. What can I do for you?'

'I'd like a word with you, in my office.'

'Of course, but I'm out following up some—'

'*Now*, please, DS Hudson.'

Then the line went dead.

Chapter 62

'I've absolutely no idea what you're referring to, ma'am.'

Joseph Hudson was working hard, trying his best to appear aggrieved and mystified, but DCI Simmons wasn't buying it.

'That's strange because DI Grace was very clear in her testimony—'

Hudson didn't like her use of the word "testimony", as if this was already an official investigation.

'—and she said you *explicitly* threatened her with exposure if she initiated disciplinary proceedings against you.'

'Exposure of what?'

'Your past relationship. Or are you denying that that took place?'

'No, no. We were involved for a while. But it was brief, casual, it didn't mean anything...'

'So why are you intent on undermining her?'

'I'm not and to be honest, ma'am, I resent the accusation. I'm trying to *help* her, but we're overrun at the moment, can't seem to catch a break in any of our cases—'

'So her reports that you're prioritizing your own investigative enquiries to the detriment of the rest of the team are untrue, are they?'

'Categorically. I'm just trying to bring *someone* to book for *something*.'

'And you deny questioning her authority in front of the team? Going against all established protocols—'

'We have robust exchanges. That's normal. It's one of the strengths of the team—'

'That's strange, because from where I'm sitting the team looks weak and divided.'

'Well,' Hudson shrugged, 'you'd have to talk to DI Grace about that.'

'Actually, I'd rather talk to you, as I strongly suspect *you* are the root cause of all the disharmony and unrest.'

'That's totally untrue. If you should be hauling anyone over the coals, it's Grace. The problems we're facing are due to her, not me.'

'Look, DS Hudson, we could go around in circles on this, with you denying every accusation put to you, so perhaps we should just cut to the chase?'

Hudson said nothing, uneasy about where this was heading.

'DI Grace has told me about your past liaison and I'm obliged to pass this knowledge on to the powers that be. To that end, I've drafted my report and will pass it to HR ASAP. I should tell you that I've accepted DI Grace's apology and explanation regarding the relationship and am recommending that no further action be taken. As you know, such relationships are frowned upon, rather than forbidden, and given DI Grace's many years of loyal service to this station, I see no reason to make a scapegoat of her.'

Hudson stared at her, stunned.

'I shall add as a postscript that you deny that the relationship has interfered with your relationship and that you have no personal animus against DI Grace as a result. Do you have anything to add to that?'

She had him trapped and she knew it. If he rowed back on his denials, he would open himself up to charges of insubordination. But if he said nothing, he would effectively be clearing Helen of any wrongdoing. It made him seethe, but for now he had no choice but to hold his tongue.

'I shall be even-handed in my official handling of this incident,' Simmons continued, 'but I want to make it abundantly plain to you that I hold you responsible for the problems the team has experienced during the last six months.'

'With the greatest of respect, ma'am—'

But his angry protest was cut off, Simmons raising her hand to stop him.

'With that in mind, I have two further things to say. First, that I want it to stop now. The insubordination, the attitude, the cultivation of division, the sniping, the rumour spreading, the leaking of sensitive information to the press.'

'That's got nothing to do with me.'

'Second, that *if* you do this, *if* you can toe the line until we've cleared this backlog of cases, then you have my word that I will give you a good send-off.'

'I'm sorry?' Hudson spluttered the words, outraged.

'DI Helen Grace is the finest officer, the finest leader, the MIT has ever had and I have no intention of throwing her under a bus to salve your ego. No, the person who is finished here is *you*.'

Hudson stared at her, unable to muster a single word in response to this vicious and unexpected ambush.

'If you do as I ask, however, I will ensure you get a glowing reference to facilitate your transfer back to Cheshire Police. Understood?'

'Yes, but—'

'Then we're done here. Thank you for your time, DS Hudson.'

Chapter 63

She sped along the street, pedalling hard, her mood rising all the while. At home, Lilah had felt trapped, as if the walls, her *life*, was closing in on her. So, in the end, she'd fled, throwing on some clothes and hurrying out to her bike, suddenly desperate to be away from her responsibilities, her troubles, from the difficult conversations she was due to have. She needed to be by herself for a while, in the open air, she needed to *breathe*.

The contrast in temperature was a shock. The house was shadowy, cool and dark, but outside, the heat radiated up off the pavement, the atmosphere sultry and oppressive. She was sweating before she'd managed to unchain her bike, but, nevertheless, it felt good to be out. The silence in the house had become oppressive, a silence filled only by her own dark thoughts, and it was better to be amongst the familiar sights and sounds of her neighbourhood than stuck in a home that had recently become a prison.

She picked up pace, her heart thumping as she powered down the street. With her helmet on and her face hidden behind sunglasses, she was unrecognizable, able to pass neighbours and local shopkeepers unmolested. This mild subterfuge made her smile, a small victory of sorts, and soon she was several streets away, straying from her usual haunts, happily anonymous.

The traffic was light and soon Lilah found herself outside the Westquay shopping centre. Securing her bike, she pushed into the crisp, air-conditioned interior, shivering as the sweat cooled and clung to her, before losing herself in the delights within. She hadn't been to the centre in ages and it appeared to her now as some kind of Aladdin's cave, so colourful, so opulent, so *happy*. It was a place designed to entertain – a place to shop, chat, eat, drink and laugh – an emporium of pleasure. Something she'd had little of lately.

Skittish, giggling, Lilah threw herself into its many diversions, gorging herself on a cupcake and gingerbread latte, before buying a dress she would never have the confidence to wear, which in turn necessitated a visit to Victoria's Secret. She felt giddy, drunk with amusement, but she went with it, gliding around the different levels of the shopping centre in a daze. For the first time in ages, she felt content. More than that, she felt alive.

Descending the escalator to the ground level, she made her way towards Schuh. The icing on the cake would be some glamorous and impractical summer shoes that she could totter around in as she embraced her new life, her new future. She had no idea when she'd wear them or who she'd wear them for, but she was suddenly gripped by the idea of having them. She had spotted a cute pair of pink platform wedges on her way in and was suddenly convinced they had her name on them.

She strode forward, confident, energized... then suddenly ground to a halt, the wind punched from her sails. For a moment, she was unable to move, unable to take in what she was seeing. This was *her* time, her moment of euphoria and release, and they had no place here. Yet here they were, a quiet, unassuming middle-aged couple shuffling slowly towards her, utterly oblivious to her presence, lost in their own private world of pain. Just the sight of them was a piercing stab to Lilah's heart and she swiftly turned away, pretending to examine something in the shop window.

In the reflection she watched the sad couple pass by, hollow ghosts clutching empty shopping bags, whilst remaining stock-still herself. The pair moved on, gone as swiftly as they'd appeared, but their presence remained with Lilah and, staring at the shiny glass, Lilah saw her own haunted face staring back at her. All joy, all giddiness had now evaporated. Now she felt hollow, cold and numb, a shadow of the woman she had been not five minutes earlier. Then again, it was all she deserved.

Chapter 64

She knocked on the door a second time, then stepped back to look up at the house. But it was dark and lifeless – there was no one at home.

Disappointed, Helen retraced her steps, hurrying back down to street level. She'd tried several times to respond to Robert Downing's urgent summons, but his phone appeared to be permanently switched off, hence her sudden, impulsive decision to visit him at home.

His office had said that he would be here, as this was one of his afternoons with the boys, yet there was no sign of the tight, family unit. Returning to her bike, Helen pulled out her phone, intent on leaving yet another message for him, but as she did so, a noise made her look up. A dark-blue Mercedes S Class had just pulled up by the curb and behind the wheel was the man himself.

For a moment, they regarded each other, Helen feeling she saw his face darken briefly, before a cheery smile once more lit up his features. Now Downing was out of the car and striding towards her, a briefcase and two files under his arm.

'Helen, nice to see you again.'

'You too. Where are the boys?'

Another slight reaction, as if he'd been caught out.

'I had to leave them with Alexia. They weren't happy about it, but sadly they're getting used to it. My work schedule is very unpredictable.'

'Big case?'

'An appeal that starts in two days, which I know very little about.'

Laughing, he gestured towards the files, subtly picking up his pace. Falling in step, Helen cut to the chase.

'You wanted to speak to me?'

For a moment, Downing looked non-plussed – Helen suddenly wondered if he *had* actually called, whether she'd dreamt it – but then his features relaxed, as recognition kicked in.

'Yes, I did. But really, you didn't have to come down here just for that.'

'What was on your mind? You sounded worried.'

They slowed as they reached the steps leading to his house. Suddenly, Downing looked uncertain, even a little sheepish.

'Well, it's a bit awkward, but I fear I might have been guilty of not providing you with full disclosure the other day.'

'In English please, Robert.'

'I wasn't entirely candid with you about Declan McManus.'

'In what way?' Helen replied, intrigued.

'Well, as you know, he called me about twelve days ago.'

'Sure.'

'And then – well, he actually turned up here, a few days later.'

Helen nodded, saying nothing. Malik and her supporting officers had been busy canvassing Downing's neighbours, eventually turning up a sighting of McManus in the vicinity not five days ago. Had this diligent probing got back to Downing, prompting his call? Or was this confession simply the product of a guilty conscience?

'What did he want?'

'Well, as I said before, he was touting for business, wanted to work for us in an investigatory capacity. Now he wanted to prove his worth, to *buy* our interest, if you will.'

'How?'

'He claimed to have some material relating to a case I was working on, a nasty stalking scenario involving threats to person and property. He claimed to have evidence *proving* that the defendant had done this kind of thing before with a previous girlfriend. As lead prosecutor, he wanted to furnish me with names, texts, even a recorded phone conversation – for a fee, of course.'

'And?'

'And I told him to bugger off. It's completely unethical and, besides, I wasn't at all uncomfortable with him turning up at my house.'

'And that was the last you heard from him?'

'Absolutely.'

He nodded, as if his duty had been discharged, signalling that he had nothing more to tell.

'And can I ask why you didn't tell me this first time around?'

Downing paused, seemingly displeased to be delayed further, dragged back into the conversation.

'It was silly, really,' he confessed sheepishly. 'I was just think-ing on my feet and – and I was worried that if you knew that he'd contacted me twice, that it might look as if the firm had some kind of ongoing relationship with him, which categorically wasn't the case.'

'And that was all?'

'That was all,' Downing responded decisively. 'Ridiculous, really, but I wanted to put matters straight, give you the full picture, in case it helped at all...'

Helen nodded, but said nothing, ignoring his tacit appeal for a progress report.

'Right well, if that's all...'

'Nothing else worrying you?' Helen asked.

'Only how I'm going to get across this lot in time.'

Raising the weighty files, he flashed a weary smiled at Helen and hurried up the steps. Helen watched him go, taking in his fussy urgency, the way his house key tumbled from his grasp, as he wrestled with the lock. Something *was* bothering him, though what, exactly, would remain a mystery, as the barrister now slid the key home, disappearing quickly inside, the front door closing firmly behind him.

Chapter 65

'Why won't you talk to me?'

'Because there's nothing to say.'

Belinda was trying to sound authoritative, but it seemed to have no effect. Carol continued to stare at her, her expression a mixture of anger and supplication.

'I just want to know if there's anything that I – that *we* – need to be worried about?'

'Such as?'

'You tell me.'

There was defiance now, but Belinda could see through it. It was anxiety – *fear* – that was the real driver here.

'Look, Carol, we could talk in circles about this, but I don't see the point. Why don't we just go out for a drink, chat about it, then maybe think about heading out for a bite to eat?'

'You want us to go *out*?'

'Why not?'

'Like nothing's happened?'

'Nothing *has* happened.'

'You were visited by the police, Belinda. At school. And not by some jumped-up PC, by a detective inspector.'

Belinda swallowed a curse. How the hell was Carol so well informed? Whom had she been talking to at school?

'CID detectives don't chase up lost dogs or stolen handbags. They deal with serious crimes...'

'Obviously.'

'So why were they visiting *you*?'

And there it was on a plate. A deep concern, an unpleasant accusation, concealed in a heartfelt question.

'Because they had some questions about Eve.'

Carol eyeballed her, begrudgingly grateful for the information, but alarmed nevertheless.

'What sort of questions?'

'Just background, that's all. You know that they haven't made any progress yet, so they're just casting around, seeing if they've missed anything. They wanted some more info on her background, her timetables, her routine, whether she had a boyfriend on the go... If you ask me, they're clutching at straws, but they've got to try. For her parents' sake, if nothing else.'

'So did they talk to other people? Members of staff, pupils who knew her?'

'Of course. They didn't come all that way just to talk to me, did they? What could I give them anyway? I told them she was a diligent student with a very bright future ahead of her. Which I'm sure they knew already.'

Carol's body language relaxed slightly. She desperately wanted to believe that it had just been a routine visit, but clearly wasn't ready to commit just yet.

'And that's it, is it? Nothing more than that?'

Belinda took her in. There was so much being left unsaid, so much suspicion, anger and hurt hovering just beneath the surface. Carol was like a wounded animal seeking to be put out of its misery, so crossing to her, Belinda laid a gentle hand on her shoulder.

'Nothing at all. It was routine, that's all.'

'Honestly?'

'Honestly. So, don't fret and, please, *trust me ...*' She pulled Carol to her, wrapping her arms around her. 'There's nothing to worry about.'

Chapter 66

Emilia eyed Joseph Hudson warily, uncertain how to tackle him. She had never seen him seem so agitated or preoccupied before. They were in a quiet, side-street bar, a venue carefully chosen to avoid prying eyes, yet the experienced officer seemed utterly oblivious to his surroundings, his bottle of beer untouched in front of him, lost in his own dark thoughts.

'What's happened, Joseph?'

He shot her a brief glance, but didn't respond.

'Has something gone wrong?'

Her tone was sharper now, more urgent. She'd been trying to get hold of Hudson *all day* and now, when finally he did surface, he refused to speak. This was hardly in keeping with the spirit of their past conversations, which had always been free-flowing and illuminating.

'Is it anything I can help you wi—'

'What's the collective noun for a bunch of bitches?' Hudson interrupted, finally breaking his silence.

'I'm sorry, you've lost me.'

'That's what we've got at Southampton Central. Simmons and Grace, joined at the hip. The sisterhood, protecting each other at all costs.'

Emilia didn't care for his misogyny, but let it go. She needed to find out what was going on.

'Have a drink, Joseph. Take a breath. And then tell me what's happened.'

Begrudgingly, Hudson obliged, taking a long draught of his lager.

'Helen and I had a bit of a set-to last night,' he explained. 'Strong words were exchanged and she obviously went running straight to mummy. I was hauled in front of Simmons first thing this morning and given my marching orders.'

Emilia couldn't hide her surprise, nor her alarm. Hudson was the best source, the best ally she'd had at Southampton Central for years.

'You're out?' she asked, scarcely believing it.

'That's what they want.'

'So, what are you going to do about it?'

'I don't know yet. I'll think of something. But in the meantime, I want us to step up our attack on Helen. No point holding back now.'

'What did you have in mind?'

'A full-on character assassination. I want to drag her name through the gutter.'

'Right...'

'If you've the appetite for it, of course?' Hudson responded, unnerved by Emilia's guarded response.

'Sure, but I'll need ammunition, something I can actually *use*.'

'Oh, there's plenty of stuff, believe me, starting with the fact that she's fallen off the wagon.'

'Really?'

Emilia couldn't hide her surprise. Helen Grace was famously teetotal.

'She admitted as much to me the other day and, to be honest, it makes perfect sense. She's been all over the place lately, lacking her usual energy, dynamism ...'

'If you say so.'

'She used to have a real problem with alcohol, legacy of her childhood, I guess, which makes her return to the bottle all the more worrying.' He sounded concerned, but there was a smile concealed within his grimace.

'I can certainly do something with that,' Emilia replied, after a moment's thought. 'Ties in with our general narrative about a loss of control, failure of leadership ...'

'Exactly.'

'Plus, it allows us to dig up her childhood again – the murders in that filthy London flat, the damaged kid whose demons continue to haunt her. It's all good stuff, and it'll do for a start, but it's not enough to unseat her. I'll need more.'

'And you'll get it. There's juicier material to come, trust me. Illicit liaisons with members of staff, misuse of office ... Certainly enough to remove her.'

'Tell me more.'

Emilia's interest was piqued now. Perhaps Hudson really *did* have the ammunition to destroy Helen Grace.

'In time. Let's do the drinking angle first, then go from there. I want a concerted campaign, not a one-off. A slew of allegations and negative publicity day after day that will eventually make her position untenable.'

He spoke with such vicious zeal, such confidence, that Emilia began to wonder if he'd done this kind of thing before, perhaps in previous postings. She was tempted to ask, but knew it wouldn't pay to get distracted, not now that she'd finally got Hudson talking. So, instead, she remained quiet, nodding her head in the right places and diligently taking notes, as the accusations and bile poured forth. Now that he'd got started, it appeared Hudson would be hard to stop, which is exactly how Emilia wanted it. This was why she had cultivated him, what their whole relationship had been designed to achieve. Soon, very soon, the final assault would be launched against the unsuspecting Helen Grace.

And when it was, she wouldn't know what had hit her.

Chapter 67

'I don't understand...'

Andrew Sutcliffe's anguish was hard to take, but there was no question of sparing him or his wife.

'You're saying that – that Eve's attacker *wasn't* some kind of maniac?'

It seemed strange that the idea of his daughter being attacked by a crazed rapist might be a *desirable* thing, might offer some kind of certainty for the grieving couple, but Helen could see that her enquiries had disturbed Eve's parents. They had been given a narrative – an awful narrative, which nevertheless made grim sense – but that was now being questioned, leaving them shaken and upset. Helen was about to respond, but once more DC Malik took the lead. She had handled them brilliantly so far, as was her way.

'We've been looking into it in great detail, obviously. There *was* a serial attacker with a similar MO, whom we were initially interested in, but he was arrested ten days ago in Berwick and is still in custody, so we had to discount him from our enquiries.'

Jean Sutcliffe stared at Malik, tight-lipped, blank. It was almost as if her words weren't registering.

'And we've had no local incidents or arrests which fit with the precise nature of the attack on Eve...'

'So, we're having to look at other possibilities.'

Husband and wife turned as one to face Helen.

'You said in your previous testimony that Eve didn't have a boyfriend?'

'That's right.'

'She hadn't mentioned anyone? Hadn't brought anyone home?'

'No,' Andrew said firmly. 'Nothing like that. Eve wasn't interested in boys. She liked to study, play music, sports. She had her head screwed on.'

He gulped as he said it, grief choking him. Instinctively, his wife reached out to him, entwining her fingers in his.

'And can I ask,' Helen continued gently, 'if you ever felt that her romantic inclinations might lie elsewhere? That it was *girls* she was interested in, not boys?'

Andrew Sutcliffe looked stunned by the question. 'No ... no, that never even entered our heads. Why would it?'

He seemed determined, defiant, but Helen's eyes were on Jean. As soon as Helen had asked the question, Eve's mum had dropped her eyes, wanting to duck the enquiry.

'Mrs Sutcliffe?'

As Helen spoke, Andrew turned to his wife, expecting a firm reiteration of his denial. But she kept her eyes glued to the floor.

'Did Eve ever mention anything like that to you? Any crushes? Any feelings at all in that direction?'

'I really don't see what that has to do with anything ...'

Andrew was staring at his wife, perplexed and rattled.

'Look, Mrs Sutcliffe, I know it's difficult, that this is very personal,' Helen persisted, 'but we do need to get a full picture of Eve's life if we're to make sense of this terrible tragedy.'

Silence, save for the slow tick-tock of the carriage clock on the mantelpiece.

'DC Malik and the team have been going back over Eve's

purchases, internet history and so forth, and it does suggest she might have been a lesbian, or at least have been keen to explore that side of her personality.'

'Jesus Christ. What are they talking about, Jean?'

'For God's sake, Andrew, let them talk...'

For a second, her husband was silenced. DC Malik seized the opportunity.

'Eve used her Kindle a lot, right?'

'She was always a keen reader,' her mother agreed, a sad smile pulling at her lips.

'According to her purchase history, she bought at least one book a week, sometimes more. A lot of them were classics, books relating to her school work, I'm guessing, but half a dozen of them were erotic novels, novels aimed at young lesbians.'

'Also, her internet history revealed an interest in that area,' Helen added. 'She'd googled lesbian dating sites for teens, read articles about coming out, even, on occasion, accessed online pornography. All very mild stuff, of course, but always featuring women, never men. So, you can see why—'

'She spoke to me once.'

The words slipped quickly from Jean. It was almost as if she wanted them out and done with as quickly as possible. From her husband's stupefied reaction, Helen could see why.

'When was this?'

'A year or two back, when she was fourteen or so.'

'What did she say?'

'Just that she thought she might have feelings for girls. She – didn't want advice or anything. I think she was just testing the water, to see how I'd react.'

'And what did you say?'

'I told her to be patient. It might be a phase or a crush, lots of girls go through that at her age. Best to wait and see before making any hard-and-fast decisions.'

Helen suspected that Andrew Sutcliffe would not have been so gentle, but even so there was enough discouragement and disapproval in Jean's voice to suggest that, subsequently, Eve might have kept her feelings to herself.

'And that was it? She never mentioned anyone that she was interested in romantically?'

A curt shake of the head. And now her husband took over once more.

'What makes you think that there *was* someone? We certainly never had any reason to think there was...'

Helen took a breath, weighing up how much to share, then took the plunge.

'Again, this may be difficult for you to hear, but the post-mortem examination suggested that Eve had been sexually active.'

'No, no, she was just a girl...'

'I understand that, of course I do, but it's clear that Eve was not a virgin, which is why we're keen to discover if she was involved with anyone, prior to her death...'

Both parents looked shell-shocked, reeling from this revelation. They had lost their beloved daughter – now they were wondering who their daughter was.

'To which end,' Helen continued swiftly, 'can I ask you about her association with Belinda Raeburn?'

Stunned silence.

'She taught Eve, I believe?'

'That's right,' Andrew mumbled.

'Did they spend a lot of time together?'

'Yes, of course. Eve – well, it's not immodest to say that Eve was her star pupil. Eve worked really hard in the run up to her music GCSE exam, plus she was hoping to be leader of the first violins for the National Youth Orchestra this summer, so they spent a lot of time together...'

There was defiance, but pride too in his assertion.

'And these lessons took place at school?'

'Yes, mostly.'

Even as he said it, he darted an anguished look at his wife. A long silence followed, before Jean finally took up the reins.

'There were – there were private lessons too. They were mostly at the weekend, at Belinda's flat.'

'I see. And were there phone calls, messages and so on, between them?'

'Yes, but only to make arrangements for lessons. Of course, they tailed off after she'd done her exams.'

'That's the thing,' DC Malik intervened. 'We don't think they did. We had a more detailed look at Eve's call history this morning and, if anything, the regularity of calls and messages *increased*. Up until about six weeks ago at least, when Belinda Raeburn suddenly stopped responding. Eve called, sent messages asking to talk, but received nothing in response.'

'Did Eve seem upset at all in the weeks leading up to her death?' Helen overlapped. 'Did you notice that she was depressed, unhappy at all?'

There was a long beat, then a meaningful look from wife to husband.

'Yes, now that you mention it, she was... she was very down in those last few weeks. I thought it was just the come-down after her exams, plus the anxiety of waiting for the results.'

'But it did surprise us at the time,' Andrew added, in support of his wife. 'It wasn't like Eve to be so blue. She was generally a happy, confident girl...'

As he said it, the bitter reality crushed him once more – his bubbly talented daughter was gone. Helen really wanted to spare him – spare *them* – any more pain. But there was one more question she had to put to them.

'Last thing, then, can I ask when Eve first met Belinda Raeburn? Properly, I mean.'

'Well – well, it would have been when they first started one-on-one lessons.'

'Which was...?'

Jean gave her husband another anguished look, then: 'Well, it was about a year ago...' She paused briefly, her mind in tumult, as she concluded: 'Just before her fifteenth birthday.'

Chapter 68

'OK, so we now have a potential motive for Eve Sutcliffe's murder.'

Helen's voice was firm and decisive, despite the many questions that remained. She had issued a general alert, summoning the team back to Southampton Central. Everyone had complied and they were now crammed into the incident room, even Joseph Hudson, who stood at the back of the crowd, avoiding her eye. Helen knew Grace Simmons had spoken to him, given him both barrels, and he seemed compliant for now. Helen felt relieved and empowered by this, launching into the briefing with renewed confidence.

'Since our chat with Eve's parents, DC Bentham has been going over Belinda Raeburn's professional history…'

'And it appears she moved around a lot, never staying at any one school too long,' Bentham elaborated. 'Looked at one way, she's just restless, itchy feet and all that. But it may be there's another reason why she kept moving on, or was *moved on*…'

'Half an hour ago, I spoke to the head teacher of Stanborough Ladies Academy in Berkshire,' Helen added. 'One of her previous postings. He wasn't very forthcoming; in fact, he was decidedly coy, but when I put my suspicions to him he pretty much confirmed that he'd had to dispense with Raeburn's services because of a possible inappropriate relationship. He won't name names or go further unless we make it official, but this does suggest that Raeburn might have a history of this kind of thing, of actively seeking out romantic or sexual relationships with her female students.'

'Even though she's got a long-term partner?' DC Edwards queried.

'Stranger things have happened,' Helen returned briskly. 'Now, maybe previous victims kept quiet, or perhaps it was deemed best to keep everything under wraps once she'd been moved on. Whatever, in this instance, I don't think Eve Sutcliffe was prepared to be tossed aside, to go quietly.'

'Have a look at this printout of her call history,' DC Malik said, handing out the sheets. 'She called Raeburn once, twice, occasionally three times a day in the weeks leading up to her death. We didn't think much of it when we had her attacker down as male and sexually motivated, but looked at with a fresh pair of eyes, it's intriguing, especially as Raeburn failed to answer the calls or respond in any meaningful way, despite having done so assiduously, earlier in their relationship…'

'This might suggest that Eve wanted to continue their liaison, or at least let her older lover know how she was feeling,' Helen added. 'Who knows, perhaps she'd even threatened her? If their relationship was exposed, then it would have had profound consequences for Raeburn. It would have cost her her job, her relationship and perhaps even her liberty, as Eve Sutcliffe was still a minor.'

'It would have meant a stretch, no question, plus she'd be on the sex offenders register for life, rendering her totally un-employable,' DC Osbourne agreed. 'It would have *ruined* her.'

'So what are we saying?' Hudson had finally raised his head

above the parapet, his scepticism all too clear. 'That this music teacher killed Martin Hill *and* Eve Sutcliffe?'

'No, it's worse than that,' Helen countered. 'Much worse.'

Now she had their attention. All eyes were on her, as the team tried to fathom the connections between these baffling murders. Turning to the murder board, Helen pointed to the picture of Alison Burris, the young NHS manager stabbed to death nearly a fortnight ago.

'Alison Burris was killed by a person or persons unknown, potentially benefitting this man – Amar Goj. He wasn't to know Burris had already emailed his boss with her suspicions and presumably he wanted to silence her...' She moved her finger to the middle-aged man's smiling face. 'Goj in turn murdered Declan McManus. He had no motive for doing so, no connection to the dead man, but *someone* must have benefitted...'

She then moved on to the picture of Belinda Raeburn.

'Two days later, Belinda Raeburn murders Martin Hill. Again, Raeburn has no history of violence and no connection to the dead man, but—'

'But perhaps she had a debt to pay?' McAndrew added, suddenly getting it.

'Exactly. We know that Raeburn didn't kill Eve Sutcliffe, she was involved in a summer school concert at the time of the murder, but Eve's death was certainly conveniently timed, saving Raeburn from exposure, from ruin.'

'So who benefits from Martin Hill's death?' DC Edwards challenged.

'His wife, Lilah,' Helen replied. 'She's painting a rosy picture of their relationship, but I don't buy it. I think he was a controlling, violent presence whom she was probably glad to be rid of...'

Helen paused to catch her breath. Turning away from the board, she addressed the team directly.

'We've been struggling of late, I'll be the first to admit that. Struggling to find credible suspects for a series of violent crimes – carjackings, sexual assaults, racist attacks. I think there's a reason for that. All of these victims – Burris, Sutcliffe, McManus, Hill – were killed by people who had no obvious motive or connection to them.'

'The perfect murder...' Hudson breathed, shaking his head in disbelief.

'Almost. In fact, if it wasn't for tiny mistakes by Goj and Raeburn in the execution of these crimes, we wouldn't have any leads at all...'

Hudson looked like he was about to respond, but Helen carried on quickly.

'We thought we were facing an unprecedented crime wave. But actually we're facing something much more sinister, something *joined up*.'

Helen let this thought land.

'All the murders were made to look like one thing, when, in fact, they were something else entirely. Think about it – Eve's body was stripped, but she wasn't sexually molested in any way. Was that because her killer wasn't interested or couldn't go through with it? Perhaps her murderer was even a woman; we have no way of knowing for sure. Likewise, the stripping of Alison Burris's car. The obvious, easy things – like the info screen – were removed to make it look like theft, but the expensive hand-stitched leather seats were left intact. What self-respecting car thief would do that? These are only small details, but they're things that have been nagging at me, things that only make sense if someone was trying to disguise the true motive behind the crime.'

Silence, as the team processed these troubling thoughts, then finally DC McAndrew spoke up:

'So are we saying that they all know each other? That Goj, Raeburn and the others are in this together? That they're co-ordinating these murders in order to help each other out?'

'Perhaps they're in some kind of club,' Hudson added, drily.

'Well, that's what we've got to work out,' Helen responded defiantly. 'Which is why I want you to drop every other line of enquiry.'

'You can't be serious.' Now the sarcasm was gone, Hudson's protest sincere. 'I can link Lee Moffat to *every one* of these crimes—'

'Lee Moffat is no longer of any interest to us,' Helen replied coolly. 'And I'll say it again, so there's no confusion…'

She let her eyes drift over the faces in front of her, some of whom were friendly, some of whom were not.

'I want us to drop every other avenue of investigation and drill down into the lives of Amar Goj, Belinda Raeburn and Lilah Hill. I want us to focus on possible contact – phone calls, messages, movements. A place they might all go, a way that they can connect. Any evidence of communication, of conspiracy, of premeditation, I want to know about it straightaway. We've been clutching at straws for a while, but these guys hold the key to cracking this case…' she turned to the murder board, gesturing at the photos – 'now we just need to find it.'

Chapter 69

She slipped inside the house, slamming the door behind her. Her head was pounding, her dress clinging to her and, buckling under the strain, Lilah dropped her bag, leaning against the wall for support. It was cool to the touch, the relief pleasurable, and she stayed there, glued to it, sucking up the respite after what had been one of the most difficult days of her life.

Her whole existence had turned on its axis. The past week had played out like some kind of bad dream, a never-ending nightmare, in which the next moment of disaster or despair was just around the corner. What should she do now? What was the *right* thing to do? Every decision seemed fraught with danger.

Peeling herself off the wall, she snatched up her bag and headed for the kitchen. It felt leaden in her hand, weighed down by her impulse buy on the way home, but there was bounty within, something she badly needed. Depositing the moleskin bag on the worktop, she undid the zip to reveal her groceries: a family-sized bar of Fruit and Nut, two cans of lemon Fanta and, in between them, a bottle of gin.

Opening the cupboard, she pulled out a glass. She didn't waste time with ice, lemon or the mixers, simply unscrewing the bottle and pouring two inches. Slowly, deliberately, she raised it to her lips. A moment's hesitation – a prayer for the dying – then she downed it in one go. The effect was electrifying, the alcohol burning her throat, even as her body reacted with something close to euphoria. A pleasant glow spread through her and with it a surge of adrenaline, of excitement, of pure unfettered joy. Laughing, she poured another two fingers in and drained that. Then another.

Now she paused, placing the glass noisily back on the surface. She didn't want to rush this, didn't want to burn through the bottle in five minutes. Not when it made her feel *this* good. Suddenly, the whole awful situation – the graffiti on the door, Martin's murder, the distressing events of the day – seemed at a safe remove. Out there, the world was dangerous, hateful and unforgiving, but here, safe in her little house, everything seemed fine. She knew relief would be temporary, that she was just anaesthetizing herself, but she was fine with that. It was her funeral, after all.

An evening of pointless hedonism lay ahead, a thought that made her giddy. The room seemed to be swaying slightly, threatening to disconnect her from reality, and she gripped the corner of the work surface to steady herself.

'Get a grip, now. Take it slow…'

She whispered these words to her better self, urging caution. And even as she picked up the gin bottle for another shot, she paused, replacing it on the surface and delving into her bag once more. She needed some sustenance, and the dilution of a mixer, to truly savour the abandon that lay ahead. Digging out the chocolate, she grabbed the cold cans and placed them next to her glass, but even as she did so, her gaze was drawn to something else, something that stopped her in her tracks.

She didn't want to look at it, but somehow she felt compelled to. And even though she longed to tug at the zip, to hide it from view, she found she couldn't. So instead she stood there, barely moving, barely breathing, staring at the mobile phone burning a hole in the bottom of her bag.

Chapter 70

The house was as quiet as the grave. Normally this would have crushed Robert, but today he was glad of the silence, the stillness. It was how he needed it.

Crossing to the front door, he double-locked it from the inside, then made his way to the rear of the house. The slider was already secured, but he checked it anyway, before returning to the hall to pick up his briefcase. Now he didn't hesitate, striding up the stairs, past the twin's room, past the master bedroom and on up, eventually cresting the third-floor landing. Now he paused, placing his briefcase on the floor and grabbing the long metal pole that lounged against the wall. Reaching up, he slipped the crook through the hook, and moments later, the loft ladder descended, beckoning him upwards. Grabbing the bag, he obliged, ascending quickly, disappearing into the shadowy loft.

Inside, he flicked on the light, and hauled up the ladder. He knew he was being ridiculously overcautious, but he couldn't risk discovery, not when he was so close to the end. If an eagle-eyed neighbour or unfortunately positioned camera should catch a sight of him, then all he'd sacrificed, all he'd risked would have been for nothing. And that was unthinkable, especially when the stakes were so high.

Crossing to the workbench, he swept the tools aside, placing the briefcase in their place. Clicking it open, he removed the legal briefs, the magazines – all useful cover – to reveal the important contents beneath. The phone and, next to it, a 9mm Glock pistol.

Sliding on disposable gloves, he picked up the gun, weighing it in his hand. It was heavy, far heavier than he'd been expecting, but oddly the weight was reassuring, seeming to suggest power. He looked down the sight, then released the magazine, checking that all eight bullets were in place. Satisfied, he clicked it back into position, then raised the gun in both hands, as if aiming at an invisible foe.

The next part was tricky, dangerous even, so he took his time, easing the safety catch off to make the weapon live. Tentatively, he placed his trigger finger in position, holding it there, willing his hands to be steady. Satisfied, he reinstated the safety catch, only realizing now that he had held his breath throughout the entire operation.

Putting the gun down, he exhaled, laughing at his own stupidity, but his relief was short-lived. Right on cue, the mobile phone concealed in his pocket started ringing. The ring tone was low but insistent, demanding his attention, urging him to answer. And, of course, he was powerless to resist. Because this was it.

The moment of truth.

Chapter 71

Her wheels bit the tarmac, propelling her through the darkened streets. Helen had spent the evening driving the team forward, searching for connections, clues, leads, urging them on until they were dead on their feet. At that point, she had finally relented, sending them home to grab some rest, albeit with a solemn promise to be back on the case first thing in the morning.

Helen had lingered a little, keen to set some final lines of enquiry in motion, before departing herself. It had been a long, gruelling, surprising day, but it was with energy and optimism that she had strode towards the bike park. Last night, she had been in a dark place, floundering in their investigations, on the defensive with a vengeful, assertive Joseph Hudson, but now she felt very different. Finally, they were making progress, and though the next few days still promised to be incredibly tough, for the first time Helen scented victory.

Firing up her bike, she'd roared away and was soon gliding down the streets she knew so well. She had ridden these roads so often that she had to actively disengage her autopilot, so as not to drive straight home. She would head there shortly – she desperately needed a shower and a good night's sleep – but there was somewhere else she needed to be first.

Ever since her early morning interview with Grace Simmons,

she'd been on tenterhooks, nervous as to how the day's events would play out. She knew that Simmons would be as good as her word, would tackle Hudson about his insubordination, his lies, his threats, but she had no idea how Joseph would react. Would he fight back? Would he double down, going straight to Peters? Or would he bide his time, waiting for an opportunity to regain the initiative? Helen suspected the latter, he had been angry and hostile in the team briefing earlier, but suddenly Helen was desperate to know how the interview had gone. To get a full debrief from Simmons on their showdown.

Her superior lived in a pretty little house in Shirley and Helen made it there in less than ten minutes. Killing her engine, she slid off the bike and strolled up the path, admiring the floral borders that Simmons tended to at the weekend. She lived alone, following the death of her husband, and though occasionally she got lonely, Simmons's house and garden kept her occupied – her release from work, stress and the general travails of life.

Smiling to herself, Helen wondered if *she* would ever end up in a place like this. It seemed highly unlikely, in all honesty, so for the time being she would have to enjoy its pleasures through others. She knocked on the door and stepped back, waiting for her old friend to answer.

There was no movement inside, but the TV was on, so rocking back and forth on her heels, Helen waited for the door to open. It was hot and sticky tonight, and Helen craved a cold drink to soothe her parched throat. Stepping forward, she knocked again. But still there was no response.

Puzzled, she angled a glance towards the living room. The lights were on, but the curtains were drawn, shielding the occupant from view. Digging out her phone, Helen rang Simmons's number and straight away she heard her familiar ring tone. Looking up, she tried to work out where the noise was coming from – yes, her instinct was right, it was coming from the living room. But if Grace Simmons was in there, watching TV, why wasn't she answering?

The phone rang out, going to voicemail. Worried, Helen stepped forward, pounding on the door. Still nothing. Her anxiety spiking now, Helen made her way down the side-access passage. The gate at the end was locked, but Helen vaulted it easily, landing quietly on the other side. Now she was hurrying up the path towards the back door, testing its handle, but to her disappointment it was locked. Frustrated, she rapped on the glass.

'Grace? It's me, Helen. Are you home?'

Her voice sounded loud and intrusive in the calm of the suburban garden. Self-conscious, Helen was about to leave, when she spotted something, something that confused and alarmed her. The back door looked onto a small kitchen and, through the doorway of that, the hall could be glimpsed. This in turn led into the living room and Helen now spotted something lying in the doorway to that room. It was a hand – no, it was an arm, lying motionless on the ground.

Horrified, Helen dialled 999 immediately, urgently requesting an ambulance. Then she did the only thing she could do, slamming her elbow through the pane of glass in the back door and sliding her hand through to find the lock. Five seconds later, she was in, racing through the kitchen and into the hall.

The sight that greeted her took her breath away. The TV was on, a plate of biscuits and a cup of tea on the coffee table, and next to that was Grace Simmons, spread-eagled on the floor. There were no obvious signs of disturbance or of violence, so, kneeling down, Helen gently called her name.

'Grace, can you hear me? It's Helen.'

No response. Helen reached underneath, turning her friend

over, but still Simmons didn't react. She was warm, which was a good sign, but terribly limp in Helen's arms.

'Grace, please respond, it's me ...'

Her voice was tight, strangulated. Terrified, Helen now placed her fingers underneath Simmons's throat, searching for an artery. She was practised at this and soon found it, but dissatisfied with her findings, she tried again, and again. But the result was the same. There was no pulse, no sign of life at all.

Her colleague, her mentor, her friend, was dead.

Day Five

Chapter 72

'I appreciate this must have come as a profound shock to you, as it did to me. So, if you need to take some time off, I'll completely understand...'

Chief Superintendent Alan Peters sounded sympathetic, but Helen wasn't sure he meant a word of it. In fact, she sensed that he was baiting a trap for her to walk into. The pair of them had never seen eye to eye and, without Helen's mentor to protect her, she now feared Peters would use Grace Simmons's tragic death to sweep the decks clean.

'I'm fine, sir,' Helen replied quickly, though of course she was no such thing. 'I'll continue to lead MIT and if you need me to cover any of DCI Simmons's duties—'

'It's OK. I'll deal with those.'

Helen wasn't sure she liked Peters' tone; it sounded very much like he was planning to hoover up Simmons's powers and responsibilities, leaving Helen more exposed than ever, but she let it go for now. She had more pressing things on her mind.

'Do we know any more? About what happened?'

'Well, the early indications are that it was a heart attack. The paramedics were pretty convinced about it and I spoke to her son first thing this morning. Apparently, she was diagnosed with chronic heart disease nearly a year ago ...'

He was looking at Helen for a reaction, but her shock was genuine.

'I had no idea, sir. She certainly didn't say anything to me.'

'Nor me,' Peters returned, bristling. 'Though God knows why. I would have been happy to sanction sick leave, or retirement, for that matter, but for reasons that are unclear, she chose to keep it to herself...'

Helen had a pretty good idea why she had stayed on and it crushed her. Simmons had always wanted to support Helen, to aid her career in any way she could, having persuaded her to join the police force over twenty years ago now. Had she sacrificed her life in a selfless attempt to help her protégée? If so, it was a bitterly cruel end to their friendship.

'I did – I did wonder...' Helen found herself saying, fighting the emotion that was rising within her – 'if something was up. She hasn't been herself for a while, less present, perhaps a little more tired than usual.'

'So I'd noticed. But why? Why would she conceal something like that? Pride, I suppose...'

'And professional duty,' Helen added quickly. 'For her, policing was a vocation, not just a job.'

Peters nodded absently, but said nothing.

'Well, sir, if that's all...'

'How are we doing on the McManus case?' he asked, looking up sharply.

'Good. In fact, we're making progress on *all* fronts at the moment,' Helen replied confidently.

'Any chance of an arrest? Something to give the baying mob? We've got a press conference scheduled for this afternoon, which I guess I'll be taking now. Abigail thinks we need to give them something, just to stop the relentless attacks.'

Mention of Southampton Central's media liaison chief

immediately sent a pulse of anger coursing through Helen, but she kept her response civil.

'Soon, sir. Very soon. The team are working flat out on several new leads and, if we're done here, I'd like to—'

'Do you want me to say something to the team?' Peters interrupted. 'About DCI Simmons, I mean, and what's likely to happen next?'

'If it's OK with you, I'd like to do it.'

Her response was polite, but firm. Peters conceded, seemingly glad to have been spared this unpleasant duty, waving her on her way. Thanking him, Helen took her leave, heading fast away down the corridor. There was no question of anyone other than her bringing the team up to speed, of paying tribute to a fallen colleague, mentor and friend. It would be hard – one of the hardest speeches she'd ever had to make – and she wondered if she'd be able to get through it. But a part of her hoped it might be a rallying cry, a way of healing divisions, of knitting the team back together. If so, that would be a fitting legacy for an inspirational leader and public servant.

Striding along through the seventh floor, Helen tried to push all other concerns – Hudson, Peters, Miller – from her mind, eating up the distance to the incident room and buzzing herself in. As she did so, two dozen heads turned towards her. The team were already here and they had clearly heard the news, many looking pale and tearful. They were professionals to a man and woman, but they were also human beings.

'OK, guys, gather round. I've got something to say to you...'

They all got to their feet, crossing the incident room swiftly to form a crescent shape around her. Helen took them in, sober, courteous, purposeful, doing a quick head count before starting. She wasn't sure why she was doing so... until she concluded her tally. They were one short. Subconsciously, she must have noticed this, even before her brain caught up, and running an eye over the assembled faces, she swiftly identified the missing body. Perhaps she shouldn't have been surprised, but this didn't make her outrage any the less.

Where the hell was Joseph Hudson?

Chapter 73

'That's very kind of you, DS Hudson. A lovely thought...'

Janet Briars, Grace Simmons's PA, whimpered even as she said it. She looked utterly shell-shocked, her eyes red from weeping. There was no question, her boss's death had come completely out of the blue, but still Joseph wondered if there was more to it than that. Briars was no spring chicken, a station lifer who was herself approaching retirement. The sudden death of someone only a few years older than herself was bound to have a profound effect. Was Briars even now reflecting on her own mortality?

'Should I put these with the others, or...?'

Hudson nodded to the bouquet he'd bought on the way in this morning. The florist, which was only a stone's throw from Southampton Central, had clearly had several visitors before *he* arrived. News of Simmons's demise had broken just after 6 a.m. and her fellow officers had been quick to pay tribute in any way they could. The station Twitter feed and Facebook pages were awash with glowing messages and her office was now a repository for floral tributes.

'Of course, go ahead,' Briars replied, eventually mastering herself, and gesturing him to enter her office.

Hudson obliged and was immediately struck by the aroma

– musky, perfumed, beguiling. Over a dozen large bouquets sat on the desk, leaving precious little room for his offering.

'Perhaps you could just put them on the chair for now?' Briars said, sounding a little embarrassed. 'I'm sure I can find a good spot for them later.'

'Of course.'

He rounded the desk and placed the bouquet on the chair. The act seemed faintly comical, his ultimate boss replaced by a bunch of flowers, and he would have been tempted to laugh had the loyal Briars not been present. Fortunately, her phone now started ringing.

'Would you excuse me for a minute, DS Hudson?'

Once more, Briars sounded upset and flustered. Joseph Hudson gestured at her to go, and she did so gratefully. Moments later, she was on the phone, commiserating with the caller.

'I just can't believe it, Emma. We're all in shock here…'

Keeping one ear on the conversation, Hudson approached the desk, feigning interest in a few of the bouquets. Then, once he was sure he was safe, he diverted to the object of real interest. Simmons's in-tray was full to the brim, neither she nor Briars being the most efficient administrators, and his heart sank at the number of files that lay stacked on top of one another. This seriously upped the chance of delay and discovery, but there was nothing for it, so he flicked open the first file.

It was a summary of the Force's current operational commitments, so he moved on, digging out the second file. This was a report about cost-cutting within Southampton Central. It would have made for interesting reading, but not now, so he moved on. The third file concerned media liaison, so again he moved on, flicking feverishly through the multitude of buff-coloured files.

'Well, it's very sweet of you to call, Emma. I know the family will appreciate the sentiment…'

It sounded as though Briars was winding up, so Hudson picked up the pace, flicking open the files, examining the top sheet, then moving on. Still he'd had no joy – where the hell was it? Was it possible she'd filed it already? If so, the damage was done and his defeat was assured. Surely she couldn't have been so efficient; they'd only had their interview yesterday morning.

On he went, faster and faster.

'OK, thanks again.'

Faster still, his vision a blur of words and lines. Now he heard Briars hang up.

'Fucking hell—' he hissed.

But now he ground to a halt, spotting a familiar word: Hudson. Yes, here it was. Grace Simmons's signed report concerning her discussion with Helen, her admonishment of him and her recommendation that the former should not be disciplined. Greedily, he snatched it up, even as Briars entered.

'Everything OK in here, detective sergeant?'

'Absolutely. I was just admiring these bouquets. They're – beautiful.'

'Aren't they?' Briars responded, choked. 'If you'd like to stay a while—'

'No, it's fine. I've taken up enough of your time, already.' He crossed to her, placing a comforting hand on her shoulder. 'Thanks for everything, Janet. And chin up, eh?'

She offered him a sad smile and he took his leave. As he did so, a smile lit up his face. It had worked. He had paid his respects, appearing as the grieving colleague and, as a result, Simmons's official rubber-stamped response to the liaison between Helen and himself was now safely tucked inside his jacket, never to see the light of day.

Chapter 74

'She was the best and brightest of us. Someone who devoted her life to police work, to this place and to the people she swore to protect.'

All eyes were glued to her, young and old, long-servers and fresh faces alike, clearly moved by what they were hearing.

'She believed in giving the best of herself every single day, of doing her utmost to serve the people of Southampton. Above all, she believed in this—' she gestured to the half-circle of officers in front of her – 'the importance of the *team*. Of working together, as one, without ego or agenda to do the important job we've been given. To get justice for those who've been let down by life…'

Was it her imagination or did she detect shame on some of the faces in front of her?

'So, let's honour Grace Simmons by remembering why we're here, remembering what we all swore to do when we took the badge. Let's get justice for these poor people.' She gestured to the board, where the faces of Martin Hill, Declan McManus, Alison Burris, Eve Sutcliffe and others started back at them. 'Let's put an end to their families' misery. Let's get the job done.'

Nods, purposeful and spirited, from many in the team. Pleased, Helen gestured to them to resume their duties.

'Right, go to it.'

Turning, Helen strode to her office, feeling oddly cheered. It had been one of the worst nights of her life – sleepless, anguished, guilt-ridden – but her speech had buoyed her up, filling her with energy and purpose. She had meant every word of her speech – Grace Simmons had always been a touchstone for her, a model of dedication, duty and excellence. She just wished she'd said it to her whilst she'd had the chance.

Passing into her office, Helen pushed the door to behind her. She was keen to crack on with their investigations, but first she needed a moment to gather herself. To reflect on what she'd lost and what she now had to do, to ensure Simmons's legacy was properly honoured. But, as ever, her attempt to find a moment's peace was doomed; a rap on the door snapping her out of her introspection.

She turned, half expecting it to be Joseph Hudson, come to offer some lame excuse for his absence, but to her surprise DC McAndrew now entered, sheepish, but determined.

'So sorry to bother you, guv—'

'Not at all, my door is always open.'

'It's just that I found something last night I thought you'd want to see. I was going to call you first thing this morning, but then I heard the news about—'

'It's OK,' Helen said, ushering her inside. 'What have you got?'

McAndrew approached, clutching a printout. 'Well, as you suggested, I went back over the available evidence from the Eve Sutcliffe murder. Given what we said yesterday, I looked at it with a fresh pair of eyes, ignoring the sexual motive and, well, I found this—'

She handed Helen the piece of paper, a still from a CCTV feed. In the picture, a slender middle-aged woman could be seen walking towards Lakeside Country Park. Dark-haired, with a fullish face, she wore sunglasses, jogging gear and a small rucksack and, though her face was turned to the ground, she was nevertheless fairly well captured.

'This woman entered the park around fifteen minutes before Eve Sutcliffe. She left roughly five minutes after the time we estimate Eve was attacked.'

She handed Helen another CCTV still. This image captured a woman of similar build leaving the park, wearing a cap and black joggers and trainers.

'It's a different person, right?' Helen queried, intrigued.

'That's what I thought at first,' McAndrew responded. 'She's wearing a cap, but no sunglasses, different-coloured joggers this time, *but* the little rucksack she's wearing is the same and look at her hands ...'

Helen scanned the two images, immediately seeing the connection.

'She's wearing gloves.'

'Exactly. In both of the pictures this woman is wearing gloves, *despite* it being seriously hot that day, over thirty degrees, according to the Met office records.'

Helen took this in, staring intently at the CCTV grabs.

'So, you think she *changed* whilst she was in the park?'

'Or had reversible clothes. But the rucksack and gloves give the game away. Question is, why was she there for such a short time and why did she want to disguise her appearance?'

'You're sure she's not just a jogger, albeit a very fashion-conscious one?'

'I went over weeks and weeks of CCTV from the vicinity of the park during the initial investigation. This woman doesn't turn up on any other day, except this one. Also, there are other CCTV spots, mostly around the perimeter of the park. None of those pick her up, so her jogging route must have been a very limited one, which is odd, given she was in there for twenty-five minutes—'

'Perhaps she was attending an open-air class.'

'There weren't any scheduled for that day.'

'Or a personal trainer.'

'There's no evidence of that, and, believe me, I've looked. But that's not the interesting part...'

'Go on,' Helen replied, intrigued by McAndrew's evident excitement.

'Well, the point is, I *recognize* her. In fact, I've spoken to her.'

'So, who is she?' Helen replied, genuinely surprised.

'I'm ninety-nine per cent certain that it's Amanda Davis.'

Even as McAndrew said it, alarm bells started ringing. It took Helen a moment to place the name, then it hit her like a sledgehammer.

'That's the wife of the guy—'

'Who was killed in an aggravated burglary a few weeks back. Her husband was very rich, liked to brag about it in the press, so we put his death down to that. But looking at the file again, only a handful of the most obvious items were stolen from their house during the burglary. You'd think if you were willing to kill, you might make it worth your while. Look for a safe, take the TVs, the top-of-the-range audio equipment...'

Helen said nothing, stunned by McAndrew's report. In many ways, it made perfect sense. A half-hearted 'burglary' and a brutal, failed attempt at 'sexual assault', both, in fact, clumsy attempts to disguise cold-blooded murder. It fitted the pattern of the other killings, the logic, the approach, crystal clear, but still the implication of McAndrew's discovery was devastating.

Just how big *was* this thing?

Chapter 75

Lilah picked her way through the cars, keeping low to the ground.

Her body was tense, her senses alert, expecting danger. If she was spotted, if someone clocked her and called out, she would turn and run. Run and never look back. But so far, everything had gone precisely according to plan.

Crouching down next to the wheel arch of a pristine Nissan, she peered round the bonnet, taking in the scene. There were dozens of cars here, scores even, all in the process of being hoovered, cleaned and polished, ready to be driven back to various Hertz outlets throughout the city. Some time ago, the company had made the decision to centralize its cleaning operations, all cars now delivered to this industrial estate in Freemantle, meaning she had a host of options to choose from.

Scanning the handful of finished vehicles, Lilah weighed up her options. Should she go for the Toyota SUV nearest to her or one of the other cars that were slightly further off? They would be riskier to get to, but were closer to the exit, so there was less chance of someone slamming the chain-link gates shut before she'd had a chance to escape. Plus, they were smaller, less conspicuous, more ubiquitous – Fiat 500s and the like – and less easy to pick out in the Southampton rush-hour traffic.

Yes, that was it. She would aim for the red Fiat that was roughly forty feet from where she was hiding. Taking a deep breath, she braced herself for what was to come. How she regretted her gin bender now; she felt drained and nauseous, her head pounding and her mouth bone dry. She felt *awful*, as if she'd gone twelve rounds in the ring, barely able to put one foot in front of the other. Yet there was no question of wimping out. This had to be done *today*.

Swallowing down the bile that was rising in her throat, she tried to focus. All she really wanted to do was climb into bed and pull the duvet over her head, but she was here to do a job, so once more she scanned the yard, searching for potential dangers. Happily, there weren't many cleaners on site today and those who were here seemed to be hard at work, their heads buried in the poky interiors, their forms lost in the arcing mist, as their high-pressure hoses buffeted metal and glass.

This was it, then. Now or never. She crept forward, scurrying over the scrubby ground to the safety of the high-sided Toyota. She braced herself for discovery, fully expecting to be challenged, but the world continued to go about its business, unaware. Round to the front or round to the back? Scuttling backwards, she leaned into the Toyota, praying its alarm wouldn't scream out at her. Most of these cars were unlocked, the keys still in the ignition, but, even so, she could catch a bad break...

Fortunately, all was still. Taking a deep breath, she tried to calm herself. Her heart was pounding, beating in rhythm with her poor head, but she had to press on, so now she broke cover, this time crawling over the ground on her hands and knees to the red Fiat. Reaching up, she grasped the handle and tugged. But to her horror, it wouldn't move.

'What the fuck...'

Swallowing her expletive, she gathered herself and tried again.

This time she squeezed harder and to her immense relief, the catch gave, the door inching open. This was the most difficult, most dangerous, part of the operation. She would have to sit upright in the car, fully visible to anyone who turned her way, and pray that the keys were in the ignition...

Peeking inside, she saw them dangling down, tantalizing and tempting. Mastering her fear, Lilah scrambled into the vehicle, sliding into the seat, keeping herself low. Peeking through the windscreen, she was pleased to see that there was no one nearby, though a couple of the sprayers had paused to chat, tired out already from their early shift. She didn't dare shut the door, for fear of alerting them, so she slipped her seatbelt on and gently turned the key in the ignition.

The engine purred into life and she took full advantage. Slipping the car into first, she began to edge forward. As soon as she did so, the car's warning system started to ping loudly. Desperately scanning the dashboard, Lilah noticed that a yellow triangle icon was flashing next to a picture of an open door. The onboard computer clearly didn't like the fact that the driver door was ajar, but she didn't bother to shut it. She could see heads starting to turn, so, instead, she jammed her foot down on the accelerator, ramming the gear stick into second.

The car leapt forward, the engine roaring, as the revs shot off the scale. She was over-gunning it, torturing the gears, but speed was of the essence now, the vehicle shooting forward towards the open gates. The ground was rough and uneven, the car bouncing around, and Lilah felt the driver door beginning to swing open. Desperately, she reached out, grabbing it and slamming it shut. Immediately, the sound of the outside world receded, a blessed relief for her pounding head. Looking up, she realized she was nearly free and clear. The gates were just ahead of her, wide open and welcoming, and she sped through them now with a profound sense of relief.

She had done it. She had got the car, stealing it from under their noses. Even if anyone had spotted her, they wouldn't have anything to say, except that someone dressed in a burgundy hoodie and jeans had stolen one of their cheaper models. Lilah suddenly felt a surge of optimism, of joy, but as she looked in her rear-view mirror, her joy was tempered by the sight of one of the workers staring after her, his phone clamped to his ear.

He was presumably calling the police, phoning it in. Which meant the clock was ticking. The only question now was whether she could stay at liberty, keep the car under wraps for long enough, until the time came to use it.

Chapter 76

'This really isn't a good time, Helen...'

Alexia Downing was clearly having a bad morning, the presence of a police officer in her kitchen doing little to improve her mood.

'I've got to drop the boys off at my mum's and the traffic's going to be terrible...'

'I wouldn't be here if it wasn't important,' Helen replied politely.

'Even so, can it wait until later? I'm already late for work—'

'No, I'm afraid it can't.'

Something in Helen's voice gave Alexia Downing pause. Helen could see the crease of concern in her features, the growing sense that something bad had just landed on her doorstep. Tossing two dirty cereal bowls into the sink, Alexia cried, 'Boys? Teeth, then blazers and bags. We leave in ten.' Turning back to Helen, she smiled tightly whilst gesturing to her to sit. Helen returned the compliment, but didn't respond to her ultimatum. She would be the one who decided when their interview was over.

'I'd like to talk to you about Robert.'

'Right...'

It was said cautiously, tightly, as if she was loath to give anything away. Was this out of loyalty to Robert? Or just anxiety strangling her response?

'I understand you're currently in the middle of divorce proceedings—'

This was unnecessarily formal – Helen had bumped into Alexia socially a few months back and had commiserated with her on the break-up of her marriage – but it was how it had to be.

'That's right.'

'Could you tell me how things are progressing? Is it running smoothly or is it protracted? Is it harmonious? Acrimonious?'

'It's a bloodbath.'

She said this with no sense of triumph, or even bitterness. Just excessive, pained weariness.

'It's been going on for months now. I had hoped we could settle it out of court but that's going to be impossible.'

'Because?'

'Because Robert wants equal custody. And I won't sanction that.'

'Right. Can I ask why?'

'Because his professional and personal situation won't allow for it. He works too hard and is often away for days at a time. He has no partner, no family locally, so who'd look after the kids when he's working? When court proceedings overrun?'

'So it's purely a matter of logistics?'

'Of course. The boys have been through enough disruption already. What they need is stability, parents who'll actually be around.'

'You and your new partner?'

'That's right. Graham is his own boss, so he's very flexible. And I can generally choose my hours, fitting them around the kids. We're only in this mess this morning because Robert dumped them on me out of the blue last night. It really is bloody typical of him.'

Concern arrowed through Helen now, unnerved by this sudden change in Robert Downing's plans, but she kept this to herself.

'And can I ask what type of arrangements you'd suggested regarding the custody of the children?'

There was a short pause, Alexia for the first time looking a bit self-conscious.

'Full custody.'

'I see,' Helen responded, surprised. 'So, he wouldn't get to see them at all or—'

'Of course he'd get to see them. During the holidays, on special days, the odd weekend, but it would be when we – when I thought it appropriate.'

She said it defensively, aware it might sound cruel, but defiantly too, as if convinced it was the right course of action.

'And was this your position from the off? When you started proceedings?'

'Yes.'

'Why was that?'

'What do you mean?'

'Well, I'm not judging you or Robert, I know nothing of the circumstances, but usually people only push for full custody when there's a serious problem, a question of safeguarding or—'

'Like I said, it was just a question of logistics. You know what Robert's like—'

'Yes, I do. And I know that he adores his kids.'

'That's never been in doubt, but that's not the point…'

'I also know *you* a little. And you don't strike me as being cruel or irrational or vengeful—'

'It's nothing like that.'

'Then what? Why were you – *are* you – so determined to cut him off from his sons?'

The question hit home, Alexia Downing looking both angry and upset. Was there regret too, that a happy marriage had come to this?

'Alexia, please. I need to know. For Robert's sake, for your sake, for the boys…'

At their mention, Alexia shot a look upstairs, where the boys could be heard laughing. Then, taking a deep breath, she continued in a low voice, 'Look, I don't want the boys or Graham knowing about this, but when – when Robert and I were together we occasionally used recreational drugs. Amongst friends, when we were away from the kids…'

'What drugs?'

'Cocaine, ecstasy,' she replied, dropping her eyes. 'Cannabis, of course…'

'And?'

'Well, it was common in our circles and we only did it occasionally, as we both had high-powered jobs to hold down. It was a weekend thing, really.'

Helen said nothing, letting the silence do the work.

'But when our marriage hit the rocks, when it became clear that I'd found someone else and was planning to leave him – well, Robert started using drugs more regularly.'

'Coke? Ecstasy?'

'At first.'

'But then…?'

'Well, after I'd left, taken the boys, I think it got steadily worse.'

'In what way?'

'I think – well, I heard from friends – that he was using more and more, that he had resorted to stronger drugs.'

'Such as?'

'Well . . .' she replied, breathing out hard, 'crystal meth was mentioned.'

It clearly hurt her to say this, the idea of her husband resorting to Class A drugs, driven to it by their break-up.

'Obviously, now I was seriously worried. He was still seeing the boys, still a part of their lives, so I went round to his house unannounced. He was in a really bad way. He looked like he hadn't slept in days, was unshaven – plus, the house was a mess. He claimed he'd had a bug, but I knew he was lying. That was when I decided to push for full custody.'

'So why on earth is he still seeing the boys, still looking after them?'

'Well, after that visit, he seemed to clean up his act. He applied for a temporary access order, which the courts granted, of course.' It was said bitterly.

'But why didn't you bring up his drug use *then*? Surely it would have been relevant.'

'I wanted to, but my lawyers advised me against it. We only had hearsay and rumour to go on at that point; it would have been his word against mine.'

'Because you had no hard evidence.'

Even as Helen said it, another piece of the jigsaw slid into place.

'Yet *still* you're pushing for full custody. Something you'd be unlikely to get – unless the situation had changed. If somehow you managed to get concrete evidence of Robert's drug use – well, that would change *everything*. In that scenario, you'd be nailed on to get what you wanted, cutting Robert out of the boys' lives completely.'

Alexia Downing continued to stare at the table.

'Does the name Declan McManus mean anything to you?'

Alexia's eyelids fluttered but she said nothing, staring down at the table.

'Did your lawyers instruct McManus to investigate Robert, to tail him?'

A long, heavy silence.

'Alexia, if you did, if *they* did, I need to know. *Right now.*'

And now, finally, Alexia capitulated, nodding briefly.

'They said they'd used him before,' she said, her voice shaking. 'That he got results.'

'And did he? Did he get the evidence you needed?'

'I don't know.' Her voice cracked now, a single tear running down her cheek. 'McManus told the lawyers that things were progressing well, then suddenly he went quiet. Next thing we know, his name's all over the papers, because he's been attacked, killed.' She let out a brief sob, desperately trying to hold herself together.

'And at any point did you think that *Robert* might have been responsible for the attack on him? Or might have sanctioned it at least?'

There was silence as Alexia appeared to wrestle with her conscience, then, finally, she looked up. And Helen now saw her eyes were brimming with tears.

'Honestly? I have absolutely no idea.'

But Helen did.

Chapter 77

'You *really* think Downing's involved in this?'

Chief Superintendent Peters looked incredulous, clearly concerned that Helen *had* finally lost the plot.

'Yes, I do. He was the first person I spoke to in connection with the McManus murder and from the very start I've felt that something was *off...*'

'Even so, it seems very far-fetched.'

'According to his wife, Robert Downing's drug use was out of control. If McManus had obtained evidence – testimony, footage even – of Downing using a Class A drug, then that would be it, his life as he knew it would be over. He'd lose custody of the kids, be struck off by the Bar Association, could even be hauled up in court. He would be humiliated, disgraced – the same fate faced by Belinda Raeburn and Amar Goj, before their particular tormentors met a nasty end.'

'I can see there are some unpleasant coincidences, connections even,' Peters responded, 'but where's the evidence? Where *is* the footage? The testimony? What did Alexia *have* over her husband?'

'We don't know; in fact, we may never know.'

Not an answer that satisfied Peters, but Helen had to be honest.

'Think about it. Someone, presumably Amar Goj, tried to access McManus's home, then later stole his laptop from his car. My guess is that whatever evidence McManus had obtained about Downing was on that laptop. Having secured it, Goj then targeted the man himself, in the process destroying any paper trail that might lead back to Downing, or his wife's lawyers...'

'But why had McManus not passed the evidence on? You say Mrs Downing is not aware of anything McManus uncovered...'

'I think that perhaps McManus spotted an opportunity to sting Downing first.'

'Blackmail?'

'I can't see any other reason why McManus would contact his target personally. He called him once, then a few days later collared him face to face, at his home. He doesn't gain anything by doing that – he was supposed to be *shadowing* Downing, not confronting him. My guess is that he was trying to extort money from him.'

Peters said nothing, regarding her suspiciously, apparently unsure whether to entertain Helen's line of thought or dismiss the whole theory as wild speculation.

'And Downing confirmed that he was accosted by McManus?' he eventually responded.

'Yes, he confirmed as much to me personally.'

'Why would he admit that?'

'To cover himself. I think he was worried we'd find out that McManus had been in his street, that they'd talked, and he wanted to shut down that avenue of investigation. So, he made up a story about McManus touting for work with his firm.'

'A reasonable enough explanation, surely?' Peters replied.

'Sure and maybe it's true, but DC Malik spoke to a number of the clerks and partners at Downing's chambers this morning. They've never been approached by McManus, nor did Downing raise the matter with them. Moreover, why would McManus choose *now* – when he's actually *tailing* Downing – to make a bid for work from him?'

'Leverage?'

'Possibly, but I'm sure evidence of Downing's criminality and drug use could have been put to far better use,' Helen countered. 'He could have extorted thousands of pounds from him if he'd wanted to. Now I don't know what Alexia's lawyers were paying, but standard retainers aren't great.'

'Presumably McManus could have extorted large sums from Downing and then *still* handed the evidence to her lawyers, making it a double pay-out.'

'I certainly wouldn't have put it past him.'

Peters said nothing in response, lost in a sea of troubling thoughts.

'I'm requesting surveillance, sir. A twenty-four seven watch on Robert Downing and Lilah Hill. If my theory's correct, then it's very likely that they are even now planning criminal acts, possibly including murder—'

'This is the bit I don't get,' Peters cut in. 'Downing stood to lose everything, but then a total stranger comes to his rescue, murdering McManus despite having no connection to the case or indeed to Downing himself. Why would Amar Goj do that?'

'To pay it forward. Someone dispensed with Alison Burris for him, conveniently making it look like a carjacking. So now the onus was on him.'

'And how do they organize this scheme? Are they all on some kind of WhatsApp group? Murders R Us? How is it plotted, executed?'

Helen didn't care for his tone – suspicious, disbelieving – but replied evenly, 'I don't know. Not yet. But it's the only thing that makes sense, given what these individuals stood to lose, their total lack of motive and the concerted attempts to conceal the true nature of the murders. I think if we keep eyes on Downing and Hill, if we intervene before they can follow through on their half of the bargain, then we stand a good chance of discovering how this enterprise works.' Helen stopped, out of breath, out of arguments. In Simmons's absence, she needed Peters' backing, but she could see that he was sceptical.

'And you're *absolutely* certain,' he queried, 'that Robert Downing, a respected local QC, is actively involved in this, in a plot to *kill?*'

Helen took a moment, before looking up to meet his gaze.

'Yes, I am.'

Chapter 78

He picked his way down the gloomy corridor, taking care not to make a noise. Bare light bulbs hung from the ceiling, emitting a weak glow, meaning progress was painstaking and slow. Discarded clothing, drugs paraphernalia, even used condoms, littered the floor, meaning extreme caution was necessary.

Step by step, Robert Downing's anxiety grew. He didn't want to be here, could never have imagined himself doing this a few months back, but he had no choice. Gripping the gun in his hand, he tried to summon his courage. In a few minutes it'd all be over, then he would be free. What he was planning was ruinous in every sense, but if he could pull it off, if he could win this high-stakes gamble, then he could still be happy, could still make a success of his life.

If he *did* manage it, he had already vowed to lead a decent, upstanding existence, spending as much time with the kids as possible, taking on pro bono work whenever he could, giving generously to charity. Who knows, perhaps he would even try and find love again. There had been many happy moments with Alexia, before it all went so disastrously wrong.

Had the break-up been his fault? He had blamed her, for her disloyalty, her infidelity, but perhaps it was he who'd been to blame. He was obsessional, single-minded, whether it was with work, drug-taking or any other arena of his life. Once he was in, he was *in*, often to the exclusion of all others, even those he loved the most.

This single-mindedness, his total focus, had cost him dear in the past, but perhaps it would serve him well now, allowing him to see this thing through. He could only be a few hundred feet from his quarry now. Stepping over a discarded sleeping bag, he kept going, on and on down the dimly lit corridor, as if being sucked ever deeper into a vortex. To Robert, this seemed about right. Today might be a new beginning, but it was also an end. There would be no way back from this.

Reaching the end of the corridor, he turned left, walking carefully down an identical walkway. Shivering, he gripped the gun a little tighter. This place gave him the shivers, so empty, lifeless and shadowy. It seemed to possess a brooding menace, yet in reality it was just another casualty of the downturn. Construction of this new, out-of-town storage facility had almost been completed when the finance suddenly ran out, leaving the vast, cavernous collection of corridors and lock-ups to fester and rot. Since then it had been used by junkies, hookers, runaways and, lately, by Gary Bleecher.

The moneylender – or loan shark, to give him his real title – lived in the centre of town, in a comfortable mews house. But he conducted his business out here, away from prying eyes. The very remoteness of it was a bonus to Bleecher, but so was the feeling of unease and discomfort it fostered in its visitors. Anyone turning up here to borrow or repay money would realize how easy it would be to come to grief, even to disappear, without anyone being the wiser. What must the poor, desperate folk have felt, Robert wondered, as they trudged these lonely corridors, knowing they were about to hook themselves to a brutal, pitiless man.

Yes, this was good. This was how he had to think. What he was about to do went against everything he believed in – as a lawyer, a father, as a human being. But if he could convince himself that he was doing the world a favour, ridding it of a festering parasite, perhaps liberating scores of debtors in the process, then it might be easier. Yes, he had to think that dispatching Bleecher was like crushing a cockroach: nothing more, nothing less.

Reaching the end of the corridor, he paused. Light slipped from underneath the door, alerting Robert to the fact that he had reached his final destination. Behind this battered door was his victim. Easing the safety catch off the gun, Robert reached out a gloved hand, teasing the door gently open.

This was it, then. There was no going back now.

Chapter 79

'You can't just barge in here – this is a place of business.'

DC Bentham didn't break stride, powering forward.

'I apologise for the intrusion, but like I said, this is a murder enquiry.'

'Even so, if you don't have a warrant...'

'I'm not conducting a search and this is a shared office, not a private residence, so I have every right to be here.'

This wasn't strictly true, but it gave the office secretary pause for thought. She kept pace with Bentham, anxious and alarmed, but said nothing, instead looking around her desperately, as if seeking support. Bentham was glad of the silence, keen to focus on the task in hand. There was no question now that Helen Grace was onto something, so it was vital that the team made contact with their new suspect as soon as possible, regardless of the discomfort or embarrassment it might cause.

Amanda Davis worked as Finance Director at a firm special-izing in luxury yacht production, occupying an expansive office in their HQ in Ocean Village, but Bentham had no interest in her professional standing. He was more intrigued by the murder of her husband, Alastair, and whether she might have had a motive for wishing him dead. At the time, his murder had been written off as a burglary gone wrong, but now it seemed clear that *he* was the real object of his assailant's presence in the family home, not the handful of watches and jewels that had been taken on the night. Had he been unfaithful? Was he abusive? Did he have some kind of hold on her? Or was it just a financial thing, Davis standing to inherit a very tidy sum as his widow?

The names flicked by as he marched down the corridor, past a series of closed doors. He dismissed them all as irrelevant, before suddenly grinding to a halt. Here it was, the name 'Amanda Davis' etched in large gold letters.

'DC Bentham, please, if you could just—'

Ignoring the secretary's protests, Bentham grasped the handle, pushing inside. Sliding his warrant card from his pocket, he held it up, even as he stepped inside to confront the suspect. He had a speech planned, knew what his tactics would be, but it was immediately apparent that none of these would be required. The office was empty. Worse still, the desk was immaculately clear.

'Where is she?' he asked urgently, turning once more to his pursuer.

'That's what I've been trying to tell you. She's on leave.'

'Is she ill?'

'No, nothing like that. She's on holiday. At least, I think it's holiday, it could be compassionate leave. Anyway, the point is that she left the office about a week ago, to visit her parents in Sydney.'

'Sydney, Australia?' Bentham countered, incredulous.

'Is there another one?'

Bentham stared at her, lost for words. Davis was an important suspect, potentially the key to unlocking this strange case, but apparently she was on the other side of the world.

'When did she go? Exactly?'

'Well, as I said, it was a week ago, so it would have been the tenth ...' the young woman replied.

'Are you sure of that?'

'Absolutely, I booked her tickets myself. It struck me as a bit odd at the time, but it wasn't my job to question her arrangements.'

'Odd how?'

'Just that it was so soon, that's all.'

'Meaning?'

Now the secretary paused, as if wary of speaking ill of anyone at the firm, before continuing quietly: 'Well, it was just that – that she flew to Sydney the morning after her husband's funeral.'

Chapter 80

He crept forward, his shoes caressing the concrete floor. Gary Bleecher was only twenty feet away from him and utterly oblivious to the danger.

The loan shark was deeply involved in his work, furiously bashing away on an aged laptop, altering figures in a spreadsheet. He seemed consumed by what he was doing, as if a moment's lack of attention might cost him money, something which, presumably, would have been abhorrent to him.

Still Robert moved forward, inching slowly closer, until Bleecher was only ten feet from him. The slovenly middle-aged man was a big target, it would be harder to miss than hit from his range, so now he slowed, his finger quietly releasing the safety catch, before sliding onto the trigger. Taking a silent breath, Robert gathered himself, taking in his victim. Bleecher was unshaven and unkempt, sporting greasy, uncombed hair and a tired Adidas tracksuit. If he really was a successful loan shark, as Robert's research suggested he was, then it was hard to imagine where the money went. Clearly personal appearance, bling and the ostentatious display of wealth was not his thing. Or was this just a ruse? An attempt to stay below the radar of police interest whilst he quietly salted away thousands? Whatever, his scams, his manipulations, his bare-faced thuggery were about to come to an end. It wasn't a nice way to go, it wasn't a nice place to *die*, but there was no other way.

Gathering himself, Robert raised the gun to eye level. As he did so, the gun brushed again his jacket, glancing off one of the metal poppers. Instantly, Bleecher tensed, then slowly rotated his neck, craning around to see who – or what – was behind him.

Confusion gripped his features – who the *hell* was this guy? – then concern, as his eyes came to rest on the gun.

'I'm sorry,' Downing breathed, as he squeezed the trigger.

Nothing. Shock registered on Bleecher's face, even as a spike of terror pulsed through his assailant's body.

Robert squeezed again, but the gun clicked awkwardly. He pulled harder on the trigger, the barrel waving wildly now, but he couldn't get it to move. The bloody gun was jammed.

And now Bleecher sensed his opportunity. Charging forward, he threw himself at his would-be assassin, the pair of them crashing onto the dusty ground. Now he was climbing on top of the floored lawyer, scrabbling to get his fat hands round his neck. Robert tried to fend him off as best he could, striking him with the butt of the gun, but it seemed to have no effect. Bleecher's blood was up, his desperation to survive writ large on his sweaty, contorted face.

This was a bare-knuckle struggle now. A fight to the death.

Chapter 81

'She wants me gone. Out of the team, out of this station, out of the Force.'

DS Hudson modulated his accusation carefully, trying to imbue it with the perfect balance of personal hurt and professional disappointment. So far, Chief Superintendent Alan Peters had been polite and receptive, but this was the moment of maximum danger, when he might unravel Hudson's testimony.

'She actually said that to you, *explicitly*?' Peters asked, right on cue.

'Absolutely. She collared me at the bike park two nights ago. I'd challenged her during the evening briefing, called into question the direction of the investigation, and she didn't like that. She completely lost it, told me there and then that she would not rest until I was gone, no, until I was *finished*.'

'DS Hudson, Helen Grace may be many things, but she's not vindictive or insecure. Why on earth would she target you like that?'

'Because we used to be lovers.'

Peters, who'd looked dismayed for the majority of this conversation, now turned deathly pale.

'Lovers?'

'Yes, sir. For about nine months or so.'

'Did anyone else know about this?' Peters demanded.

'No, sir. We kept it to ourselves.'

'I bet you bloody did.'

'Sir, I want to go on record to say that I know it was wrong, both the relationship and the secrecy. I hold my hand up to that. But as to what followed—'

'What *did* follow?' Peters asked sharply.

Looking as sombre as he could, Hudson took a breath, then replied, 'Well, I ended it, sir. It was fun to begin with, but in truth, Helen's not who I thought she was. So, I brought things to a close. And she wasn't happy about that, not happy *at all*. I don't know if she felt slighted or rejected or what, but ever since then she's conducted a campaign of harassment against me, with the express purpose of driving me out.'

'And she'll confirm this, will she?' Peters asked sceptically.

'I've no idea what she'll say, but you must have picked up on it, sir. The general sense of disquiet, the problems of morale, the lack of progress. An MIT unit only prospers if the DI and her deputy work hand in glove, yet for the past few weeks, months even, she's ignored, frustrated and belittled me at every possible opportunity. Ask a member of the team – DC Reid, DC Edwards – they'll tell you. We have leads – concrete leads that could have led to an arrest already, that could have put the press pack right back in their place, yet DI Grace deliberately sidelined my lines of enquiry in an attempt to suffocate me.'

'What leads?' Peters demanded bluntly.

'Lee Moffat.'

'Never heard of him.'

'But you *should* have, that's my point. And would've, if DI Grace had taken it seriously as an avenue of investigation.'

'Who is he?'

'He's the prime suspect in the Declan McManus case, who

can also be *directly* linked to the murder of Alison Burris and Martin Hill.'

Hudson could see that this had landed. Peters clearly had no idea that there had ever been another suspect – a really good suspect – in play.

'And DI Grace's theory that the murders are committed by a group of connected individuals?'

'It's fantasy-land. Crazy stuff. We've all had our doubts about DI Grace's wellbeing for a while now, wondering whether she's been doing this too long or been overwhelmed by the current situation, but honestly, this is *something else*. She's clutching at straws with this bizarre theory. Moffat, by contrast, is a career criminal with strong links to three of the victims, who'd be a sizeable scalp if we can bring him to book. And we *will*, I'm sure of that, but only if I'm given licence to pursue legitimate lines of investigation, and if the obstacles to me doing so are removed.' He dared put it no more strongly than that.

'Believe me, sir, I don't want to be the one telling tales and I certainly didn't envisage landing this on you. But we've hit a crisis point and I don't believe any progress can be made unless radical action is taken. But, obviously, that has to be *your* call. All I can do is alert you to the problem.'

Sitting back in his chair, Hudson's expression spoke of fatigue, contrition and sadness. But inside, he was hopeful, excited even. Peters look troubled, which was good, but determined, which was even better. Their conversation had played out as well as Hudson could have hoped and, for the first time since this whole campaign had started, Hudson suddenly felt optimistic, no, more than that, he felt *convinced* that he would win out, that the demise of Helen Grace's career was now all but inevitable.

Chapter 82

It was all over. There would no escape now.

Robert Downing had fought for all he was worth, but it was no use. He wasn't a fighter, wasn't used to this kind of confrontation, nor did he possess the physical strength to counter his weighty assailant.

Bleecher was on top of him, his hands locked around Robert's neck, squeezing as hard as he could. He looked possessed, bug-eyed, his features twisted into an awful expression of rage and violence. He didn't want to kill Robert, he wanted to crush him, to destroy him. Robert could smell his acrid sweat, could feel the spittle landing on his face, could sense Bleecher's desire to kill. This was a man steeped in violence, a man who would do whatever was necessary to survive.

Still Robert struggled, but his arms were pinned down by Bleecher's knees and he could gain no purchase. The gun was in his hand, but was jammed. Even if he could have raised it, it would have gained him nothing and, as Bleecher's hands tightened on his throat, he felt all hope desert him. This was how it would end for him – Bleecher's awful, glistening face would be the last thing he'd see.

Suddenly, unbidden, an image of the twins popped into his head. Would they ever find out what had happened to their dad?

That he ended his life here on a dirty concrete floor? Or would his fate remain forever a mystery, his body buried in some grim wasteland? Would they go to their graves thinking their dad had deserted them?

Robert was losing consciousness, stars studding his vision. Bleecher was swearing viciously, enjoying his triumph, but it was not him Robert saw now, but Freddie and Joshua, laughing, joking, running to him. The image, rather than tormenting him, seemed to rouse him. From nowhere, energy suddenly coursed through his veins and he bucked once more, desperate to throw his attacker off. Bleecher wasn't expecting this sudden resistance and wobbled violently, only just managing to stay on top by shifting his position. Again, Robert bucked, sensing an opportunity. Bleecher swayed backwards, his weight carrying him to the left, and now Robert struck, bringing his knee up sharply into the man's groin. Off balance, unprepared, Bleecher crumpled in on himself, his breath exploding from his open mouth. With one last push, Robert heaved him off, the large man landing with a crash on his back. Even now Bleecher's fingers were scrambling for purchase, but Robert was quicker, scrambling onto his knees, grasping his prone attacker. An arm came up to repel him but Robert batted it away with his spare hand, the hard metal of the gun smashing into Bleecher's stubby fingers. The loan shark cried out in pain, his attention momentarily diverted. Robert didn't hesitate. Raising the jammed gun high above his head, he held it there for a second, screamed out in fury, then brought it down hard, driving it into the man's fleshy face.

Chapter 83

DC Malik was staring up at Robert Downing's house, as Edwards asked:

'Do you want to go or shall I?'

He offered this up even-handedly, as if there was a choice, but it was clear that he had no intention of moving. And though they were the same rank, there was no point in Malik pushing back, of forcing *him* to get off his fat arse. Edwards had been at Southampton Central significantly longer than her and with that came a strange, unspoken superiority. She didn't get that from her female colleagues, of course, just the men, but sadly it was par for the course.

'I'll go. I could do with the exercise ...' she replied quietly.

Smiling thinly, DC Malik climbed out of the car. Though she hated Edwards's casual assertion of authority, there was nevertheless a part of her that was *glad* to be free of him. With each passing day, the atmosphere within the team seemed to be worsening, with individual officers overtly taking sides. Edwards had made no secret of his support and admiration for DS Hudson, but that was not a choice Malik could support. To her mind, Hudson was reckless, self-interested and underhand, a threat to the cohesion and smooth working of the team. She could never voice this in front of Edwards, of course, so perhaps it was better to be out on the street, rather than stuck in a poky car making small talk.

Pacing away from the vehicle, Malik turned to look up at the house. They had been stationed on Wentworth Road for over two hours now, waiting for Robert Downing to put in an appearance. But so far their surveillance had yielded nothing, other than extreme boredom and pins and needles. Stretching, Malik began to walk along the road, pretending to consult her phone, whilst actually casting an eye towards the impressive terraced house opposite.

It was four storeys high and impressively finished, the front door gleaming with the confidence of fresh paint. The house was a status symbol and until recently would have been an attractive family home. But now Downing lived alone, a spurned single dad. What arguments, what disagreements, what events had taken place behind those locked doors that had led the eminent barrister to this sorry pass? Suddenly Malik burned to know, but there was no sign of the man himself, no opportunity to shake the answers out of him. Where was he? Was it possible that even now he was engaged in some desperate act, hoping to pay back those who'd saved his skin? Or was his unusual absence just a coincidence?

Checking her notebook, Malik dialled Downing's home number, not once breaking stride. She was at least forty yards from the house, on the other side of the road, but even so, she heard the landline ring, a faint melodic trill. It rang, six, seven times, then cut out, as the voicemail clicked in. There had been no movement within, no disturbance at all, except the ringing phone. Clicking off, Malik walked a bit further, before casually exercising an about turn, heading back in the direction of the car. Even as she did so, however, her phone started ringing, making her jump. Alarmed, she darted a look towards the house, worried

Downing might be inside, executing a call back, but looking down at the caller ID, she realized it was just her boss calling.

'Guv?' she said quietly, scanning about her to make sure she wouldn't be overheard.

'Just checking in,' Helen Grace replied down the tinny line. 'Any sign of our man?'

'Not yet. We've been here two hours now and there's no sign at all. What would you like us to do?'

'Sit tight. As soon as there's any movement, let me know.'

'Of course.'

Ringing off, Malik headed back to the car with a heavy heart. Surveillance work was always challenging, but this outing seemed even more difficult than usual. If walls could talk, the handsome terraced house would no doubt reveal the full horror of this deadly scheme, and Downing's part in it. But, for now, it was giving up nothing – dark, brooding and as quiet as the grave.

Chapter 84

He turned the key in the ignition, killing the engine. Suddenly he was surrounded by silence – lifeless, suffocating silence.

The car park at the Riverside Park Sports Field was deserted, the athletes long since departed. In one sense this was comforting, no witnesses to clock him or the car, but it was also unnerving and eerie. He longed to be away.

Teasing the door open, Robert hauled himself off the plastic sheeting that clung to the driver's seat, climbing out and shutting the door gently behind him. Then he was on his way. The important thing now was speed. He was covered in blood and would have a hard time explaining his appearance should he bump into a late-night dog walker, or, worse still, a police officer.

Hurrying away, he stepped over a small fence, taking care not to leave any trace. Blood coated his trousers, his shirt, his skin and hair. He felt stained by the act, as if drowning in sin, and wanted desperately to be rid of it. Even now, he could feel the blood congealing on his skin, attaching itself to him. He wondered if he would ever be able to rid himself of the feeling.

Scurrying across the field, he found a gap in the bushes. Pushing through the narrow space, he descended, scrambling down the bank towards the River Itchen. This had always been his intended disposal site, overlooked and out of the way, but in his imagination he'd always appeared calm and collected, clean and untouched, carefully disposing of the evidence. The reality was very different. He was blood-soaked, trembling and scared.

Bleecher was dead. That was the only positive from an evening when pretty much everything else had gone wrong. There was no question he would have left forensic evidence – blood, sweat, prints – at the scene, but as Robert had no criminal record this needn't necessarily count against him, *if* he could cover his tracks. This was why the next few minutes were so important.

Pulling the bin bag from his pocket, he looked around. By the river's edge were a couple of small rocks and he scooped them up, dropping them into the reinforced bag. Now he undressed, tearing off the damp, sticky clothes that clung to him, depositing them in the bin liner. Shirt, trousers, belt, socks, shoes, even underpants, everything went in. Now he added the final, but most important piece, flinging the gun inside, before tying the bag together with a secure double knot. He tested it – once, twice – then flung the bundle as far as he could from the bank. It landed with a satisfying splash, then there was silence once more.

Shivering, Robert wrapped his arms around himself. The original plan had been to bring his change of clothes down to the river with him, but there was no way he could do that – the chance of cross-contamination was too high. So he would have to scurry back to the car naked. At least, if anyone clocked him now, they would think he was a naturist or a pervert, rather than a killer.

Kneeling down by the river's edge, he scooped up some water, desperate to wash off the blood that caked his arms, neck and face. As he did so, however, the sight of his face stopped him in his tracks. He didn't recognize himself – the crazed expression, the unkempt hair and the awful blood spatters on his face.

Suddenly he was back in that room, that awful, airless room, straddling his victim. Bleecher had tried to kill him, would have killed him, but Robert had the loan shark at his mercy, straddling his arms with his knees. Now he was raising the gun, bringing it down hard on the defenceless man's face. Once, twice, three times. He felt Bleecher's nose break, heard the air escaping from his lungs as his victim groaned, but still he didn't stop, pulverizing the man's features. He could feel the blood hitting his face, spraying up at him, a few droplets landing in his eyes, blinding him temporarily. Only then did he stop. Only then did he see the terrible carnage beneath him.

Snapping out of this nightmare, Robert realized he was crying, his tears diluting the stains on his face. Bereft, broken, he scooped up great handfuls of water. He couldn't bear to look at himself anymore, to see what he'd become, so on he went, until his hair was dripping wet, his face frozen by the cold water. Now he did chance a look and this time was pleased to see that no trace of Bleecher remained, he was whole and clean once more.

For now, the job was done. Robert was shivering violently, the cold mixing with shock, so he rose quickly. Casting one last look at the river, which now concealed his secrets, he offered a silent prayer for salvation, then turned, hurrying off into the darkened undergrowth.

Chapter 85

'The light's pretty good in this still and you can see her clearly. It's taken from a CCTV feed from the municipal pool on the Horsham Road.' Helen flicked a look at the officers crowded around her, then carried on. 'From the time-coding we can see that this woman arrived two minutes after Eve Sutcliffe. Eve used the pool twice, sometimes three times a week, usually staying for around forty-five minutes to an hour. This woman—' she gestured to the middle-aged brunette in running gear – 'stayed for less than ten minutes. Certainly not enough time to change, swim and change back again, but still she paid her money and followed Eve into the locker room. Now maybe she just changed her mind, didn't fancy it, but it was on this day, at around this time, that Eve's bag was stolen from her locker.'

She let the team process this, before turning to them once more. Barring Malik and Edwards, all her officers were present, even Joseph Hudson. He had failed to show up this morning for Helen's rallying cry, hadn't even mentioned Grace Simmons's death in her hearing and seemed to have no intention of accounting for his whereabouts during what had proved to be a very busy day. Worse still, he seemed strangely cocksure, apparently unworried that he was about to be exiled back to Cheshire. But she couldn't let herself be distracted by his mind games – not now that they were finally making progress.

'DC McAndrew uncovered another image that I think you'll find useful…' She turned to McAndrew, who stepped forward, pinning another CCTV grab to the board.

'This was taken two days later,' McAndrew told them. 'It's from a camera outside a cash and carry on Oakmont Avenue, just by the Common. This was the evening Eve complained to her parents that she thought someone had followed her through the park. It was dark and she couldn't be sure, so she didn't contact the police, but she was certainly rattled. The camera picked Eve up, walking towards the park around 10.30 p.m. – this person was only moments behind her.'

The officers leaned in, drinking in the image.

'Now obviously you can't see a face because she's wearing a hat, but her build and hair length is a match for the woman seen *both* at the swimming baths and at Lakeside Country Park. And look at the trainers. They're the same brand and dark colour on all three occasions…'

'So far, so circumstantial,' Helen added, nodding her thanks to McAndrew, as she took over. 'But it's an intriguing coincidence and means we can potentially link this individual to the bag theft, the stalking incident *and* Eve's murder.'

A ripple of excitement spread through the team.

'The suspect's name is Amanda Davis. She's a Finance Director at a luxury yacht firm and, more importantly, she's the only person who links all three events…'

'So she was stalking Eve?' DC Reid queried.

'Possibly, though we haven't found any evidence of her having targeted Eve at the girl's house or school, so she'd clearly done her homework, was being careful.'

'So, what do we do now?' Reid continued. 'Bring her in? Put a watch on her?'

'Amanda Davis is currently in Sydney, Australia,' Bentham piped up, 'visiting her parents. All attempts to contact her have so far yielded nothing, but we're going to liaise with the police there. Their CID department should be waking up about now. Obviously, we need to speak with Davis ASAP, so she can account for her movements on the night of Eve's murder, but the critical thing now is the question of motive. Amanda Davis jetted off to Australia the morning after her husband's funeral – Alastair Davis was beaten to death in what appeared to be an aggravated burglary just over a fortnight ago.'

Several eyes strayed to the murder board, where Alastair Davis's gaunt features stared back at them.

'DC Osbourne has done a bit of digging on the couple,' Helen continued, ceding the floor to the junior officer.

'So on paper they look like a successful, aspirational couple,' Osbourne told the assembled officers. 'She's got a high-powered job, he's a self-made tech millionaire. They've got the big house, fancy cars and are regular, generous entertainers. They lead a very visible, very public life, promoting themselves and their exploits on social media constantly, but there was a side to their relationship that remained hidden.'

Osbourne handed out photocopies of a charge sheet.

'You'll see from this that, three months ago, Mrs Davis complained that she'd been sexually assaulted, a charge she later withdrew. I've redacted the identity of the alleged attacker, but it wasn't her husband. A similar thing had happened eight months previously – an accusation made, charges readied, then the complainant withdrew the charge.'

'Under duress? From the attacker?'

'Or from her husband. It's interesting that both alleged attacks took place in sex clubs, during sex parties or prearranged orgies.'

'They were swingers?' DC Reid asked, suddenly interested.

'Looks that way. We can see from his bank records that they had memberships at several sex clubs. Interestingly, there's no record of *her* having paid for or set up any of these memberships, and from the brief conversations we've had with members of Southampton's swinging community, it appears Alastair was the driving force in terms of their attendance—'

'So she was coerced into doing it?'

'Quite possibly. It's certainly intriguing that the charges she made – which were detailed, specific, angry – were suddenly and swiftly withdrawn. It's notable, also, how regular their visits to these clubs were – three, sometimes four nights a week. How she managed to do that, often staying out all night, *and* hold down a demanding job is hard to fathom.'

'What are we saying?' Hudson demanded, finally speaking up. 'That she wanted her husband dead? She wanted out?'

'Well, that's what we need to work out. Which is why running her to ground is—'

'If that's really what you're saying,' Hudson interrupted, 'then surely by extension we should be re-examining Alastair Davis's murder too?'

'That's exactly what we *are* doing.'

'Because if you follow your theory through,' Hudson continued, 'then it suggests that some random punter with no connection to Davis lay in wait in his living room and stove his head in at the first available opportunity.'

'Well, I wouldn't put it quite like that,' Helen replied calmly, turning to face him. 'But that's precisely what I'm suggesting.'

Already Hudson was shaking his head.

'So how far does this go back? Are we going to have to

re-examine every murder in the last six months? The last year? Two years? And why? Why are all these people suddenly doing this?'

It was a blatant challenge to her theory, to her authority. One Helen couldn't duck. So, turning to face Hudson, she replied: 'That is what I intend to find out.'

Chapter 86

She retreated to her office, shutting the door carefully behind her. Helen's brief spat with Hudson had been aggravating and concerning, but nevertheless it underlined some important avenues of investigation, or, put another way, some gaping holes in her theory.

Helen felt certain she'd correctly identified the perpetrators of the most recent murders – Goj, Raeburn and now Davis – potentially having enough evidence to warrant the arrest of those who were still in the land of the living. But the CPS would want more before they'd consider charging them. Motive *could* be established in all three cases, presuming they were right about the unhealthy dynamic between Amanda Davis and her husband, but the CPS lawyers would want more on the connection between the attackers. Had they communicated? How did they know each other? How were the murders planned, coordinated, executed?

This last point continued to nag at her. All of the murders were meticulously conceived, the perpetrators making only fleeting appearances in the victims' lives before making their move; so fleeting, in fact, that it would have been possible to miss their involvement entirely, had it not been for a couple of lucky breaks. They didn't appear at their victim's place of work or at their homes, yet still seemed to know their movements well enough to steal a bag, to follow them through a park, to commit a murder unseen and undetected. There was no sign that they'd been tailing them, stalking their prey over weeks and months, so how were they so clued up on their timetables, their movements? Also, why did they appear in their victim's lives in the days preceding the act itself, why not just murder them and have done with it? Davis had robbed Eve, then stalked her, before finally taking a hammer to her in the darkened park. Goj had tried to break into McManus's flat, then stole his laptop from his car, before committing his deadly arson attack. Belinda Raeburn had made an abusive phone call, daubed a swastika on Hill's house, before attacking the unfortunate man in a deserted alleyway...

Even as Helen thought this, it struck her: the rule of three. Each of the perpetrators had committed three acts of criminality, culminating in murder. Looking at it now, there could be no question that there was a pattern. This further unnerved Helen, more evidence of the precise, meticulous nature of this chain of killings, but it threw up some interesting questions. Why three acts? What was the purpose of this mini campaign of intimidation and violence? Was it simply to unnerve the victims, so that they would complain to friends, the police and so on, drawing attention to the *alleged* motive for their eventual murder? Was this done deliberately, then, to make Martin Hill's murder look like a racist attack, or Eve Sutcliffe's murder look sexually motivated, when actually they were nothing of the kind?

It was a seductive explanation, but even now another possibility occurred to Helen. It was notable that the three acts increased in criminality and unpleasantness as they unfolded, the first 'crime' being remote, focusing on the victim's personal possessions or property, the second being more risky for the perpetrator, involving breaking into a car, daubing someone's home with graffiti or following a young woman through a park. In any of these situations, the perpetrators could have been challenged, surprised, confronted even. The risk level was high, though of course not as high as in the third challenge – the murder itself – where the danger of arrest, injury or even death was acute. Was this escalation deliberate? Did it mean something? Was it possible the three acts had been deliberately designed like that as some kind of *test*?

Helen was so lost in thought that it took her a moment to realize she was no longer alone. Looking up, she saw Joseph Hudson standing in front of her. Alarmingly, the door was closed and he had a determined look on his face.

'Can I help you, DS Hudson?' Helen asked, angry to have been wrenched from her thoughts.

'Oh, you know how you can help me, Helen,' he replied. 'Step aside. Hang up your boots and make way for a younger man.'

'Get out of my office,' Helen spat back, anger flaring within her.

'I'll go when I'm good and ready. I have something to say first.'

Helen was tempted to bawl him out, to drag him from the office, but the blinds were up and they were clearly visible to the rest of the team, so, instead, she swallowed down her fury.

'You see, I know all about your little cosy chat with Simmons. How she wanted to help you whilst shitting on me from a great height. But here's the problem, she's gone now. Your protector's *gone* ...'

He smiled as he said it. Helen had to use every ounce of strength to restrain herself from punching him in the face.

'And guess what? Her signed directive to HR about the incident is gone too. I burnt it this morning.'

Helen couldn't conceal her astonishment, or her disgust.

'Have you gone mad?'

'Not at all, I've never been able to see more clearly,' Hudson purred. 'To see what needs to be done, what *will* be done. You see, I don't think Chief Superintendent Peters will be so forgiving about your errant behaviour – sleeping with fellow officers, misusing your powers to force them out, doing secret deals with Simmons, lying, cheating, conniving to save your own skin, all whilst failing to make arrests on *any* of the current investigations. I think he'll take a very dim view of the whole situation and will be forced to take *action*.'

'In your dreams.'

'Too right. I *have* dreamed of this, dreamed of the moment when, finally, I'll have you on your knees...'

He said it salaciously, his twisted desire clear, making Helen feel nauseous. How had she ever had feelings for this creep?

'You know, once I admired you, Helen,' he continued, moving in closer. 'Then I wanted to be with you. But now—' he moved in still closer, until their noses were only inches apart – 'I'm going to destroy you.'

Chapter 87

She froze on the spot, suddenly alive to the danger. Her key hovered by the lock but she made no move to slide it home, Lilah's gaze drawn to the reflection in the glass. Her front door had glazing in it, to allow light into their dingy hallway, but now, with no illumination within, it caught the light from the lamp posts, providing a reflected view of the street behind her. Lilah hadn't noticed anything untoward as she hurried home, but now she clocked it. A shape on the far side of the street. A shape that looked very much like someone sitting in a car, watching the house.

'What the fuck –?'

She knew she had to stay calm. It might be nothing, she might be imagining things, so sliding the key into the lock, she hurried inside. Normally, she would have thrown on the lights in the hall, the living room, the kitchen – she hated darkness – but instead, she dropped her bag and hurried upstairs. Crossing the landing, she crept over to the bedroom window and, using the heavy curtains as cover, peered back down on the street below.

Even as she did so, her heart skipped a beat. There was no question about it now – there were two people sitting in a car not forty yards from her house. The lights were off, the engine stilled and, though she couldn't see their faces, she could tell by the angle of their bodies that they were looking at her house, looking at *her*.

Were they police officers? If so, what were they planning? Were they about to spring the trap? Rush up the steps to arrest her? Or were they just going to wait and watch? What did they *know*?

A dozen jumbled thoughts tumbled over one another. Had they been following her earlier, when she stole the car, when she deliberately ran those red lights under the watchful gaze of those traffic cameras? No, there had been no obvious reaction to these minor violations, no one pursuing her down the empty city streets. What about when she parked the car? Had she been clocked then? No, she was sure she would have noticed something; the refuse tip where she'd secreted the car for the night was so remote, there was no way anyone could have tailed her there without drawing attention to themselves. So why were they here? How had they got a *lead* on her?

It didn't make any sense, but their presence in the dark-blue Mondeo was a clear sign that something had gone wrong. Did they suspect her of some kind of involvement in Martin's murder? Did they have positive evidence of his ill treatment of her? Or did they have some inkling of what *she* was planning? Was such a thing even possible? Sweat was forming on her brow as the questions continued to cannon around her brain. There were no answers to these nagging anxieties, no indication of what the police knew or what they intended to do. But as Lilah stared out into the darkness at their shadowy, menacing presence, one thing was beyond doubt:

The stakes had just got a lot higher.

Chapter 88

'What the hell did you tell her?'

'I told her the truth, Robert. Something you used to be acquainted with.'

'What *exactly* did you say?'

Now Alexia hesitated, as if uncertain how to respond to her ex-husband.

'Well?' Robert barked.

'I told her about McManus...'

'That you instructed your lawyers to spy on your own husband?'

'With good reason, as it turned out.'

'Meaning?'

'Do you really want me to spell it out?'

She cast an anxious eye towards the boys, who were sitting on their Trunkies watching TV, occasionally casting anxious glances towards their parents.

'This is bullshit,' Robert breathed, angry and unnerved.

'So you deny that you were hooked on drugs? Crystal meth, crack, whatever—'

'Of course I do. I would never put myself in that position, put the kids in danger in that way.'

'Oh Robert, would you look at yourself...'

It was said more in sadness than in anger, which made it all the worse. Alexia did seem genuinely upset by his appearance and he didn't need to cast an eye into the hall mirror to know why. He had spent ages cleaning himself, trying to make himself look respectable, but he had scratches on his cheek and looked decidedly odd, his aged Nike top zipped up to his chin. His croaky, hoarse voice didn't help either, making him sound fractured and husky.

'What's happened? What have you got yourself into?'

'Nothing, I've told you. I ran into a low branch when I was jogging, I really don't know why you're making such a fuss.'

'Why do you think?' she hissed, angry, upset. 'I have to think of the boys.'

'They are *safe*,' Robert fired back at her. 'They've always been perfectly safe, nothing bad is going to happen to them.'

'And what happens when Helen Grace comes back? When she arrests you?'

'She's not going to arrest me. I've done nothing wrong.'

'So you can honestly look me in the eye and tell me that *none* of what she suggested is true? That you had no involvement in McManus's death?'

'None, whatsoever, I swear.'

'I don't believe you.'

'Then I'm wasting my time here. Boys, we're going!'

There was a brief pause, then: 'Can we finish this?' Freddie cried, from in front of the TV.

'No, we need to go NOW.'

The words shot out, harsh and unpleasant, provoking grumbling compliance, as the TV was reluctantly switched off.

'I don't want you taking them...'

As Alexia spoke, she grabbed his arm, determined to detain him. Angered, he took a step forward, shoving his face into hers.

'Try and stop me.'

Tears filled her eyes, but there was fear there too.

'They are my boys – legally, emotionally, in every way that matters – and they are coming home *with me*.' He fired the words at her, only now becoming aware that the boys were standing directly behind him.

'Come on, then, lads, say goodbye to your mum and we'll be on our way.'

He walked past Alexia to the front door, not once looking back. He heard tearful farewells, whispered words, then the sound of the boys' Trunkies being dragged along the ground. Marching across the drive, Robert unlocked the car, opening up the boot. Moments later, their bags were safely stowed away, the boys strapped into their seats. Only now did he chance a look at them, but the sight that greeted him broke his heart.

Both boys looked sad, even tearful. But worse than that, much worse, they looked scared.

Chapter 89

Helen pushed out into the smoker's yard, slamming the door shut behind her. The scrubby space in a forgotten corner of the station was deserted, the noise of the door echoing around the gloom. Pulling her cigarettes from her pocket, she lit one up, inhaling deeply. She hadn't had a smoke in over a week, but she needed one now.

Joseph Hudson's ambush had been totally unexpected and was all the more effective for it, raising urgent, worrying questions. Was Hudson planning to go to Peters with his charges? Was it possible he'd already done so? And if so, on whose side would Peters land? Helen had never been close to the station chief, could sense his distrust of her, and feared she already knew the answer.

Helen was furious with Hudson, but also with herself – she should have expected some reaction to Simmons's death, to the loss of her protector – but she was also shaken. She hadn't expected Joseph's response to be so swift or so determined. It wasn't just what he'd said that had alarmed her, he was prone to exaggeration and his desire to oust her from Southampton Central had been clear for a while now. No, it was the way he'd said it that had shaken her. He looked unhinged, wild, as if he would stop at nothing to bring her down, whatever the personal cost might be. Helen had faced many formidable foes over the years and knew from experience that the most dangerous adversaries were the ones who had nothing to lose.

The nicotine was having the desired effect, thank goodness. Even now, she felt a little calmer, a little more focused. In times of professional stress, she had usually sought out Grace Simmons, but of course that wasn't an option now. The poor woman was lying in a mortuary across town, her life force snuffed out. Which only left one person. One person she knew she could rely upon.

'Hello, stranger. How are you?'

Charlie's voice – warm, informal, friendly – nearly undid Helen. But she kept her voice steady as she responded.

'I'm OK, thanks. You?'

'Yeah, all good.'

'And how are my favourite girls?'

'Oh, a nightmare. You can have them, if you want...'

Even as Charlie said it, Helen heard shouting, then laughter in the background. It didn't sound like a nightmare to her, it sounded like a happy family home. Something she had never possessed and probably never would.

'Hold on, I think they're coming my way,' Charlie continued. 'Would you like to say hello?'

'Of course, but I was wondering... would you mind if I popped round?'

'Now?'

'If it's not convenient, that's fine, but—'

Helen was already backtracking, feeling foolish and weak. Her nerves were still jangling and she desperately wanted to be amongst people she could trust, but it was pathetic to intrude upon another family like this. But even as she was about to offer an apology and retreat, Charlie replied:

'Well, the wheels have already come off, so we might as well make a party of it. When can you get here?'

Helen felt a flood of relief, overjoyed that for a brief time she might be afforded some sanctuary.

'That's great. I can be there in about ten minutes?'

But even as she said it, her phone started vibrating. Surprised, she looked down to see that DC Bentham was trying to get hold of her. Part of her was tempted to ignore his summons, but as usual her better side won out.

'Actually, can I buzz you back in a minute, Charlie? I've got another call coming through.'

'Sure thing.'

'Thanks.'

Clicking off, Charlie accepted Bentham's call.

'DI Grace.'

'Sorry to bother you late in the day, guv—'

It was a call Helen had received countless times over the years and she knew what was coming next.

'—but we've found a body.'

Chapter 90

Alan Peters sucked in his cheeks, staring down at the carnage in front of him.

'Sorry to be the bearer of bad news, but I thought you needed to see it.'

Peters barely registered Abigail Miller's words, his eyes fixed on the copy of the *Southampton Evening News* that lay open on his desk. Miller had skipped over the front page, directing Peters' attention instead to the double-page spread inside. Here a deeply unflattering picture of Helen Grace stared back at him, flanked by a lengthy article from Emilia Garanita. The photo of his most senior officer was terrible – it appeared to have been taken near the Martin Hill crime scene and showed Grace looking dazed and confused. And beneath it was the damning headline: 'Boozing whilst losing'.

Alarmed, Peters speed-read the article, the gist of which was that the famously abstemious Grace had cracked under the pressure of recent events, hitting the bottle and reverting to damaging, self-destructive behaviour. Usually Peters would have dismissed this rumour mongering out of hand, but now he hesitated.

'Do you think there's any basis to it?' he muttered gravely, turning to Miller. 'I mean, where's Garanita getting this stuff from?'

'The article says "a source close to the investigation", which, I'm guessing, means someone in Grace's team. Whatever *she* says, we know there's a leak. We also know there have been issues of morale in the team, grumblings that she doesn't have a grip on things. So, yes, I think we have to ask ourselves if alcohol may be a contributing factor.'

Peters said nothing, staring down at the hapless image of Helen Grace.

'We also have to consider how we're going to respond. This is a full-on assault on the competency of both DI Grace *and* Southampton Central. We can't let it pass, we have to respond, because, trust me, these headlines are going to make waves.'

'You think?' Peters retorted sharply. 'You can bet your bottom dollar I'll have the mayor *and* the police commissioner chewing my ear off tonight.'

'Exactly, so we need to speak to DI Grace, see what she's got to say.'

'Well, I would if she was here, but there's been another murder.'

'You're kidding me?'

Miller blurted out her response, unable to conceal her shock. But Peters shot her such a dark look that the media liaison chief backtracked.

'Anyway, like I say, you'll need to hear Grace's side of the story before you can make any *firm* decisions. Perhaps if she co-operates, comes clean, then there might be a way we can manage—'

'And why would she do that? I expect her to deny *everything*, to hunker down and try to ride it out. That's what I'd do, if I were her.'

'So how are we supposed to respond? Just sit on our hands, whilst the body count mounts day by day?'

Angered, Peters turned to Miller, unimpressed by her bluntness, but this time Miller showed no signs of retreating.

'Listen, sir, I know operational command isn't my area, so tell me to shut up if you want, but facts are facts. We've made no arrests, have no tangible leads and DI Grace is currently stalking a local barrister of unimpeachable good character. We're a laughing stock, a joke.'

Peters couldn't deny Miller's damning assessment of the situation. Suddenly he felt exhausted and depressed by the whole damn thing. He had never faced challenges on so many fronts before, nor felt so powerless to remedy them.

'Now, you've shown admirable loyalty to DI Grace, as a good station boss would. But if that faith isn't repaid, if it's felt in the wider world, even in her own team, that DI Grace has lost her authority, her equilibrium, her ability to lead, then what's to be gained by continuing to support her?'

It was a fair point, one Peters couldn't refute.

'I hate to say it, but perhaps it *is* time for a fresh pair of eyes?' Miller ventured.

'You think I should cut her loose?'

It felt odd, but also a relief, to say it out loud.

'I think you should protect the reputation of Southampton Central,' Miller replied firmly.

And there it was, in a nutshell. This station was *his* domain, his career, his legacy. Failure to grapple with the lawlessness and violence gripping Southampton would be *his* failure, the end of what had been a highly successful career. But even as he thought this, he hesitated. To dispense with Helen Grace would be highly controversial and problematic, given her track record and standing within the Force. Could he really make that call?

Perhaps he *had* to make that call, given how far the rot seemed to have spread?

He was so deep in thought, caught on the horns of this impossible dilemma, that he was oblivious not only to Miller's presence, but also to the sudden appearance of his secretary in the doorway. A sharp rapping on the door now snapped him from his introspection.

'Sorry to bother you, sir ... it's just that I've got the police commissioner on the phone and he seems *very* keen to talk to you.'

And in that moment, Chief Superintendent Alan Peters had his answer.

Chapter 91

Helen ducked underneath the police tape, marching towards the uniformed officer.

'Where is it?' she demanded, dispensing with all pleasantries.

'Down the corridor and to the left. DC McAndrew's managing the scene.'

Nodding, Helen took in the dilapidated building in front of her. It was an awful, cheerless place, a cheap, prefabricated unit that had been designed for maximum profit with minimum investment. Clearly the storage business had never got off the ground, however; the building which had been quickly thrown up now well on the way to falling down. Helen eyed the darkened doorway with mistrust, it looked like the entry to the underworld.

Ducking inside, she held up her torch, the powerful beam illuminating a long, lonely corridor. Her shoe coverings made a strange swishing sound on the dusty floor, almost as if some dark spirit was whispering to her, making her shudder. She was not prone to being spooked, but something about this place unsettled her. Perhaps it was the hangover of her confrontation with Joseph earlier. Perhaps it was the overriding sense of decay, of corruption, that clung to the place. Or perhaps it was just her knowledge of what lay in store.

Hurrying down the corridor, she angled left. And now she heard voices. The characteristic purposeful voices of officers on site. She hastened towards them, soon finding herself standing opposite DC McAndrew in what appeared to be some kind of storage unit-cum-office. There were papers everywhere, an upturned table and, amidst the wreckage, a man lying flat on his back.

'Any idea who it is?'

'No ID on him,' McAndrew replied, shaking her head. 'But the laptop might tell us something.'

Nodding, Helen stepped past her towards the body. The victim was a portly, middle-aged man, probably in his late forties. If this was his office, he clearly didn't care much for appearances, a trait that seemed to extend to his person. He was dressed in dirty jogging bottoms and a velour tracksuit top which had seen better days. His trainers, too, were tired, one of them hanging off his left foot, presumably having been dislodged during the struggle. Clearly there had been an epic confrontation – this was obvious from the upturned furniture and scattered personal effects, but also from the numerous cuts and scratches on the man's hands. But it was not these injuries that Helen's eye was drawn to. Instead her gaze settled on what remained of the man's face.

It was an awful sight. The man had not just been beaten, he had been crushed. His nose was broken, his eyes sockets fractured, his teeth knocked clean out. Whoever had done this must have been driven by rage or desperation, such was the brutality of the attack. The man's whole face seemed to have sunk in on itself, like a morass of crimson quicksand. He didn't even resemble a human being anymore, just a body which had once had life. It was hideous to behold and Helen shuddered once more.

Whoever had done this didn't just want to kill their victim. They wanted to obliterate him.

Day Six

Chapter 92

'Come on, people. I want photographs completed and the images on the system within the hour, please...'

The please was an afterthought. Politeness was not DS Hudson's strongpoint, a fact that shone through now, as he strutted the crime scene, handing out orders and ultimatums. Helen Grace was elsewhere this morning, paying a visit to Robert Downing, meaning DS Hudson *was* the SIO on site, but that didn't make it any easier to swallow. Then again, Meredith Walker had never liked this presumptuous, self-regarding upstart. How she longed for the return of DS Charlie Brooks.

Shooting a knowing look at the photographer – which was returned with interest – Meredith resumed her task. The main confrontation site had been extensively photographed at first light, meaning Meredith could get in amongst the papers, the personal effects, not to mention the victim himself. She had sifted the blood-spattered documents, the empty Lucozade bottles and Pot Noodle tubs, but had found little of any interest, so had then turned her attention to the laptop instead. She assumed this belonged to the victim and had hoped it would furnish them with useful information concerning identity or motive, but even her cursory initial examination put paid to that idea. Repeated attempts to turn it on yielded no response and, teasing up the damaged keyboard, Meredith soon discovered why. The circuit board, the battery, everything within the laptop's titanium casing seemed to have melted. It would have to be taken away and examined at the lab, but Meredith already had a strong suspicion about what might have caused the damage, the white residue of what looked like industrial acid clinging to the microchips and processors.

Disappointed, Meredith bagged and labelled the computer, before turning her attention to the dead man. It would be for Jim Grieves to determine cause of death, though this appeared to be in little doubt, but still there might be important clues that could be garnered even now, before the body was taken away. Kneeling down next to the man's devastated face, Meredith ran an eye over his torso, arms, hands. There didn't seem to be any obvious hair or fabric in his hands, though Jim might well harvest DNA from under his nails or in the creases of his palms, as there had clearly been a sustained struggle. She was intrigued to note, however, that his scruffy velour tracksuit top had been torn in several places – analysis of these rips could well yield important clues, especially if they had been torn by hand. Meredith now found herself making a mental inventory of the clothes she would pore over later, once they had been removed from the body – the tracksuit top, the shabby jeans and, of course, the trainers. If the victim had met his killer elsewhere and brought him here, then dirt, pollen or vegetation caught in the grooves of his soles might help them uncover his last movements, perhaps even the identity of his attacker. Turning away from his shoes, Meredith resumed her examination of the torso, spotting first a bulky watch on his left wrist, and then a gold medallion that lay helpless on his traumatized neck.

It was a strange piece, at odds with the cumbersome watch and ostentatious rings on his fingers, being rather small, even insignificant by comparison. She would have expected this guy to go for something bigger, something more in the Tom Jones line, but, handling it now, she realized that it was small and also extremely light. In fact, to her it felt very much as if it must be hollow.

Intrigued, she cupped it in her hand, running a finger gently round the edge, until she found a catch. Teasing it with her finger, she gently increased the pressure, until the face of the medallion suddenly popped open. Curious as to why this kind of bloke would be wearing a locket, she peered inside. Immediately, she had her answer. Because nestling neatly within the locket, safe from prying eyes, was a tiny microchip.

Chapter 93

'This is an outrage. A bloody outrage ...'

Helen let Downing's words wash over her. The warrant she had just handed him gave the lie to his protests.

'This is a family home, *my* family home.'

'It's the principal address of a key suspect and, as you well know, we have every right to search it.'

Sensing that Helen could not be browbeaten, Downing changed tack.

'Look, Helen, I've got the boys here. They're freaking out ...'

'And I'm sorry about that. Could Alexia take them? I can ask our FLO to call her on your behalf.'

Downing hesitated, clearly torn. He didn't want to have to call his ex, but nor did he want a stranger to do it.

'All right, I'll call her, but this is all a massive misunderstanding.'

The scratches on his cheeks and hands suggested to Helen that he was lying, but she said nothing by way of response.

'If you could just give me five minutes ...'

As he spoke, he made to leave the room, but Helen laid a hand on his arm.

'I'd prefer it if you did it here.'

This clearly wasn't a request, so with great reluctance Downing complied, moving away from her to conduct a hushed conversation in the corner of the room. As he did so, half a dozen officers in sterile suits, gloves and masks walked past him, fanning out to conduct a fingertip search of the property. From the landing above, Downing's two boys watched on, open-mouthed.

Finishing his call, Downing returned to Helen, all signs of friendliness, of bonhomie, well and truly gone.

'She'll be here in ten minutes,' he said tersely.

'Then I suggest we get the formalities over with.'

Stepping forward, Helen lowered her voice, conscious of the audience above, delivering the standard caution in hushed tones.

'Robert Downing, I'm arresting you on suspicion of murder. You do not have to say anything, but it may harm your defence if you do not mention when questioned something you later rely on in court. Anything you do say may be given in evidence.'

Downing surely knew these words by heart, but they seemed to have a profound effect on him now. The blood had drained from his face; he seemed shocked, flustered and afraid.

In fact, he looked every inch the condemned man.

Chapter 94

'Get out of my sight. I can't even bear to look at you...'

Carol was incandescent, every word dripping with bitterness and bile. Belinda wanted to calm her, to console her partner in some way, but what the hell could she say? Every accusation was true, every insult justified.

'Please, Carol, I never meant to hurt you...'

'By fucking one of your students. *Again.*'

'It was a brief affair. It meant nothing.'

'Like the time before? And the time before that?'

Crossing to the wardrobe, Carol flung open the doors. Snatching up a suitcase, she hurled it at Belinda, before scooping great piles of her clothes from the rail and dumping them on the floor.

'Please, Carol, you don't have to do this...'

'Yes, I do. In fact, I should have done it years ago.'

'We can get through this.'

This weak assertion got the withering response it deserved. Belinda wanted it to be true, wanted to believe they could recover from this latest betrayal, but she knew in her heart that it was over. Already this morning, she had been suspended from her post at school, following a formal accusation of impropriety by

Eve Sutcliffe's parents. It was perhaps fitting that her relationship should die too, sacrificed on the altar of her lust.

Gathering up her clothes, Belinda laid them in the case, but they felt heavy, leaden, even, the task almost beyond her.

'Carol, I want you to know that I do love you.'

'Oh please, spare me.'

'That I always *will* love you.'

It was true. She did love her. It was just not the kind of love Carol needed or craved. In truth, it never had been. Carol had always been a worshipper, rather than a soulmate, a solid, dependable partner who would always love more than she was loved. When Belinda had finally abandoned her erratic, neglectful parents all those years ago this had seemed enough – it was the stability and dependability she craved – but it had never really satisfied her, if she was honest with herself.

'And I'm desperately sorry for having hurt you. You deserved better, much better.'

Carol continued to stare at her, her eyes pinpricks of cold, grey hatred.

'Look, I know we're through. That I've hurt you too many times, but you should know that the years we spent together meant something. All the good times we had together, that wasn't a lie, and... and I hope that somehow in the future we might be friends again, because... because I would hate to lose you...' She felt a lump in her throat, then tears sliding down her cheeks. She was desperate, desolate, suddenly fearful that she would never see her loyal, loving partner again.

'Well, it's too late. Because you have.'

Grabbing the suitcase, Carol marched from the room, almost running down the stairs, in her haste to be rid of her. Belinda followed, watching as her irate partner wrenched open the front door, tossing the bag outside.

'Carol, please—'

But this time her lover didn't let her finish, grabbing her by the collar and manhandling her out of the house, screaming at her as she did so.

'I never want to see you again, as long as I live ...'

Belinda wanted to stop her, wanted to beg for a further hearing, but she didn't get the chance, the front door slamming firmly shut in her face.

Chapter 95

She peered down through a gap in the curtains, her heart thumping. They were still there, parked just across the street, watching and waiting.

Part of her had hoped the police would be gone by now, that it was just a one-off, a spot check to ensure she hadn't left the area. But in truth Lilah Hill knew that they would still be there, patiently plying their trade, hoping for her to make a mistake. That could be the only explanation for their sudden appearance, some misguided notion that she would incriminate herself in Martin's murder. That was crazy, of course, his death had been nothing to do with her, but that must be why they were spying on her. They couldn't have any idea of her current situation, of what she was planning to do. Could they?

She had hardly slept, a dozen scenarios, each worse than the next, filling her thoughts. She'd gone over and over the events of the last few days, minutely analysing her actions to see if somehow she had unwittingly drawn attention to herself. Dismissing this as improbable, she'd then started to wonder if the whole thing was a trap, some sick game deliberately designed to entrap and destroy her. But that seemed preposterous too, all the evidence suggesting that this thing was *real*. Which left her in a difficult place.

The police were on the wrong scent. They rightly sensed that her relationship with Martin was flawed – DI Grace suspected him of being violent and controlling – and that she might therefore have had some hand in his murder, even if she hadn't committed the act herself. So far, unless they bent the truth or fabricated evidence, they would find nothing against her that would stick. But their presence *did* present practical problems.

Today was the day, the moment when she would kill, when she would perhaps finally be free, but how could she do so with a police escort in tow? It was ridiculous, almost funny, the idea of them trailing her, hoping to pin one murder on her, whilst witnessing another. In reality, however, it was awful, beyond unfortunate, a crazy cosmic coincidence that made her feel sick.

What should she do? There were other ways she could leave the house, of course, other than by the front door. She could venture into the garden, scale the back wall... but would they be waiting for her there too? If she was caught, sneaking away down the back alleyway, how would she explain herself? Even if they didn't apprehend her immediately, how would she shake them off? She wasn't trained in these things, she wasn't a *spy*, for God's sake.

The curtains fluttered in front of her and, looking down, she realized that her hand was shaking. She was still clutching the phone – part of her was tempted to hurl it to the floor, to scream out in anger and distress, but there could be no room for weakness, not today. The deed couldn't be postponed, it had to be now, everything had been leading up to this moment. But could she really go through with it, with the odds now stacked against her? Was she brave enough to face arrest and exposure to see this thing through? These were questions that couldn't be ducked, that must be confronted head on.

It was decision time.

Chapter 96

'All I'm saying is that sometimes you have to make *choices.*'

Joseph Hudson lingered over that last word, looking at each of the three faces in turn. He was talking quietly but decisively, and it was clear that Edwards, McAndrew and Reid were taking in every word, alive to the importance of both this meeting and Hudson's message. They'd known something was up when he'd pulled them away from operational duties to a private meeting in the Lamb and Flag, a quiet boozer a stone's throw from Southampton Central – now they knew what.

'I'm not saying that DI Grace hasn't done good work in the past or that she hasn't been a good leader, boss, even friend to you—' Hudson let his gaze linger on Ellie McAndrew, who of all of them was the most likely to harbour doubts about participating in this coup. 'But you have to live in the present. To deal with the situation in front of you. Change is coming and it's coming *fast.* Perhaps today, perhaps tomorrow. As you are the most experienced officers in the team, I didn't want you to be blind-sided. Nor did I want to be underhand. DI Grace *will* be called upon to account for her attitude, her actions, and it may be that you are asked to corroborate my version of events, specifically that she deliberately ignored a viable suspect and took great pleasure in belittling me and dismissing valid lines of enquiry.'

There was no immediate reaction, but Hudson felt he was on safe enough ground to continue.

'Now, maybe DI Grace will fight her corner, try to cling on, maybe she won't, but either way, I wanted to outline to you how *I* see things going forward. And I wanted to ask for your support. Because I can't achieve anything unless I have my best people with me.'

He smiled warmly, receiving encouraging nods from Reid and Edwards in response. McAndrew, however, hardly reacted. She clearly understood the way the wind was blowing, but perhaps was finding it difficult to let go.

'Change is hard, I get that,' he continued in an emollient tone, 'but it's also natural and beneficial. People rise, people fall and everyone's career has a shelf life. Helen Grace's has come to an end and, whilst that's sad, we have to look forward, to a better, brighter future. So, the only thing you have to ask yourself is whether you want to be *on* that train . . . or whether you want to go down with a sinking ship. It's not an easy choice for you, I'm sure, but it *is* a clear one.'

He let that notion settle for a moment, before adding:

'Which is why I'm asking you to be courageous. To back me at this crucial moment for the team, for the station. Why I'm asking you to *do the right thing*.'

Chapter 97

'You're lying to me, Robert.'

The lawyer maintained eye contact, but didn't respond to Helen's accusation. He'd hardly said a word since entering the interview suite.

'You love your boys to distraction, I know you do. And you live for the time you spend together. Yet suddenly yesterday you dump them on Alexia and rush off to the office, putting your work schedule ahead of *their* needs...'

'It wasn't what I wanted, of course it wasn't, but I had no choice,' he replied, reluctantly.

'Why? I've spoken to the clerks and it wasn't like there was any emergency. A case that suddenly needed fielding. Your appeal had been postponed, I hear, so—'

'I'm just very behind because of all the stuff that's been going on with Alexia. I've been distracted, I admit it. I've taken my eye off the ball and, as I've got a couple of big cases coming up, I felt I needed a bit of extra time to get on top of things...'

'So how long were you at the office last night?'

'Three or four hours?'

'Any of the clerks see you?'

'No, it was late. In early, out early, that's how they work.'

'You didn't go anywhere else? To pick up some files? Get something to eat?'

'No, I've told you, I was there all evening.'

Helen let the lie float in the air for a moment, before replying, 'You own a Mercedes S Class, don't you?'

'You know I do.'

'Registration number OE18 RDY?'

'Yes...'

'It's a prestige vehicle, very desirable. For affluent professionals like yourself, but also thieves...'

'What's your point, Helen? I'd like to get back to the boys.'

'My point is that the S Class has a built-in transponder. A transponder that's constantly sending out information about the car's whereabouts, just in case it falls into the wrong hands...'

And now for the first time, Downing looked uneasy.

'Following your arrest, we ran a check on the vehicle's movements. And guess what? Your car *was* in the city centre near your office, but only momentarily, then it moved on, heading out to Thornhill, where it was stationary for well over an hour. From there, the car returned to your wife's house, but not before it was stationary for a while near the River Itchen. Now... you say you were at the office all night, so you can understand my confusion.'

Robert Downing stared at her, refusing to be intimidated, but Helen had him on the rack, staring right back.

'You'll perhaps be aware that a man was murdered in the Thornhill area last night. His name is Gary Bleecher, he's a loan shark. Anyway, he was beaten to death in a vicious attack.'

'Don't know him.'

'Never met the guy?'

'Course not. I don't need to borrow money. I don't know this man, and I certainly wouldn't have attacked him.'

'So where did all those scratches come from?'

Downing paused, instinctively glancing down at his hands.

'You're scratched on your face, your hands, and, despite your best attempts to conceal it, you clearly have significant bruising on your neck. So why don't we skip the denials and cut to the chase. What happened last night, Robert?'

'I don't know this man,' he muttered in response.

'Doesn't mean you didn't kill him. I'm guessing it was a pretty violent struggle, perhaps he fought back, tried to strangle you. If I was in that situation, if I felt my life was in danger, I think I'd do pretty much anything to protect myself.'

'It wasn't me.'

'Robert, look at me.'

For a minute, Helen thought he hadn't heard her. Then, slowly, he raised his gaze to meet hers.

'You know me, you know my reputation. So you know this isn't going to go away. I think you went to Thornhill last night. I think you murdered Gary Bleecher—'

'No, I'd *never* do something like that. You must know that, Helen.'

'So why were you there? Why drive all that way? What happened to you?'

There was a long pause, Downing staring at the ceiling, the door, at the walls, anywhere except at Helen. Then, finally, he lowered his eyes and now, as he spoke, Helen was surprised to see tears in his eyes.

'Look, I – I don't want the boys to know about this, nor Alexia, but the honest truth is that – that I went to Thornhill to end my life. I'd reached the end of the road – emotionally, mentally, physically. I've tried to be a good dad, a good husband, but I've failed. Failed in every way—'

His voice was quivering with emotion now, his whole body shaking.

'So I drove as far away from the house, the office, my life, as I could. There are areas out there where no one goes, where you can be totally alone. And I sat there in my car for an hour, writing a note to the boys, to Alexia. There are several abandoned buildings there where I thought I might do it, but then some guys turned up – kids, skaters, druggies, I don't know – so I changed my mind, drove to the woods near the river instead. I don't know why I chose that spot, it was just somewhere familiar, somewhere I knew. I got the rope out of the car and I did it, I hung myself—'

Now he gestured to the bruising, pulling down his tracksuit collar to reveal the full discolouration around his neck.

'And if I'd got it right, I wouldn't be here talking to you now.' His eyes were brimming with tears now, but he soldiered on. 'But I didn't. The rope broke and I fell to the ground—' He held up his damaged hands, touched his face. 'And as I was lying there, I knew. Knew that I couldn't do it, couldn't leave my boys. In spite of everything, I had to make it work somehow...'

He looked at Helen through misty eyes now, expecting sympathy. But Helen's face betrayed no emotion.

'It's a sad story, Robert. And beautifully told. But I'm afraid I don't believe a word of it.'

He continued to hold her gaze, but did Helen glimpse a flash of anger behind the tears?

'You're a man who has everything to live for, everything to fight for. A good job, lovely kids, a bright future. We've spoken to Alexia – *I've* spoken to her – on a number of occasions and she says you've been uncharacteristically bullish of late. Moreover, when you turned up last night, she said you were far from despairing. Angry, aggressive, perhaps even in shock, but certainly not suicidal.'

'Well, she would say that, wouldn't she?'

'Why?'

'To blacken my name, of course. She'll do everything in her power to drag my reputation through the gutter, so she can steal my boys from me—'

'Is that why she hired Declan McManus to spy on you?'

'I'm sorry?'

'We spoke before about McManus; you insisted he'd contacted you looking for work. But that wasn't true, was it? The truth is that he'd found out about your drug habit and hoped to extort money from you...'

'For God's sake, Helen, what is this?'

'Was it crystal meth? Were you really that far gone, Robert?'

'No, of course not, I – I'd never...' But suddenly he seemed to have lost his natural eloquence.

'You see, I think this is how it works,' Helen continued. 'Amar Goj killed Declan McManus to get you off the hook, stealing his laptop and torching his files in the process. Suddenly you were in the clear; you could happily look forward to your day in court with Alexia, confident in the knowledge that she'd have nothing on you. But your salvation came at a price – and that price was Gary Bleecher.'

'This is lunacy, sheer lunacy—'

'I'm assuming someone was badly in debt to Bleecher, needed him *gone*. You had no connection to the loan shark, the murder wouldn't be traced back to you or the instigator, except that Bleecher had a microchip on him, with details of all those who owed him money, details we're currently poring over. It should reveal who had a motive for killing him and ultimately help us link the instigator of this murder back to *you*.'

'No, no. This has *nothing whatsoever* to do with me.'

'Oh, come on, Robert. Give it up. Your DNA will be *all over*

Bleecher's body. Blood, sweat, skin cells. You won't be able to wriggle out of this one.'

Downing shook his head repeatedly, violently, but said nothing.

'I know you killed him. And I know why.'

'Listen to yourself, Helen. This is beyond crazy. I don't know the guy, I have no motive.'

'But you do, we've established that. Following the break-up of your marriage, your drug use escalated. McManus knew that he had the power to destroy you—'

'No.' The word spun out of his mouth, hard, aggressive, definitive.

'Alexia's obviously already been telling tales, so I won't deny that I was a user,' he continued tersely. 'Cocaine, ecstasy and the like. And yes, I may have had a few bad experiences after she left, but I am not an addict. I was never an addict. I had my issues, but I dealt with them. I got treatment and now I'm clean. I've been clean for weeks now, so no, I had no motive for killing anyone, for wanting anyone dead.'

He sat back in his chair, his arms folded in defiance. Something he'd said, however, had piqued Helen's interest, rendering his fervent denials irrelevant.

'Can I ask where you got treatment?'

Downing continued to stare at her, his eyes narrowing slightly.

'Or rather who treated you?'

There was a long, long pause, the silence in the room suddenly oppressive and claustrophobic, then the lawyer replied: 'No comment.'

Chapter 98

'Excuse me, coming through…'

Two startled secretaries stepped aside, making room for Helen to pass. She was running down the corridor, desperate not to waste another second. Reaching the lift bank, she punched the button, then seeing that the lift was stuck on the fifteenth floor, charged through the doors into the stairwell.

Down, down, down, she flew, taking the steps five at a time. Colleagues saw her coming and made way – they had grown used to her over the years and knew not to impede her. In under a minute, she had reached the ground floor, bursting through the doors and racing towards the custody area.

'Where's the fire?'

Anthony Parks was smiling at her, that customary twinkle in his eye, but Helen had no time for banter.

'Robert Downing…'

'What about him?'

'Have you got his custody details to hand?'

'Course. What're you after?'

'I want to know what he had on him when he was brought in.'

'Not very much, if memory serves—'

He busied himself, punching the keyboard with pudgy fingers.

'Phone, car keys, wallet, a pair of reading glasses, that was about it.'

'Anything else?'

'No, nothing – though he did have some stuff in his car. The search team bagged that when they went through it this morning. I've got the details here ...'

Helen watched him intently as he typed.

'Here we go. A road atlas, a hi-vis jacket, warning triangle ...'

'Anything personal, Anthony?' Helen interrupted.

'A couple of things. There was a book of photos, family snaps, I believe. And I think they found a bottle of pills in the glove compartment.'

'What kind of pills?'

Parks peered at his screen once more. Helen realized she was holding her breath, even as he eventually replied.

'Naltrexone.'

Helen breathed out, relief and excitement coursing through her body.

'Where is it? Where's the bottle?'

'I've got it here, give me two ticks.'

He walked off to the secure storage area, returning a moment later with a small bottle of pills, encased in a transparent bag.

'Any good to you?'

Helen snatched it from him, eagerly reading the label. And there was the answer to his question, in black and white. The name of the drug, the quantity and regularity of the dose and beneath it the name of the prescribing physician.

Doctor Alex Blythe.

Chapter 99

'Yes or no? It's a simple question.'

Alex Blythe opened his mouth, but nothing came out. Initially hostile to her intrusion – he'd had to send one of his clients away mid-session – he now looked flabbergasted, stunned by the volley of questions being fired at him.

'Look, if I have to pull you in to do this at Southampton Central, I will,' Helen continued.

The young psychiatrist clearly didn't like the idea of *that*, finally finding his tongue.

'Yes, Robert Downing was a patient of mine.'

'For how long?'

'Three months or so.'

'Drug addiction?'

A slight pause, a shred of resistance, of professional modesty, still remained. Blythe shot a troubled look down at his loyal springer spaniel, who stared happily up at him, then muttered: 'Yes. He'd got himself hooked on crystal meth, couldn't shake the habit. He'd even tried heroin on a couple of occasions – I think that's what eventually scared him into seeking help.'

'And Belinda Raeburn?'

'Look, what's all this about, inspector? I'm not comfort—'

'Answer the question.'

Her tone was cold and unyielding. Blythe blinked, unsettled, worried, before reluctantly responding:

'Yes, she was with me for a couple of months, no more than that.'

'And what was *her* issue?'

'Well, there's a very complicated name for it, but basically it's love addiction. She was hooked on the adrenaline, the buzz, the joy of new relationships – that heady feeling you get when you realize that someone else shares your feelings.'

'And did she happen to mention that these new "loves" were underage?'

'I'm sorry?'

'Fifteen-year-old girls, possibly even younger on occasion ...'

Now all resistance seemed to evaporate, the young psychiatrist stunned by what he was hearing.

'No, of course not. She said they were young women, nineteen, twenty years old—'

'Well, they weren't. They were girls. One of whom was brutally murdered ten days ago.'

'But – but surely you don't suspect Belinda of—'

'What about Amanda Davis?'

He stared at her for a moment, wrong-footed by the sudden change of tack.

'Was she a patient of yours too?'

'Yes,' he conceded, hollow now. 'A long-term patient.'

'What for?'

'Well, Amanda – Amanda was an extreme case. Hyper sexuality linked to her bipolar condition. People popularly call it nymphomania, but there's no such thing, not really. When she was in a downward spiral, she was very down, would hardly leave the house. But when she was in a manic phase, she was pretty much out of control. She'd always substituted sex for affection and during her manic upswing she would deliberately seek out extreme sexual encounters.'

'In sex clubs?'

'Clubs, dogging sites, swingers parties. During those phases, she would sleep with as many people as she could, do whatever they wanted, losing herself in the experience. Obviously, I counselled her against it, it wasn't safe, but she found it very hard to kick the habit. Not least because she had a domineering husband who encouraged her wild behaviour.'

'And what about Lilah Hill?'

Alex Blythe broke off his account, staring at Helen as if she was practising some form of witchcraft, such was her ability to penetrate others' secrets.

'Yes, yes – but she's a relatively new client. We've only scratched the surface of her issues.'

'And what's her form of addiction?'

'Alcoholism, a fairly serious case of it.'

And there it was. All the suspects, all the perpetrators, neatly lined up in a row. All of them receiving treatment from Alex Blythe.

'You're the link.'

The words hovered in the air, terrorizing the young psychiatrist. 'The link to *what?*'

'All these individuals have committed murder or have plans to do so.'

'No, no. I've told you before, that's *impossible*...' He was desperate, insistent. 'You tell me Amar Goj is a killer, and I say he can't be. Whatever trouble he was in, it's not in his nature to hurt others.'

'The evidence doesn't lie.'

'And the others? Amanda, maybe, yes, I can see her getting into a difficult situation, a dark place – but Lilah? Robert?

Belinda? These are well-educated, professional people with their whole lives ahead of them. However troubled they were, however desperate, they wouldn't *kill*...' Blythe protested.

'You'd be surprised what people can do when they're backed into a corner. My only question is who made them do it.' There was a brief pause, as the weight of her accusation made itself felt.

'You think – you think *I'm* involved in this?'

'What other explanation is there? You're the only one who knew their secrets.'

'But I was trying to *help* them.'

'I only have your word for that.'

'No, no, you're *not* pinning this on me. I've done nothing wrong.'

He looked petrified, shrinking into himself as he spoke. Where he had once seemed charismatic and impressive, now he just seemed weak, pitiful even.

'So how *do* you account for it?' Helen continued, keeping up the pressure.

'I can't...'

'Then you're the link.'

'No, I'd never use confidential information against my clients. It goes against everything I believe in—' He was staring at her imploringly, but he could sense her disbelief. 'I've dedicated the past fifteen years of my life to helping people. Why would I undo all that by doing something so – so sick?'

'That's what I intend to discover.'

This bald statement of fact seemed to undo him, the fight in him suddenly evaporating.

'Right, can I suggest that we continue this discussion at Southampton Central—'

'Look, if I co-operate, can we – can we try and keep my name, the name of this practice, out of the papers?'

It was said more in hope than expectation.

'Co-operate?' Helen queried.

'Yes, if I tell you what I know, can we—'

'We don't do deals, Dr Blythe. You'll tell me what you know, freely and willingly, or I'll charge you with obstruction of justice.'

Another hammer blow, the psychiatrist looking ever paler.

'Fine. If you're not going to talk, I can put the cuffs on you right now—'

'I had a data breach, OK?'

'I'm sorry?'

'Three months ago, I – I had a data breach. Someone, some organization, gained access to my systems.'

'How?'

'Malware. I received an email purporting to be from a scientific journal that I subscribe to – only it wasn't that at all, it was a way of someone getting past my firewall, remotely accessing my computer, my files, once I'd clicked on it. It was a stupid, stupid mistake; I hadn't noticed that the email address didn't quite match the regular one, and I let them in.'

'What then?'

'Then nothing. I was aware that my system had been breached, that files had been downloaded, and I was expecting whoever did it to make contact. To demand payment, protection money, whatever the scam is these days. But I never heard anything, still haven't ...'

Helen stared at him, weighing up his words. 'Why didn't you report it?'

'Why do you think?'

Helen was taken aback by the aggression in his response.

'I've spent *years* building up my practice. What do you think would have happened if I'd reported the breach, if it somehow got out that my patient files had been accessed, *stolen* – all my clients' most private confessions, problems, issues out there in the public domain? I would have been ruined. People come here because they need to talk, talk without being judged. They don't visit me so that their secrets can be paraded for all the world to see...'

'So you did nothing? Said nothing?'

And now she saw his shame.

'Look, I should have said something, of course I should. But I was scared. Scared of what it might mean for me. For *them*...'

'So you kept your mouth shut to protect yourself.'

'Yes.'

'And as a result of your cowardice, I've got five bodies to deal with.'

The full horror, the full *cost*, of his actions seemed to sink in now, the stricken psychiatrist looking up at Helen, as he concluded: 'Please believe me, inspector, I *never* meant to hurt anyone, but I didn't know what to do for the best. I just hoped it would go away, that it would pass—' he seemed to be in physical pain, anguished by what he'd done – 'and I never, never in my worst nightmares thought it would lead to *this*...'

Except it had. And now both of them would have to deal with the consequences.

Chapter 100

Helen pushed through the doors, spilling back out onto the street. Immediately, the fierce heat hit her, almost stopping her in her tracks. Today seemed to be even warmer than yesterday, the temperature searing, suffocating even, a fitting accompaniment for her troubled mood.

She had come here convinced that Alex Blythe was responsible, preparing herself for a showdown that she felt sure would be difficult, perhaps even dangerous. If he was the mastermind of this sinister game, who knew how far he'd go to protect himself and preserve his liberty? But there had been no confrontation, just capitulation, the excuses and explanations spilling from him freely as he stared down the barrel of his ruin.

Did she believe him? Was it possible that he was telling her the truth? Her head said no – he *had* to be the link – but her heart argued against it. He had seemed genuinely shocked, as if he couldn't quite believe what he was being told. Moreover, he had put up a passionate and spirited defence of his clients, insisting they weren't capable of murder. Helen suspected he was right to do so, that they *had* been law-abiding members of society for most of their adult lives. But perhaps he didn't know what she knew, didn't know just how far they had fallen.

This was not a scenario she wanted to countenance. If his

shock was genuine, if he *was* telling the truth, then her life had just got a lot harder. Helen had at first believed that the perpetrators somehow knew each other and had made their grim arrangements between themselves. Then she'd believed that it was Alex Blythe who was pulling their strings. Now another, even more sinister possibility presented itself. Was there some unseen nemesis out there, making these vulnerable people dance to his or her tune? Committing multiple acts of murder without ever revealing, or implicating, themselves? And if so, who?

The thought made Helen's head spin. Tracing a cyber hacker would be virtually impossible, especially if they had taken basic precautions, such as routing their operations via another country. They could do this, carefully concealing their tracks, and still operate unhindered in the UK. How then to track them? How had they communicated with Goj, Raeburn and Downing? Could this be used against them? Maybe, but it seemed like a fond hope – the architect of all this bloodshed and misery having remained perfectly concealed until now.

Reaching her bike, Helen paused. Instinctively, she wanted to believe that Blythe was lying – and she would waste no time in getting a warrant to examine his computer, his systems, to test his story – but one thing gave her pause for thought. Earlier, when she was speaking to Robert Downing, her adversary had looked *scared*, the experienced lawyer appearing more intimidated by the mastermind of this enterprise than by Helen, even though she was backed by the full force of the law. And she had seen that same look on Alex Blythe's face just now, as she pressed her case. Was it possible that he knew more than he was letting on? Knew just what the shadowy figure behind all this mayhem was truly capable of?

Turning now, she looked up at the psychiatrist's first-floor office. And, to her surprise, she found the callow psychiatrist looking down at her, watching her retreat, as if wanting to be sure that she was really gone. Curious, she held his gaze, hoping to see something that would reinforce her suspicions – some anger, some defiance, perhaps even a sense of triumph. But there was nothing like that. Blythe appeared rigid, ashen, tortured. He did not remotely resemble a victor, a predator, an evil genius. Quite the opposite, in fact.

He looked *haunted*.

Chapter 101

She stood by the battered metal drum, staring down at its grim contents. The park was always busy in summer, meaning the bins were overflowing with rubbish. This suited Lilah down to the ground and she didn't hesitate, digging down through the discarded Coke cans and sandwich wrappers, carving out a deep hole amidst the detritus. Knowing full well that she would excite people's curiosity if spotted doing so, she retrieved the phone from her jacket pocket.

This thing, this small piece of technology manufactured thousands of miles away by faceless low-paid workers, was both her route to salvation and her captor, and she was pleased to be getting rid of it. It had burnt a hole in her pocket for the last two days now, a deeply uncomfortable reminder of the terrible enterprise she was engaged in. But its use was now at an end, the story nearly finished, so removing the back cover, she fished out the SIM card. Scrubbing it with a disinfectant wipe, labouring to remove any sign of her ownership, she snapped it in half, enjoying the hearty 'click' as it fractured in her hands. She dropped one half into the bin, before pocketing the other half for later disposal. Then, piling a heap of rubbish on top of the snapped card, she dismantled the phone, removing the battery from the handset, preparing to dispose of them too.

Chancing another look up, she was dismayed to find that someone was approaching – a young mum chatting happily to her toddler. There was no opportunity to delay, to savour her moment of freedom, so now she dropped the phone parts into the metal container, piling more trash on top of them to obscure them from view. Darting a glance to her left, she saw that the young mum was oblivious, engaged in earnest conversation with her little boy. Still, it wouldn't do to take chances, it would be better if she wasn't seen at all today, so taking one final look at the bin, she turned on her heel and hurried back towards the car.

Chapter 102

'How the hell did they lose her?'

Helen couldn't conceal her incredulity or her anger.

'Well, they had eyes on her at home last night and again this morning,' DC Osbourne answered hurriedly. 'They saw movement on the first floor around 9 a.m. Since then, there's been nothing.'

'Have they tried calling the house?'

'Several times, but no joy. Mobile too, but it's turned off. Twice DC Bentham has knocked on the door, intending to pass himself off as a colleague of Martin's, but there was no movement on either occasion, no sign that anyone's in the house. The curtains are all open, so it's not like she's gone to ground. Anyway, they're worried that she might have slipped out somehow.'

'Where were they stationed?'

'Out front, in the road.'

'What about rear access?'

'There's no back gate, just a high wall. It's possible she may have left that way...'

'Did they *not* have someone stationed there?'

DC Osbourne paused, wary of antagonizing his boss still further. Helen knew she was being unfair, that she was shooting the messenger, but her interview with Alex Blythe had left her rattled, as if she was once more losing a hold of this troubling investigation. Now one of the principal players, a woman who was perhaps even now plotting to commit murder, had gone missing.

'No, I don't think they did. They felt it was unlikely that she would attempt that escape route, as it was quite physically challenging, plus they reasoned she'd have no need to do so, as she didn't know she was being watched. They had been very cautious in their approach—'

'Clearly not cautious *enough*. She was obviously aware she was being tailed and found a way to disappear without being clocked. Now why would she do that unless she was up to something?' But even as she vented, the storm blew itself out. 'Look, sorry, I know it's not your fault but—'

'But we need to find her.'

'Exactly. We might only have hours to stop her doing something awful, so we need the team to pull out all the stops. Phone triangulation, traffic cameras, live CCTV feeds, plus we need every beat copper issued with a recent photo of her, so we can track her down. If we can do that, then maybe we can save a life and perhaps find out what the bloody hell is going on, what mess Lilah and these others have got themselves in. Talking of which, do we have any idea where Belinda Raeburn is?'

'We think she's somewhere in town, though we haven't pinpointed exactly where. I spoke to her partner – well, her ex-partner, this morning. She wasn't exactly in the mood to talk – it sounds like Raeburn's lost her job at the school and been booted out of the flat she shared with Carol Shepherd—'

'So she's lost everything.' Even as she spoke, Helen's mind was turning. 'Which may help us,' she continued quickly. 'Belinda Raeburn killed to protect her livelihood, her career, her relationship...'

'But now she's got nothing to lose.'

'Right. If anyone's going to be inclined to tell us what, or who, is driving this, then she is. Same drill as Lilah Hill, I want the guys on the street notified and I want the team to track down every friend, relative and colleague she knows locally. Is she staying with them, hunkering down until the storm blows over? Let's check out hotels, B&Bs, but also the main travel hubs too, in case she's decided to leave town. If you think she *is* still here, then let's check out what her regular commitments were – classes and appointments she'd keep, duties she'd attend to, regardless of her current situation. We need to do anything and everything to try to locate her. Have you got all that?'

'Sure thing...'

'Then let's get to it.'

Helen was looking at Osbourne quizzically, puzzled as to why her urgency was not translating to her junior, who looked uncertain, even bashful. And now Helen clocked something – Osbourne was not staring nervously at *her*, but instead at something just above her right shoulder. Turning, she realized why he had suddenly clammed up.

Chief Superintendent Alan Peters was standing in the doorway.

Chapter 103

'You cannot be serious?'

Helen couldn't contain her horror.

'We're so close to cracking this thing, you can't possibly take me off the case—'

'I'm afraid the decision's already been made. I should say that it's not one I made lightly—'

'You're firing me?'

It didn't seem possible, but it was true. The station chief was standing in her office, clutching a copy of the *Southampton Evening News*, apparently intent on relieving her of her command.

'I'm suspending you, pending a full internal enquiry. Once that's completed, we'll review your position here, then take a decision. In the meantime, DS Hudson will assume operational command—'

'No, no, no, no, no...'

Helen hadn't anticipated this – it was immediately clear to her that she had been badly outflanked. Hudson clearly had Peters' ear and was suddenly in the ascendency, meaning she'd have to fight back with everything she had.

'He's not the right person for the job; he cannot lead the team—'

'Why?'

'He's not suited to it, in terms of temperament, experience or capability—'

'You spoke very highly of DS Hudson when you appointed him,' Peters countered quickly.

'That was then. Now I know different.'

'Maybe, but from where I'm standing, DS Hudson appears to be a committed and effective officer. In fact, he's the only detective on the team who's come up with a credible suspect for these murders.'

Once again, Helen was taken aback. Clearly Peters had been well briefed, Hudson giving him chapter and verse on *his* lines of enquiry.

'Lee Moffat is not a credible suspect,' she hissed.

'I don't see why not. He's violent, amoral, has a clear motive for the McManus murder, not to mention strong links to the Alison Burris killing *and* that of Martin Hill…'

'It's circumstantial at best—'

'Which is presumably why you kept it from me?' Peters' face was set, his anger clear.

'I didn't bother you with it, sir, because it doesn't stack up.'

'You know that for sure, do you?' Peters persisted. 'You've personally looked into it, discussed it with your deputy, weighed up the evidence…'

'Well, no,' Helen admitted. 'I don't need to; I know it's a blind alley.'

'Copper's hunch, eh?'

'Not all. I'm just going on the facts, the leads we've unearthed. We have a much clearer picture of what's going on now—'

'So, if Lee Moffat isn't behind it, who is?'

Once again, Helen paused, surprised by the aggression behind the question.

'We don't know for sure, but we are certain this is all the work of one individual...'

Peters exhaled, long and loud, shaking his head. 'So we're no further on than we were when we last spoke.'

'I didn't say that. My team is working flat out and—'

'Can I ask if there are any *other* reasons why you might feel Moffat is not a credible suspect?'

'No, like I said, it's just a question of weighing the evidence and—'

'So your dismissal of that line of enquiry has nothing to do with your personal animus against DS Hudson?'

'I'm sorry?'

'For God's sake, Helen, we're way past the time for lies and subterfuge. I know that you and Hudson were lovers.'

Peters nearly shouted his accusation, several heads jerking up in the incident room beyond. Helen stayed stock-still, in mute shock, stunned that Hudson had confessed *this* to Peters.

'It's true that we were together briefly...' she stuttered.

'Something else you saw fit to conceal from me.'

'Which was wrong of me. In fact, the whole thing was a stupid, stupid mistak—'

'A mistake which has poisoned relations within the team,' Peters interrupted. 'Fatally undermining its effectiveness at a critical moment in the policing of this city.'

'No, sir, that's not true—'

'And all because you were angry that he had called time on the relationship, because you were embittered and upset—'

'No, that's not how it was at all.'

'And determined to force DS Hudson out.'

And now Helen saw it. The simple cunning of Hudson's plan. Getting in first with Peters, playing the victim, painting her as the vengeful woman scorned. Now she saw the full extent of the forces ranged against her, and how weak her position was.

'Look, sir, I don't know what DS Hudson has told you, but it was *me* who ended the relationship, because of what I'd learned about Joseph Hudson's character. And I was happy to do so, believe me—'

'So you've never threatened him?'

'Absolutely not.'

'Never told him he should move on?'

Helen paused, once more thrown on the defensive. 'On a couple of occasions, I suggested that it might be better if he transferred to another station, perhaps back to Cheshire...'

'So he *is* telling the truth.'

'No, I – I never threatened him. It was a suggestion, nothing more.'

It sounded feeble and Peters was quick to pounce on it. 'I'm afraid I don't believe you, DI Grace. Where DS Hudson has been frank and contrite, you have been evasive, deceitful and uncooperative. In order to further your own ends, you have attempted to destroy a decent man's career, in the process leading the team on a wild-goose chase, dragging the reputation of this station through the mire.'

He tossed his copy of the *Southampton Evening News* onto the desk. Helen had seen the headlines the previous night, but had ignored them. Now it was hard not to stare at the vicious character assassination, Emilia Garanita's damning headline 'Boozing whilst losing' goading her from the desk.

'Which is why I have no choice. I'm officially suspending you pending an—'

'No, sir, you can't, please—'

'I've made up my mind,' he concluded savagely. 'DS Hudson's in, you're out.'

Chapter 104

'You're kidding me?'

Emilia Garanita laughed as she said it, staggered by what Hudson had just confided.

'Why? Do you find it odd that someone would be attracted to me?'

'No, of course not,' Emilia recovered quickly. 'I just didn't know Helen Grace was capable of forming meaningful connections with another human being.'

'Well, she is. And it was meaningful, for a time.'

'And how long did this go on for?'

Emilia scribbled a brief note in her pad, but never took her eyes off Hudson. They were hidden away in her car, out of sight, out of mind. She was certain he was supposed to be elsewhere, but he seemed increasingly careless of his professional duties, intent only on bringing his superior down.

'Eight, nine months or so—'

'Right,' Emilia murmured, genuinely surprised. 'And you managed to keep it a secret from your colleagues all that time?'

'From colleagues, friends, even *you*,' he replied with a hint of triumph. 'Relationships between serving officers aren't completely forbidden, but it is severely frowned upon, especially if you're at the same station. It's even worse if you're in the same team, working together every single day.'

'Of course, I can see how that would get – complicated. So, why did it end, if you don't mind me asking?'

Her politeness was all pretence. Having stumbled upon this gossip, she fully intended to ring every last drop of juice from it.

'I called time on it,' Hudson replied quietly. 'I thought I had the measure of her, but I was wrong. She turned out to be controlling, paranoid, even violent...'

'Go on,' Emilia cooed, scribbling furiously.

'Anyway, she was enraged when we broke up, made it clear to me that I had no future at the station. She started giving me grunt work, duties barely fit for a DC. She also openly denigrated me in front of fellow officers whilst spreading rumours about me behind my back, trying to turn the team against me.'

Emilia doubted this was true, but wrote it down nevertheless. First-hand testimony like this was worth its weight in gold, however dubious its veracity.

'What did you do?'

'Well, I challenged her on it, said I would take it up with HR, and that's when she threatened me.'

'Threatened you how?'

'She promised to ruin me. She told me that not only would she drive me out of Southampton Central, but she would also ensure that I never worked for the police again.'

'But why? Why all this hostility towards you?'

'Because I wouldn't go quietly. Because I was prepared to stand up for what's right. Remember, I'd done nothing wrong. We were in a relationship, then we weren't. Fair enough, shit happens. But to victimize me like that, to try and force me out, *destroy me* like that, simply because I'd tired of her attentions? Think what would happen if this was the other way around, a male boss victimizing a female lover. He wouldn't last ten minutes.'

'And nor should DI Grace,' Emilia responded knowingly. 'We live in an equal opportunities world these days.'

'Putting aside the morality of it,' Hudson continued, 'she's guilty of misuse of office, abuse of her position, constructive dismissal, harassment. They'll throw the bloody book at her. I've already complained to Peters, things are in train—'

'Which way do you think he'll jump? Will he back her?'

'I doubt it. He's a straight man, a time server. He's always disliked Helen's disregard for established protocols and rules. You ask me, he'll be happy to get rid of her.'

Emilia stopped writing, stunned by what she was hearing. She had come today hoping for some more juicy titbits, but had got more than she could possibly have bargained for. Illicit relationships, abuse of power, a celebrated officer who'd gone rogue ... It had the makings of a story that would run and run, one which might very well bring the curtain down on Helen Grace once and for all.

Chapter 105

'Please, sir. I'm asking you to give me more time. A day, two days at the most, to bring this thing to a close.'

Helen had never begged a superior for *anything*, but she had no choice. Her career, her future, was hanging by a thread.

'Can't be done. I've let this situation drift for too long.'

His tone brooked no argument, but Helen had to try.

'Look, sir, none of what you've been told is true. DS Hudson has twisted the facts to suit his own ends. It was *me* who ended the relationship, *me* who was threatened as a result. I went to Grace Simmons about it, she spoke to DS Hudson, wrote up a report for HR backing *me*—'

'So where is this report? I haven't seen it.'

'Joseph Hudson got hold of it, destroyed it before it could be submitted.'

It sounded far-fetched, even ludicrous, prompting Peters to shake his head in weary disbelief.

'Even if that *were* true, why did you not come to me about it, then?'

'Because I thought I could handle it myself. But obviously I misjudged DS Hudson's determination, his desperation to bring me down.'

'And I'm to take your word for that?'

'Of course not, sir, but I *am* the senior officer here, one who's achieved a great deal since I took over the team—'

'Who has also repeatedly broken the rules, ignored protocols, frequently placing both yourself and your fellow officers in danger.'

'Yes, my methods are a little unorthodox—'

'Who's barely escaped suspension *on a number of occasions* previously and who has a penchant for killing suspects, rather than bringing them in.'

'That's not fair,' Helen returned, enraged at the accusation.

'You're a renegade, Helen. A loose cannon. Which is why we end up with headlines like *this* . . .' He cast an angry glance at the newspaper on the desk between them.

'But you must see what's going on?' Helen countered forcefully. 'What this is.'

'It's a fucking PR disaster,' Peters replied curtly. 'That's what it is.'

'For the last few months, DS Hudson's been conducting a campaign against me. He's the reason these stories keep appearing, why Emilia Garanita is always in the right place to snap an unflattering photo and stick the knife in—'

'That's a very serious allegation, DI Grace,' Peters warned.

'Sir, you asked me before if I had doubts about anyone in the team, if I felt one of my officers might have been feeding information to her. I'll admit I wasn't entirely truthful in my response. I *did* have doubts and now I know for certain – Joseph Hudson is the leak.'

Peters didn't look minded to accept this accusation. He had his view of events and didn't want it muddied by her counter claims.

'He's been manipulating this situation from the off—' she cast an arm towards the murder board – 'waiting for the right moment to strike, using all this bloodshed and tragedy for his own selfish ends. All because he can't bear being bested by a woman, because he can't bear being rejected.'

'As I said previously, DS Hudson tells a very different story.'

'I bet he does.'

'He says you confronted him in the bike park two nights ago, explicitly threatening to run him out of Southampton Central...'

'No, that's not true. Not one single word of it.' The words erupted from Helen, loud and decisive, silencing Peters. 'He threatened *me*. That's the sort of man he is. The kind of man who'd abandon his wife and child, who'd sacrifice colleagues and friends on the altar of his own ambition. I knew that well enough by the time I confronted him in the bike park, which is why I specifically mentioned the drinking during our argument that night.'

'You've lost me,' Peters replied tersely, looking confused and angry.

'I thought Hudson was leaking information to Garanita, so I decided to test that theory. I didn't walk into that ambush totally unprepared.'

'You're saying you deliberately *lied* about the drinking?'

'*Of course.* I haven't touched a drop in over thirty years, you must know that.'

'You mentioned it purely to see if that "information" would be leaked to Garanita?'

'Exactly. And this is the result.' She gestured to the paper, but Peters didn't take his eyes off her.

'Even so,' he continued, for the first time looking a little uncertain, 'I only have your word for any of this, leaving us no further on.'

'Not exactly,' Helen countered. 'Joseph Hudson *is* lying, he *is* the leak. And I can prove it.'

'How?' Peters demanded, incredulous.

In response, Helen placed her phone on the desk. 'Because I recorded the whole conversation by the bike park, in the hope of exposing Joseph Hudson. That was my plan all along.'

Peters looked incredulous, but before he could respond, Helen continued: 'Would you like to hear it?'

Chapter 106

Helen marched away from her office, leaving a stunned Peters in her wake. Her superior had listened to the recording twice, was still digesting its contents, but Helen didn't have any more time to waste. She had a killer to catch.

She made good progress across the room, moving rapidly to the murder board. She needed a moment to gather herself, to refocus her thoughts on the investigations in hand, to provide the leadership the team so desperately needed. But she knew it would be far from easy. In truth, she was still reeling from the events of the last few hours.

She had been the victim of the grossest possible betrayal, an attempted coup by her own deputy. The effects of this would be profound and damaging, not least on her own officers, several of whom might have been seduced into supporting his bid for power. She had her suspicions as to who they were and she would have to deal with them later; her first priority was to neutralize Joseph Hudson. Whether Alan Peters would help her was unclear, he was still processing the morning's revelations, but he had at least granted her a stay of execution. Meaning she was still at liberty to deal with Joseph Hudson herself if she had to.

Resolved, determined, she completed the last few steps to the murder board, wrenching her mind back to the case in hand, to her conversation with Blythe, to the telling questions that remained unanswered. But even as she did so, she spotted DC Bentham approaching, a look of excitement on his face.

'Good news, ma'am. We've got her. We've got a trace on Belinda Raeburn.'

Chapter 107

Helen roared through the city streets, weaving in and out of the congested traffic.

The team had done their homework, unearthing a local friend whom Raeburn was staying with, through him discovering that Raeburn was currently at her weekly class at the Pure Box gym on Ogle Road. According to the receptionist there, Raeburn had signed in for her eleven o'clock class as usual, but would be leaving shortly, as the class had just finished.

Firing a look at her bike's display, Helen saw it was two minutes past the hour. All thoughts of Hudson, Peters and the rest now well behind her, she upped her speed, swinging wide past a van, before executing a wild U-turn, doubling back so that she was now heading the right way along the Western Esplanade. It was not a manoeuvre she would normally attempt, but the one-way systems in the centre of Southampton were designed to hamper progress and she could ill afford delay – if they lost sight of Raeburn now, they might spend the rest of the day hunting for her. Her phone had been off for over twenty-four hours now, presumably in an attempt to avoid her troubles, making it hard to keep track of her. So it was imperative that they bring her in. Gentle pressure, strategically applied, could crack this investigation wide open, Helen felt sure of that. Raeburn had nothing left to lose, whilst Helen held all the cards, all the leverage, not least the prospect of charges relating to the murder of Martin Hill and her inappropriate relationship with Eve Sutcliffe.

Swinging left onto Portland Terrace, Helen raced down the wide avenue. Ogle Road was just up ahead and Helen signalled to turn, praying privately that Raeburn was still in the vicinity. Even as she did so, however, she saw the teacher emerge from the mouth of the street, slinging her gym bag over her shoulder, before heading down Portland Terrace.

There was no question that it was Raeburn – the svelte figure, the long blonde hair, the smooth, swinging gait – so Helen increased her speed. Would Raeburn crack straightaway or would this be a hard-fought encounter? Either way, Helen just wanted her back in the interview suite, under lock and key, confronting the many questions that lay in wait for her.

Helen was bearing down on her fast, the teacher unaware of the danger, but now Raeburn surprised her, checking up and down the road, before stepping off the pavement. Helen had assumed she'd head further into town, but in fact she now seemed to be heading for the NCP car park. Was she parked there, planning to head off elsewhere? Or was she planning to cut through it to Westquay? If so, Helen would have to dump her bike and pursue her on foot, which would complicate matters. Concerned, Helen started scanning around for somewhere she could park, but as she did so, she noticed something else.

The road had been clear when Raeburn had checked for traffic, but as she stepped down onto the warm tarmac, a car had emerged from a side street. A small red car. For one crazy minute, Helen thought it might be Emilia Garanita, but now she clocked that it was a Fiat, not a Corsa. This should have put her mind at ease, but in fact the opposite was true. For the car had lurched out of the side street at some speed and was now roaring towards Raeburn. It seemed a crazy manoeuvre and at any minute Helen expected the driver to spot Raeburn and slow down. But the driver now hit the accelerator, increasing her speed as she approached Raeburn. The latter, who was wearing headphones, seemed lost in her own world, oblivious to the approaching danger. Helen, by contrast, could see it all too quickly – a sudden vision of what was happening forcing itself into her consciousness. How could she have been so stupid? So slow?

Ripping back the throttle, Helen urged the bike forward. Her speed ratcheted up – fifty miles per hour, sixty, sixty-five – and, even as she raced towards Raeburn, she yanked up her visor.

'Belinda!' Her scream was hoarse and ineffective, drowned out by the roar of her engine. 'Belinda! Get out the way!'

But it was too little, too late. Raeburn *did* now look up, but only to see the car bearing down on her. Helen could only watch in horror as the Fiat barrelled into the terrified teacher, sending her fragile body cartwheeling into the air.

Chapter 108

The car roared on, as a horrified Helen watched Raeburn's broken form crash down to earth, bouncing off the tarmac, before lying still. Immediately a piercing scream rang out, a passing shopper horrified by what she'd just witnessed, but Helen's attention was drawn not to this sudden interruption, but to the red Fiat that was now speeding towards *her*.

She had been so shocked by what she'd just seen that she hadn't thought of her own safety, her bike grinding to a halt as the attack on Raeburn took place. Tensing, Helen now gunned the throttle, preparing to speed away from the approaching car, but even as she did so, the Fiat screeched to a halt. The car was not ten feet from her now, the blinking driver shocked to see the lone rider blocking her path. Helen, however, was not surprised. There was a grim logic to the murder that she could have foreseen – and prevented – had she been quicker on the uptake. Which is why she glared at Lilah Hill through the cracked windscreen with contempt, rather than shock. The team had been chasing two suspects all morning, little thinking the pair would cleave together in such brutal fashion.

Time seemed to stand still, the two women staring at each other, then more screams intruded, breaking the moment. Lilah Hill seemed to come alive, suddenly aware of the danger she was in. She rammed the car back into gear, spun the vehicle around, speeding away in the direction she'd just come from. This took her back towards her prone victim, but mercifully escape was uppermost in her mind now, Hill veering around the fallen teacher and away down the street.

Helen had a split second to make a decision. Stay with Raeburn or pursue Hill? Already a gaggle of shoppers were hurrying towards the prone woman, phones clamped to their ears, and this decided Helen. Snapping her visor back down, she tore away from the scene, intent on pursuing her attacker. The Fiat was already a way off in the distance, but Helen felt sure she could catch her – if she was quick.

Her tyres dug into the tarmac, her speed steadily climbing. As she sped along the street, her eyes darted constantly this way and that, searching for pedestrians. This was a busy shopping area, full of teenagers, families, pensioners, and it was possible that one might emerge at any time, stepping out in front of her, so she kept her senses alert, scoping the way ahead for danger.

Hill seemed to have no such compunction, however, intent now on escape. She ripped down Castle Way, then straight onto French Street. This was much narrower, a relic of the city's Tudor architecture and popular with tourists and locals alike. The chances of a collision here were even greater; Helen's heart was in her mouth as she pursued the fleeing suspect over the bouncing cobbles. Mercifully, luck was on their side, and Hill reached the end of the street unscathed, Helen breathing a silent sigh of relief.

Now Hill would be likely to encounter trouble. She would emerge almost directly opposite the Red Funnel ferry terminal. Here there were traffic lights, but also a steady stream of traffic, as holidaymakers made their way to the port. Even from this distance, Helen could see the lights were red, but to her surprise,

Hill didn't hesitate, roaring through the stop signal and skidding wildly out onto the ring road.

A truck missed her by inches, its horn blaring as it swept past. Hill seemed unabashed, clipping another vehicle in the adjacent lane but nevertheless managing to straighten up before speeding away. Helen, by contrast, had to break sharply, wasting valuable seconds waiting for a break in the opposing flow of traffic.

Cursing, she tapped her Bluetooth, dialling into the incident room. A gap now opened up in front of her and she sped forward once more, even as the call connected.

'Incident room?'

She recognized DC Osbourne's distinctive tones over the noise of her engine.

'This is DI Grace. I'm currently in pursuit of a red Fiat, registration number K R one nine R F F, heading anticlockwise on the A33. The suspect is currently heading away from the Red Funnel port – request full tracking and intercept.'

'Straight away. Who is it?'

'Lilah Hill. Quick as you can please.'

Ending the call, she fixed her eyes once more on the speeding car. The Fiat was sixty yards ahead, even now weaving in and out of the lanes in a desperate attempt to maintain a lead. Raising her speed, Helen zeroed in on her, intent on making up the distance between them. But the pursuit had just become a lot more hazardous. The ring road, which circumvented Southampton before colliding with the M27, was one of the city's main arteries. As such, it was always busy. This might play in Helen's favour, slowing or even stopping Hill, but it might also mean casualties, something Helen was acutely aware of.

The sensible thing to do would be to hang back and monitor the situation, staying in touch with the fleeing suspect, whilst waiting patiently until Hill could be apprehended safely. But it would be difficult to execute a hard stop on such a busy thoroughfare and Helen's strong instinct was to divert Hill off the ring road before she reached Mountbatten Way. Looking down at her speedometer, she saw she was already doing sixty mph, but now she yanked this up by another twenty, determined to narrow the gap between them.

Hill seemed to sense this, upping *her* speed, but even so, Helen gradually began to reel her in. The Fiat was nippy, but not built for high-speed pursuits and was no match for Helen's Kawasaki. And even as she approached the fleeing car, Helen spotted her opportunity. Wrenching back the throttle even further, she sped past, before pulling back into lane directly in front of her. The Mayflower roundabout was just ahead of them, a crash there was a distinct possibility, but Helen sought to cut Hill off by dramatically dropping her speed, forcing the pursuing car to brake suddenly. There was a loud skid, Hill's tyres protesting wildly, as the car slewed towards her. For a moment, Helen thought they might connect, and braced herself for the impact, but at the last minute, Hill wrenched the wheel round, shooting off the main road and onto a slip road that ran along the water's edge.

Helen had achieved her principal goal, but even so Hill was now speeding away from her so, spinning around, Helen followed suit, slipping off the main road. Roaring after the fleeing Fiat, she glimpsed the turning heads in Mayflower Park, young parents and their toddlers intrigued by the high-speed pursuit playing out in front of them. But Helen kept her gaze firmly fixed on the vehicle in front. This was a less populated area of the city, mainly comprising storage depots and business parks, but still danger lurked, the Fiat swerving even now to avoid a courier's van. Helen followed hot on her heels, giving the van a wide berth, before upping her speed once more.

They shot past the old Odeon, then a row of trade outlets, the two vehicles neck and neck now. At any minute, Helen expected the Fiat to swerve towards her, but Hill remained grimly focused on the way ahead and now Helen saw why. Twenty feet away there was a roundabout. If Hill hung a right there she could be back on the ring road, speeding away from town. The suspect seemed to sense this, angling a look to the flyover above. Ramming her foot on the accelerator, Hill raced towards the junction, barely braking as she careered *over* the roundabout, heading for the third exit and the slip road back to the A33.

Helen had been expecting this move and was quicker, leaning into the turn and bypassing the roundabout altogether, risking life and limb by going against the flow of traffic to get to the exit first. She made it – *just* – the Fiat's bumper almost clipping her tyre, as Hill sped away from the roundabout. Now the slip road lay before them – a hundred feet of open tarmac up to the ring road. Yanking back on the throttle, Helen eased away from her pursuer, opening up a ten-foot lead. Hill raised her game, determined to escape, which is what Helen had been counting on. And now, as she neared the junction, she tugged hard on her brakes, simultaneously wrenching the handlebars around. As she'd hoped, the bike skidded to an elegant halt, spinning slightly in the process, so that she now formed a human roadblock across the entry slip. It was a foolish, reckless thing to do – Helen could see Hill's shock, knew that she only had a split second to make a decision. Would she try and avoid a collision or would she drive straight through her, adding another casualty to her hit list? It was a crazy strategy, Helen risking her own life to bring the fleeing suspect in, but her instincts proved right. Hill was not a seasoned killer, and the young woman wrenched the steering wheel sharply to the right, the car veering wildly away, just missing Helen as it did so.

Her speed was still high, her desperation to escape as keen as ever, so Helen was not surprised as Hill now yanked the steering wheel back the other way, desperate to skid out and away onto the ring road. But Hill had left it too late. The solid concrete wall of the flyover was fast approaching – too fast – the vehicle's momentum carrying it inexorably towards it. Seconds later, there was a huge crunch, metal and fibre glass cracking horribly, as the car slammed into the wall, stopping dead in its tracks.

Chapter 109

'You're absolutely sure about that?'

'Yes, sir. DI Grace called it in not five minutes ago.'

Chief Superintendent Alan Peters gripped the phone, speechless. He could scarcely credit what DC Malik was saying – Lilah Hill had just killed another suspect, Belinda Raeburn, in a hit-and-run incident in the centre of town. Stranger still, DI Grace had been on hand to pursue the culprit along the A33, until Hill had totalled her vehicle, ramming it into a concrete wall. It seemed improbable, not to say impossible – he'd been locked in a heated meeting with the detective inspector barely an hour ago.

'What's the condition of the suspect?' he eventually replied, regaining his composure somewhat.

'Reasonable, I think. She's being checked out by paramedics, but it sounds like the airbag did its job. As soon as she's passed fit, DI Grace is going to bring her back to base.'

'OK, keep me posted,' Peters concluded, with more equanimity than he felt.

Hanging up, he slumped into his seat, staring blankly at the phone, as if wondering what bizarre, unexpected development it might yet throw at him. The past few weeks had seemed like a bad dream, each shocking development swiftly followed by something even worse. They'd had a string of unsolved murders, then a motley group of unconnected suspects, now a chain of killers who seemed to be turning on each other. Was Robert Downing even now sitting in his cell, plotting some weird and wonderful way to target Amanda Davis in Australia? Or vice versa? It seemed crazy, ridiculous even, yet Peters couldn't deny that it appeared that Helen Grace *had* been right after all, that her apparently far-fetched theories had some basis in fact.

It was bewildering, but throw into the mix the bizarre goings on within the team as well, and you had an investigation the like of which Peters had never experienced before. Was there any part of this situation that was predictable or straightforward? Apparently not and, as if to underline the complexity of the situation, his secretary now buzzed through on the intercom.

'DS Hudson for you, sir.'

'Thank you, Jackie.'

Moments later, Joseph Hudson strolled in. He did not have the air of a man under pressure. In fact, he seemed in good spirits.

'I presume you've heard the news, sir.'

Peters nodded absently.

'We've taken a hit,' Hudson continued soberly, 'one dead, one injured, a stolen car written off. But on the plus side, we do now have Hill in custody. It's just a pity we couldn't have got to her slightly earlier.'

His face was rueful, laced with regret, yet his criticism of Grace was too clumsy to miss. Peters was tempted to agree with him – Grace's pursuit *had* been characteristically reckless – but he hadn't summoned Hudson to pour fuel on that fire, so he kept his counsel.

'I'm going to suggest that I lead the questioning on this one, once Lilah Hill is in custody,' Hudson continued. 'DI Grace has done more than enough for one day...'

'Well, that's very generous of you,' Peters responded swiftly, 'but that might not be possible.'

'Sir?'

'I didn't ask you here today to discuss the case. DC Malik's already brought me up to speed on today's developments.'

Hudson nodded tightly, reinforcing Peters' suspicions that the DS and his young Asian colleague did not get on.

'No, I wanted to talk you about the allegations you made against DI Grace. I should stress from the start that what we are about to discuss may end in disciplinary proceedings, so if you want to have a Union representative present—'

'That won't be necessary. I've nothing to hide.'

'Good, then let's press on. I've heard your version of events, and now I have DI Grace's. And I must say that what she revealed to me was very illuminating.'

'I've no doubt she tried to defend herself.'

'Indeed she did. Rather successfully, I might add.'

DS Hudson said nothing, regarding Alan Peters with unease.

'We discussed your shared history, the breakdown in relations and specifically the conversation in the bike park. Unbeknownst to me, and I assume you, DI Grace recorded your little chat in order to *prove* that you were leaking confidential information to Emilia Garanita. I'm happy to play you the whole thing, if you like, but for now I'm going to start near the end...'

Peters opened up the voice memo app on his phone and moments later Hudson's voice rang out loud and clear in the hushed office.

'You'd love me to come running back to Mummy, wouldn't you? To be a good little boy because you're feeling the heat. Well, you can forget it, Helen. I wouldn't piss on you if you were on fire...'

'What the hell?'

'I mean it. We had something, could have been great together, but you dismantled all that with your clumsy accusations, your paranoia, your lies. Which is why I'm going to bring you down.'

Peters stopped the recording and turned to look at Hudson once more. He was expecting anger, denials, accusations, but for once Helen Grace's accuser looked speechless. In fact, he looked like he'd just seen a ghost.

Chapter 110

'You've got some bloody front, barging in here, barking questions at me.'

The officer from the Professional Standards Department eyed Emilia Garanita coolly across the conference-room table, as he slowly slid his warrant card back into his jacket pocket.

'I wasn't aware of any barging, or barking, for that matter,' he replied coolly. 'We simply want to ask you a few questions.'

'Even so, this is the private offices of the *Southampton Evening News*, my place of work—'

'Which is why we want to wrap this up as quickly as possible,' the police officer responded, 'so we can have a nice little chat now, sort this out, or we can come back tomorrow, but I should warn you that if we are made to return, it will be with a warrant to access all your computers, phones, devices, as well as any written files, private notebooks or Post It notes that we deem relevant to our enquiries. After all, acquiring confidential police information for personal or professional gain is a very serious offence.'

He was still grinning, but it was the smile of a killer. Emilia felt sure Detective Sergeant Cooper had done this dozens of times before and had probably heard every lie, evasion and obfuscation. Unusually, she felt intimidated by this guy and his smooth, dead-eyed patter.

'What did you want to ask?' she replied firmly, disguising her discomfort.

'I should say that this is off the record for now,' he replied quickly. 'I won't be recording our conversation, though obviously we may need to do a follow-up under caution at Southampton Central, should that become necessary.'

'Well, I guess that's kind of hard to know, isn't it? As you haven't actually asked me anything yet...'

That smile again, insincere but well practised.

'We're investigating an allegation of police corruption. Specifically that a serving officer in the Major Incident Team at Southampton Central has been passing confidential information about ongoing police investigations to this newspaper, using *you* as the conduit. Do you have anything to say in relation to this?'

'I'm afraid not,' Emilia shot back. 'It's news to me, if you'll pardon the pun.'

'To the best of your knowledge, then, you haven't had any direct communication with DS Joseph Hudson, either by phone or in person, during which he has passed confidential information to you?'

There was no lead-up, no preamble, just a sudden and direct accusation. It felt very much to Emilia like entrapment, as if they were willing her to say 'no', so they could then pounce on her lies. She had committed this offence many times before, of course, with a dozen or more police officers, and so part of her was tempted to laugh it off. And yet... it was a serious criminal offence, one which might threaten her career, not to mention her liberty.

'I'll ask you again,' Cooper repeated, snapping her out of her internal debate. 'Has DS Joseph Hudson ever contacted you directly, with the intention of leaking privileged police information to you or this paper?'

Once more, Emilia shifted in her seat. She was a seasoned journalist, adept at dodging the slings and arrows that came her way, but there seemed little room for manoeuvre today. She'd had great hopes for her working relationship with Hudson, but their alliance was now at end – to save her own skin she would *have* to throw him to the wolves. Once again, she cursed both her bad luck and Helen Grace's apparent invulnerability. She had tried her best to unseat her nemesis, had thought she'd finally got her on the ropes, but once again she had failed. Turning to face Detective Cooper with a resigned air, she asked:

'What do you want to know?'

Chapter *III*

Lilah Hill stared back at her, sullen, hostile.

Looking at the suspect, now hunched on a seat in the interview suite, Helen once more questioned the wisdom of quizzing her so soon after the crash. Hill was ashen, obviously still badly shaken, and her breath smelt strongly of alcohol. Set against that was the fact that Hill had sustained no serious injuries, seemed sobered by the traumatic experiences of the day and was staring down the barrel of a murder charge. Despite her misgivings, therefore, Helen knew she had no choice *but* to confront her. Lilah Hill had killed someone not three hours ago, right in front of her. Moreover, she might yet prove the vital link in this case, *if* she was prepared to talk.

Despite her desire for answers, Helen nevertheless knew she had to approach the interview carefully. This was a woman who appeared to be on the edge of a nervous breakdown, endlessly fidgeting in her seat, picking at her nails, her clothes, her hair. A woman on the brink of total collapse.

'Lilah, I need you to talk to me.'

Hill continued to pick at her nails.

'I know you're not a cold-blooded killer, that you would never have killed Belinda Raeburn unless you felt *compelled* to do so ...'

Hill didn't react, didn't even blink, her attention glued to her fingers.

'Now I don't know who's got at you, what they've said or done to make you kill, but there's no point in you taking the fall for them. If you were coerced – forced, blackmailed, threatened – if someone *made* you do this, then the courts *will* have to take that into account.'

It was a good offer, the best she was going to get, but still Hill didn't look up. Helen was sure the suspect understood what she was saying, but something was preventing her from engaging. In spite of the gruesome events of the morning, this saddened Helen – she was sure Hill was at heart a decent person, who'd somehow ended up in a terrible place.

'Please try and understand the seriousness of the situation, Lilah…'

Helen softened her tone, trying to appear as friendly and unthreatening as possible. And now Hill finally stopped fidgeting.

'There's no way you can wriggle out of a murder charge, no way you can claim it was an accident. I was there, I saw you do it. Plus, we have two witnesses who'll confirm that the car used in the attack was stolen yesterday from the Hertz depot by someone wearing a burgundy hoodie. The same hoodie you were wearing when you deliberately ran all those red lights yesterday. The same hoodie you're wearing *today*.'

Hill blinked, the weight of the evidence against her starting to make itself felt.

'It *wasn't* an accident. It wasn't even manslaughter. It was premeditated, cold-blooded murder.'

Another reaction, that final word punching through.

'It's the most serious charge there is. And there's no way you can avoid it. *But* you're still young, Lilah, which means you have a choice—'

If Helen could've taken the young woman's hand in hers, she would have done. She meant every word she was saying, desperately hoping their fragile suspect would make the right decision.

'You can choose to spend the rest of your life behind bars, hated, reviled, misunderstood. Or you can come clean.'

Helen let this register, before continuing: 'Tell me what happened, tell me what pushed you into this awful corner, and I can help you. This doesn't need to be the end, Lilah…'

Hill's shoulders started to shake, tears filling her eyes. Helen could feel the pent-up misery, the desperation. She had never seen anyone look so despairing, so stricken, so *hollow* before.

'If you help us now, if you serve your time, make reparations, then you *still* have a chance, a chance to have a life, a meaningful life…'

A stifled sob, half expelled, half swallowed. Hill looked like a woman at war with herself, torn between confession and denial.

'So, please, take your time, start at the beginning. Tell me who made you do this.'

Helen's hand was laid palm up on the table, as if urging Hill to share. Helen desperately wanted this to be over, for their suspect to finally bare her soul.

'I can't…'

Helen could feel Hill backing away from her, as she stuttered out the words.

'Why not?'

'I can't, I'm sorry.'

'If you're scared, if you're concerned for your safety, we can help—'

Hill dropped her gaze, picking at her nails viciously. She

seemed desperate, possessed almost, wanting to pull the skin from her fingers, to make herself bleed.

'Lilah, talk to me. I'm your only hope here, the only person who can help you...'

Another stifled sob as the self-harm ramped up. It was like the young woman wanted to destroy herself, but Helen had to reach out to her, to give her one last chance.

'Whatever's happened, we can deal with it. You and me *together*. So, please, tell me what's worrying you.'

She moved in closer, almost whispering now.

'Tell me what you're *afraid of*.'

There was a long pause. Helen watched Hill intently, desperate to see some signs of softening, some willingness to co-operate. But when the young woman looked up, the tears now dry in her dull, deadened eyes, Helen realized that she had already made up her mind.

'I *can't*.'

Chapter 112

'Why isn't she talking? She must know she can't wriggle out of this.'

Helen was back in the incident room, the team crowded around her. They'd clearly all been hoping for a confession, for a breakthrough in this troubling investigation. Helen had had to disappoint them, but was not content to accept defeat, pulling the entire unit together to review the evidence and plot their next move. Everyone had responded, everyone except Joseph Hudson, who seemed to have vanished off the face of the earth. Helen didn't miss his presence today, however. She needed the whole team pulling together at this critical juncture – even now she was pleased that it was DC Reid who'd asked the question, an erstwhile ally of Hudson's.

'I don't know for sure,' Helen replied. 'It may be that she thinks she *can* pass this off as a hit-and-run, an accident of some kind, and that the less she says, the less she incriminates herself. But I don't think it's that, not really. You can hear from the recording that she sounds scared. Whoever's behind this clearly has a hold over her.'

'Because she feels they can get to her, even though she's in custody?' DC Malik queried.

'Possibly, but there are other ways of exerting pressure, of commanding loyalty.'

'You think she's *grateful* to whoever's behind this?' DC Edwards asked. 'Glad that her partner was killed?'

'Maybe, though I sense she's torn about that, partly relieved, partly guilty. So, if it's not gratitude, and it's not purely fear, then it must be because admitting to murdering Belinda Raeburn is somehow *better*, more acceptable, than revealing the truth.'

'I'm not sure I follow.'

'Think about it. Amar Goj stood to lose everything, so he took action. Belinda Raeburn and Robert Downing too. Lilah Hill's life by contrast seemed set fair. She was grieving her husband, sure, but she was actually *liberated* by his death. His murder could not be explicitly linked to her, there's no suggestion she ordered it, so even if there *was* a quid pro quo, even if she *had* promised to kill Raeburn in return for Martin Hill's death, she wouldn't have to go through with it, *unless* she genuinely feared for her own life if she refused, or if there was some other sword of Damocles hanging over her, compelling her to commit a desperate act.'

'You think we've missed something on her?'

'I think we've barely scratched the surface. We need to go way back, looking at former lovers, friends, jobs, any family issues. We need to turn her life upside down. She's got no criminal record, no previous brushes with the law, but there must be something we've overlooked, something shameful, or criminal, or ruinous. I can't think of any other reason why a basically decent, ordinary woman would willingly take a stranger's life.'

'Why Raeburn anyway?'

Edwards had now raised his head above the parapet.

'Why was she targeted? Surely . . . surely the point of this whole thing is that none of the links in the chain can be connected? The perpetrators don't know their victims, can't be linked to each other in any way. But these two *can*. They were both suspects in ongoing investigations, now perpetrators. It seems untidy, doesn't fit the pattern. Why would the architect of all this mayhem draw attention to their scheme like that?'

'Maybe they don't have a choice,' Helen replied firmly. 'Maybe we've got them rattled now. The whole scheme works perfectly only if the perpetrators are never identified. The original plan must have been for the murders to go unsolved, to appear as random carjackings or hit-and-runs or racist attacks, but as soon as the real motives and real perpetrators are identified, it starts to unravel. Belinda Raeburn was a potential weak link. She killed to protect her job, her relationship, her livelihood, but lost everything anyway. There was nothing to stop us targeting her now, persuading her to tell all, so better that she be silenced. Maybe she was deemed to be vulnerable, that Hill and Downing would be more resilient in holding out. I think whoever's behind this is cleaning out the stables...'

There was a brief pause as the team considered this, then DC Malik returned to the fray.

'So, what now, guv?'

'Well, I think we probably all agree that this whole enterprise is the work of one individual or body. That it wasn't Downing, Hill and Raeburn forming some kind of sinister collective to solve their problems...'

'We've looked into that, extensively,' DC Bentham offered. 'There's no evidence of any contact between the different perps.'

'So somebody else is coordinating this – contacting them, threatening them, giving them targets, timings and crucial information about their victims' movements. There's no reason why Raeburn should have known that Martin Hill used that cut-through every day, nor that Lilah Hill should have known where Raeburn went to the gym. Somebody must have given them that information, given them a set of instructions. How?'

'We've examined their phone histories, messages, emails,' DC McAndrew offered. 'I can't see any common contact, any overlaps, at all. It's possible they might have some covert means of communication, a burn phone or whatever, in which case it's going to be virtually impossible to chase it down.'

'But someone would still have needed to *give* them the phone,' Helen insisted. 'Or the details of a dark-web chat room, or whatever. Someone would still have needed to communicate with them, directly or digitally. So how did that first contact take place?'

There was silence as they processed these thoughts, searching for answers.

'Surely it *has* to be Blythe?' DC Malik ventured tentatively.

This was what Helen had been thinking, but she was glad someone else had said it.

'Go on.'

'Well, they all had regular weekly appointments with him. Confidential, private meetings...'

'In his very discreet city-centre office,' DC Reid overlapped.

'He's got no assistant, right?' McAndrew added.

'So there'd be no record of who came and went, who he'd been seeing,' Malik agreed. 'Or what state they were in when they left. Whether they were angry, upset, scared...'

'What's more, if they were smart,' Helen added, a new thought occurring, 'they would continue to see him afterwards. Best not to alter their weekly schedule in any way, to draw attention to themselves... which means he could continue to keep an eye on them, or perhaps even enjoy their discomfort, their anguish, post the killing.'

It was an unpleasant notion, but one Helen instinctively felt was right.

'How are we doing on Blythe's alleged data breach?' she continued.

'No joy so far. No other breaches or cyber attacks were reported at that time, so unless it was a one-off... obviously, we'll need to examine Blythe's systems, but so far we haven't been able to raise him.'

'So right now we've only got his word that there *was* a data breach. He might just have been buying himself time. What do we know about Blythe specifically?'

This question was aimed at DC Bentham.

'Not very much, to be honest. Local boy, brought up by his mum after his parents' divorce. Did well at school and university and has been a practising psychiatrist for nearly fifteen years. No partner, no kids, has a flat in Upper Shirley. Doesn't post, tweet or insta. Keeps himself to himself.'

'Any criminal record?'

'No. No previous, no cautions, nothing. He was questioned a few years back following an incident with his ex, but, honestly, that's the only interesting thing about him.'

'Who was the ex?'

'Gina Brown.'

'And what do we know about her?'

'Well, she's married to a Mark James, they live down in Bournemouth, but *previously* she'd been engaged to Blythe. It ended badly, to put it mildly. She broke it off and Blythe was *not* happy, apparently feeling betrayed, spurned. A few months later, this happened—'

He handed her a printout of an article from the *Southampton Evening News*. Helen took in the date, July 2018, then the name underneath the photo – Gina Brown – before raising her eyes to the image itself. As she did so, her hand went to her mouth.

Captured in the photo was the *same* young woman whose picture she'd seen lovingly framed in Alex Blythe's office. But this time the subject was not grinning and posing for the camera. Instead, she was staring directly forward, shocked, desperate, *anguished* – the lower half of her face blistered and raw, freshly ravaged by a terrible acid attack.

Chapter 113

'I can't talk right now. I'm sorry, I just *can't* . . .'

Gina Brown was hiding behind the front door, hoping that if she didn't engage, Helen would turn tail and retreat. But there was no question of that – Helen had broken several records, not to mention laws, burning down to Bournemouth in record time. There was no way she would be denied access, however shocking or upsetting her sudden appearance might be.

'It is vitally important that I talk to you, Gina. About what happened to you, about your relationship with Alex Blythe . . .'

The mere mention of his name seemed to cause Brown physical pain, her whole body reacting, as she continued to hug the door.

'I've got nothing to say about that and as you can tell I'm *trying* to get the baby down . . .'

The raucous strains of a baby's cries could be heard from upstairs.

'Then perhaps your husband could take care of it. Is he home?'

Gina hesitated, which gave Helen the opportunity she needed.

'Please, Gina. I wouldn't be here unless I *had* to be. It's a matter of life and death.'

And now, finally, the seriousness of the situation seemed to sink in; Helen's fearful hostess reluctantly stepped aside to let her enter.

'I should start by saying that nobody knows I'm here. And that everything you tell me is off the record...'

Gina nodded, but said nothing, cradling her mug of tea. The pair of them were sitting in her modest living room, surrounded by the trinkets, photos and souvenirs of a happy family life. Whatever she'd been through, whatever she'd endured, clearly Gina Brown had survived, prospered even, carving out some happiness for herself. Tonight, however, she looked far from content, appearing cowed, tearful, even afraid.

'Alex Blythe is unaware of our interest in him, or that I'm having this conversation with you. The last thing we want to do is to upset or alarm you. Genuinely, you're perfectly safe, Gina. All I need from you is some information.'

Gina stared into her tea, but made no attempt to drink it.

'What do you want to know?' she muttered, seemingly determined not to make eye contact.

'How did you and Alex first meet?'

Another reaction, but this time it was not fear Helen saw. It was embarrassment.

'I was his patient...'

'Right, you went to see him because...?'

'Because I had a problem. I... I'd had a nasty motorbike accident the year before. I was on some fairly heavy pain medication during my recuperation and well, I found it hard to wean myself off it afterwards.'

'You engaged Alex Blythe's services to help deal with your addiction?'

A doleful nod.

'How long did you see him for?'

'Professionally, three months or so. Personally, much longer ...'

'Go on.'

'Well, I was motivated to get off the medication, so the treatment worked. I was so grateful to him, I felt he'd given me back my life. Turned out he felt the same.'

'Because?'

'Because he was lost, at sea ...'

'How so?'

'He was directionless, unhappy. You have to understand that from the age of six it was just him and his mum. She'd tried for years to have a baby, had gone through several rounds of IVF, then on the last throw of the dice, she conceived. Alex was her little miracle and she worshipped him, gave him whatever he wanted, told him whatever he wanted, day after day after day. Then suddenly she was gone. Late diagnosis breast cancer. Died just before his twenty-second birthday.'

'Leaving him alone in the world.'

'After that, he didn't seem to have *anyone*. The odd flirtation, I guess, but nothing serious. Then we met. I was so happy, so pleased to be "normal" again, that I doted on him. For a time, I thought we were happy, that we might have a future, which is why I let him persuade me to get engaged ...'

'But your heart wasn't in it?'

She shook her head. 'Alex didn't want to be loved, he wanted to be worshipped. And he was very controlling, would get very cross if I didn't behave *exactly* how he wanted me to ...'

'Because no one had ever called him on this behaviour, because he'd always been indulged?'

'Maybe, I don't know. *I'm* not the psychiatrist ...' The bitterest of humour, laced with anger and hurt.

'So you decided to get out?'

'I was deeply unhappy, felt trapped, suffocated even. Then one day I met Mark, at my singing group. And he was so genuine and gentle and kind – and I fell in love, *properly* in love with him.'

The hint of a smile. Helen cast an eye to the ceiling – the baby was quietening down and she could hear Mark's footsteps as he walked back and forth, trying to pacify the infant.

'What happened then?'

Now Gina hesitated, as if scared to reopen the box.

'Gina?'

'Look, I could have handled it better, I – I did see Mark for a bit whilst I was still with Alex. I just didn't know what else to do. Alex was so happy, so gung ho about the wedding, telling colleagues, acquaintances, anyone who'd listen, about what a great couple we were, what an amazing day it was going to be. He was making more and more plans, spending more and more money, so one day I just came out and told him that I wanted out.'

'And how did he react?'

'Well, at first he didn't believe me. Thought I was trying to goad him, to trick him. Then, when it finally sunk in, he went crazy. Called me every name under the sun, said some awful, awful things, even hit me on one occasion. To me it seemed like he was having some kind of breakdown, so I just grabbed my things and made to leave. Then suddenly he was crying, saying that he could change, but I knew he wouldn't. Alex loves one person and one person alone. So I left.'

'And after that?'

'After that—' she said, taking a deep, pained breath, 'it got even worse. Phone calls, messages, calling me a whore, accusing me of leading him on, of deliberately humiliating him. I tried to reason with him, but that only seemed to make it worse. My car got smashed up, my office was vandalized—'

She seemed to be struggling to breathe, as if she was about to suffer a panic attack. Helen was tempted to tell her to stop, but Gina seemed determined to continue, to finish her story.

'On and on it went, day after day, then suddenly it stopped. At first, I thought that maybe he'd met someone else, or finally seen reason. But looking back, I know now that it was what *I'd* done that caused the change.'

'What was that?'

'I – I'd posted on Facebook about my engagement. Mark had asked me to marry him and, of course, I'd said yes.'

'And so Alex saw that it was pointless? That your relationship was at an end?'

'In a way. But it was also the start of something else...'

'Revenge?'

Gina exhaled, long and hard, before nodding.

'He deliberately severed contact, tried to distance himself from me, from the situation, but he was just biding his time.'

She looked up at Helen, tearful defiance writ large. Gina looked good, there was no question about that, she had made a new life, a new image, for herself, but the pain, the damage of the past, was still etched into her features.

'You're sure it was him?'

'What do you think?' she fired back, gesturing to her face. 'This happened the night before I was due to be married.'

Helen stared at her, sickened by the twisted timing of the attack. 'There were never any other suspects, any other explanations?'

'Don't be ridiculous. Who else would do something like *this*?'

'Was he questioned?'

'Sure, once he got back to the UK.'

'I don't follow.'

'Well, Alex is many things, but he's not stupid. He was at a conference in Copenhagen on the night of the attack.'

'So he had a rock-solid alibi.'

'He'd never leave anything to chance.'

'And the individual who *did* attack you?'

'We never found out who it was,' she said bitterly. 'Some guy in a hoodie and cap. He came up behind me, I barely saw him.'

'And the police couldn't link the attack back to Blythe?'

'Course not. Alex had no friends, no family, no mates, no one who'd do something like that for him. So how could they?'

Helen's mind was suddenly whirring with possibilities, even as Gina concluded:

'But he was behind it, I know he was. It was *him*.'

Chapter 114

Helen hurried back to her bike, deep in thought. What had once seemed a hopeless situation, a catalogue of unconnected murders, now seemed anything but. Even now the various pieces of the jigsaw were coming together, dancing in front of Helen's eyes. What mattered now was that she grasp them, sliding them firmly into place.

It seemed highly probable that Blythe's twisted scheme had its genesis in the attack on Brown. A jilted lover wreaks a terrible revenge on his ex-fiancée, marring her face, her fortunes, even as she stood on the brink of happiness. Helen could picture the scene now – a younger, greener Alex Blythe persuading a desperate, vulnerable patient to commit a drastic act, convincing them to throw sulphuric acid in the face of a total stranger. Had that client been persuaded, bribed, threatened even? No, that seemed implausible and unnecessary. Presumably blackmail would have been much simpler, the unwitting patient having already confessed his darkest secrets, his deepest shame, to his trusted addiction counsellor. It was at once horribly sinister and oddly brilliant, Blythe's victims *willingly* giving up this informa-tion, telling their psychiatrist things that they wouldn't dream of confessing to their family, friends or colleagues. They *trusted* him – then Blythe used that trust against them in the worst way possible.

Helen had no idea how Gina's attacker had transgressed to allow Blythe to manipulate him in this manner. But what she was certain of was that this whole thing was born of that episode. How Blythe must have revelled in the power, knowing that he had *forced* one of his clients to disfigure another human being, without any possible comeback to him. It was a foolproof scheme. To rat on Blythe would, in effect, be to confess to the attack itself and what incentive was there to do that, when the police had no leads? Better to keep quiet, then, let sleeping dogs lie.

This, then, was the spark that lit the fire. The attack on Gina Brown must have been personally satisfying, but why stop there? Why not force those poor, vulnerable wretches who abased themselves in front of him to go *further*? To commit the ultimate act of violence? It would be intoxicating, empowering, irresistible. It would be like playing God.

It would have required careful planning, as none of the needy professionals who sought out his discreet services were natural-born killers. The stick, the threat of exposure, would only motivate them so far. Perhaps some could be persuaded to kill, but others would surely resist; resist until all hope was lost? Why then not add a carrot too, by first disposing of the person that threatened *their* happiness, their livelihood, even their liberty? That way they would be doubly tied in, in debt to Blythe for their sudden liberation, but now utterly in thrall to the knowledge he alone had of their vices, their peccadilloes, their *crimes*?

And now it hit Helen like a thunderbolt, Blythe's own words suddenly coming back to her. When they'd first met, he'd talked about his clients' unrealistic expectations. What was it he'd said?

'When my clients first present, they want me to wave a magic wand, to make it all go away.' Was this what he'd done for them? Ensuring one client's problems disappeared by ordering another client to murder their tormentor? Once more, Helen shivered. This was beyond criminal, a scheme the like of which she'd never encountered before. It was a way of torturing his poor clients, of drenching Southampton in blood whilst never lifting a finger himself. It really was God-like, awe-inspiring, yet simultaneously utterly chilling.

Climbing on her bike, Helen pulled her phone from her pocket. Finally, the picture was becoming clear and the imperative now was to mobilize the team. For weeks now, they had been chasing their own tails, blundering down blind alleys, chasing up false leads, persecuting innocent parties, when in reality the situation was incredibly simple. This whole thing was the product of one man, and one man alone.

Dr Alex Blythe.

Chapter 115

He stood perfectly still, staring out into the inky darkness. The grey Vauxhall Astra had been stationed in the street opposite his office since just before midnight, but, oddly, the occupants had not exited the vehicle, instead sitting in the shadows, watching and waiting. From there, they wouldn't be able to make him out – the blinds were down, the internal lights off – but Alex Blythe could see them by peeking through the tiny gap between fabric and frame. It was a strange stand-off, an odd kind of communion between hunter and prey, as the world carried on its business unawares. Drunk office workers stumbling home, gaggles of teens running down the street, lovers hurrying past arm in arm – all manner of people passed between them, little realizing the life-and-death drama they were caught up in.

The police officers had arrived two hours ago and since then they'd done nothing, lingering with intent, but lacking the confidence, the imagination, perhaps, to act. Satisfied that they weren't about to storm the building, Alex Blythe moved away from the window, returning to his desk. A quick glance at his laptop revealed that the auto-cleanse programme was almost complete, all files destroyed, the computer's hard drive wiped clean, so he moved on to the shredder. Grasping the last set of paper files, he began feeding them into the mouth of the beast, watching with grim satisfaction as its rear end spewed out the finely cut strands of paper. The sight of this destruction was strangely enjoyable, but tinged with sadness too. He had spent years amassing this treasure trove of secrets, confessions and crimes. What a waste it seemed to just toss it all away. All that anguish, all that shame, all that *leverage*.

Still, there could be no question of taking any chances now – all concrete links to Raeburn, Hill, Downing and the countless other wretches he'd treated *had* to be destroyed. It was a pity, sacrilege really, but there was no other way. The only saving grace was the power of his memory, which was prodigious, almost photographic in its recall. This might yet prove useful and, if nothing else, would provide entertainment and distraction for him as he replayed their tearful confessions and naked pleas for help.

The last strands of paper fell into the bin. Switching the shredder off, Blythe did likewise with his laptop, before picking it up and hurling it to the floor. It hit the tiles, cracking them instantly as the machine came apart, the keyboard springing clean off to reveal a mass of circuitry underneath. Now he didn't hesitate, striding forward and stamping on it, repeatedly, aggressively, his foot pounding the unfortunate device until it was just a mass of smashed glass and broken microchips.

Exhausted, sweating, Alex Blythe leaned back on his desk, taking a moment to catch his breath. In the corner of the room, Bella whimpered plaintively, suddenly scared of her master, but he ignored her whines, his mind on higher things. He stood on the threshold of the endgame and took a moment now to drink in his surroundings. This place had been his sanctuary, his playground, for so long. He'd enjoyed his time in this cloistered, confessional space and he revelled in the memories, breathing in the pain, the distress these four walls had witnessed over the years. Here he had blossomed, thrived, even as the mindless world thrashed around him, ignorant and blind, little realizing the extent of his ambition. He had beaten them all, abused, tortured, controlled the poor excuses for human beings who willingly raced into his embrace and he had *enjoyed* doing so, but every show had its climax, a point after which the curtain must come down. That moment had now arrived and he would bow out with no regrets. It had been fun whilst it lasted, but as the old saying went, all good things must come to an end.

Day Seven

Chapter 116

Helen paced her flat, the floorboards creaking as she marched back and forth. Following her interview with Gina Brown, she had retreated home to process, plot and strategize, yet she remained restless and dissatisfied. They were so close to ending this thing, but *still* they were not ready to deliver the killer blow.

Crossing to the balcony, Helen looked out over the city, trying to calm her thoughts, the anxiety that was steadily growing inside her. Dawn was just breaking, the first slivers of light glistening on the rooftops, heralding the new day. Standing there, Helen wondered what the next twenty-four hours would bring. Triumph and salvation? Or more death and destruction?

Helen felt sure she knew why these crimes had happened, who had engineered them, but calling Blythe to account for his actions would be far from simple. She had never come across an adversary like him, someone so adept at keeping themselves in the shadows. In Helen's eyes he was responsible for at least seven murders, probably more, but the fact remained that as things stood, not a single witness, not a single perpetrator, had pointed the finger at him, identifying Blythe as the architect of the bloodshed and misery. Amanda Davis was AWOL in Australia, Amar Goj and Belinda Raeburn were dead, and

Robert Downing and Lilah Hill still refused to talk, for reasons that remained unclear.

Without a witness or victim directly accusing the psychiatrist of blackmail, coercion and incitement to murder, the CPS would never bring charges. Even if Helen pulled Blythe in now, as she was *sorely* tempted to do, they would be left empty-handed. They might be able to link Blythe to the perpetrators of the murders via his files, presuming he hadn't destroyed them, or by appointment reminders and location services on his victim's phones, but the threshold of evidence would need to be higher, *much higher*, if they wanted to bring him to book. They needed a smoking gun – a voice, or series of voices directly accusing Blythe, insisting that it was the twisted psychiatrist who'd set this terrible chain of events in motion.

Returning to the kitchen table, Helen looked down at her files. Lilah Hill's mug shot stared back at her – she had been sifting through what they knew of her life for the past few hours. Helen hadn't changed, hadn't even showered on her return, diving straight into the information DCs Malik and McAndrew had gathered about the woman who now languished in the custody cells. She had refused to cooperate, issuing blanket 'no comments' to all the questions put to her, yet in Helen's mind, she remained their best hope of a breakthrough.

Downing was an accomplished lawyer and a tough adversary. He would attempt to wriggle out of any involvement, despite the weight of forensic evidence that was growing against him. He was adept at defending himself, plus he had a lot to lose, not least access to his kids. Lilah Hill was by contrast an amateur, a law-abiding advertising executive who'd never been in trouble with the police before. Moreover, she was all alone in the world, vulnerable and shaken, with no one to support her in her hour of greatest need.

If they *could* crack her, if they could get her to talk, then they might still be able to put Alex Blythe behind bars. What they lacked currently was leverage, something to bring her to the table. Helen had been wracking her brain for hours, poring over her files, searching for something, anything, to open her up, yet still it eluded her. Lilah's trajectory through life seemed fairly standard, prioritizing romance, hedonism and career in her twenties, before segueing into building a home and looking after body and spirit in her thirties. So far so ordinary, with the twist that alcohol had been ever-present in her life, even in her later, healthier years, when she cycled, meditated and gym-classed for all she was worth. The apologetic messages to friends after she'd caused a scene, the numerous off-licence transactions on her credit card statements and the frequent googling of organizations such as Alcoholics Anonymous was all evidence of the power of her addiction. She had clearly struggled with it for years, before eventually contacting Alex Blythe as the last throw of the dice.

In some ways, it made perfect sense. Advertising was a tough business. Executives were forever precariously hanging between success and failure, between landing an account and losing one, which meant the party culture – for which read drinking culture – was well established. Drink, drugs, sex, it was all part of the adrenalized, masculine, work hard, play hard ethos. And Lilah Hill seemed to have gone for it, playing her full part in the bacchanalia. The team had printed off and scanned numerous photos from Hill's Facebook page and the pictures from her twenties were certainly illuminating. There was a panoply of photos of Hill as a young woman, drinking shots in a crowded bar, sitting proprietorially on a brand-new Mercedes, kissing a colleague lasciviously on the cheek whilst winking at the camera. It was a period of unbridled hedonism, a picture of careless youth, all a far cry from the misery Hill now found herself wallowing in. How had her life gone so wrong?

It seemed impossible, looking at the pictures of her early years, that she should now be imprisoned in a cell, facing a murder charge. For Hill had clearly tried to clean up her act, prioritizing exercise and clean living, whilst she continued to fight her addiction to booze. This made her involvement with Blythe, or rather her subjugation by him, even more bemusing. There were numerous struggling alcoholics out there, so how had he been able to manipulate her, force her, to do something so out of character? Every other aspect of her life – her charity cycle rides, her love of community projects, her involvement with local church groups – seemed to suggest she was a model citizen. What on earth did he have on her?

Lilah had always been a binge drinker, that was clear. But, oddly, it was after she made certain changes to her life – cycling rather than driving, buying organic, local food rather than expensive, carbon-heavy imports, committing to sustained weight loss – that her drinking really ramped up. In her twenties, it had been a few days' excess, then a few days off, judging by her spending patterns. But in later life, drinking was a daily occurrence, Hill seemingly favouring spirits, given the levels of cash she was burning through day by day. Why was this? Why had her condition suddenly worsened, even as she tried to get a grip of other aspects of her life? And what had Blythe spotted there to take advantage of?

Tiring of her investigation, Helen's eyes strayed back to the photos from the morning's tragedy. Raeburn's crumpled body on the road, her possessions scattered about her, the black skid marks left by the Fiat that had skidded to a halt just in front of Helen's bike. Immediately, she was rocketed back there, to the moment when the two women had locked eyes. It had struck her at the time, and it impressed itself upon her again now, that it had not been triumph or anger in Hill's expression. No, it had been horror.

And now a thought landed, an idea that suddenly seemed obvious, but which she had overlooked until now. Picking up her phone, she dialled the incident room and was pleased to hear McAndrew on the other end.

'Can you access the PNC for me?' she said without introduction.

'Sure thing. What are we looking for?'

Casting a look at the photo of Hill, posing on her brand-new Mercedes, she replied:

'Any RTAs involving a Mercedes SLR, reg BG14 JYB ...'

There was a pause, then:

'Nothing involving that vehicle, I'm afraid.'

Helen pondered this. 'OK, then do a wider search. Any RTA, collision, hit and run, anything that might have involved a vehicle of that make or model in Southampton ...'

McAndrew was already typing. As she waited, Helen cast an eye over the files in front of her, but this was merely a distraction, her attention was totally focused on McAndrew's response.

'I've got something that *might* fit the bill. A hit-and-run in Freemantle in December 2015. A teenage boy left for dead in the road near his home ...'

'I remember it,' Helen replied, suddenly excited. 'No one was ever caught for it. His parents make appeals every year. What was his name? Billy ... Billy ...'

'Billy Anderson.'

'That was it, Billy Anderson ...'

'Anyway, there was only one witness, an elderly neighbour. She didn't see the incident, but thought she clocked a dark-blue Mercedes saloon racing away from the scene.'

'Which road was it in Freemantle?'

'Barrow Road.'

'And Hill worked in Ocean Village, right... so if she'd been heading home late at night, say from a Christmas do, she might have used that route.'

'For sure, it's a well-used cut-through, much quicker than sticking to the main roads.'

'And if she was in a hurry, had perhaps been drinking...'

Helen returned her attention to Hill's Facebook site, flicking through the posts from 2015, 2016, 2017... It seemed clear now that Hill's sudden decision to cycle everywhere, and the escalation in her drinking, had occurred around Christmas 2015. There appeared to be no pictures of Hill with that car, or indeed any other vehicle, after this date.

'Do the Hills still own the car?'

'Hold on a minute... No, according to DVLA records, they sold the Mercedes in January 2016. Odd really, given they'd only bought it five months earlier. Must have taken quite a hit on it...'

'Any garage bills from that time? If Hill was responsible, then there'd presumably be significant damage to the car?'

More typing, then: 'Can't see anything obvious in her account... though there were some significant cash withdrawals in early December, totalling... two thousand, five hundred pounds in total. If she wanted the repairs done discreetly, she would have paid cash presumably.'

And now the final piece slotted into place. The hit-and-run was infamous locally, Billy's shattered parents continuing to campaign for justice, renewing their appeal for witnesses annually on the anniversary of his death, hoping against hope that someone's conscience might be pricked. But Lilah Hill had opted to stay quiet, swallowing her guilt to save her own skin. What toll had this taken on her? And how vulnerable had it made her? Had Martin Hill known about this, using it against her, forcing her to stay in a relationship she found claustrophobic, even toxic? And what of Blythe? Had she confessed her guilt to *him* during their sessions, delivering up her soul on a plate? Helen suddenly felt convinced that this was what had happened, that this was the key to understanding Blythe's hold over her.

But the boot was on the other foot now. Now it was Helen who had the knowledge, the leverage, and she intended to use it to the full.

Chapter 117

The strip lights flickered on as she strode across the dirty concrete floor towards her bike. Seized by a conviction that she now had the means to force Lilah Hill to confess, Helen was determined not to waste a second. The custody officers and her lawyer might protest, insisting that she'd endured enough questioning already, but Helen knew that she was within her rights to summon her to the interview suite once more.

Tearing across the grimy basement, Helen vaulted onto her Kawasaki. Sliding on her helmet, she fired up the ignition and kicked off the brake, moving away. Seconds later, the automatic gates rose and she sped through the gap, up and away onto the street.

It was deserted, so Helen tore along the empty thoroughfare, enjoying the breeze that battered her body. Though early, the temperature was already high, after a sultry, oppressive night, and it felt good to have the soft balm of the breeze swirling around her. After weeks of frustration, fear and anxiety, Helen now felt assured of victory, that justice would prevail, that finally Blythe would be brought to book. Many lives had been ruined, much blood had been spilt, but at long last, they were nearing the end of the road.

Reaching a four-way junction, Helen slid left onto Oswald

Road, ratcheting up her speed, responding to the kick of the bike as it leapt forward. She was only minutes from Southampton Central, her commute eased by the absence of traffic. Her progress was serene, unstoppable, complimenting her mood, and she powered forward. She was impatient to be in front of Lilah again, to get this thing done. Each metre gained was a metre closer to the station, to the resumption of hostilities.

Crossing Fairfax Road, she glimpsed Southampton Central in the distance. The tall granite-and-limestone building stood out against the skyline, beckoning to her. She was about to tug on her throttle again, but finally her luck ran out, the lights suddenly changing from amber to red, the first obstruction in an otherwise seamless journey.

Dropping her speed, Helen came to a halt by the stop line. Exhaling, she tried to gather her thoughts, to prepare herself for what lay ahead. Even now, however, she was to be denied this moment of peace; her phone buzzed in her pocket, demanding her attention. Tapping her Bluetooth helmet, she answered:

'Grace—'

'Guv, it's DC Bentham.'

He sounded tense, which immediately concerned her.

'Everything OK?'

'Fine – but I wanted to run something by you.'

'Go on…' Helen replied, flicking a look at the lights, which remained red.

'Well, I've been going through the information that was recovered from Gary Bleecher's microchip, the one we recovered—'

'From his locket. What of it?'

'Well, Bleecher had a full copy of his files on it, everyone who owed him money, in various spreadsheets and lists—'

'And?' Helen prompted.

433

'Well, it's probably nothing, but one of the names on the list rang a bell. Anthony Parks.'

Helen's blood ran cold. If someone who worked at Southampton Central was in Bleecher's debt, then it was possible that Blythe might have some kind of a hold over them, was even now prompting them to take action.

'He works in the custody depart—'

'I know who he is,' Helen interrupted tersely. 'Where is he? Is he on duty today?'

There was a pregnant pause, then Bentham replied:

'Yes, he clocked on half an hour ago.'

Chapter 118

The door swung open, but she didn't move. Lilah Hill remained where she was, sitting on the edge of the wire-framed bed, staring at the ground. She had been in this position since first light, when she'd finally given up the futile attempt to sleep, preferring to contemplate her ruin in an upright position instead. It made her feel less supine, less beaten, though this was an illusion – her ruin was total, whichever way you looked at it.

Since her interview with DI Grace, Lilah had been in freefall, unable to comprehend how she could have come so low, so quickly. A week ago she had been in a bad place – claustrophobic, trapped, crushed by guilt – but it was bearable. She had her job, a handful of friends, the occasional moment of heady liberation. How she would take that sentence now, how she would love the privations, pain and misery. But that option was gone, now she faced a life behind bars. How naïve she'd been to think that she could get away with something like this – now she had a double stain on her conscience. She would be tortured by Raeburn's death every bit as much as she was by Billy Anderson's, she knew that. The latter had coloured her life for years now – she had been poleaxed when she'd spotted his broken parents in Westquay a couple of days ago – and Raeburn's would do so too. Presumably Raeburn had parents, friends, a partner, a life. A life which *she* had snuffed out. Anderson's death had been accidental at least, even if Lilah's cowardice then and in the years after was unforgiveable, but Raeburn's was something altogether different, something much, much worse.

A shadow fell across her and she became aware of the custody officer looming over her.

'Come on, Hill. You know the drill.'

The words were hissed at her, angry and tense. She hated him for his aggression, his coldness, but in truth it was all she deserved, so hauling her frame off the bed, she turned to face the wall, her arms stretched out wide. How she hated this rigmarole, the indignity of it, the not-so-casual brushing of her breasts, as she was examined for weapons, contraband or anything that might be used to try and effect an escape. How laughable it all seemed to her – she wasn't going anywhere.

He was standing right behind her. Closing her eyes, she braced herself for what was to come, hoping it would be over quickly. She knew that more questioning awaited her upstairs, but somehow even that was better than being stuck in here. Any company, even that of DI Grace's, was preferable to this.

'Come on, let's get this over with...' Lilah urged.

She was angry now. Why was he stringing this out?

'Fair enough,' was the muttered reply.

Immediately, Lilah's eyes flicked open. Suddenly, inexplicably, she felt alarmed. There was something heavy in the man's tone, his voice thick with tension, even regret? Fear arrowed through her, but before she could react, she felt something slide around her neck. She tried to grasp it, it was smooth and leathery, perhaps a belt, but even now her attacker was pulling it tight, forcing the air from her throat. She gasped, terrified and airless, kicking her legs violently as she clawed at the belt, but now he was pulling it *tighter*. Try as she might, she couldn't get any purchase on it, couldn't turn, as he hugged her body to his, all the while increasing the pressure on her throat. Her vision seemed to be crowding in on her now, she was seeing stars, the fight fast going out of her, as the world began to fade. She'd known she might be in danger, but had never expected it to come *so quickly*. Now she would pay the price. She was helpless to resist, powerless in his clutches, utterly unable to fight back.

This was the end.

Chapter 119

She hit the ramp hard, roaring into the car park. Ignoring the line of bikes to her right, Helen sped straight towards the building's staff entrance. She was driving too fast, endangering anyone who might cross her path, but she had only one thing in mind. She had to get to Lilah Hill.

The doors now loomed into view and Helen dismounted, leaping clear of the still-moving bike. Her beloved Kawasaki skittered across the surface, the front wheel spinning wildly, but she was already sprinting away towards the doors. Seconds later, she'd buzzed herself in and was haring down the corridor towards the ground-floor stairwell. Bentham was no doubt racing towards the custody area himself, making his way down from the seventh floor. It was just a question of who'd get there first. And whether they would be too late.

Why had they not spotted this earlier? As yet, Helen had no way of knowing for sure if Parks *had* been prompted by Blythe to target Hill, but something told her that that's *exactly* what was happening, that this most precise and premeditated of serial killers would stop at nothing to tie up loose ends. The thought made Helen feel nauseous – she shuddered to think what Hill might be enduring even now – but there was no time for recriminations or regret. The clock was ticking.

Reaching the doors, she hauled them open. The stairs down to the custody were short, fifteen at the most, and Helen took them in one go, leaping from the top, guiding herself in with the handrail. She hit the ground hard, but was immediately on her feet, tearing away down the corridor. Busting through another door, she found herself in the internal custody area, only a few paces from the gateway to the cells. There was no sign of Bentham yet, and even as she hurried forward, she heard the lift *ping* behind her. He had been fast, but not fast enough, meaning *she* was now Lilah Hill's best hope.

Marching forward, she roared at the guard on the gate.

'Open up!'

The man looked puzzled, even slightly alarmed. Helen saw him reaching for the alarm button and, realizing her mistake, tugged off her helmet.

'It's me. DI Grace...'

Angrily, she yanked out her warrant card, thrusting it at the Perspex screen that separated them.

'I need to see Lilah Hill *now*...'

'Sure, sure...' the flustered man responded. 'But if you wait here, she'll be right up. Officer Parks has just gone to get—'

'NOW!' Helen bellowed, kicking the screen.

Bentham was haring up behind her and this seemed to decide the custody officer, who slammed the release button, buzzing them in. Pushing past him, Helen sprang forward, bursting down the corridor.

'Cell Ten...'

The custody officer's panicked cry slowly died out, as Helen raced away. This was it, then – Parks was with Lilah *right now*. Would they be in time to save her? Or would Blythe triumph once more?

'Lilah?'

Helen's cry was shrill and angry, yielding no response.

'Lilah?'

Louder this time, more breathless, almost drowned out by Helen's pounding footsteps. But now it got a response. The door of Cell Ten flew open and a figure darted out, racing away down the corridor. Helen had a split second to decide and, skidding to a halt, gestured to Bentham to follow the fleeing suspect, before hurrying into the tiny cell.

As she'd feared, Hill was lying on the floor, a leather belt discarded next to her. Tossing her helmet onto the bed, Helen knelt down beside the prone woman, gently cupping her face and turning it to her. The sight took her breath away, not just the livid bruising around her neck, but the ghostly pallor of her face. Desperate, anguished, Helen felt for a pulse – but found nothing. She checked again, but still came up short. Why the hell had she been so stupid? How had she not seen this *coming*?

Lowering Lilah to the ground, Helen sat astride her. Placing her hands on her chest, she began to pump.

'One, two, three, four…'

Leaning down, Helen squeezed the woman's nostrils together and, parting her lips, breathed into her airways. Then she resumed pumping her chest.

'Come on, Lilah, come back to me…'

Again, she breathed into her mouth, but the woman remained inert beneath her.

'Please Lilah—'

Helen was surprised to find tears pricking her eyes. She was desperate, panicking, wanting more than anything to save this woman, this one life, from Blythe's grim circus of death. Hill had done terrible things, wicked things, but, still, she didn't deserve to die like this, choked to death by a total stranger in a poky, airless cell, the plaything of a man she'd once trusted with her life.

'Please—'

Still she pumped the young woman's chest, but with little hope of response. Leaning down, she expelled more air into the woman's lungs, one last, desperate attempt to foster life into the corpse beneath her. She knew it was fruitless, that she was kidding herself, but she had to try.

And now, to her immense surprise, Hill's right eye flickered, then slowly opened. She was utterly bemused, her eyeball swivelling wildly, but there was a spark there, signs of life.

'Dear God...' Helen breathed the words, even as Hill's other eye opened.

For a moment the two women stared at each other, one semiconscious and reeling, the other tearful and relieved, when a noise behind them made Helen turn. It was Bentham, sweaty and grim-faced, standing in the doorway.

'No luck, I'm afraid...'

He seemed gutted, crestfallen.

'I've already put out a general alert. How're we doing here?'

He asked it tentatively, as if fearing the worse. But it was with real emotion that Helen replied:

'We're OK, we'll *live*...'

And it was true. Hill had come close to death, very close, but she would survive. After all the bloodshed and mayhem of recent weeks, it was perhaps scant consolation, but it was a victory nevertheless, the first time since this all began that they had been ahead of the game, the first time that they had frustrated the sinister intentions of Alex Blythe.

Chapter *120*

The barrel charge slammed into the door, shattering the heavy lock. Withdrawing it, the officer swung again and this time the door came off its hinges, landing on the floor with a deafening bang. Standing back, he now let the quartet of armed officers charge inside.

DC Ellie McAndrew was right behind them, scurrying up the stairs in their wake. Her heart was pounding, her senses on fire. She didn't normally take part in raids – traditionally, this was DS Brooks's role and, more recently, DS Hudson's. He should have been here today, leading the charge, but he'd suddenly and inexplicably been removed from the investigation. Rumours were already beginning to circulate that he'd been disciplined, perhaps even suspended, but that made no odds now. What mattered was that she had to pick up the slack, leading the team as they apprehended Dr Alex Blythe.

Loud noises above now grabbed her attention, the heavy tread of the armed officers accompanied by aggressive cries for Blythe to give himself up, to surrender. Would Blythe come quietly? Or would he put up a fight? It seemed unlikely that he would pose much of a threat, given his stature and profession, but who could say, given the prolific killer he had turned out to be?

You never knew how these things would go, hence the knot in McAndrew's stomach.

Reaching the head of the stairs, she pushed through into the main room. It was a simple, welcoming space, with table and chairs and a water dispenser. Off it, were several smaller rooms, including the bathroom and storage area. The blinds were down and it had been hard to get any eyes on the man himself, but the desk light still burned, leading the surveillance team to speculate that Blythe *was* still present. They had seen him enter the space some hours earlier, but had heard or seen no movement since. McAndrew had feared that he was either holed up, awaiting the final confrontation, or perhaps had even taken his own life, aware that the net was tightening around him.

But looking around the large room that doubled as his office and consulting space, McAndrew realized that she was wrong on both counts. A laptop lay smashed on the ground and around it lay reams and reams of shredded papers, like confetti at a wedding. Blythe had known he was being watched, that he faced arrest, and had taken action accordingly.

The armed officers emerged from the clutch of doors that led off the main meeting room, chorusing 'clear' in unison. This left only one option now and this time McAndrew took the lead, racing over to the rear window, which opened onto the building's fire escape. She wasn't surprised to find it unlocked. Pulling it open, she clambered out onto the metal walkway. Stairs led down to a yard and then onto a rear alleyway, but that would have led Blythe to an awaiting surveillance team, so instead McAndrew headed up.

She took the stairs three at a time, driving herself onwards. She crested one flight, two, three, then suddenly she was on the roof, confronted by a majestic vision of Southampton at first light. But it was not a vista that thrilled her today; in fact, quite the opposite. For it was now clear that there were a dozen different routes Blythe *could* have chosen to make his retreat, climbing over the rooftops of the adjoining buildings to safety.

Cursing, McAndrew pulled out her radio. She had come here with high hopes, desperate to make the first major arrest of her career, but had come up empty-handed. They had not been careful enough, nor had they been quick enough, allowing the devious psychiatrist plenty of time to escape.

This bird had flown.

Chapter 121

She was losing her. Helen knew she had to move fast.

'Look, Lilah, I know you're hurting. I know you're scared. But you have to trust me. We can protect you and we *will*. You have my word on that.'

Lilah Hill was lying in a bed at Southampton University Hospital. The medical staff had satisfied themselves that there was no immediate threat to her life and she was now awaiting tests to assess the damage to her throat and neck. They had, with some reluctance, allowed Helen to interview her, but their key witness seemed reluctant to talk.

'I will personally take charge of the situation. We'll find you a secure medical facility where you can recuperate, then later a safe house whilst you await trial. You will be under guard and surveillance at all times, safe and sound. I can't make you any promises beyond that, but trust me, there is no point shielding Alex Blythe anymore. He wants you dead – I think the events of this morning have made that clear.'

Lilah Hill blinked, but said nothing, tears slowly sliding down her cheeks. Even now she was still coming to terms with the fact that Blythe had ordered her death – and very nearly succeeded.

'Your best bet now lies in helping us bring him in. Once he's caught, under lock and key, facing trial, he won't be able to hurt you anymore. But whilst he's out there, talking to God knows who, doing God knows what, there's a threat. It may be minimal, given everything we can do to protect you, but still—'

Finally, Helen's words started to sink in, the damaged young woman nodding.

'Good. Now I promise I won't prolong this, I know you need to rest. But I need some honest answers to some straightforward questions, OK?'

Another tiny nod.

'Did Alex Blythe order you to steal that car, to run those lights?'

'Yes.'

One word, croaked and with much effort, but it was what Helen needed to hear.

'Did he tell you to kill Belinda Raeburn?'

'Yes.'

She dropped her head as she said it, too haunted, too ashamed, to maintain eye contact. Leaning forward, Helen lifted her chin, forcing Lilah to look at her.

'I'm not here to shame you, Lilah. I just want the truth.'

Hill met her eyes unflinchingly this time, a shred of her old resolve seeming to surface.

'Did he tell you where she'd be? When to do it?'

Hill nodded. 'He – knew everything about her.'

'And when did he tell you to do this?'

'He told me to steal the car three days ago.'

'At your regular weekly session?'

'Yes.'

'And the rest of it?'

'He – he called. I had a burn phone he'd given me. I – I dropped it into the bin in a park, you know, before I—'

She didn't need to finish her sentence.

'And why did you agree to do it?'

A heavy silence, as she swallowed down the rising emotion, grimacing even as the pain flared up her throat.

'Was it because of Billy Anderson?'

Her body was shaking, her eyelashes heavy with tears.

'Were you responsible for his death?'

Hill made a sound, half sob, half word, but her intent was clear. She wasn't going to deny her guilt, but couldn't find the words.

'Was Alex Blythe the only person who knew about this, other than Martin?'

This time, Hill inclined her head, not trusting herself to speak. Once again, Helen was struck by the simple brilliance of Blythe's operation. His clients willingly vomited up their souls, only to have their honesty turned back on them.

'Blythe threatened to reveal this information about you, unless you agreed to kill Belinda Raeburn?'

'Yes – he – he said he'd tell my family, my friends, the police—'

'So, in your head, you had no choice but to comply.'

She looked ashamed, deeply ashamed, but still managed to mutter a reply. 'Yes.'

'And, if it came to a trial, you'd be prepared to swear to that in court? That he coerced you into killing a total stranger, someone you'd never met before, someone whom you had no personal animosity towards?'

'Yes, yes.' Her response was more forceful this time, anger punching through.

'Good. Last question, then. Did you always meet him at his office on Church Street?'

'Yes.'

'You never met him anywhere else? A café? A flat? A bolthole somewhere?'

'No, it was always at his office.'

Helen had suspected as much. Blythe was too shrewd an operator to have given any clue to his life beyond the hushed space of his office. It was impressive, his self-control, his discipline, but it made their lives harder now. The architect of all this bloodshed was out there, no doubt intent on disappearing from Southampton, possibly from the UK, for good. With no sightings, no concrete leads as to his whereabouts, what should they do?

Where should they start this deadly game of hide and seek?

Chapter 122

He watched her emerge from the hospital. Her Kawasaki was stationed in the visitor car park, a beast amongst the sea of mopeds that were clustered in the far corner, and Helen made for it now without delay. He, meanwhile, was standing by a pay station, poised to intercept her, following her progress intently. Helen appeared totally oblivious, head down, lost in thought.

Striding to the bike, she flipped open the saddle. She was clearly in a hurry, which meant he had to act now. Scanning the car park for potential witnesses, he abandoned his cover, marching directly towards her.

Time seemed to speed up now – he covered the distance between them in seconds – then suddenly he was upon her. Reaching out, he grabbed her shoulder, but even as he did so, she span, grabbing his arm and flipping him around, until he was pinned down, his face pressed into the hot leather of the saddle.

'Jesus Christ, Joseph. What the hell are you doing?'

'I need to talk to you—' he protested, his face still pressed into the seat.

'We've said all we need to say to each other.'

'Please, Helen—'

For a moment, Joseph thought she wasn't going to let him up, that she would keep him here, pinned down, humiliated. Then, finally, she relented, releasing her grip, stepping away from him, whilst eyeing him cautiously.

'For God's sake, Helen, I haven't come here to *attack* you.'

'It pays for a girl to be careful.'

'Like I said, I just want to *talk*...'

He held out his hands in supplication. Now she seemed to relax, dropping her guard, but keeping a wary distance.

'Go on, then. Because I've got somewhere I need to be.'

'Look, things have got out of hand. We've both said things we regret...'

'Excuse me?'

'And if I upset you or alarmed you, then I'm sorry. What I said before – well, it was just bluster. I was angry, humiliated. I wanted our relationship to work, I *really* did, but suddenly things had all gone so wrong.'

'This is Class A bullshit, Joseph, and you know it. You threatened me.'

'I was lashing out, that's all. But you're right, I *was* out of line. So, I wanted to apologise to you, sincerely...'

He couldn't have been more genuine, more open-hearted, but still she seemed resistant. Her body was coiled tight, her face set.

'Too little too late, Joseph. But I accept the apology.'

She made to move off, but he laid a restraining hand on her.

'Please, Helen, I know the last few months have been difficult – for both of us – but it doesn't have to end like this. I'm a good police officer and I can be a good ally to you.' He had no idea if this was true, but he had to say it. 'We can start over, be the team we used to be. God knows, we need every hand on deck at the moment...'

She looked like she was about to interrupt, so he carried on quickly.

'That's what I want. Ignore all the other nonsense; I just want to be a good copper, to *contribute*. And I can be again, with your help. If you could find it in your heart to have a word with Peters, see if you could get him to reconsider—'

And now to his horror, Helen started laughing.

'You're unbelievable, you know that?'

'I don't see why—'

'Besides it's too late.'

Four simple words, but devastating to hear.

'You're being investigated by Professional Standards, Joseph. They've already opened an investigation on you regarding numerous counts of police corruption. There's nothing I can do, even if I wanted to. The train has left the station.'

'But an intervention by someone of your standing—'

'No, no way. It wouldn't go any good, and besides, I don't want to. It wouldn't be the right thing to do.'

'What do you mean by *that*?'

'You're a bad police officer, Joseph. You lack control, you lack empathy and you've never been a team player. You always put your own interests first and that is the very *opposite* of what a good officer does. You are here to serve, not to serve yourself.'

'Helen, please...'

'So save me the sob story, Joseph. You got *exactly* what you deserved.'

Breaking free of him, Helen climbed onto her bike. Moments later, she was gone, roaring away fast to the exit, leaving Joseph Hudson alone in the car park, to reflect on his total and utter defeat.

Chapter 123

He stood on the edge of the busy highway, watching the trucks roar by. He was anonymous, unnoticed, a blip in people's rear-view mirrors, but he would not remain so for long. Soon his name would be infamous, synonymous with criminality, corruption and deceit.

A patrol car roared past in the outside lane, blue lights flashing. Instinctively, Anthony Parks took a step back, fearful of discovery, but they seemed little interested in him, haring off to some other emergency. His respite would be temporary, however. A general alert would already have gone out to every beat copper, every CID officer, every data analyst – even now they would be checking traffic cameras, triangulating his phone, raiding his home, talking to his family. The thought of it made him feel sick – what would his poor parents make of it, his loving, innocent, affectionate parents who were so proud of their son? They had done nothing to deserve the censure, the judgement, the grief that was coming their way. It was his fault and his alone.

How had it ever come to this? How had he messed up so *badly*? It scarcely seemed believable that ten years ago he was a happy teenager, ducking and diving, taking his chances when they came. He knew that the roots of his affliction lay back then, a fondness for gambling cultivated in the seafront arcades, but still it was an exciting time, a good time. How he wished he could be back there now, making different choices, taking another path. But it was too late for that, he had blown the chances he'd been given in his life, using the modest salary he earned as a trainee prison officer to fund his trips to the bookies. The dogs and horses hadn't been kind, so he'd tried to make up his losses on the fixed-odds betting terminals, with predictable results. Soon, he was squandering his monthly salary in a matter of days, getting ever deeper in debt. He'd maxed out his credit cards, borrowed, then stolen from friends and, when finally he ran out of options, sought a black-market loan.

His association with Gary Bleecher had not been enjoyable, the sweaty parasite appearing to be his friend, before suddenly upping the interest payments. Soon he was in a real fix, fearful for his limbs, even his life, as Bleecher promised to make good on his threats. Then suddenly, miraculously, the danger evaporated, Bleecher clubbed to death by an unknown assailant. He'd been euphoric, over the moon, but the sting in the tail wasn't long in coming, the pitiless Dr Blythe ordering him to murder Lilah Hill. He had been disbelieving at first, but his new addiction counsellor was implacable and seemed to have a reach that was both impressive and terrifying. There seemed to be no limit to who he could have killed, so what choice did *he* have but to comply with his awful request?

He had hated it, hated it with every fibre of his being, but still he'd been determined to see it through. And this morning it had seemed simple, easy really. He would enter her cell and moments later come haring back, slamming the alarm and reporting an attempted suicide. Of course, there would be nothing 'attempted' about it – he would have strangled Hill moments earlier, ensuring she was dead before leaving the cell. Perhaps he should have known that something would go wrong, though he never expected DI Grace to come bounding down the corridor, intent on saving the unfortunate woman. How the hell did she even know what he was planning?

He had managed to escape, fighting his way past surprised colleagues, before sprinting from Southampton Central. Since then he'd been skulking in the shadows, creeping around like a common criminal, fearful, hunted, afraid. He knew he was just putting off the inevitable. He had no funds, few friends, no one who would shield him, once the gravity of his offences became clear. No, he had ruined everything, messed up his whole life, from start to finish, never once making the correct decision, forever taking the wrong path.

But that ended today. For once he was going to do something right, something that would make things better for everyone. So, muttering a silent, tearful prayer for forgiveness, he clamped his eyes shut and stepped out into the traffic.

Chapter 124

'Are we *sure* it was self-inflicted?'

Helen could barely take in the news, utterly stunned that Anthony Parks was dead, but knew she had to stay focused on the continuing hunt for Alex Blythe.

'There wasn't anyone with him?'

Chief Superintendent Alan Peters shook his head gravely.

'A handful of witnesses saw Parks deliberately step out in front of a sixteen-wheeler on the A23. It was suicide, no question.'

Helen shut her eyes, trying to push away this image. It was a hideous way for someone to go, whatever crimes they might have on their conscience.

'I'll call his family myself later,' Peters continued, 'though God only knows what I'm going to say to them. Anthony Parks betrayed his vocation, his colleagues, the very people he was supposed to protect. He's a disgrace, a bloody disgrace.'

Helen was tempted to agree, though her dismay was tinged with sadness, even sympathy. Parks had always been an engaging presence at the station and surely would never have contemplated such a cowardly attempt on Lilah Hill's life unless he was driven to it.

'I take it from your earlier questions that we're no closer to locating Blythe?'

Helen marvelled at Peters' ability to pivot from Parks's death to operational matters without a flicker of emotion.

'Nothing concrete yet, sir. But the border agencies have been notified and we've got every available officer sweeping the county for him. Blythe doesn't own a vehicle and if he tries to buy a travel ticket or hire a car, we'll know about it. It's only a matter of time before we bring him in.'

In truth, Helen was much less confident than she sounded. Peters sensed this, his response laced with mockery.

'Well, I'm glad *you're* confident, DI Grace. Though on the face of it, I'm not sure why. Blythe has been ahead of us every step of the way.'

Helen took the hit. There was more than a grain of truth in his accusation and she didn't have time to pick a fight, not whilst the psychiatrist remained at large.

'Well, if that's all, sir, I'd better be getting back to the incident—'

'Not quite.'

Helen had turned to go, but now paused.

'I didn't ask you here just to commiserate about the loss of Anthony Parks...'

Any trace of empathy was long gone. There was a hardness to Peters' tone now which made Helen uneasy.

'You'll be aware that DS Hudson has been suspended and that Professional Standards have opened an investigation into the events of the last few months.'

'Yes, sir,' Helen replied carefully.

'I've accepted your version of events, as the evidence available to me points in that direction, though of course Sergeant Cooper will want to pick over the bones of it with you in due course. For now, however, you remain in post, in the hope that we can bring this sorry saga to a successful conclusion. But I want you to know this. I don't condone your actions over the past few months; in fact, I'm shocked and disappointed that my SIO should have behaved in such a cavalier manner.'

Helen said nothing, but maintained eye contact, refusing to hang her head, to be browbeaten by this man.

'You've shown extraordinary recklessness and lack of judgement in the way you conducted both your personal and professional life, deceiving senior members of staff, fracturing team morale and compromising investigations in the process—'

'With all due respect, sir, we'd still be at square one, if it wasn't for me—'

'ENOUGH.'

Peters bellowed the word, silencing Helen instantly. Glaring at her, he continued:

'This station's reputation is already in tatters. Now we have to deal with the fact that one of our custody officers betrayed us, attempting to murder a suspect in our care. It's a disaster, an unmitigated shit show that threatens the prospects of everyone at Southampton Central. So, let me be very plain, DI Grace. We cannot afford any more mistakes, any more misfires and the last thing – *the very last thing* – this station needs right now is a renegade SIO who has no respect for protocol or procedure. From now on, *everything* is to be done by the book and to the letter of the law, or, trust me, it'll be your last act under my command. Be under no illusions, Helen…' his eyes bored into hers, his anger piercing – 'this is your final warning.'

Chapter 125

Helen slammed through the doors of the incident room, her emotions in riot. Her unpleasant confrontation with Hudson had been followed first by news of Parks's tragic suicide, then by a humiliating dressing down. Helen was enraged at the poor timing and unfairness of Peters' accusations, yet still felt shaken by the encounter. For the first time, it genuinely felt as if her career at Southampton Central was in jeopardy.

Ignoring the enquiring glances from her team, Helen marched towards the murder board, desperately trying to recover her focus. Alan Peters had her card marked now, was perhaps *looking* for an excuse to get rid of her. There was little she could do about that, she was hardly going to morph into a conventional police officer overnight, but one thing that *might* buy her some time, some breathing space, would be the arrest and prosecution of Alex Blythe. All her energies, all her fury, needed to be directed at him now.

Coming to a halt, Helen took in the photo of Anthony Parks, now pinned alongside the others on the busy display. Only a few days earlier Helen had stared at the same collage of faces and incidents, baffled by the apparently random upsurge of brutality and bloodshed. Now this tapestry of devastation looked very different – now the victims, the suspects, the various lines of enquiry were all joined up, a hideous but elegant diagram which led back to one man, whose photo graced the very centre of the board.

How she wanted to tear Blythe's photo down, ripping it into a hundred pieces. Not since her shattering confrontation with Marianne all those years ago had she faced an adversary who was so clinical, so precise, so effective. He killed without qualm or conscience, feeding off the agony of those he forced to swallow their consciences. How he must have enjoyed his puppets' torment, threatening them with exposure, then forcing them to commit a trio of increasingly criminal acts, in a twisted game of truth or dare. In so doing, he'd pulled them ever deeper into his web, desensitizing them each step of the way. They had come to him for help, for salvation, and he had made them murderers.

But even though her anger burned fiercely, she knew she had to control her emotions, to stay focused, galvanizing the team in their hunt for the fugitive. They had what they needed now – written testimony from Lilah Hill outlining his role in this awful cycle of violence. Once Robert Downing became aware of this, once they'd confronted him with the evidence the dive team had recovered from the River Itchen, perhaps he too would see sense, strengthening the growing body of evidence against the psychiatrist. This was not the end of the road; they still had no idea who Blythe's other clients were, how far this thing went back, but at least they had answers.

Of course, what they really needed was the man himself. There had been no sightings of him in the last few hours and according to Border Force, he hadn't attempted to leave the country. He was out there somewhere – but where? Did he have a support network? A friend or lover who'd put him up? Surely not, once the alert went out for his capture. What about a former client, then, someone he could blackmail into shielding him? If this was the case, then there was no telling how long he could stay hidden, his hold over his vulnerable patients seemingly absolute.

Troubled by this thought, Helen moved away, hurrying back to her office. She was due to brief the team in twenty minutes and needed to be confident and specific in her instructions. The key thing now was to be decisive, to not waste time on the obvious options, as Blythe would never allow himself to be trapped so easily. She would have to think outside the box if she wanted to catch this deadly killer.

Shutting the door, she rounded her desk, pulling a map of the South Coast in front of her. As she did so, her phone started buzzing, but she ignored it, scanning the shoreline for known smuggling sites, off-grid landing areas from which Blythe could attempt to make it to the continent. God knows this was an area that was hard to police, but the frequency of patrols had been raised recently in response to an influx of illegal migrants. Would Blythe risk such a crossing, entrusting his life to the whims of the sea? Somehow she doubted it; this was a man who liked to be constantly, supremely, in control.

Her phone rang out; Helen was glad of the respite. But then it started up again. Irritated, she snatched it up, demanding to know who it was. To her surprise, the caller didn't respond at first, so she repeated her question. But somehow even as she asked it, she knew what the answer would be.

'Hello, Helen. It's Alex Blythe.'

Chapter 126

'I'm afraid I must be brief, as I have somewhere I need to be...'

Blythe could hear the rustle of movement on the other end, could imagine Helen gesturing frantically to her colleagues, urging them to trace the call.

'I just wanted to say goodbye. And thank you. It's been fun.'

'You need to come in, Alex. You can't run from this.'

She sounded breathless, insistent, but he was bound to disappoint her.

'That's *exactly* what I intend to do. But I wanted to leave you a little gift first. And to offer some sage words of advice.'

'This isn't the time for playing games,' she cut in. 'You need to face up to this thing. You need to tell me where you are and what you're—'

'That's easy enough, Helen. I'm in your flat.'

A shocked silence on the other end, her reaction every bit as enjoyable as he'd been hoping.

'I must say, I do like what you've done with the place, especially the bedroom. Such lovely colours, such *character*...'

He ran his eye over the austere room, whose bare walls and neutral colouring spoke of an absence of love, of emotion, of security. A blank canvas for an inscrutable woman.

'Stay right there,' Helen urged down the line. 'If it's me you want to talk to—'

'I'd love to, but I'm done here. Like I said, I've left you a gift, a small token of my affection.'

His eyes came to rest on the bed. Bella's supine body lay in the middle of the duvet, the spaniel's neck lolling at an odd angle. Strange how easy it had been, her big, stupid eyes staring up at him, even as he ended her life.

'You'll find it waiting for you when you arrive with the cavalry.'

'Alex, I meant what I said—'

'Let's not waste words, Helen. I haven't got long. I simply wanted to say this. I respect you, I really do ...'

As he spoke, he made his way out of the bedroom, crossing the living room towards the door. The patrol cars would be being scrambled even now – it was time to leave.

'... but there's no question that you *have* ruined my plans. I had such big ideas, such elaborate dreams, but you've put paid to them. And whilst I applaud you for that, I can't forgive the inconvenience you've caused me, *will* cause me for months, even years to come. There must be payback, so consider this a warning.'

'Don't threaten me, you piece of shit—'

'Bluster all you want, Helen, but I'm the one who has the power here, not you. I have dozens of clients, scores of them, in fact, all of whom will be living in fear right now, terrified that I will be apprehended, that *their* grubby little secrets will be revealed. Well, here's the thing. I don't plan to be captured, but I *do* intend to make full use of the leverage I possess ...'

He lingered on the word 'leverage', enjoying its slipperiness, its power.

'I will choose a suitable candidate. I will threaten them with ruin. And then I will offer them a way out. All they have to do to free themselves is to kill a police officer. A very well-known police officer. Do you understand, Helen?'

'Go to Hell.'

'Oh, I may well do, but if I do, I'll see *you* there. Because there won't be any escape. I have a dozen willing victims in mind, people who'd stab you in the eye as soon as look at you.'

He paused to take one last look around the immaculate flat.

'Be under no illusions, Helen, this is the beginning of the end.'

And with that, he rang off, exiting the hushed space, closing the door carefully behind him.

Chapter 127

She burst through the swing doors, sprinting down the steps towards the bike park. Her lungs were burning, but Helen didn't relent, powering across the tarmac towards her Kawasaki. She knew it was probably futile, that Blythe had most likely already disappeared, but whilst he was so close by, she had to try.

Sirens wailed loudly in the background, as the squad cars fired up their engines. Helen was determined to be ahead of them, sliding to a halt by her bike and unhooking her helmet in one swift, fluid action. Swinging a leg over the saddle, she was about to turn the key in the ignition, when suddenly she ground to a halt. For a moment, she couldn't quite process what she was seeing – the catastrophic timing of it – but she wasn't imagining things. Her front tyre was flat.

Dismounting, she bent down to examine the damage. And now Helen's mystification turned to rage – a long, thin cut in the rubber was clearly visible, presumably made within the last hour. Straightening up, she scanned the bike park, expecting to see Joseph Hudson skulking away. She was all set to fall upon him, to visit her frustration and fury on her former lover, but now she paused. There was no sign of Hudson and, besides, could she be *sure* it was him? Or was someone else set on stymying her progress? Someone who'd been sent to frustrate her, obstruct her, perhaps even kill her?

'Need a lift, ma'am?'

Helen looked up to see a squad car approaching, blue lights flashing.

'Hate you to miss out on the fun ...'

The officer was staring at her flat tyre. Helen recognized him by sight and normally would have leapt at the chance – *anything* to get to her flat as quickly as possible. But now she hesitated. She didn't know this guy's name, nor that of the stony-faced officer in the passenger seat, who seemed intent on avoiding her gaze. And even if she *had*, would she have accepted their offer? Recent events had proved that it was impossible to truly know anyone.

'I'll make my own way,' she replied quickly, hurrying away.

She could tell the officers were surprised, bemused, perhaps, as to why she seemed intent on making her way on foot, but she was not going to waste time explaining. Nor did she want to confess her fears to them, her sense that *anyone* she encountered from now on might potentially harbour malign intent. She had no idea how far Blythe's influence stretched, but suddenly his reach seemed limitless, the danger ever-present.

Hitting the street, Helen cast a wary eye around, but there was no one nearby. She was quite alone. So, even as the patrol cars roared out of the station car park, Helen set off, first jogging, then sprinting away down the road. She was focused, determined, driven on by adrenaline and fear. Yet for all her intent, for all her relentless forward movement, she continued to scan her surroundings, her senses on high alert. She would not give up, she would not be broken by his threat, but as the full import of Blythe's chilling ultimatum now made itself felt, one thing was painfully clear.

From now on, she would forever be looking over her shoulder.

Credits

M.J. Arlidge and Orion Fiction would like to thank everyone at Orion who worked on the publication of *Truth or Dare* in the UK.

Editorial
Emad Akhtar
Celia Killen

Copy editor
Marian Reid

Proof reader
Clare Wallis

Audio
Paul Stark
Amber Bates

Contracts
Anne Goddard
Paul Bulos
Jake Alderson

Design
Debbie Holmes
Joanna Ridley
Nick May

Editorial Management
Charlie Panayiotou
Jane Hughes
Alice Davis

Finance
Jasdip Nandra
Afeera Ahmed
Elizabeth Beaumont
Sue Baker

Marketing
Tom Noble

Publicity
Leanne Oliver

Production
Ruth Sharvell

Sales
Jen Wilson
Esther Waters
Victoria Laws

Rachael Hum
Ellie Kyrke-Smith
Frances Doyle
Georgina Cutler

Operations
Jo Jacobs
Sharon Willis
Lisa Pryde
Lucy Brem